Madge Swindells was born and educated in England. As a teenager, she emigrated to South Africa where she studied archaeology and anthropology at Cape Town University. Later, in England, she was a Fleet Street journalist and the manager of her own publishing company. Her earlier novels, *Summer Harvest*, *Song of the Wind*, *Shadows on the Snow*, *The Corsican Woman*, *Edelweiss*, *The Sentinel* and *Harvesting the Past* were international bestsellers and have been translated into eight languages. She lives in South Africa, and her next novel, *Winners and Losers* will be published in hardback by Little, Brown in December 1999.

Sunstroke

MADGE SWINDELLS

WARNER BOOKS

A *Warner* Book

First published in Great Britain in 1998
by Little, Brown and Company

This edition published by Warner Books in 1999

A CIP catalogue record for this book
is available from the British Library.

ISBN 0 7515 2296 1

Typeset by Palimpsest Book Production Limited
Polmont, Stirlingshire
Printed and bound in Great Britain by
Clays Ltd, St Ives plc

Warner Books
A Division of
Little, Brown and Company (UK)
Brettenham House
Lancaster Place
London WC2E 7EN

To my daughter, Jenni, who has helped since she could read and by now is highly proficient in coping with an author mum and all that this entails: sorting out plot problems, helping to create the characters, making sure our friends don't recognise themselves, and propping me up when I've lost my courage.

. . . So, acknowledgements to Jenni Swindells for her ongoing encouragement and moral support, and particularly for her creative plotting and editorial assistance.

To Jeffrey Sharpe for his invaluable criticism. My thanks to John and Susan Wynne-Edwards for sowing the first seed from which this plot grew, and to Lawrie Mackintosh for his research assistance.

Prologue

Cape Town, 30 June 1993

The judge looks bleak and impersonal as he pronounces my sentence. 'Nina von Schenk Möller, I have taken into account your blameless record and your youth, but I have to take cognisance of the seriousness of your crimes. You have been found guilty on two counts of spying against the state and four counts of fraud. I sentence you to six years in prison.'

Hands guide me out of the dock and down the stairs to the cells. The prison door clangs shut and I stand staring at it, unable to turn away. The tension is like a steel wire running from my heels to my neck, pulling ever tighter. I can bear it, just as I bore the injustice and the betrayal, but my baby's pain is unendurable.

Where are you, Nicky? Instinctively I know that you're alive. Are you crying for me? Are you afraid? Dear God, protect my child, my sweet son. God, help me to survive until I'm free and I can find my baby. Help me to stay sane. If only I could understand. Why?

Part One

39 22 10 37
33 28 42

Chapter 1

There was a time when laughter flowed and the future beckoned like a star to my exploring youth. So I, life's novice, swept the world with a new broom, living snug in the belief of an all-wise fate watching over me, of the invincibility of my parents' bond, the inevitability of my adult fulfilment and the wisdom of those who managed the world. Above all, I believed in the all-healing power of love.

I grew up among the mists and mountains of the Scottish Highlands. I knew where the golden eagle built her nest in the inaccessible mountain peak of the Liathach, in the Torridon mountains. I often watched her swooping down over the loch and gliding into the forest for her prey. Then I would hear the shrill keening of a rabbit or a blue hare, swiftly silenced. Sometimes on a spring evening I would hear the eagle's anguished calls, and I knew that she had young to feed and she must kill, or die.

Summers were the best. I would steal out to play in twilight nights and see the great red deer and wild goats creep down to graze around the loch. Then I grew strong and tanned, scratches appeared all over me, and my dark red hair became sun-streaked, long and wild.

I played hard after school at all the things that beckoned to me, and as an only child in an isolated house I had no knowledge of what was for boys and what for girls. I learned to paddle a canoe in our torrential mountain streams and sail a small yacht on the loch on the stormiest of days. I grew hardy climbing the local peaks, and swimming in ice-cold water. I could handle a catapult as well as any boy I knew, track the poachers and dismantle their snares, chop wood and saw planks, but I never learned to fear. Fear was for the lower orders of mankind, not for Ogilvies. So I grew strong and arrogant in my snug harbour of happiness, in our old home beneath the pine trees, beside the loch.

Winters had their compensations, when a log fire burned in the hearth and the house was fragrant with the scent of burning pine, yew and juniper boughs. Sprawled on a black sheepskin rug by the hearth I read for hours and made new friends: David Copperfield, Tam O'Shanter and Wandering Willie. At night the fire smouldered beneath great lumps of peat and the warmth was still there at dawn to warm me before I set off for school. Mother was home more often in the winter, and sometimes Father would sweep in to endure the homage and adoration that returning warriors deserve.

We lived an isolated life in Ogilvie Lodge. Torridon was the only village within bicycle range and it was there I went to school. My mother, who loved company, was often gone for days. She would return in a flourish of bags, hat boxes and tissue paper, her eyes sparkling, her hair set fashionably. Then the house would reverberate to the beat of dance music, and her feet would be tapping in time to it as she showed me her new dresses and jewellery and the useless presents she had brought me.

My mother was a lovely dreamer of dreams, a genie who lived a dozen lives at the same time. I would sit transfixed with awe at this lovely woman, her hair long and burnished red, her large violet eyes gazing longingly out of the window towards the snow-topped mountain peaks, as she spun tales of what might have been.

Why had she chosen Father? Perhaps because he was in British Intelligence. He had been decorated three times by the Queen for services rendered to the Crown. He was altogether special, an athlete, a commander in the Navy, the local squire when he was at home, and the best shot in the district. Fluent in several languages and a perfectionist in everything he did, he was a harsh man who set high standards for himself and everyone else. Nevertheless he was full of fun, and our family was loved and revered in the local village. I adored my handsome father, with his laughing brown eyes and tousled, light brown hair.

Maria, our housekeeper, whom I loved as a mother, swore I grew more like a gypsy every day. She and her husband, Mac, reared me in a haphazard manner. They were kind and caring. Maria's kingdom was the kitchen, a vast place that served as a living room when my parents were away. Mac ran the grounds and drove the family car when needed. I never knew him by any other name. Under his careless but benign tutelage, I built a tree house when I was ten and shot my first and last bird, which I cried over for days.

When I was eleven, I found an otter by the shores of Torridon Loch, which bordered our grounds. The poor wee creature was trapped in a snare. Half dead with cold and deep in shock, he allowed me to free his leg and wrap him in my jersey. I carried him up to our home, the tears pouring down my cheeks. My cries brought Maria running. 'Nina! What's wrong, my lovie?'

'Bring a box. Be quick, please. I've found an otter . . . caught in a trap. Call Mac . . . please. Hurry, hurry, we must get him down to the vet. Maybe he can do something. He's in such pain, the poor, poor creature.'

Mac rushed me to the village, where the otter was stitched up, bandaged and given a fifty-fifty chance of survival by our vet, Dr MacIntyre. For days he lay in a basket by my bed, nibbling herrings and trout fillets and hiding when I went to school. After two months he emerged to take his place in our household and quarrel violently with our Great Dane, Brigit, named after a Celtic goddess.

I called my new friend Otto-the-Brave. On winter nights I would sprawl on the rug by the open fire, straining my eyes in the gloom to read my favourite stories to him: *Ivanhoe*, *Kidnapped* and *The Wind in the Willows*, while Brigit, who was old and felt the cold, would often creep right into the cinders.

One day, when I was thirteen, Otto disappeared. It was autumn and I pushed my way through copses of thorny branches and red berries, tramped across ditches of fallen leaves and bracken and searched around the loch. I saw the elusive red squirrels gathering nuts and the wild goats racing past, splendid in their glossy winter coats. At last I found Otto's corpse in a ditch, his head nearly sliced off by a farmer's spade from the look of things. I guessed it was the work of John Gilmore, our neighbour.

I went straight there, voicing my accusations, with Otto wrapped in my coat. The farmer was having his tea by the fire.

'You killed Otto. I'll report you to the RSPCA. You're a cruel and horrible man.'

The farmer and his wife were distraught. 'They're pests you see, lass. I never guessed it was your Otto. Here, let's give him a decent burial.'

8

They persuaded me to give up Otto's remains and they buried him in the centre of their rose garden.

Later I realised that the farmer's cruel spade had been a blessing in disguise. Where would he have gone, my poor, tamed Otto?

Within a few weeks my father had been crippled in a car crash and our world fell apart.

Bitter months followed. Father became introverted and dour. Mother fretted and cried, and disappeared on week-long trips. In her absence, Maria would tut-tut her way around the kitchen. Once I heard her say, 'What would this poor lass do without us? It's a crying shame.'

A month later Maria and Mac packed their possessions and told me that they were leaving.

'I want to go with you, Maria.'

'You're not our kin. We've been given notice. We've found a new place, but we couldn't take you there, pet, not even if we wanted to.'

From this I deduced that they did not want to. So love can be terminated with one month's notice. Mute with despair I tramped around the loch, steeling myself to face this unexpected rejection. Hours later I went home to confront my mother. She, too, was packing, but she had abandoned her suitcase to gaze in the mirror. I stood beside her, noticing that I was almost as tall as she was. She was so dainty and I was so strong.

'We're going to Bristol, Nina, to stay with Uncle Theodore.' She gazed at my reflection with her astonishing violet eyes. 'You'll learn to love him in time and we'll be happy. The town is full of shops and clothes. You'll have so many friends.'

'I don't like shopping and I don't need new clothes.'

'But look how short your dress is. Goodness, how you're

growing, Nina. You'll never find a husband if you're taller than all the boys. Don't pout, there's a good girl. You don't look pretty when you sulk and I can't stand you when you're moody.'

'I want to stay at home with Father.'

'But, darling, Father and I are parting. You'll have to live with one of us, and your father's never here. Whom do you love best, your father or me?'

How could I tell her the truth?

Days later, when the dreaded prospect of loss was almost upon me, I took my problem to my father. 'Don't send me away. I'll look after you, Father. We'll be fine together.'

Father taught me the harsh realities of life when he forced me, with a few bleak words, to confront my world.

'Nowadays people get divorced. We're not the first and not the last by any means, although perhaps the first in our family. The children suffer, but remember, you're an Ogilvie. You've had a lonely life here. You'll be better off with your mother.'

'When will I see you?' It was a cry of pure anguish.

'Me?' He seemed genuinely taken aback. 'Listen, Nina. Life seldom works out exactly as you had in mind. The trick of surviving is to accept change and make the most of what you have. Enjoy school and try to get on with your stepfather. Soon you'll be grown-up and you'll be free.'

'But I love you, Father.' I reached forward and grabbed his cheeks, pressing hard with my open palms as I struggled to batten down the worst of my rebellion.

I remember how he looked at me, so strangely. 'You're female, so you'll soon forget.'

How cold he was. At that moment I hated him.

I insisted on going to boarding school. Occasionally I

saw Father, but he was walled into his own unique hell and could not reach out, least of all to a young woman who so strongly resembled her mother. I became inviolate. At school I organised all kinds of mad adventures until the headmistress flinched when she saw me coming.

My father took up painting and became a recluse, living in three rooms of our old house, with a neighbouring couple to clean, cook and drive for him. I went to see him once a month, but our meetings were always painful. We could never get through to one another, but I was always sad to leave.

By then I knew that the world was for winners. Whatever kind of God had created life, He had no mercy for the weak or maimed of whatever species you'd like to name. Hadn't He created a system where living creatures fed upon each other and lived or died according to their strength, or cunning or brains? Kill or be killed, eat or be eaten, win or be beaten. It was a world I understood, where logic reigned and all false sentiments were banished. It was a world where I could win.

So, like the golden eagle, I searched the highest mountain peaks for my own special niche, and found it.

Chapter 2

FINANCIAL TRIBUNE,
London, 15 December 1989

Those who wield the pension funds have become key financial power players in the city, the most frightening beasts in the corporate jungle, and Nina Ogilvie, vice-chairman of Bertram Merchant Bank's Asset Management Division, is the deadliest of them all. At 28, Ogilvie controls the investment capital of 500 pension funds, amounting to over fifty billion pounds. The most powerful of corporate entrepreneurs quake when she queries their profit performance.

Witness her latest financial coup – the takeover of the national Sidor supermarket chain. Ogilvie considered Sir Reginald Sidor incompetent. She decided to back Cedric Jedrow's proposed takeover bid. Jedrow is no fool. He leaked the news that Ogilvie was backing him and from that moment the deal was as good as done. Sir Reginald, raised from the cradle to run his father's business empire, found himself out of work overnight . . .

'Fuck!'

There was plenty more. I could not believe the media could write this trash about me without my permission.

Briefly my eyes skimmed the press columns. Moments later I reached for the intercom and rang my boss, Eli Bertram.

'Nina?' Eli's voice. 'I was just going to call you . . .'

'And I know why.'

'Come right over if it's convenient.' He sounded agitated.

'Be right with you.' I replaced the receiver.

I hurried into my private bathroom. It was eight a.m. and I had only just arrived. Outside, the bitter south-east wind was gusting up to 50 m.p.h. and my hair stood up as if I'd had an electric shock. I gazed at myself in despair. I had everything I detested: tightly curled dark red hair, a pale skin and green eyes. Today I looked even paler than usual and my eyes were glittering with anxiety. I had a gut feeling that bad news was hovering about me. All this because of a newspaper report?

'Calm down, Nina.'

As I ran downstairs to the first floor I thought about Eli and my job, and this highly prejudicial personal publicity. Eli Bertram was a man I admired for he was motivated only by logic. Once a refugee from Hamburg, the only survivor of a Jewish banking family, he had fled through Europe and reached Britain where he joined the RAF and fought as a rear gunner until the end of the Second World War. In the bitter post-war years he had succeeded in re-establishing Bertram's Bank, this time in London, and in the late sixties launched his Asset Management Division. I'd joined him seven years before as a raw novice when I graduated with a degree in business economics, but I'd thrived on the cut and thrust of pure reason. Yet I relied heavily on my intuition, too, and right now my hunch told me this story was big trouble. As I strode in, I could feel my cheeks burning.

Eli leaped to his feet. At seventy-three he was still athletic, and a handsome man with his burning black eyes and mop of thick white hair.

'I won't deny we have a problem here, Nina. Now that the media have discovered you, we could have the whole pack round our necks.' Eli's eyes gleamed with amusement. 'Because you're photogenic they'll want to publish your picture, and they'll be sniffing into your private life. Dinner with Neville Wimpey, for instance, could push up his shares to absurd heights and crash them down twice as hard. I know you never give interviews but they have ways and means, as they've demonstrated here.' He leaned back, clasped his hands behind his head and stared quizzically at me. 'We're going to foil them, Nina. I suppose you know you've made a dangerous enemy in Sidor.'

'He'll have to get to the back of the queue.'

Eli shot me a swift, supportive smile, which made me feel slightly better.

'Nevertheless, yesterday, in the House of Commons, Sir Reginald warned of the danger of the asset manager's growing power. He was well supported and this could mean problems for us.'

'Losers always squeal. You taught me that.'

'Well, now. I have an idea. Coffee, Nina?'

'Mm, please.'

He pressed a button and sat frowning at his desk pad. 'I have more bad news, but we could easily leave this for another day if you'd prefer to.'

'Black Monday. Let's get it over and done with.' I'd learned to take the ups and downs of our investments in my stride, so I wasn't really paying much attention.

'It concerns Ralph Dorrington.'

A bucket of cold water in my face could not have shocked me more. Did he know? Did everyone? In-house affairs were strictly frowned upon, but Ralph and I had been discreet. Our social life took place far from the City's prying, calculating eyes. I stood up with a swift, tense movement and gazed through triple-glazed windows at the bare branches of the sycamore tree trembling in the wind.

'Why do clever women always pick the dunces? My dear, he's not for you.' Eli was trying to be gentle, but he was being impertinent.

'Perhaps because clever men choose young, dumb blondes, Eli.' I didn't have to turn round to know I'd scored a hit. Eli's third marriage had scandalised the bank's personnel.

'Listen to me, Nina. At twenty-eight you wield enormous power. You are my own discovery, a woman of rare perception, and your business instincts are infallible, if nothing else. At my age, I think I can be forgiven for taking a fatherly interest in my staff.'

'Is this conversation about me or my job? There's a world of difference. You must see that, Eli. I'm not screwing the business, only Ralph.' I flushed because I sounded so gauche. 'And could we cut the fatherly interest bit? It really doesn't work with you. I like you better as yourself. And another thing. Since I'm going to be as blunt as you, do you employ the services of an investigator to spy on us?'

'Yes.' His eyes challenged me.

I suppose I had guessed, but his confirmation infuriated me. I had always admired him.

'So why bother to flee the Nazis? You'd have felt so at home there.' I wondered dismally where I would find another job that paid like this one.

Now his blue eyes were glacial, and when he spoke so was his voice.

'I know your tactics, Nina. Shock the opposition off their guard, create a smokescreen and snipe from under it. I taught you, remember? Now shut up and listen. We're investing people's lifelines, so I must know if there are any weaknesses that might lead to bullying or constraint. I have to know if a duffer like Dorrington is hanging in here because of his fucking ability instead of his brains. The man's a pompous schmuck masquerading as a banker.'

What could I say? I knew he spoke the truth, but loyalty kept my mouth shut.

'There's worse to come. He's screwing your secretary too.'

I struggled to pull myself together. 'You can't expect to spy on people and retain their loyalty. Goodbye, Eli. I'm leaving. I'll give it to you in writing today.' I stood up and made for the door.

'Hey, come on, Nina. Running away isn't going to solve anything.'

I paused reluctantly.

'Sit down. Hear me out at least. I've had an idea. With your permission, I'll send you to South Africa for a few weeks. It's only a matter of time before that economy opens up to the world. They can't avoid change for ever. My agent there, a man by the name of Bernie Fortune, has put together a very interesting deal. A group of local entrepreneurs took advantage of US and British companies pulling out because of sanctions. They bought up these 'dumped' companies for a song. Major names, huge undertakings, but the group is too big for them to handle. They want overseas finance and expertise and Bernie's looking to us to supply it. He reckons there's a fortune to be made. Have a look around, Nina. And keep your eyes open. If the South African government changes, we must be ready to act fast. There's unimaginable wealth

17

lying underground, some of it still untouched. Capital is what the country badly needs. Those who get in first will reap the benefits.'

Once Eli found a new project there was no getting him off it. As I sipped my coffee, I was only half listening. Part of me was grieving over Ralph and hoping against hope that Eli was wrong for once, but he never was. Then Eli caught my imagination as he painted a scene of untold treasure.

'You make me feel like Ali Baba. All I need is the password.'

'Easy! It's Eli Bertram,' he retorted modestly. 'But watch out for the forty thieves.'

I couldn't help considering what a complex, autocratic, yet caring boss he was. That was Eli for you, a loyal friend or an unforgiving enemy. That was why he was so loved and feared in the City. But I also knew that I could not endure being spied on. I'd have to leave the bank. I promised myself to make a move when I got back home.

'By the time you return, this Sidor deal will be stale news,' he was saying, with a self-satisfied smirk. 'You'll have forgotten about Dorrington, and we'll settle back to normal. A month in the sun will do you good.'

Chapter 3

───❧❧❧───

'A farewell lunch,' Ralph had called it. As I followed the waiter past blue and white gingham cloths to our special table, I pondered on the ambiguity of his words. Could he be referring to my coming South African trip? We often met in this modest Italian restaurant not far from the bank. Today it was almost full and I noticed several women surreptitiously eyeing my emerald green Chanel suit.

'Hi, darling. Hope I haven't kept you waiting.' So far so good.

As Ralph stood up and assumed his strictly-for-clients smile, I saw him rearrange his face into an expression of pseudo-compassion. He was intending to voice regrets and sadness like a paid mourner at a stranger's funeral. Falseness was all about him. I saw it in the way he held his head sidelong and peered at me from the corners of his eyes and the way he squeezed my hand with both of his. But tell-tale triumph shone through his mock solemnity. He was looking forward to getting back at me.

For what? For not putting him on a pedestal? Men's egos were so damned fragile, they needed constant puffs of admiration. Let them talk non-stop all evening and they would pronounce you fascinating. Beat them at anything, and they'd put you down. I'm just no good at adoring.

So it was true, Eli was right, I realised, as I sat down.

A wave of hurt gave way to irritation at my own stupidity. While Ralph studied the wine list, I examined the menu, and waited.

Ralph had worked his way through university by modelling, and he'd scored with his fashionable so-called Establishment look: chestnut hair ruffled by the wind, eyes shining with English candour, a strong profile and a winning smile. He was a karate black belt and he kept fit. At work his self-assured image had bamboozled colleagues into believing in him. He played the role of banker perfectly, but his performance was flawed by his inability to accept that he might be wrong. He never second-guessed, never did his homework.

The wine waiter hovered. Ralph ordered ostentatiously, then turned his attention to me.

'You look lovely, Nina.'

I nodded coldly. Too late, I saw that I had lost something I valued, for Ralph had made me feel wanted and feminine. I would miss him. Perhaps the coming month abroad would give me time to take a long, hard look at myself.

'Ralph, listen, I have bad news and I'm sorry. Yesterday morning Eli told me that he's dismissing you because of the Sherborne Insurance flop and the Bahamas Marina fraud, which he feels you should have been on to. I asked him for two months' grace so that you can resign, to which he agreed. It gives you a chance to make a new start and save face. After all, you can tell everyone you're leaving because . . . well, because Diana works for me.'

There was a long silence. I decided to sit it out. Ralph gave in first and slapped the flat of his hand on the table. The cutlery tinkled.

'So you found out about Diana and me. Dear God! Suddenly everything's becoming crystal clear. Bitch! A woman scorned! Tell me about it.'

'No, Ralph. I was about to call you when you called me.'

I could not tell him that I'd been protecting him for weeks. I could never sink that low, could I?

'I've been protecting you for weeks. I covered up for you on both of these accounts, but Eli found out.'

'Well, you won't have to cover up in future.'

I took a deep breath. How the hell did he manage to keep that self-righteous look on his face and act as if I were in the wrong? There was no point in arguing because Ralph always believed what he wanted to believe, which was why he was so dangerous as an asset manager.

'Let's order,' Ralph growled.

'Salad Niçoise and a glass of water.'

'The usual, huh? Even in a crisis, you never let up. No wonder they call you the Ice Maiden.'

Did they? And who were *they*?

'What crisis?'

Ralph flinched and took a long breath. 'Jesus, Nina . . .' Suddenly he was lost for the right answer. I could see that the silence was getting him down.

'Diana and I are getting married,' he threw at me, with a touch of flamboyant spite. 'She's pregnant. I'd call that a crisis, wouldn't you?'

'For you, yes, but not for her. She's dumb and fat and ugly.'

I had spoken too loudly: heads turned at the nearest table and I flushed.

'She'll make a good wife.' Ralph was enjoying his cruelty. 'She won't compete with me. I won't have to prove myself nightly. Jesus, Nina, bed was the only place where I could be the leader. I nearly turned myself inside out to hang on to my advantage.'

At that moment so many precious memories died of

21

shame. Briefly I mourned his beautiful body. Don't men like successful women? Can they never bear to be beaten? Or was Ralph the exception?

'And she'll always think I'm the greatest. Don't blame yourself for our break-up,' he added, patronisingly. 'I'm just not up to marrying one of the City's most powerful operators.'

'I don't remember asking you. You were good in bed. That's all.' I was lying, but he believed me and flushed.

'You don't need anyone, Nina. You never did. That was the problem. I guess I should have told you sooner, though. Did Diana . . . ?' There was that false look again. 'Diana and I—' He broke off.

Diana and I said it all, but Ralph decided that he must tell me exactly what he loved about Diana.

'If I hurt her, she cries and I feel a shit. You always bring out the big guns, a missile to kill a mosquito. You always have to win.'

'Here's to your marriage.' I raised my glass, gulped some wine and hiccuped. Of all the times . . . Grabbing my napkin, I pressed it over my mouth, stifling my rising fury.

A new understanding hit me like a mystic's revelation. A man like Ralph would not want the woman in his life second-guessing him and being the boss. So why had he wanted me in the first place? Job protection? And when had he found the time to screw Diana? Then I remembered his busy training schedule: karate on Monday and Wednesday, squash Tuesday and Thursday, jogging over the weekends. Ralph was getting a paunch, which should have told me something.

'You're getting flabby. I should have noticed.'

'Please don't go all female-bitchy on me, Nina.'

How many times had that remark stopped me in my

tracks? Why had I let the bastard get away with it? This meeting was a waste of time. There was nothing left to say. I stood up quietly.

'Ralph, you're a cheat. You cheated on me, but who cares? I wish you'd stop cheating yourself. You actually believe all the comforting rubbish you tell yourself. Eli sacked you because you made too many mistakes. Face the facts and join the real world, Ralph. Goodbye.'

My exit was dignified and absolutely right. So why did I have to spoil it all?

Turning back, I placed one hand on his shoulder. 'No hard feelings, Ralph. Let's part friends. You made me feel like a woman and we had fun, so thanks. Good luck.'

His eyes lit up with a gleam of what I stupidly took for warmth. 'Why, Nina,' he exclaimed, gripping my wrist, 'creating the illusion that you were a woman was a Herculean task. I could never have coped in the long term.'

That was when I threw his wine over him. Shit!

Later, I thought it could have been worse. We could have been at Annabelle's.

Chapter 4

I left on a rainy, blustery December evening and as I filed on to the aircraft I was filled with the strange thrill of taking flight to unknown shores. I was glad to leave England, the media and the cold.

As I buckled my seat-belt I considered my goodbyes. Last weekend had been disastrous. I had flown up to Edinburgh to see my mother and her third husband, John. Not wishing to stay at their home, I had booked into the Mount Royal Hotel in Princes Street and arranged to meet them in the restaurant at seven p.m. I had arrived with a magazine, since Mother was always late, but after an hour I began to wonder what had happened. Then I caught a whiff of Chanel No. 5, heard a swish of nylon against nylon, and the click of her high heels.

Mother relied heavily on female aids, chiffon scarves, scents and jewellery. She looked fabulous in a powder blue Versace suit, with a white silk blouse. Heads still turned when she passed. She had been born beautiful, but God knows what efforts maintained her schoolgirl figure, her youthful complexion, her dark red hair without a trace of grey at the temples, her smooth throat. The amount of planning that went into her survival strategy could run a fair-sized business, I mused, and then wondered why

I was mentally sharpening my claws. Five seconds later I knew the answer.

'Darling. You look tired.' She stepped back, tilted her head down and glanced at me, pouting prettily as a child might. 'Aren't you gaining weight?'

'No.'

Something about Mother's diminutive size and her ultra-feminine attitude had always made me feel too tall. She clasped me delicately and planted a near miss of a kiss on each cheek. My nostrils tickled as her hair brushed across my face and I swallowed a sneeze, which made my eyes water. John hovered, a big, awkward, florid-faced man who had once suffered badly from acne.

'I think we'd better go straight into the dining room.' I took my mother's arm. 'This way.'

'Tell us the news,' Mother purred. 'When are you and Ralph getting married, Nina? We're dying to know. How is the darling boy?'

'We've split. He was screwing my secretary.'

There was a long, uneasy silence until we reached our table.

'I always knew he wasn't right for you,' Mother murmured bravely, as she sat down.

That had surprised me. Was she letting me off lightly?

'The trouble is, he worked for you. Let's face it, Nina, you can be very bossy and thoroughly intimidating. It's your brains, I'm afraid. No woman should be saddled with brains like yours. It was hard enough living with your father, and he was a man.'

But not man enough for you. Particularly after his accident. I never voiced the hurtful words.

'Water under the bridge, Mother. I'd rather not talk about it. Let's order the wine, shall we?'

John gave a booming laugh. 'Ease off, Rebecca. If

Nina wanted a husband, she'd get one.' His fat red fist closed over my hand. 'She's looking even lovelier, or hadn't you noticed? Your looks, but she's fresh and new.'

That must have hurt, but Mother knew how to take her punishment. John was a moody, spoiled, difficult man who needed my mother, but hated her for being old. Now he was punishing her by flirting with me. Mother would retaliate, of course. I could almost write the script as I clung to my role of neutrality.

'Believe me, Nina. Pushing thirty is not the end of the world. You've been dumped, but I'm sure Mr Right will come along. I've known women land husbands even later than thirty.'

Did she dislike me, I wondered for the first time. I grabbed my wine impulsively and sent it flying. 'Oh, hell!' Why do I let her get under my skin? 'We live in different worlds, Mother. Profits is the name of the game for me, not husbands.'

'You still have periods, I suppose, or do you only produce balance sheets?'

She had plenty of spunk, but the hurt of John's disloyalty smouldered in her eyes. How could I hurt her more by hitting back? I opted for unconditional surrender and remained mute throughout the cut and thrust of her verbal ripostes and feints. Finally, around ten, after I had listened to her interminable monologue on fashion, Mother made the final thrust. *La belle*!

'I haven't heard you laugh all evening, Nina. You never did have a sense of humour, but this City job of yours has made you terribly dull. Thank God you're getting away for a break.'

She pushed back her chair and stood up.

I rose to mumble my goodbyes.

One down, one to go! I flew to Inverness the following morning to see Father.

When I arrived Father was sitting at his easel in his study. He glanced over his shoulder and gave me a quick, shrewd scan before turning back to his painting.

'It wasn't necessary to come all this way, but good of you to make the journey,' he said, in his clipped, expressionless voice.

Father painted wildlife, mainly birds, and his paintings were meticulous, but as lifeless as the poor stuffed creatures he used for models. How sad he looked. His scant grey hair was awry, his long, bony face thinner than ever. His watchful eyes sunk deep into brown shadows reminded me of a wistful owl. It was hard to remember that he was Commander Charles Ogilvie, DSO, DFC and Bar, almost a legend in British Intelligence.

Except for his housekeeper, Angela Joyce, and her husband, Trevor, who stayed in a cottage in the grounds, he lived alone, growing ever more introverted. A smell of dust, damp and despair mingled with the stench of mothballs. A quick trip to the kitchen confirmed my fears. There was no food in the house.

Dad wasn't short of cash, was he? I knew he had inherited some capital and that he played the stock market. He owned five hundred acres of farmland, some of which he leased to local farmers. Besides this, we had good breeding herds and he had a pension. Perhaps he'd bombed with Lloyds.

'Dad. I earn far more than I can spend. Are you short of anything?'

'God, no.'

'So where's Mrs Joyce?'

'Flu.'

28

'You need stocking up. I'd better get on with it. Can I borrow your car?'

'Don't bother. Mrs Joyce will be back tomorrow. If I wanted anything meantime I could always send Trevor. He's around somewhere.'

'Dad, why don't you move down to London and stay with me?'

'Can't abide the place.'

'It's not so bad. It has its moments. I've got a lovely apartment in Hampstead on the top floor, overlooking the Heath. The flowers are lovely. I can see for miles. It's like being in the country.'

There was no response so I went off to make tea and we passed an hour exchanging meaningless small-talk. It was only later when I was almost ready to leave that I tried to tell him about Ralph.

'I met this man, well, a colleague, really, in the bank. He was a lot of fun. Good-looking, too. I'd thought we had it made, but clearly he wasn't happy. He dropped me for my secretary. That's why I'm glad to be getting away for a while. Eli sacked him for incompetence, but he blamed me. I shall miss him.'

'He's done you a favour,' Dad said, in his quiet, precise voice.

Later, with Trevor waiting in the car to drive me to the airport, I bent to kiss Father's cheek. I longed to hug him, but he did not stop painting and I was scared to nudge his brush-stroke.

'Well, then . . .'

'Take care,' he said, and that was that.

The warning bell coincided with a sudden lurch. Having set my alarm for four in order to have a good wash before the queues began, I was unwilling to vacate the toilet. *Return to your seat and fasten your seat-belt* flashed above the tiny washbasin. Within seconds the aircraft was swaying and bucking and my cosmetics were skidding over the floor. I peered into the mirror. A thin face with large, startled eyes, bloodshot and swollen, stared back.

Gathering my possessions, I squeezed past the stewardess and stumbled to my seat. The night had seemed endless, but at last the lights were switched on. A brittle, smiling attendant appeared from the galley to hand out glasses of orange juice. Breakfast and coffee improved my mood, and shortly afterwards we were circling over Cape Town's Table Mountain.

Chapter 5

A blast of the city's famous sou'easter nearly knocked me flying as I left the gangway. Wow! I hung on to my case and battled to move forward. Soon I was shuffling through passport control. I grabbed a trolley, retrieved my luggage and walked towards the exit, amazed that it had been so simple. The door slid open and I hurried through.

'This way, Nina. I'm Bernard Fortune, your host. Well, your friend, too. Call me Bernie. Meet my wife, Joy. The press got wind of your arrival, but airport management have given us an interview room, so follow me.' He grabbed my trolley.

Bloody hell! 'Well, hello there.'

So this was Eli's local agent. I studied him cautiously: olive skin, average height, excessively muscled, probably from weight-training, hairy everywhere except on his smooth and shiny head, bushy eyebrows almost concealing his ultra-expressive, predatory brown eyes. A man to beware of, I instinctively felt. I had the impression that he would run roughshod over anyone who got in his way.

'Sorry you weren't warned,' Bernie said, 'but your arrival here means a great deal to us. It lights the end of the tunnel. We've been the world's lepers for almost half a century and we've had enough if it, I can tell you. Bloody Dutchmen are on the way out. They know it, we know it, and your coming here will spell it out for a whole lot more people.'

I was getting breathless for him. To my mind, people gabble on to confuse their listener. So what was Bernie trying to put over me? And what sort of an idiot organises a press conference for a woman who's spent the night on the plane? Wouldn't tomorrow have done as well?

'What's your hurry? I'm here for a month, Bernie.'

He flushed and grinned disarmingly.

'We don't let the grass grow under our feet, Nina. Too much at stake.'

His wife, Joy, seemed over-anxious and tense. She was wearing a velvety blue track-suit with a matching ribbon round her bleached straight tresses. Her eyes were blue, her features good, and she was thin enough to be anorexic, but her skin let her down. It hung in folds under her chin, sagged around her eyes, wrinkled her brow and turned to chicken skin around her neck. Nothing that a good plastic surgeon couldn't fix, as Mother could have told her.

The media consisted of two tired-looking men and three young women. I was pushed behind the desk between Bernie and Joy.

'This is Nina Ogilvie, whom you've come to meet.' Bernie's voice was honey smooth. 'As I told you, Nina is the City of London's latest whiz-kid.'

I glanced sharply at him, but Bernie was keeping his face averted. 'She's been on the plane all night, so ask your questions and buzz off.'

The questions came haltingly at first, but ten minutes later there was still no end in sight. 'That's it. I'm getting out of here.' I moved towards the door.

'How do you cope with being a woman in a man's world?' a female voice called from behind me.

I turned with a tart comment on my lips, which froze when I saw how young and vulnerable the reporter was. Haven't we all been living in a man's world for the past ten thousand years? I pondered. So how do I cope? Perhaps by beating men at their own game.

I smiled and put up my hand. Enough was enough.

I was ushered into a gleaming 7-series BMW and introduced to a huge black man with slanting eyes and a small pointed beard. He was wearing a chauffeur's uniform that was far too tight for him.

'This is Caesar, our driver. Take you anywhere you want to go.' Bernie spoke without bothering to glance at him.

'Good morning, Caesar.' I held out my hand and he shot me an astonished smile.

As we wove between the traffic Bernie placed his hot hand on my knee. 'What a girl!' he said. 'A superb performance. Old Eli's lucky to have you.'

I knew for a fact that he and Eli were not on first-name terms. I burned at his crude flattery and pushed his hand away, hoping Joy had not seen.

Soon we were passing the most depressing slums. Mile after mile of tin shanties set among unbelievable squalor and overcrowding.

'Our latest informal settlement,' Bernie said, with a tinge of bitterness in his voice. 'Every householder owns a field, a few cows, a mealie patch at the very least in his homeland, but they flock to the cities where there aren't enough jobs for them.'

Silence would be my best bet, I decided, since I was a stranger.

We sped away, leaving the slums for pleasanter homes. Soon we entered what might have been another planet: oak-lined avenues, exotic architecture, acres of manicured lawns and brilliant flowering shrubs, styles that were Swedish, Spanish, Moroccan, Old English, Early Dutch, but they all had something in common and that was wealth.

'This is Constantia where we live,' Joy told me, with a tinge of smugness in her voice. 'You see that house up there? Lord and Lady Melcroix live there. And can you see that pink wall between the trees . . . ?'

Joy had a weakness for titles. According to her, half the British Establishment were securing their place in the sun. We turned into the driveway of a massive Spanish *hacienda* with immaculate lawns and an Olympic-sized pool. Caesar opened my door.

'Caesar, this madam has flown six thousand miles to see our country. Look after her well. See you at dinner, Nina.' Bernie smiled smoothly. 'Joy will take you shopping and that sort of thing.' He nodded coldly at his wife.

'Look here, Bernie, I can see you have a real problem catching up with the twentieth century, but try to banish this image you have of a visiting colleague's wife. I'm the colleague. Right? So I'm not here for shopping.'

'Nina . . . Nina . . . You need to meet the big boys socially first. That's important here. We're leaving for Timbavati Game Park first thing in the morning. Everyone you need to know will be present, relaxed and ready to make friends.' He frowned before favouring me with a disarming grin. I could see that he resented having to humour me. 'When in Rome, Nina. We've invited a select few to dinner tonight, so take the day off and pamper yourself. Joy's taking you shopping because you'll need a few things: khaki shorts and shirts, a bush hat, good boots. Charge it. My pleasure.'

He drove away, leaving me fuming.

Chapter 6

'Dinner at seven,' Bernie had said. Not knowing how they dressed here, I played safe with a black cocktail dress. The damp heat, plus the shower, had turned my hair into an unmanageable dark red frizz and my face was still flushed and slightly puffy from the long flight. I tied my hair back with a white chiffon scarf and added a pearl necklace and earrings.

Bernie was hovering. 'Come,' he said, propelling me firmly towards the sound of voices. 'You're late. Let's get the show rolling.'

I smirked as I entered Bernie's reception room. The décor shrieked loud and clear that the Fortunes had made it: wood-panelled walls, Persian carpets on an inlaid marble floor, old paintings in heavy gilt frames. Joy was flitting around in a midnight blue silk shift loaded with jewellery, playing the society hostess with enviable skill.

A quick glance around assured me that every wife was beautiful and none was past their mid-twenties. Clearly this was the second or third time round for their paunchy husbands. Joy stuck out like a weed in a rose garden, and twice as poignant, as she doggedly clung to her illusion of being young and attractive.

'Look at them.' Bernie blinked lovingly at his guests.

'Ugly bastards, most of them, but they don't come any better – friends from way back. Between them they're worth billions.'

Presumably the female guests were mere appendages. A white-clad waiter, complete with gloves and cummerbund, approached carrying glasses of punch on a silver tray. Taking one, I was shocked to recognise Caesar, whom I had last seen in khaki shorts weeding the garden.

'Thank you, Caesar. A man for all seasons, Bernie.'

Bernie flushed. 'Get to know the country before you start criticising, Nina.'

Grudgingly I conceded this point with a nod as Bernie grabbed my arm and steered me across the room. 'Nina, meet Theo Hamilton. He owns several diamond concessions,' Bernie blabbed happily. 'Hi, Theo, meet Nina, London's newest and only female whiz-kid. Woo her, my boy.'

'Hi, Theo.' I thrust out my hand. 'Wooing won't help. Profits will.'

Bernie was a schmuck, but Theo seemed unconcerned as he turned on the charm heavy-handedly. He looked like a Hollywood-style Roman gladiator gone to seed.

'Bernie and I go back a few decades, Nina. Under that tough skin there's a great guy. Trust me!'

The back-scratching session came to an abrupt halt as Bernie dragged me to the next group.

'Meet Steve Watson, who made his pile in Texas oil.'

Steve drooped over me like an overgrown beanstalk, while his piercing, predatory blue eyes left no doubt as to his mental agility.

'Cool it, Bernie,' Steve mumbled, without success.

'Steve owns a dozen mines and a fleet of jet aircraft. Worth ten million dollars if he's worth a cent.'

'By Nina's standards we're the *hoi-polloi*. Right, Nina?' Steve nodded knowingly at me while I froze with annoyance.

'If the cap fits, Steve . . .'

Bernie dragged me on.

Joshua van der Walt, chairman of the country's most powerful indigenous bank, assumed the manner of a monarch as he listened to Bernie's monologue and clasped my hand in his gigantic paw. 'Hello,' he murmured.

'Worth a hundred million rands,' Bernie stage-whispered, as we moved along.

God! It was endless. David McFarlane's massive head was set on wide, muscular shoulders with a paunch to match. He bought and sold mines and mining supply houses, Bernie explained, well within McFarlane's hearing.

'Don't let Bernie intimidate you. I'm just a glorified salesman. We all are.'

'Yes, I know that.' A sidelong glance revealed David's amusement. He winked and suddenly I liked him. I guessed he wouldn't patronise me again – and he had meant no harm. He was a man's man and he could only relate to the 'little woman'. I tried out a smile as he grabbed his wife.

'Honey, come and meet Nina. You two will be great pals.'

David's new wife, Sophia, looked set for a royal wedding in her amazing collection of diamonds, including a tiara, set off by a sophisticated black strapless sheath. 'Enchanted, darling.' She leaned forward, almost kissed me on both cheeks and turned her back.

By now I suspected that my fruit punch was not as innocuous as it tasted. The alcohol, plus the heat, was producing purple patches on my arms. I dreaded to see

39

what my face looked like. I could feel the trickles of sweat rolling down between my shoulder blades and gathering in my armpits. Did it show?

Bernie nudged me forward and lowered his voice. This puzzled me. 'I'm going to introduce you to Wolf Möller,' he murmured. 'It's rumoured that he's making a fortune breaking sanctions to bring oil into this country. No one knows for sure. Said to be very well connected in high places. Bit of a dark horse.'

I found myself gazing into dark blue eyes crinkling into a smile. He was lovely to look at and my glance lingered, captivated by his boyish grin. His hair was light brown, and cut very short. He was in his mid-thirties, I guessed. Sweetness and humour showed in his expression. I felt I'd found an ally in hostile territory.

As Bernie began his recitation about my work, Wolf Möller gripped my arm. 'You're embarrassing Miss Ogilvie and, besides, I read it in the newspaper. Didn't everyone? May I borrow her for a moment?'

Turning his back on the astonished Bernie, Möller led me across the terrace towards the garden.

'Phew! I couldn't be more grateful.'

'Bernie goes a bit over the top.' He stopped short and pressed his fingers on my arm.

'Listen,' he muttered, 'a Cape canary. You don't hear them often.'

As we listened to the melodious strains, I was conscious of the scent of Möller's aftershave and the way his eyes seemed to darken as he gazed towards the trees. In a matter of minutes twilight turned to dusk and the canary lapsed into silence.

'Shall we go down to the pool, Miss Ogilvie? It's cooler there.' He took my glass and poured the contents on the grass. 'I've probably killed their lawn.' He chuckled. 'I checked with their obsequious slave: aqua vita, champagne, brandy, tequila, orange juice . . . I advise you to stick to fruit juice until it cools down, Ms Ogilvie.'

As we walked towards the pool in the lingering twilight, I puzzled over his accent. German, with a long stay in America, but that wasn't all of it.

'No wonder I feel dizzy. It's so hot. Is this normal?'

'Unusual for the Cape, but further north the nights are always this exotic. Nights for fishing offshore in a small boat, scuba-diving, walking in the mountains, making love, dancing barefoot on the sand, almost anything except standing in a stuffy room full of sweating *nouveaux riches*. I was wishing I hadn't come, but then I saw you and I changed my mind. You are that rare phenomenon, a perfectly beautiful woman.'

'Wow! Slow down! Let's analyse your opening gambit. For starters, do you know Africa well?'

His laugh came often, I noticed. It was a sensual, deep-throated sound, both intimate and intriguing.

'Does anyone ever know it well . . . ? Quite frankly, I don't think so, but I've travelled extensively all over the continent. I'm always amazed by its excesses. I adore and fear and hate Africa. Like so many of its viruses, once it penetrates your bloodstream you can never be free of it.'

'So let's move on . . . Is the Cape good for scuba-diving?'

'Not really. The water's too cold. You need to move north along the Indian Ocean coast.'

'D'you know, Mr Möller, I haven't heard that description *nouveau riche* since my vague flirtation with Communism during school days. It seems to reveal an Eastern European background with aristocratic connections.'

He scowled. 'I'm German. Does that bother you, Ms Ogilvie?'

41

'Should it?'

'Yes, maybe it should.'

My silence echoed around us, but then he said, 'I find your omissions more interesting than your questions.'

I wasn't going to fall for that innuendo. 'It must be dinner-time, Mr Möller.'

'Oh, come now, Ms Ogilvie. You pounced like a tick-bird on a buffalo's back to sort out the juiciest titbits, gently sidestepping those that didn't tempt you, such as my allusions to your incredible appeal. I have an obsession for beauty, particularly in women.'

'Everyone has an obsession, Mr Möller. Mine is my work. It occupies all of my waking hours.'

'That's a temporary aberration, Ms Ogilvie. One day you will find a man who is more satisfying than your work and you will marry him.'

Somehow this intriguing man, with the scented garden and the balmy night, had conspired to penetrate my defences. I turned towards the house, but he pulled me towards him.

'Don't run away.'

'Back there I wanted to die of embarrassment, Mr Möller. Bernie's the limit. I was keen to get away, so thanks for rescuing me, but I'm here on business so let's join the others.'

He gave a mock bow. 'The pleasure's all mine. Isn't that what you British say? Only in my case it's sincere.'

There was an implied criticism there, but I wasn't feeling patriotic. I was far too busy trying to fend him off.

'Bernie's become Africanised,' Möller went on, as we strolled towards the house. 'In traditional African society an important man will commission a praise-singer, who's called an *imbongi*, to walk ahead of him and publicise his wealth, his power, his good deeds and his health. Bernie is performing this service unasked and for free. One must consider what Bernie is getting out of it, Ms Ogilvie. Could it be your fund's much publicised fifty billion that's looking for a home?'

I looked up suspiciously and saw the glimmer of mirth in Möller's eyes. Then the sound of the dinner gongs came, muted and melodious, in snatches through the trees.

'May I call you Nina? It's a lovely name. Some say it's Hebrew, in which case the literal translation is a young girl or a granddaughter, but the name really stems from early Babylonian, meaning 'goddess of the deep waters'. You are well named, Nina.'

What did he mean? 'Are you Jewish?'

He shook his head. 'I speak Hebrew because I worked in Jerusalem for a while.'

I pondered over this unusual man as we walked back in silence. You're far too smooth, Wolf Möller. I'm certainly not taking you seriously.

It wasn't often that I lied to myself so blatantly.

Chapter 7

Eighteen places were set along an ebony table on which gleaming cut glass, silver cutlery and candelabra glittered in the light from crystal chandeliers. I had been placed between Joshua and David, with Steve opposite and Sophia beside him. Lobster bisque was served by three black waiters wearing white gloves, including the faithful Caesar, working under the watchful eye of a hired butler. The fish came and went while David plied me with questions about my work.

'We study statistics, keep up with market trends, try to predict future earnings. That's about it.'

'Is "we" the royal pronoun?' Joshua boomed.

'We work as a team, Joshua.'

The temperature was soaring. I found myself staring at a massive painting of an old English scene: a brace of partridge and a dead Muscovy duck lay on a kitchen table. I could almost smell the putrefying flesh.

'Tell me, Nina,' Steve tossed out casually, 'do you ever get share options from grateful clients?'

'No.' I tried to disguise my smile. These guys had a lot to learn about subtlety.

'So, sadly, you only make fortunes for others,' Theo said. 'Just a simple, salaried woman, eh, but with a hell of a lot of clout.'

They were agile fielders, I had to admit, and they worked as a team. I sensed the guests tensing around me. Had they been waiting? It was time to take a stand.

'I don't go unrewarded. I've no complaints.' A quarter of a million pounds a year covered my needs.

David neatly took the ball. 'A salary can never match capital, Nina. With capital you can go places. I don't have to tell you that, do I? In this country we do things differently. We understand the value of a good man, – or should I say woman? Perhaps because we're so short of financial expertise we reward those who have the necessary know-how.'

'That's the neatest way I've ever heard a bribe described.'

He looked shocked. 'It's not a bribe, Nina. If you're involved in the success of a group it stands to reason you should own a slice of the action. It's a safety mechanism.'

They were trying to make it easy for me, but to my mind their group was smelling worse than the partridges.

Abruptly the men seemed to forget about me as they chatted about matters of mutual interest. Their conversation was blunt and money-oriented. It seemed that every item, animal, vegetable or mineral, had to show a profit. They discussed antiques knowledgeably, the accelerating local taste for cabernets and the need to import new vines, the need for more game parks and the soaring prices of zebra and giraffe in local auctions. I learned that there was a huge profit in buying game to be shot by overseas hunters. They wore their wealth with well-practised ease, and if they intended to dazzle me, they succeeded, but I was also repulsed.

'What a charming dress, darling.' Sophia broke her long silence. 'Such an unusual line,' she enthused. 'I don't recognise it from this season's collections.'

46

So it was war! 'I'd hate to be a slave to fashion, Sophia. Catherine Walker designs my clothes to suit me.'

'You prefer English designers? How patriotic!' Now she was openly sneering.

'Not really. I just love her work.'

When the waiter carried in a silver meat dish with a spit-roasted side of lamb, Bernie stood up to carve.

'No one else does this to my satisfaction.' He sharpened the knife with a flourish and stopped, hands in mid-air, as we heard the sound of screeching brakes coming from the road. Then came a massive crash followed by a series of loud thumps. An agonised scream was abruptly terminated, followed by groans and cries for help.

Joy said, 'Oh, God. Of all times! The roast's getting cold, darling.'

I gazed at her in shocked silence, scared by her indifference. Then I jumped up. 'We must do something.'

'You're a stranger here,' Joshua muttered, taking my arm and thrusting me back on to the chair. 'Leave it alone.'

'Rightie-ho, Joy! Smells delicious.' Bernie hesitated, looking around for approval. I gathered that he wasn't *au fait* with the correct social etiquette for dealing with the dying at a dinner party. 'Here goes!' He began to carve.

The cries were becoming louder and more urgent.

'Caesar!' Bernie turned imperiously. 'You go. We'll cope here. Make sure to call an ambulance and the police.'

A howl of anguish propelled me to my feet.

'Not our problem, Nina,' Joshua said. 'We don't want to spoil Joy's dinner.'

'Excuse me!' I shook off his arm.

Wolf was making for the door. I followed him and heard

Joshua tagging along. 'Keep close to me,' he commanded. 'Be careful.'

A torch flickered ahead as we ran down the drive-way. A flash of lightning revealed a minibus wrapped around a tree that had half toppled over, crushing the neighbouring wall. The injured lay sprawled around the road. There was so much blood. Neighbours were arriving and together we hauled the injured to the grassy verge.

I thought I heard muffled groans coming from the ditch behind a bush. Shielding my face with my arms, I pushed through the branches. A dark figure was bending over an injured woman and for an idiotic moment I thought he was helping her.

'Is she badly hurt?' I called.

He whipped around, rings, necklaces and bags clutched in one hand. I saw the whites of his eyes flash in a sea of darkness. A single movement flung me against the tree-trunk. I saw a shaved head, felt his hot breath, and smelt his rancid body odour. 'White whore!' His voice was thick with hatred. He grabbed my pearl necklace, tearing the clasp against my neck, while his other hand fumbled in my crotch. I squirmed and fought him in silence, not believing that this was happening, while his victim screamed for help.

A knife flashed towards my face. I caught hold of his hand with both of mine, trying to push him away, panting, slowly losing. Running footsteps were approaching. Dropping the knife, my attacker fled as Wolf flung himself into the ditch.

'Are you hurt?'

'No,' I panted. I took a deep breath and picked up the knife. 'He would have stabbed me. But why?'

Joshua had appeared behind him. 'These *tsotsis* prey

on the weak,' he said heavily. 'You should have stayed with us. I warned you.'

Thank God no one could see how shocked I was.

A doctor had arrived from a neighbouring house and we could hear the sirens of approaching ambulances and the police, so I walked back to the house. In the bathroom I stared long and hard at my reflection. I looked composed.

When I returned to the table Joy was none too pleased with me.

'Can you believe it? A man was actually robbing the injured . . .'

My voice tailed off as Joy shot me a pitying glance. 'So what's new?'

My plate had been kept warm: peas, pumpkin, lamb, roast potatoes, mint sauce and gravy. I drained my glass and David refilled it. The wine was dry and strong, and I felt the blood returning to my cheeks.

'My latest,' David told me. 'We brought the vines over from Italy. You must come out and see our place. Sophia's refurbishing our home.' He gazed fondly at his young starlet, who rewarded him with a bored smile.

I could not shake off a curious sense of unreality as we finished dessert.

Wolf returned as we moved from the table and, as I looked up at him, I tried to explain something that I only dimly perceived. 'This rich home, the pattern of life, it's an illusion. To me it seems we're like travellers adrift in a luxury yacht in savage seas.'

'Hey there, calm down. You've had a shock. Let it go.'

Wolf hung around chatting about local wines for the next few minutes while I got a grip on myself.

Chapter 8

The next morning we left Cape Town airport at six a.m. and arrived in Johannesburg in time for breakfast.

'Where's Wolf?' I asked Joy. There was no sign of him.

Joy shot me an inquisitive glance. 'I didn't think to invite him. It's too late now. Sorry, Nina.'

By the time we finished breakfast it was raining. A minibus took us to a runway where Steve's private jets were waiting. As we soared into a darkening sky, the pilot tried but failed to rise above the Highveld's summer storm. We were pitched in all directions. Above, around and beneath us blue-black clouds, seemingly alive, surged towards us, nuzzled and jostled us, exploded in our faces; retreated, regrouped and rushed back again. Through the near-darkness, forked lightning stabbed at us. My blood succeeded in catching up with my body when we flew into sunlight at noon.

'Phew!' Bernie said. 'That was a bad one.' I noticed he'd drunk most of his bottle of Scotch.

We came in to land on a short runway inside the game camp's living enclosure. As I stepped off the plane a wave of heat enveloped me. It was like going into a sauna, and my lungs burned, my nose dried, my eyes smarted.

Bernie put a hot arm around my shoulders and spoke in

an undertone. 'I've invited everyone you're likely to want to meet. We start work today with drinks and a buffet lunch. Satisfied? All the big fish will be here. Anyone else you come across is a minnow. Don't waste time on them. Remember that.' His whisky breath washed over me.

'When I need a big brother, I'll come to you, I promise, Bernie.' I kept my voice low so that Joy would not hear.

Bernie's bonhomie evaporated. For a fleeting moment his guard slipped and his eyes gleamed with dislike. Then the mask was back in place. 'That's a deal,' he said, as if I had paid him a compliment.

Annoyance fled when I caught sight of a giraffe towering over the fence only a few yards away, peering at us with an expression of benign curiosity. I was tossed into a state of happy anticipation as we piled into the Jeep and sped around rows of rondavels situated on a rise overlooking the river. Braking beside a grove of trees, Joy pointed to the nearest hut. 'There you are,' she said, handing me a key. 'Remember the number. See you in the lodge in a few minutes. Drinks before lunch. For God's sake, wear something light and informal. None of your linen suits here. Shorts or a skirt and a T-shirt, otherwise you'll boil, quite apart from looking ridiculous.'

Bernie shot her a scathing look and Joy closed her mouth fast.

'Thanks, Joy. I appreciate your help.'

I had a grandstand view of the river, and I guessed I had the best position. Bernie was sparing no efforts to please me. My hut was charming inside: a large circular bedsitter, with cane settees, a grass mat, comfortable chairs, a bed and a cupboard. I strolled down the sloping lawn to the fence overlooking the river far below.

A tall buck steps from the reeds, its coat burnished silver in the brilliant sunlight. Ethereal and graceful, it moves to the sluggish water as if gliding through a dream. I long to be a part of the beauty, but it remains inviolate and tantalising. Scent and sound embrace me: toasting fragrant herbs, the fetid aroma of the water buck, the heady chant of cicadas and, overpoweringly, the birdsong. I am struck by the intensity of the moment. I flow and merge, intricately bound into the fabric of the bush. No longer a spectator. Paradise.

Chapter 9

The cocktail party, on the other hand, was more like hell.
I paused in the doorway, suddenly aware that shorts and
T-shirts were not for me. Compared with these birds of
paradise, their honey tans set off by the brilliant colours
of their elegant sports clothes, I looked as if I'd been
buried alive for a couple of years. I should have worn
slacks, but it was too late and too hot. Too bad.

A woman nearby turned towards me. 'My God.' She
gave a high-pitched neigh. 'Did you just fly in from
Alaska?'

'It felt like it.'

I was drawn into the group, introduced, and subjected
to a polite third-degree as the women tried to place me in
their status scale. What were their guidelines? Not class,
fame or achievements but wealth, I soon discovered.
Their conversation was foreign to me as they discussed
the merits of hired caterers and butlers, where to dump
the kids during the school holidays, the pros and cons of
the more fashionable slimming farms.

The husbands, sporting khaki bush gear, seemed to
prefer their own company as they gathered around the
bar. Stern-eyed and predatory, they were all larger than
life, deeply bronzed, with hairy legs, thick as saplings,
and sinewy muscles. Sun and space had brought about

a strange transformation, for they were hardier and tougher than the European stock from which they had sprung. I sensed that to these magnates, life was yet another corporation to be stripped down to asset level and exploited.

'Hey, Nina.' Bernie approached me from the bar. 'Come over here.' He tugged at my arm. 'Johan's a valuable contact, and an amazing fellow.'

'Cut the eulogies, please, Bernie.'

Johan, a middle-aged brute of amazing girth, with grizzled, crew-cut hair and a battered nose, appraised me coolly. I guessed that he had calculated the cost of my clothes, my age, my IQ and my fucking ability in one sweeping glance. He came out from behind the bar, took my arm and led me to a bench covered with a hairy skin that prickled my bare legs when he drew me down beside him.

First came a glass of wine. 'Try this, Nina. I'd be interested in your educated verdict. It's from my estate.'

'Excellent! I love it.' Clearly, owning a vineyard was the ultimate status symbol.

Johan smiled pityingly and I realised that I should have said much more.

'Taste this, my dear,' he went on, in a gruff undertone. 'You've never tasted meat like it in your life.'

He speared a long sliver from a marinating tub beside him and held it poised, dripping red wine into the tub. The drips ceased and I watched in fascinated horror as the fork moved towards me.

'Open,' he commanded.

Cupping one hand under the meat, he shielded my clothes while the fork moved towards my mouth.

'Mm-mm.' I shook my head and closed my mouth.

'Don't be a coward. Open your mouth.'

'It's delicious, Nina. Try it. You must,' the men chorused.

Oh, Eli, you owe me danger pay.

'Nina, give it a go.' That came from Bernie, and it sounded like a plea.

'D'you know why it's so delicious, so tasty, so sweet? It's because the buck felt no fear. Fear taints the meat. To my mind abattoirs should be banned. The pain of being herded together, the anguish of watching the others die, knowing their turn will soon come . . .'

Oh, God! 'Is it kosher?' I interrupted him, with sudden inspiration. 'No? Well, in that case, I'm afraid . . .' I rose, trying not to smile in the face of Bernie's embarrassment. I'd make my peace with him later.

Advancing as far as the doorway, I hovered and looked back. They seemed to be waiting uneasily, as if they had missed their cues. I was reminded of a staged charade playing out a hidden message. I, too, had a role to play, but what was it?

Chapter 10

Pushing my hat in place, I abandoned the party and wandered over the sloping grass to a grove of tall, graceful trees, heavy with gigantic pods, shuddering in their deep pools of shadows. The wind blew the spiky arms of the acacias, scattering yellow blossom and rocking the weaver birds' nests in time to the undulating yellow grass. Beyond the trees was a game track, cutting steeply through tall reeds to a near-dry tributary of the river far below. I slithered down and reached the shady riverbed. Far above, the trees waved their large leaves in sparkling sunlight.

It was so silent. I took off my shoes and crept uphill a short distance to examine a clump of tropical palms fringing the shore. I caught sight of monkeys watching me from way up in a tree, but then a sudden sense of unease sent me scurrying to the bank. Yet nothing was around so why worry? I sat on a rock in the shade, enjoying the heat and the joy of being alone. Then the bush came to life with the cicadas' heady vibrations, then birdsong.

Twigs snapped behind me like gunshots. I stood up and backed into the bushes, trying in vain to calm my panic.

Moments later, Wolf stepped out of the reeds and I almost yelped with relief. I wanted to call out but the intensity of my feelings alarmed me. Needing time to pull myself together, I remained hidden.

My first impression was of his gracefulness. He was tall and slender. He wore only a loose khaki vest and brief shorts with a hunting rifle slung over his shoulder. I could see the lean strength of his limbs. He was barefooted and his hair looked lighter in the sunlight, his skin darker, his eyes more brilliant.

He studied my footprints, pausing where I had admired the palms. He's part jungle, I thought, wary as a buck, stealthy as a cat. Moments later he pushed aside the bushes and leaned over me.

'Ah! So I've found you, Nina, luckily for you. Don't you know you're breaking the rules? You could have been killed and eaten by now.'

I tried to hit back. 'And you're gatecrashing the party. Joy said you weren't invited.'

'So you asked her?' He gave a strange smile, as if he were filing some vital piece of information. 'I'm glad you thought to ask. I missed you, too. Luckily Bernie's party didn't book the entire camp, so, as you rudely remarked, I gatecrashed the party. I saw you sneak off, but when you didn't return I started to worry. You're safe, no harm done. May I examine your legs?'

I couldn't help laughing. 'Give me one good reason why you should?'

'Here's two. Snake bite, ticks.'

'I'd know if I'd been bitten by a snake, wouldn't I?'

'Strangely enough, people often don't. There's a tick on your ankle. One's not bad considering you're sitting in a nest of them.' He was enjoying himself. 'Take a look at the grass, Nina. You're far from home and this is not a zoo.'

'You're joking!' I looked around and saw that every

stem had a small black knob at the end of it. Suddenly I was on my feet brushing my shorts vigorously.

'Keep still. Ach! Wait a minute. There's more on the back of your thighs. You would think you would feel the little beasts, but not so. You'll have some nasty marks. If you start feeling nauseous in a week's time, see the doctor. Tick-bite fever is not pleasant, particularly the first time.'

'Have you had it?'

'Can't avoid it if you live in the bush. Some people say you can only catch it once, but I've had it several times. Come over here, Nina. You paused by this rock, yes? Did you know you were being scrutinised?'

'By whom?'

'Take a look through my glasses, under that tree.' He pointed upriver.

I focused and found myself gazing into the fierce tawny eyes of a male lion. Adrenaline surged through my veins. I wanted to run, but controlled myself. I counted four lionesses, but there were probably more. After a while I handed back the glasses.

'They've been watching me.'

'Uh-huh.'

'How do we get out of here? Will they attack?'

'Probably not, since it's noon. They aren't hunting and they fear *Homo stupido* as much as *Homo sapiens*.'

'Thanks for the compliment.'

'Let's go. Stay close.'

'I'll be your shadow. Is the gun loaded?'

'Of course.'

Wolf climbed ahead, pushing his way through the reeds and hauling me up behind him. When we reached half-way he squatted on the grass in the shade of some bushes.

'We're probably safe here. They avoid the camp in daylight – but don't venture out alone again.' He laughed. It was a pleasant laugh that began as a rumble in his belly and moved up to his throat. 'You're a country girl at heart, Nina, despite your business success, so learn about the bushveld. If you need a teacher I'm volunteering. The bushveld can be deceptive and dangerous.'

'I was foolish.' I gazed around wistfully. 'Everyone's gorging themselves, and then they'll be sleeping. They go out at five. They said there's nothing to see until then, but they're wrong, there are the trees and the birds. I wouldn't have missed this walk for anything.'

'I'll drive you around wherever you want to go. I hired a Jeep at the airport.'

'I wish . . . but I'm Bernie's guest.'

'Too late for lunch, so why worry?'

'Why are you trying so damn hard, Wolf?'

He smiled. 'Nina, my sweet, if you don't know why, then I can't tell you. If I tried, you would wonder what my angle was.'

He was right. I was already wondering what he wanted to sell me.

He smiled disarmingly, but I was not fooled. He was not as straightforward as he tried to pretend.

'Nina, please be careful. I like you and I won't say this twice, so listen to me. You've stepped into a jungle.' He reached out and held my hand.

'And you rescued me.' I laughed shakily, for his touch had set my blood racing.

'There are far more dangerous jungles than out there, Nina. And you are the quarry. Don't say I didn't warn you.'

His choice of words intrigued me. For a moment I had the oddest idea that he meant himself. Then I remembered how I had felt as I stood in the doorway of the lodge. Clearly he was talking about Bernie's friends.

'Come on, Nina. Move it. I'll drive you wherever you want to go.'

As I scrambled up the steep slope behind him, I felt strangely drawn to him. I knew I had found a friend in this hostile territory.

Chapter 11

By mid-afternoon the heat had intensified, scorching the veld. The land was crying out for water, but the purple rainclouds hung far back on the horizon.

Wolf was the perfect guide. He knew the names of the trees and shrubs, the birds and their calls and habits, and he had a talent for spotting the unusual: nail-sized tree frogs emerging from their cocoon of spittle and scurrying to a nearby waterhole, a nest of vultures, white and fluffy, in the bowl of a half-decayed tree, an iguana in a shallow stream.

'I wish it would rain. It makes me sad to see the parched grazing. The buck are so thin.'

'For me, Nina, the cruelty of creation is an enigma. This Christian God of love whom I worship also created a world of incredible harshness. The strong eat the weak, that's the philosophy of the gutter but it's nature's way too, and when we impose a system of kindness and security, we become lazy and degenerate. Sometimes I think winning is the only virtue worth having.' He wiped his forehead with an oily engine cloth. 'God, it's hot.'

'I learned early that it's wise to win. I used to long to be strong and invincible, like the golden eagles in the mountains around our lochs.'

'And now that you're older?'

'I still have to win. I work in a tough environment, but I love it. I like to pit my wits against the competition.'

'And what about the rest of you?'

I frowned. What was he talking about? 'There is no "rest of me".'

'Womanliness, femininity, confidence in your sexuality. All those qualities seem to be in hibernation.'

'I can do without such disadvantages.' I laughed harshly. I could almost hear my father's voice, saying, '*You're female so you'll soon forget*.' The memory still hurt, but I wasn't going to tell Wolf.

'Don't laugh like that. You sounded like Sophia. Imagine a world peopled with Bernie's friends and their hard-arsed wives.'

'They're not so bad when you're past their defences.' His probing was beginning to irritate me. I said, 'It's too hot to think, let alone talk. I can't believe this heat. It even hurts to breathe. My lungs are seared.'

After this I refused to be drawn into revealing more of myself, so Wolf spent the afternoon telling me about his home in East Germany, the estate where he had been brought up, and his idyllic childhood. He had adored his mother and he had been spoiled, he told me. I fell asleep in the middle of his monologue.

In the late afternoon, Wolf tensed and caught hold of my arm.

'Hey! Wake up! Look over there, Nina.' I could sense his excitement as I searched the bush, seeing nothing unusual. His arm encircled my shoulders and drew me towards him.

'There! Under that tree.'

At close quarters I could smell his musky sweat. There was an awesome ache in my groin and my lips had to be

forcibly restrained from touching his neck, his shoulder
and the beautiful line of his jaw.

I turned my attention to the tree. 'Wow!' I yelled. She
was tall and stately and her flecked, haughty eyes locked
with mine. Moments later she turned abruptly and took to
the tarmac in front of us, as four more lionesses emerged
from the bushes.

'They know exactly where they're going,' Wolf whispered. 'They're after something. We might be lucky.'

He drove slowly, keeping well behind the pride, but
half a kilometre further on, the leader veered off the
road and disappeared back into the undergrowth, her
pride hard behind.

'Shit!' Wolf braked. 'We'll wait here. They might
come back.'

He put his arm around me and drew me close to him.
After a while he bent forward and gently kissed my throat.
When I gasped, he pushed his hands behind my neck and
kissed me on the lips. Time stood still as my ego became
my mouth and melted into his.

After a while he sat up. 'Let's go find them,' he said,
with a grin. He winked at me and turned to the map.
'There's a water-hole two kilometres away in the direction
they took.'

I smoothed my hair, wishing I had held back. We raced
along a bad by-road that meandered through scrub and
over small koppies. I was breathless and choked with dust
by the time we found the water-hole, lying concealed
under a cliff ledge. Wolf parked the truck nearby to give
us a grandstand view.

'Now we wait. Look over there, Nina.'

A shadow under a grove of trees seemed to move
and flow as a black shape emerged from the safety of
the bushes. I peered through the shimmering vista at a

lone black buffalo, old and scraggy, propelled by thirst to venture forward in a curious stumbling gait, head lowered, fierce, bloodshot eyes scanning its surroundings.

'It's come a long way by the look of it,' Wolf said. 'I've heard half the water-holes have dried.'

The buffalo drank for a long time and stayed in the shallow water as if unable to move away.

Wolf leaned back and flattened his palms against the roof of the cabin.

'It might be a long wait. Mind if I sleep? Lean against me if it's not too hot.' He pulled me into the crook of his arm.

I couldn't get his proximity out of my mind, but the heat intensified and after a while I closed my eyes and fell into a trance-like sleep.

We woke to an anguished bellow and saw the old buffalo fighting off an attack by two lionesses. Tiredness fled as fear surged. I leaned out of the window, trying to will my strength towards the exhausted beast.

Time and again the lionesses lunged in, and the heroic buffalo fought them off with its horns and hoofs. At last it tired and swayed as it wheeled about, head down, bellowing with rage.

A young lioness, reckless with hunger, leaped forward for the kill, but missed her timing and the buffalo ripped her pelt with its horn. She limped back, as the larger cat sprang at the beast's throat. She hung on from underneath its torso. Strong forelegs wound around its neck and her fangs sank into its jugular vein. For a moment there was only blood, dust and pounding feet. The water turned crimson as the tired old beast staggered to deeper water, hoping to drown its burden. Moments later it sank to its knees with a despairing moan. The lionesses hurled themselves on to it, hauled it to the bank, already ripping at the soft underbelly.

The buffalo gave one last despairing bellow and succumbed.

I was shuddering violently. A deep shame welled through me at my weakness, but I could not stop. 'It fought so bravely. Oh, my God. That was so awful.'

'And now it's wonderful. Look over there.' Two more lionesses were hurrying towards the kill, four cubs loping behind them.

As we sat, watching the life-giving feast unfold, I felt strangely bereft. It was as if my former values had perished with the buffalo. I had been confronted with more compelling needs than the weighing up of assets and liabilities. I felt bruised by the day. Somewhere, I thought, I've got everything wrong.

By the time we left, the jackals were gathering and the western sky was crimson. The sun sank and, within minutes, day had turned to night.

Chapter 12

A gathering of people around an African camp-fire brings about a metamorphosis. Acquaintances become friends and friends are drawn into a mystical oneness – perhaps it was the firelight, or our closeness on the rough wooden benches, or just the cries of predators around us. A wild boar sizzled over the embers, while chops and boerewors slowly browned on the grid. Joy, a romantic at heart, had not needed much urging to rearrange the seating, shifting Theo to the left, so that Wolf sat on my right, with David opposite. Bernie's eyes smouldered with disapproval, but he couldn't do much about it.

David's voice boomed out, 'A new sky, hey, Nina? Have you seen the Southern Cross before?'

'No. I don't even know where it is.'

Wolf pulled me close against him to look along his pointing arm. 'Got it?' he asked.

'No, well, maybe, yes,' I admitted, happy to search the heavens for half the night.

'The Africans have a story about the Southern Cross,' David went on. 'To them it is the holiest of all the constellations. Some tribes think that it's the tree of life, placed there to guide wanderers in the night.'

David's lecture came to an abrupt halt as a gunshot rang out nearby.

'He's got it,' he exclaimed. 'Good! Now we can get back to normal.'

Shortly afterwards Johan came in carrying his rifle and the carcass of a baboon, which he handed to Theo.

'Bury it fast and deep,' he growled.

'What happened?' I asked David.

'A deformed baboon has been raiding the camp. The workers think it's a *tokoloshe*. They've taken off. That's why we're eating here tonight. There's hardly any staff left.'

'What's a *tokoloshe*, for heaven's sake?'

'Superstitious nonsense,' Wolf told me. 'There's no such thing.'

'A dug-up corpse,' Joy called.

'An evil spirit,' someone insisted.

'A curse.'

'A ghost.'

'A zombie.'

No one seemed to know for sure.

'No, no, listen to me,' David said. 'A *tokoloshe* is neither mystical nor supernatural. It's an evil creature, sometimes human but occasionally a baboon, created by deprivation and cruelty during its formative years. The Africans are wise people. They know that a child surrounded with evil in its formative years becomes Satan's slave.'

'I can believe that, David.'

I was unprepared for Wolf's annoyance. 'Stop talking bullshit, Nina.' He scowled at me.

'No, you're wrong, Wolf,' Joy cut in on him. 'Even in modern society, cruelty and pain invariably breed monsters.'

'You must see that it's not an African phenomenon, Wolf. Back home the prisons are full of kids from bad homes.' I glanced up, half smiling, expecting to get through to him, but he shot me a look of fury.

'If David says so, then naturally it must be so. You people amaze me. Your minds are clouded with mumbo-jumbo, perhaps because you were reared by black nannies. I can't sit and listen to this crap. Goodnight, everyone.'

I couldn't believe Wolf could be so rude. As I watched him stalk out, I was so sure he would turn, laugh and apologise, but he didn't.

'What's got into him?' Joy asked me.

I shrugged and tried to hide my hurt.

'The point is,' David went on, as if nothing had happened, 'while Westerners believe in a force of goodness all about us, and the eventual triumph of good over evil, the locals see an amoral force, ultra powerful and impersonal, which can be used for either good or evil. That's why evil frightens them so. This poor, maimed baboon was mistaken for a *tokoloshe*, so the workers fled. That's why we had to kill it.'

David couldn't get off the subject, but I wasn't really listening. I felt sure Wolf would return soon. I kept looking for him while we ate supper. Theo moved next to me to fill the gap, but he waited until after dessert before mentioning business.

'Come and see me when we get back to the Cape, Nina,' he said. 'I've a few investments that might interest you.'

At his words, a hush fell around the table.

'I'll do that. Look forward to it,' I muttered.

'Could we forget business for once?' Sophia said sharply. It wasn't a request and Theo bowed towards her and touched his forehead in a mock salute.

After that, dinner became more of a party and our laughter rang out into the night. David and Theo were quick and clever, and Bernie could match their wit. Even Joy came out of her shell and enjoyed herself. I had a great time and stayed late, hoping that Wolf would return, but he did not. Finally I put some chops and sausages on a paper plate, and wrapped it in a napkin.

'My, you have a gargantuan appetite,' Joy called. She got up and gave me a swift hug. 'Take care, Nina,' she whispered, as she let go.

It was hard to get to sleep that night. A family of meerkats raided the dustbin, bushpigs came running by, snorting and squealing, the hyenas' weird calls seemed to echo inside my head and it was so hot. I lay and thought about Wolf, and the way I felt about him. I worried about the difference between love and lust. Did I believe in love? I wasn't sure. Was Wolf right when he said I had erected intimidating barriers to keep emotions at a safe distance? Did I take refuge in logic to avoid emotions? Eventually I fell asleep and dreamed.

I was wandering in the veld but it became dark and I found myself lost in the near-dry riverbed. I sensed that lions were stalking me through the long grass and, panic-stricken, I began to run. They were gaining on me. I could smell their hot, fetid breath. Then I heard Wolf's voice nearby. The reeds parted, but my cry of welcome froze on my lips. It was the deformed baboon, but its eyes were Wolf's.

Such are the dreams of the African night.

Later the wind rose and whined through the roof and I woke again to hear scuffling in the thatch. Moments later something unbelievably foul fell on me. I was covered with putrid hair and the stench was terrible. I screamed and tore at the stinking thing, trying to get it off my face and my hair.

'Oh, God!' I fumbled around the edge of the circular wall towards the door and finally found a switch.

As light flooded the room, I saw the debris of a deserted bird's nest scattered over the bed and floor: ancient matted feathers, old bones and droppings dark with age. An owl? I guessed it had been dislodged from the thatch by the gusting wind.

'Nina! Are you all right? Nina! Answer me or I'm breaking the lock.' Wolf's voice.

'Hang on. I'm coming.' I grabbed a towel. Wrapping it around me, I opened the door and stared at him as he stood silhouetted against the night sky. His eyes reminded me of my dream. I frowned at him.

'Good God! What happened to you? Looks like the *tokoloshe* got you.'

'For a few moments I had that in mind.'

He began to laugh as he plucked feathers out of my hair. 'What a stench!'

'Oh, Wolf! It was horrible.' I meant the dream more than the nest. I made an effort to pull myself together. 'Absurd, really. It's nothing. But it was so dark. I couldn't see a glimmer of anything. Not my hand in front of my face. I thought of huge hairy poisonous spiders, or worse.' I drew him into the room. 'Look at the bed. Covered in filthy old feathers and bird droppings.'

'It's nothing. Feathers can't hurt you. I thought you were a bush girl.'

'Don't humour me. Well, I guess I'd better clean up. Thanks for coming over.'

Wolf was staring up at the well at the peak of the thatched roof. 'The cleaners should have noticed it. Abandoned months ago, by the look of the debris.'

I began to sneeze. 'I'm allergic to feathers,' I gasped. My nose and ears and every membrane in my head were blocking and itching madly. I couldn't see, couldn't even breathe properly. I felt myself being pushed towards the shower. I heard Wolf strike a match and light the geyser, and then the welcome warm water washed away the stench and the filthy feathers. My towel fell as I felt Wolf spread my hair under the water. I didn't care that I was naked. I just wished I could stop itching. Wolf was wiping the debris out of my face and ears and eyes.

'Imagination can be a dangerous thing, Nina.'

I felt his body push close against mine and I realised that he was naked. His erection was prodding at my belly.

'Sorry! Naked women turn me on,' he muttered, close to my ear.

I put my arms around his waist and held tight as the water cascaded over us.

'Close your eyes, Nina. Hold this cloth over your face. Where's the shampoo?'

'On top of the wall.'

Locked together under the warm water, we were almost one as our arms clasped each other. Wolf's smooth, wet skin touched every part of mine. But it wasn't enough. Not nearly enough. I gasped and hung on to his strong neck as his arms strengthened around me, crushing me against him. His lips were on mine and I felt myself melting into him.

Chapter 13

'Would you like coffee, Wolf?'

It was almost dawn and we had decided to drive out into the bush when the camp gates opened and return to join the others in time for breakfast. Wolf was sitting on the balcony staring through my binoculars towards the river. He put them down and turned to me with such a sweet smile.

'That was good sex, Nina. We go well together. I have the strangest feeling that I was the first man to excite you so much. But don't say anything, that would break the spell. And yes, please, I'd love some coffee. Then I must shower. We should try to be waiting at the gates when they open. That's when you see the most.'

He turned back to study the river and I paused to gaze at the moonlight on his shoulders and his hair. You're beautiful, Wolf. One doesn't say that to men, so I won't, but looking at you turns me on, particularly your lovely hands. How sensuous and knowledgeable those hands are when we make love. And then there's your eyes, which seem to be lit by an inner glow. I've never seen eyes as brilliant as yours.

For a moment I was lost in daydreaming. I had squandered my virginity the night before the start of my A level exams.

It might have been fright that led me to bed the head
boy of our neighbouring school under the hedge behind
the games shed. This hit-and-miss amateurish coupling
had been wholly unsatisfying but it had loosed the genie
in the lamp, a genie who slept for months, but woke
trembling and brimful of desire at the sight of true male
beauty. How I hated myself for this weakness. It was a
flaw that could destroy me, as destructive as the San
Andreas fault.

'I expected you to come round last night, Wolf, so I
brought you some supper. Chops and things. They're
in the wire safe behind the kettle. I have some biscuits, too.'

'Smart girl! Why did you expect me to come?'

'To apologise.'

Wolf got up to fetch the chops and munched them
happily. 'Would you like one?' he asked.

'No, thanks. I'll make do with coffee.'

'I wanted to come. If I'd known you had food I'd have
come sooner.'

'That figures.'

'David irritates the hell out of me. Full of bull! Half
the things he says are made up on the spur of the
moment.'

'He seems very knowledgeable.'

'He sounds it. D'you know anything about ancient
tribal beliefs?'

'Absolutely nothing.'

'That's how he gets away with it. I know a great deal
about local flora and fauna. I've heard him talking utter
rubbish as if he were a sage.'

'So now he's suspect, whatever he says.'

'Exactly. And you agreed with him and that pissed
me off.'

He caught hold of me and hugged me close to him. Once again the magic surged through me as I gasped and pressed against him. Touching his back was like touching iron.

'How did you get like this? You don't even look strong.'

'At the gym.'

That was a lie. Mind your own business, Nina.

'Well, here we are, Nina, two independent adults, both hard-headed, single-minded achievers, both feeling at risk to this powerful sense of togetherness, but sensing it, nevertheless. I think you feel afraid. You equate caring with hurting.'

'You're fishing. It's just that we're still strangers. We don't know each other.'

'Is that your feeble attempt to keep me at bay? Do you really believe that talking and making love are the only ways to get to know each other? D'you believe that our sum total is what you can see and touch? What about intuition? What about thoughts and psyches merging? I don't believe we're strangers. I think you're very perceptive, particularly about me. As for me, I seem to have known you all my life.'

He was right, but I was glad not to talk about it. I decided to be honest. 'I have no faith in lust. I couldn't trust a friendship based on such an ephemeral thing. It's not real.'

'You amaze me, Nina. It's the basis of love between every man and woman. It's nature. It has created every great love story, it has made history. Don't denigrate sexual lust. I love you for your wild tangle of deep red hair, the way your delicate nose tips ever so slightly at the end, your candid, warm green eyes. I may never love you quite so much for your ability to judge a good investment.'

'How about goodness and morality?'

'I have no desire to fuck a nun.'

'You're making fun of me.'

'Sometimes I see you as a lost girl. When did you become lost, Nina?'

I stirred uncomfortably. Perhaps when Otto died. Or was it earlier? 'You're talking nonsense, Wolf.'

'I don't think so. Perhaps I'll rescue you and take you home. You're a very sensuous woman, Nina.'

'Don't! I'm not here for long.'

'Are you sure?

'Of course.'

'I'm going to shower.'

I leaned back in the chair, in that curious half-waking, half-sleeping state, thinking about Wolf and the way it had been, wondering how to prolong my stay here.

A bird bursts into song. Looking up, I see that the eastern sky has turned pale grey. Another bird wakes, then another, and hundreds more burst into a magnificent hallelujah. The sky turns pink and red, then crimson. An elephant trumpets and the camp comes to life. Morning has broken and I thrill to this scene of indescribable beauty.

Chapter 14

By Monday night we were back in Constantia, colonialism's last outpost, which seemed to me like the world's last dinosaur, splendidly archaic as it ambled its blinkered way through a fast-changing world. Back in business mode, I was ready to leave at eight a.m. for my hectic round of meetings.

I returned at four to Joy, who was only too happy to have someone to entertain. We would ride, swim, play tennis, or send for the helicopter Bernie shared with Theo and tour the Cape peninsula. Each night saw a succession of rich expatriate Europeans gracing Joy's table.

On Wednesday morning, Bernie placed a large envelope on the breakfast table beside me.

'Theo asked me to give this to you on the off-chance that you're interested in investing in his group. I told him you'd need facts and figures before you'd talk to him, so here they are.'

And what a profitable picture they painted. But they didn't seem quite believable to me, and I wondered how I could check the information.

A few days later I flew to Johannesburg for meetings and spent the first two days chasing up pre-takeover balance sheets of the group's many companies. The result was astonishing: total debt had amounted to 200 million rands prior to the merger. How had they managed that?

After some lavish lunches and dinners, and a costly visit to a British-owned, Johannesburg-based intelligence company, I had the story.

A few years back, most American, British and European companies had been pulling out of South Africa because of sanctions. It was a buyers' market and Bernie's friends had climbed in, boots and all. Consequently, they all suffered at least one big loss.

It was Joshua, the banker, who had had the bright idea of putting all the losers together under one umbrella, disguising the size of the debts with creative accounting and hanging in there until the country's image improved. Then they planned to find a sucker from overseas to purchase the majority holding.

But how could Bernie prejudice a long and profitable association with Eli by dumping the loss on Eli's bank? Yet why not? He was one of the losers, after all, and his failing property company had been taken into the group.

And I had been voted for the post of Fairy Godmother. I decided not to say a word until Bernie contacted me.

Back in Cape Town, Bernie cornered me before dinner. 'Theo's pressurising me, Nina. Have you had a look at the figures? Did you mention our deal to Eli?'

'I don't put deals to Eli. I make up my own mind,' I told him coolly.

'Phew!' He whistled. 'You must think I'm some kind of an oaf, but I don't often meet high-powered women like you.'

Sarcastic bastard! 'I'm not high-powered. Just an efficient analyst. It's my job.'

'So what do you think?'

'About?'

'Oh, come off it, Nina. About investing in Theo's group.'

'Why do you call it Theo's group? He seems to have the least to lose. Joshua owns twelve per cent of the holding company, but he stands to lose the most, since his bank's on the line. Why not call it Bernie's group since you own eight per cent.'

Bernie blanched. 'Where did you get this information?'

I ignored his question. 'You and your friends put your losses together under one umbrella and created a magnificent PR campaign boosting Theo as the whiz-kid. Why him, I wonder?'

'Because he's the captain.'

His reply made no sense to me. 'I get the picture, Bernie. Once you've succeeded in selling fifty-one per cent of the group, all of you plan to sell your shares surreptitiously and wash your hands of the mess. But, Bernie, no one could get these companies out of the red.'

'Theo's a marvellous administrator. He'll pull the group right.'

'I'll be cheering on the sidelines.'

Bernie went off in a huff. As I stood there pondering, a photograph hanging on the wall caught my eye. It showed a group of young men in sports gear, smiling self-consciously at the camera. Wasn't that a youthful Bernie in the front row? And who was holding the rugby ball? Why, Theo, of course, the captain. And there was David at the back, and Joshua. *The Western Province Rugby Team*, I read, but the date was obscured.

By the time Bernie returned I was laughing. 'I'd heard rugby was important to you guys, but blood brothers for life is stretching it a bit.'

'What are you? Some sort of a witch?' he snarled, caught off guard for once.

'But how could you land Joshua in a mess like this? Sooner or later the debt will pull his bank under, with or without overseas finance. How could you pull down a friend, Bernie?'

Bernie gave me a strange, inscrutable look from which I gathered there was a plan for Joshua's rescue, too, but clearly he wasn't prepared to reveal his strategy. I decided to probe further.

'Eli would never consider a business liaison with someone who shopped their business colleagues.'

I was hitting below the belt, I knew. Not very ethical, but neither was Bernie. I had plenty more where that came from, so it took me only half an hour to get the information out of Bernie.

'Josh is covered by a secret Reserve Bank scheme to bail out major banks if they have a massive bad debt,' he admitted, shamefaced. 'The loss has to be big enough to get the pay-out. That's the point.'

Now it all made perfect sense. Oh, Eli, I said to myself. That accounts for fifteen of the forty thieves. And you did warn me.

The Christmas season was a whirl of parties, culminating in a ball at Bernie and Joy's house on New Year's Eve. I felt sure I would meet Wolf, but no one knew where he was. I told myself that it didn't matter anyway and threw myself into my work, pulling off several good investment deals for Eli over the following days.

When Wolf's call finally came, the sound of his voice propelled me back to the game park.

'Nina? Are you well? Enjoying yourself?'

'I'm having a wonderful time. And you? I expect you spent Christmas with the family?'

That had been beneath me, I decided, but it was too late now.

There was a quiet chuckle. 'I was in Europe. Nina, I need your help.'

His voice was so impersonal it hurt.

'I'm trying to find backing to develop a small but potentially valuable claim I own in Namaqualand. I'd like to show it to you. You might have some ideas on how I can find investors.'

It was a business call. Oh, hell!

'How about lunch, Nina?'

'Why not?' I replied woodenly.

'Or, better still, if you have five days to spare, I could take you there. It's interesting terrain. We could fly up and spend a couple of days in Namibia. That's a fascinating country and there's plenty of investment potential if you need an excuse to come.'

'I don't need excuses.'

'Fine. I must warn you that it's very hot at this time of the year. We'd sleep out and rough it. Does this appeal to you?'

It doesn't, but you do. 'Sounds fascinating,' I lied.

'How about leaving early on Sunday morning?'

'Sunday it is.'

I replaced the receiver and stood staring out of the window. Why had Wolf invited me to Namaqualand? Because he needed the cash to develop his mine? There was no question about my motives in agreeing to go: I wanted his beautiful, lithe, sexy body, and I longed to feel his sensuous lips touching mine.

I brought myself smartly under control and went to bed. From now on I would stick to business, I promised myself.

So why was my heart singing and my mind obsessed with a countdown to Sunday morning?

It was a silent, balmy night and the full moon, the temptress, flaunted her exotic beauty as she followed her destiny. I gazed in sullen envy, examining my obsession from all angles, wondering how I had managed to fall this far so fast. I tried to analyse my emotions and take control of them, but I found myself whispering, 'Wolf, Wolf.'

Chapter 15

It was Sunday morning. In the hazy dawn light I watched Wolf gazing with pride at his South African-built Bosbok, which still bore its war camouflage and a few bullet holes. I tried to share his enthusiasm, but the word metal-fatigue slipped unbidden into my mind, chilling me.

'I picked it up for a song,' he purred, running his hands lovingly over the wing. 'They said it was obsolete.' He shot me a rueful glance that was part amusement, but part apology for his illusions. Wolf was a dreamer, intent on extracting the most adventure from every situation. His blue eyes sparkled with laughter and his teeth glistened as he gave me a silly, lopsided grin. 'It's good for another thousand miles at least.'

As if I hadn't guessed. 'Christ!' I exploded. 'And you expect me . . . ?' I realised belatedly that I was chewing my thumbnail so I pushed the offending hand into my pocket.

'Relax. Honestly, I stripped it down, replaced the worn parts. Don't be nervous, Nina.' His expression dared me to be cowardly, so I climbed in and buckled up. We took off, almost scraping the trees at the end of the airfield. Then we were up and away, my stomach lurching and falling as the Bosbok rose over thermals and fell into troughs.

'It's the cool sea breeze causing the bumps,' Wolf shouted in my ear. He banked towards the sea. Soon the mountains were left behind and all I could see were flat farmlands, a hazy sky with no hint of a cloud, and a grey sea. I blinked in the glare as the crimson sun rose stealthily over the horizon.

We skirted the shoreline, moving north at 260 k.p.h. over desolate, sunbaked beaches, peppered with offshore islands of rocks, black with seals or white with guano. Inland, gravel plains and low barren hills stretched for miles with an occasional huddle of stone cottages.

'Living here must be a disaster,' I called, above the roar of the engines.

'For them, yes.' He pointed down. 'Tin claims were worth mining a century ago. Cornish miners came out here, sprayed their seed around. Later, when the mines were depleted, they went home, or died, but the flotsam and jetsam of their brief sojourn lingered in the bays and along the shoreline. The men catch fish, but selling it is another matter. I've been trying to interest a few businessmen in setting up a fishmeal plant. At least there'd be a market for the fish.'

I could see the pain in Wolf's eyes as he gazed down at the hovels. His compassion intrigued and attracted me, perhaps because it had no place in my world. Until now, the sole object of my labours had been the accumulation of wealth. Wolf really cared and I envied him this quality.

Hour after hour we flew northwards. It became hotter and more of an effort to keep alert. Eventually I slipped into a heat-induced torpor and woke to feel Wolf's hand gripping my arm.

'Swallow,' he commanded. 'We're coming in to land.'

Moments later we were bumping over the uneven runway,

skidding to dead slow and taxiing towards a long, low, corrugated-iron hangar. Wolf reached across, opened my door, and a blast of hot air surged into the cabin. Dazed, I stumbled out into a furnace. The game park had been cool compared with this.

'Wow! Real Lawrence of Arabia stuff.' I tried to sound blasé.

A khaki-coloured old man with peppercorn hair and Oriental eyes approached at a trot and took our gear. By the time we reached the broken-down farmhouse I was soaked with sweat.

I examined the two-foot-thick walls, pitted with ants' holes, the rough cement floor, the old thatch full of cobwebs, and shuddered as a hand-sized spider scampered into the corner. 'Did they actually make a living here? I can't imagine what it must have been like. Unrelenting labour from dawn till darkness, just to survive.'

'Something like that, I suppose. Come and look here.'

I joined Wolf in the next room where old photographs hung around the walls. Sepia-toned and faded, they showed a stern-faced family dressed in the fashions of the last century, the men in shirts without collars and ties, the women tired, scruffy, with shocked eyes. There were some old tins, cutlery, a bucket and a box full of kitchen paraphernalia.

'Who were they?'

'Cornish miners brought out to mine the tin deposits around the turn of the century. This family saved enough cash to buy this land, but the drought and the heat defeated them. They left their possessions and quit. The poor fools. They never knew they were sitting on a gold mine. Better than a gold mine – rare-earth deposits spread over fifteen thousand hectares. Can you believe the size of it? Fifteen thousand! And it's right underneath our feet. One of the richest deposits in the southern hemisphere.'

'What exactly is rare-earth?' I asked.

'Mainly radioactive elements, to put it very simply. Substances such as lanthanum, thulium, and so on. Some are used to make magnets. Some are both rare and much in demand. But it will take a minimum of ten million dollars to get the mine to a viable position, set up a processing plant, bring over experts.'

'Those poor people. I can't get my mind off them. How they must have longed for Cornish rain and fertile Cornish soil.' I sat on a stool in the front room and gazed out at the barren plains. Then I realised that Wolf was staring curiously at me.

'You hate it here.'

'Not really. It's a bit remote.'

'Don't worry. We'll be back in civilisation by tonight.'

'I thought you said . . .'

'This is not for you. Even I can see that. I'll fetch the geologists' reports.'

I watched him go. Nina, you're a fool! For a few silly days I had imagined that the game park meant more than it really had. Feeling badly let down, both by geography and chemistry, I wished I hadn't come.

Wolf had done his homework. The reports were thorough. They had been produced by independent analysts and backed by a geologist Wolf had flown in.

'Wolf, this is not the kind of investment my company makes, but I could find investors for you. There's a couple of Swiss mining entrepreneurs keen on getting into Africa and I know a few of the big guys in London who have most of Mozambique and Zambia tied up. Someone's going to bite. Would you prefer an outright sale or some sort of a share in the mining operation?'

'Outright sale, Nina. I'm badly over-committed. I have so many irons in the fire, and I have my eyes on a huge copper claim. Let's go. I'll tell you about it while I drive you round. To tell the truth I feel bad about this. I hate to trade on our friendship.'

So it was merely friendship now. I forced a smile.

Chapter 16

The sun was past its zenith, but there was little relief from the blistering heat of the late afternoon. Wolf wanted me to admire every damned hectare of his claim.

'Look,' he said, pointing towards the sea. 'Jackals.' He passed me the binoculars. Four emaciated, moth-eaten, timorous creatures were snapping and snarling over the carcass of a dead seal.

'Not much fun being a jackal round these parts,' I murmured.

Something about my voice bothered him. He made a heroic attempt to cheer me. 'Let's go and catch supper. I'm a pretty good cook. Take one squid, and one pot of water and, hey presto, *consommé au Möller*. The best!'

It was amazing to stand at the water's edge, one foot in the teeming sea, the other on eroded land.

'Let's cool off,' Wolf said. He stripped and dived into the white foaming surf. He was a good swimmer, naturally. Wolf seemed to be good at everything.

He belly-surfed back on a wave. 'Come on, Nina. It's too hot not to swim.' I couldn't agree more, but my bikini was back at the ruin and my underwear lacy and transparent.

'Too late to be modest, Nina. I've seen all of you,' he yelled.

I stripped off. The icy sea took my breath away. The temperature was almost freezing, but the water was crystal clear and full of fish. When Wolf swam out to deeper water with a net I followed him, diving down briefly to watch him scoop up two huge crayfish. He thrust his hand into a hole and retrieved a small squid.

Numb with cold, I raced back, dressed and helped him collect driftwood for the fire, before jogging along the beach. By the time I returned, the crayfish had boiled to a bright pink.

Wolf was heating an inch of cold water in an iron pot over the fire. To my horror he popped the live squid in. The little creature heaved off the heavy iron lid and began to scramble out.

'Damn!' Wolf dived for it. I got there first and hurled it into the sea.

'Why, Nina?' He looked amazed.

'If you have to ask, you'd never understand. So let's forget it.'

'I hate bleeding hearts,' he told me, solemnly. He said much more about the perfidious English who scorn fur coats but eat lamb chops. I wasn't listening.

Wolf recovered his temper, produced a bottle of cool wine from the icebox, two tomatoes and rolls and we dined in style.

'Feeling better?' Wolf asked. He reached out and squeezed my hand. 'You're hurting, Nina, but I don't know why. I was surprised when you agreed to come.'

He refilled my wine glass and waited for my reply, but I'm a firm believer in silence when faced with impossible questions.

'Why did you come, Nina?'

'What do you want me to say?'

He smiled. 'Perhaps something like this. "I'd rather be with you in this barren terrain than dining out with some eligible London banker." Voicing the words makes me aware of their absurdity. I should never have invited you here.'

'So why did you?'

'The truth?'

'The whole truth and nothing but the truth!'

'I had an ulterior motive.'

'You're telling me. Fifteen thousand hectares!' It still rankled.

He ignored the taunt. 'This is how I live a large part of my life. I'm often out prospecting, travelling, staking claims, selling them.'

I doodled in the sand.

'I'm crazy about you, Nina. I want you to know the score now. You see, I hope you'll come with me sometimes. Could you endure this rough life from time to time? Would you marry a man like me, Nina?'

I was so shocked for a few moments that I could hardly get my thoughts together. I had longed for romance but only in the here and now. I didn't want to lose Wolf, but I had no intention of marrying him or anyone else. The concept of permanent liaisons left me cold.

'Is that a proposal?'

'It's a run-up to it.'

'Make the run-up last a minimum of six months.' Help! But I'll be back in London long before then.

'Oh, Wolf. I'm sorry. I'm not being straightforward with you. I feel so much for you, but it's the wrong place and the wrong time. I love my work. I can't let go of it. And, besides, in my world one good fuck doesn't mean a commitment. Living together doesn't mean for ever. People grow. Sometimes they grow apart. I live in the present.'

'You may regret those words, Nina. But fair enough. I would expect a rough ride from a girl like you.'

His eyes lit up with a reckless, sexy glow and then came that teasing smile again. 'What about two good fucks?'

Suddenly he was sprawled on the sand beside me. His hand reached out and gripped my ankle, pushing it outwards as he ran his lips over my calves and up to my inner thighs. His lips and tongue moved down to my toes and back up again, slowly, while I writhed and tried to stifle my groans.

'Hey, hey, Wolf. Slow down,' he muttered. He reached up and pulled off my T-shirt, unfastened my bra and kissed my breasts, tugging at my nipples while he eased off my shorts.

'There's no one around for hundreds of miles,' he assured me. 'Except jackals. Old Piet won't leave the homestead.' Then he stripped off his clothes.

It is extraordinarily sensual to be naked in broad daylight. The wind caressed my bare skin, making me feel more alive than I had ever felt before. When Wolf held me in his arms it was the most thrilling sensation. Every part of me came alive and clamoured for more. I was brain-dead, just a body of thrilling sensations, my ego had descended to my loins, and like a nestling bird I clamoured greedily for more, and still more. And Wolf, a skilled and sensitive lover, gave me all that I demanded.

The sun had set, but we lay locked in each other's arms beside the sea, my heart at peace as I hummed a silly love song. A golden glow had miraculously transformed the landscape into a place of incredible beauty. I hadn't noticed until now the intensely lovely colours of the rocks, the tiny lichen that covered the stones, the tenacity of life in the face of such awesome conditions.

Then caution took over.

'You must understand that I put my career first,' I explained, carefully. 'My career is my life. I've studied and worked very hard to get where I am. I would never be irresponsible enough to throw all this away.'

'Then let's enjoy whatever time we have together.'

I can't say that his answer pleased me.

Chapter 17

On my first morning back in Cape Town I discovered some startling information. The rare-earth claim was extremely valuable but Wolf did not own this underground treasure trove, merely the gravel plains and the ruined farmhouse on the surface. He had purchased the land fairly recently, but the mineral rights had been sold six years before to a South African mining conglomerate.

How could a man with Wolf's training and business expertise be so naïve? Eventually I called him and gave him the unwelcome news.

'I've been had. Shit!' The rest was in German. 'To be honest, I can't afford the loss, Nina,' he explained, when he'd calmed down. 'I should have had you with me when I bought the claim. Will you see if you can bail me out?'

'I'll give it a try.'

Over the next two days I persuaded the mining house to name their price for the claim, added on the price of the land, plus a profit for Wolf, and offered the deal to two Swiss mining entrepreneurs I knew. Quoted in sterling, the price didn't sound so bad. They promised to fly over.

'If the deal's as you describe, we'll buy,' Hans Zogg told me.

I called Wolf to tell him what had transpired. Now we just had to wait. 'By the way, Nina, I was about to call you. Are you free for dinner tonight?'

I was. And the next night. And soon we took it for granted that we would spend our spare time together.

When I'm happy, my face becomes a mirror of my innermost emotions. I cannot hide my elation. When I'm angry, or depressed, no one knows. Wherever I went now, my new friends asked me jokingly if I was in love.

'No,' I replied to one and all, aware that I was lying.

'Well, whatever you're doing, keep it up,' Bernie's secretary said, which echoed most of the remarks I was receiving.

Wolf and I drew closer as we tried the best restaurants, went dancing and endured a little of the social whirl. Weekends, we flew to some remote part of the country to prospect for new deposits. I became adept at putting up a tent, making a fire for cooking, and tramping for miles over difficult terrain. I even learned to shoot for the pot.

Joy cornered me at dinner one evening. 'To what do we owe the pleasure of your company?'

'Oh, Joy!' I gave her a hug, which was unlike me. 'Wolf's in Germany.'

'So when are you two announcing the engagement?'

'It's nothing like that,' I said.

'For you, maybe,' Joy argued. 'But Wolf will want to make it legal. He's that type.'

Prophetic words! Wolf proposed the following night and remained absent for days when I turned him down.

Why do my fears only surface at night when I'm vulnerable?

I woke around four a.m. and lay awake, staring into darkness, plagued by the suspicion that Wolf had tried to cheat me with the Namaqualand mine. If I hadn't checked so carefully I might have ruined my reputation.

'Be careful, Nina,' a voice seemed to whisper in my head.

I mentally listed what I knew about Wolf. He was a geologist and an entrepreneur. He had been born and brought up on a large estate near Beeskow, East Germany. He had gained his degree and his doctorate at Dresden University and he had come to South Africa to prospect for minerals, hoping for the big break.

Two days ago, over lunch, I had tried to draw him out. Eventually he had admitted that Bernie was right and he had succeeded in breaking international sanctions by bringing oil into South Africa by a circuitous route. 'Only for the cash to keep going,' he had insisted. 'I really wasn't keen to do it.'

But then I thought, Wolf is the most exciting man I've ever met. He has a charm that cuts through all defences, but he's also a very private person, hiding his personality. An undercover man. I've tried, but failed, to draw him out. He has been trying to persuade me to look at the old house he's bought near the Fortunes'. He wants me to help him revamp it, he says. It would be fun, but I might fall in love with the place.

Unable to get back to sleep, I continued to analyse Wolf. He offers his love with the utmost delicacy, but also with confidence. His eyes beam humour and they tell me that he finds me alluring. Has he any idea how attractive he is with his lazy smile, and his startling blue eyes?

When I went downstairs for breakfast there was no sign of Joy. It was a lovely morning, so I asked the housekeeper for some toast and a cup of coffee and sat on a bench in the garden. Too late I realised that Joy was on the telephone in the room behind me.

'Please . . . !' Her voice was hardly more than a whimper. 'I love you, Louis. Haven't I proved that? I've done so much for you. Don't do this to me!'

Ashamed of eavesdropping, I tiptoed into the garden and sat on a bench. Caesar was weeding the flower-beds. I waved, and thanked him for the flowers he had picked and sent to my room with the maid.

When Joy arrived I saw that her eyes were puffy. She looked sad.

'What you need,' her chin tilted defiantly, 'is a trip to the gym. A girl's lost without a tan here.' Her pride crumpled. 'Help me, Nina. I have to go somewhere and I'd really appreciate your advice . . .' Her voice tailed off, but her eyes were pleading.

'I'll cancel my appointment, Joy. It wasn't important, just research.'

The décor was silver and black, the room as large as two tennis courts, the equipment new and costly, the clientele rich. Plastic women. Masks instead of faces, cheeks and necks drawn taut, eyes pulled up and sideways so that they looked vaguely Oriental, cute man-made noses.

Since Mother had had her face-lift I could recognise cosmetic surgery a mile off, but here it was the norm rather than the exception. I watched the women moving in a desultory way around the circuit of exercise machines. Their hearts weren't in it, so why were they bothering?

My instructor, sleek, tanned and narcissistic, demonstrated the routine without once shifting his glance from his mirrored reflection. Gold chains sparkled, his eyes glistened, and once or twice he smiled at himself.

In no time I had finished the circuit. The tanning beds were unbearably hot and they'd given me a headache. I staggered to the showers, changed, and found my way to the canteen where everyone, including Joy, had gathered for coffee.

The tension puzzled me, but I soon realised that the object of the women's attention was the men's changing room. At intervals young men in track-suits, towels flung over their shoulders, sweating faces, damp hair, emerged like gladiators into the arena. The women, predatory as jungle cats, slipped silently off their stools to stalk their prey.

I could sense Joy's anxiety as she drummed her fingers against the table.

'Let's go,' I suggested, without much hope.

Her fingers touched my wrist. Suddenly she was pleading. 'Hang on a bit, Nina. It's important.'

The door swung open. I heard a sharp intake of breath as Joy stiffened and squared her shoulders. She gazed imploringly at the husky figure in the doorway.

Adonis himself could not have been more confident of his sex appeal. Was he Greek, I wondered, or Italian? Gold medallions slung from a thick chain nestled among a mass of curly black hair, which covered his torso. He was tanned to a crispy brown, his hair was black and wavy, his profile haughty. From the bulge in his swimsuit, I gathered that he was well hung and flaunted it. His glance scanned the women, and homed in on one of them, but it wasn't Joy.

There was a snap as she broke a nail against the table-top. Presumably this was Louis. He turned towards us, shrugged disarmingly, gave a fluttering wave of his hand and walked towards another.

'So that's who he's fucking. Maria Bradford! She's

chairman of a property trust fund, a financial genius, they say. The lousy bastard!' Joy lurched forward, but I pulled her back.

'Don't make a scene, Joy.'

'Is it that obvious?'

'Well, yes. And I overheard you on the phone. I didn't mean to listen but I was there. Believe me, I understand.'

When we reached the car her story poured out: the desperation of the ageing wife with no family, no one to care for and absolutely nothing to do all day, since everything was done by maids. Her feeling of inadequacy for no one needed her. The money she'd squandered on Louis, and Bernie's anger at her credit-card totals. She'd bought him a car on credit and the bastard wouldn't give it back.

I grieved for her.

'Time flies,' she whispered. 'You don't realise this until men start overlooking you. Bernie's fucking a mentally defective teenager who used to be in his typing pool.' Joy seemed to need to let it all out. 'She turns him on. He'd marry her, if he had the guts to dump me. If she manages to get pregnant, he might try. He always wanted kids, but I didn't. I regret that now. Most of his friends are on the second round of wives. No doubt you've noticed.' Tears were rolling down her cheeks.

It was my turn to grieve and it didn't take long for Joy to notice. I was home early the next afternoon, so she organised tea in the garden.

'You might as well tell me what's happened,' Joy demanded.

'Wolf proposed. I turned him down and I haven't heard from him since.'

'You love him, don't you?'

'I think I do.'

'So go for it, Nina.'

'It's too soon. Besides, I have my career to think of. I love my work. I can't give it up.'

Joy took my empty cup and turned it upside down on the saucer. Then she studied the tea-leaves.

'Right now I'm seeing you at your retirement party. You look scared and lonely. At what age do they retire staff at Bertram's?'

'For goodness sake, Joy, that's decades ahead.'

'True, but the time will come, and when it does, what sort of memories will you have? Balance sheets, board meetings? Will you have children? Nowadays I wish to God I'd opted for kids.'

'Stop it, Joy.'

'Perhaps you're waiting for Mr Right?'

'I don't think I'll meet anyone much righter.'

She shot me an 'I-know-best' glance and nodded sagely.

'You can be damned annoying at times, Joy. The truth is, I can't bear to give up Bertram's.'

She gave me a silly secret smile and changed the subject.

I threw myself into my work and almost succeeded in putting Wolf out of my head. I was becoming well known in local business circles, and soon it became apparent that businessmen were bypassing Bernie and approaching me with their ideas. This was a problem, but there wasn't much I could do about it.

Then came the news that the Swiss mining entrepreneurs to whom I'd offered the rare-earth deposit had agreed to the price. We had a deal. I called Wolf to give him the good news, and we met for lunch at Mariner's Wharf.

We sat on the balcony overlooking the fishing harbour, watching a school of dolphins circling a shoal of fish while greedy gulls divebombed the operation. As we picked our way through crayfish, prawns and calamari, Wolf told me about his Constantia house and all the plans he had made for it.

'Why don't we take the afternoon off and go there?'

'I can't. I have an appointment. Wolf, can't we be friends? Does it have to be all or nothing in your world?'

'Of course not. Besides, I never give up. I would have called you, Nina, if you hadn't called me. I can't get you out of my head. Don't you feel the same way?'

'I do, believe me, I do. It's just that I'm not ready for a commitment. It's too much too soon.'

'I understand your fears, Nina, but isn't there some way you can have the best of both worlds? Wouldn't Bertram's consider letting you remain here? I saw Bernie today and he told me he had resigned from Bertram's. He's far too busy with his own interests.'

That surprised me. 'I hope Joy didn't talk him into this for me.'

'D'you think Eli Bertram would offer you Bernie's position?'

'Not at first. He's called twice this week demanding that I get back to London at once. I asked for more time because I have a couple of good deals on the go. If he knew for sure I was staying here I think he'd give me the job, but he'd rather I returned to London.'

Dear Eli. I'd long since forgiven him for spying on me. I would miss him if I stayed here. I'd miss the London scene, too.

'I feel isolated here, Wolf. Financially speaking, it's a bit off the beaten track.'

Wolf's blue eyes lost their happy glow. 'That's precisely what I said to you in Namaqualand. How could love and marriage compare with the incredible excitement of making more and more money for Eli Bertram?'

He kissed me softly on the lips and called for the bill.

'Let's get back to work,' he said, 'or you might miss out on a couple of rands.'

Chapter 18

I found it hard to resist the intensity of my feelings and my conviction that this rare gift of love should be nurtured. Yet however much I considered putting our relationship before my career, I could not overcome my reluctance to give up my freedom. So far, the men in my life had been offered only a passive role, prince consorts, every one of them. Wolf deserved better, and I realised that I'd have to take the plunge if this relationship was to survive. Thoughts of that awful gym with its ageing, lonely women and arrogant toyboys made me feel cold inside.

More time was needed, I decided. Wolf was in too much of a hurry, but I had to make a choice between him and London. Fate seemed to be hustling me.

Eli called the next morning to confirm Bernie's resignation.

'Find a replacement, Nina. Narrow the field down to four and send them over for interviews.'

'Eli, I was just going to call and ask you for more time here. I'll take Bernie's job for a while. You won't get better and you know it.'

'I need you in London, my dear.'

'Don't get me wrong, Eli. I love my work, but it's not enough. I need a private life, too. Maybe this isn't it, but give me time to find out.' I found it hard to explain to Eli how I felt, although I tried.

'You've taken me by surprise, Nina.'

Eli's voice sounded tinny over the long distance, but I could hear he was upset.

'I want to sleep on it. I'll cable my decision tomorrow.'

Eli's reply was brief: 'Have it your own way, Nina, but beware. You might have a touch of sunstroke. Your London resignation is not accepted at this stage. I consider your absence to be a sabbatical. You can have Bernie's job on a temporary basis for six to twelve months while you see how you go. Your position here will be waiting for you. Keep me advised of your intentions.'

When Wolf called the next day I was overjoyed to hear from him. He suggested that I meet him at his Constantia house, which was standing empty for the time being.

'Be warned, Nina. It's a mess, the whole place needs cleaning and renovating.'

He was right, it was a mess, but it was also charming. I arrived early and wandered through knee-high grass, where the lawn should have been, scattering guinea-fowl. The huge rambling garden backed on to a vineyard, and a gate led to paths that wound up through the forested mountainside. The pool was cracked and hadn't been used for years, but it could be repaired.

I found an unlocked door and walked inside. The windows were thick with dust, but when you cleaned the glass you could see the mountains, or to the north the Indian Ocean glittering azure blue in the distance. The house had high ceilings and graceful, yellow-wood-framed windows. The floors were laid with reddish quarry tiles

Sunstroke

and the atmosphere was of an older, more stately, elegant age. The only sound was birdsong.

Wolf was late. He arrived to find me washing the grime from a particularly lovely stained-glass window.

'Marry me, Nina,' he said, as his opening gambit.

'I've come to suggest a compromise. I'll live with you for a while, and if we're happy I'll marry you later. And, Wolf, I won't give up work. Don't expect me to. I have Bernie's job. You were right. He's resigned.'

Wolf went wild with joy, picking me up, swinging me round and singing some foreign song.

Then he calmed down. 'Let's settle our terms now. A successful relationship is based on good negotiations. Perhaps we need a secretary to draw up a contract.'

'I don't think so, Wolf.'

'I like double beds.'

'So do I.'

'I like to stay home at least four evenings a week.'

'That's okay. I'll have so much work.'

'I like to travel a lot.'

'We've been through all this, Wolf.'

'I like children.'

'So do I.'

'Three or four?

'Maybe. Who's counting?'

'That's it, then, Nina.'

'Seems to wrap it up.'

'When do we start?'

'Soonest, I suppose.'

'We can't just move in. There has to be some sort of a ceremony, or a division. How about a holiday?'

'I'd love a holiday, Wolf. How long can you take off?'

'Three weeks, I guess, and you?'

'A month, if we need it.'

'Nina, I've just acquired a Land Rover. I have to go north soon. Would you like a trip through Africa, take in the falls, some game parks, maybe the Kalahari?'

'Oh, *yes*.'

'When can you be ready?'

'I need a week to wrap up a few appointments.'

'Fair enough! See you, then.'

'Oh, see you, Wolf.' That surprised me. Perhaps he had an appointment. 'Do you have keys to lock up here?'

'Come here, you idiot. You aren't getting off that lightly. We're going to christen our home.'

Chapter 19

Three weeks later we were bumping over a dusty gravel path in Chobe, Botswana. We drove through a dense forest, and passed through glades where the light was brilliant and the grass swayed in the wind. Cresting a hill, our path swerved to the north and before us now we saw the tree-tops falling away steeply to a broad, sluggish river. We could see the yellow road cutting a waving course through the deep dark green, and beyond, a broad expanse of twinkling azure blue. Far off, along the riverbank, we saw a huge and splendid hotel, designed like a Spanish *hacienda*, facing across the wide waterway towards the Caprivi Strip, which separates Botswana from Angola.

Wolf was in a hurry to make the hotel before sunset. We sped downhill, sending bucks and baboons fleeing in all directions. Dishevelled and covered in dust, we arrived at Reception, to find that the hotel's paddleboat was leaving for the sunset champagne cruise. 'Let's go,' Wolf said, on the spur of the moment. We dumped our bags at Reception and reached the gangway as the steamer left the wooden wharf.

'Jump!' Wolf yelled, clutching my hand.

The passengers were European and Asian and this was their first trip to Africa. They gasped at the impala along the banks, and I smiled indulgently at their naïve remarks.

Herds of elephants waded into the deep river water to bathe, the mothers prodding their squealing infants ahead of them. Hippos surfaced lazily to protest as we passed. Fish eagles lined the banks on every tree-top. We wondered why until we saw the boatswain take a bucket of fish and fling its contents over the water for the great birds to swoop and catch, while the tourists aimed their cameras and begged for more.

It was dark when we returned, happy, tired and full of champagne. We dined by candlelight and returned to our suite overlooking the river.

'Oh, Wolf, it's wonderful,' I said, breathlessly. 'Thank you, darling.'

Wrapped in each other's arms we fell asleep, too tired to make love.

It was our fourth night at Chobe when I woke in the night sensing that Wolf was not beside me. There was no light in the bathroom. I sat up, listening, and heard him tiptoeing down the stone steps to the garden. There was a bench on the grass below our room, and when Wolf whistled a few moments later I realised he was waiting there. Someone called quietly and Wolf replied. It was someone he knew well, I could tell by his greeting, but the language was unfamiliar.

Then nausea welled up and I hurried to the bathroom. Lately I'd been feeling tired and I'd become prone to headaches, nausea and sleeplessness. Perhaps I was pregnant. It was only three weeks since I had stopped taking the pill. Surely it was too early to start feeling sick. I began to think of all the tropical diseases I might have picked up on our holiday. Perhaps I'd been drinking too much wine at dinner. I decided to give it a miss for a couple of weeks. I washed my face, put on a dressing gown and switched on the light. Wolf did not return. After a while I decided that it was absurd to worry. This was something he had planned. I called room service for a sandwich and a glass of hot milk, and settled back to read my book.

Wolf returned at dawn. He looked annoyed to find me awake.

'What's going on, Wolf? Who were you talking to?'

'No one. You must have been dreaming.'

'Don't lie. Down there . . . hours ago. You met someone you know – you whistled to him to show him where you were. Clearly you had arranged to be here. Why did you let me believe that we found this hotel by accident?'

He stared at me without answering. It was unnerving.

'Don't stare at me like that.'

'Like what?'

'As if you're a stranger. And you look so angry. I'm going back to bed.'

As I crossed the room to shut the door I saw his briefcase lying on the floor. I pushed it out of the way with my foot. It was empty. Yet he had been guarding it for days.

'What were you doing out all night?'

'Never mind,' he said, in a strange voice. He scowled as he picked up the bag and put it on top of the wardrobe.

'Why didn't you tell me you can speak Russian?'

'Russian? No, Nina. We were speaking in an Angolan tribal dialect.'

'Pull the other leg, Wolf. You were speaking Russian. Why shouldn't you have learned it at school in East Germany? That's a lot more believable than knowing a remote Angolan dialect. Sometimes you're so silly.'

'Nina, I can't take this much longer.'

His tone made me quiver. 'Take what?'

'Being spied on.'

'I'm not spying on you, but I'm not stupid, either.
I woke up. You weren't here. I wondered where you
were. I heard your voice and I listened. Then you
went away with this other man and you stayed away
all night. I'm bound to wonder what the fuck is going
on.'

As I walked back to bed the dreaded nausea overtook
me again. I clapped a hand over my mouth and raced to
the bathroom, slamming the door behind me.

Wolf followed me in. He held my shoulders and stroked
my back. When I had finished throwing up, he wiped
my face and hair with a damp cloth. Then he pulled off
my nightdress, flung it in the bath and wrapped a towel
around me.

'Nina.' His voice caressed me. 'You're ill. Poor darling.
You're so white.' He wrapped his arms around me and
gently dried my face.

'I feel terrible, Wolf. Every time I wake up I throw
up.' I clung to him, but part of me was standing back
and watching my behaviour. I found myself pathetic. I
shuddered. Why was I capitulating? Was I too scared to
ask what was going on?

'Come back to bed, darling. I have to tell you something
about my early life.'

When we were locked in each other's arms, and the
lights were off, he said, 'As you know, I was brought up
in East Germany. I learned to hate the Soviet system. I
hate all oppressors with an intensity that you will never
understand. Lucky Nina. You never learned to hate. It
has left me with a sour taste in my mouth about any
kind of oppression, particularly any form of colonialism.

So now, Nina, I help the local freedom movement and I can't tell you how.'

'Is this dangerous?' I asked.

'Yes.'

'Is it legal?'

'Depends whose side you're on. It's something I have to do, darling. Sometimes one has to take a stand for what one believes in. Now, Nina, trust me. I'm on the side of the oppressed. I help poor, suffering people. That's all.'

I snuggled into his arms, smothering doubts and suspicions. If he was a modern-day African Robin Hood, setting himself against oppression, how come he helped the right-wing South African authorities by breaking sanctions to bring in oil?

We made love, which wiped away my doubts and confusion. Later I gave myself a stern ultimatum: leave him or trust him, Nina. Make your choice. It's one or the other, my girl.

I made my choice and fell asleep.

Chapter 20

It was the same yet not the same. I circled the Land Rover
cautiously. 'Someone's been in our vehicle. Searched it,
maybe.'

'What makes you say that?'

I glanced curiously at Wolf. 'Can't you see the difference?'

'I cleaned it.'

There was that uptight expression again. The look that
told me to back off. I climbed into my seat, leaned back
and tried to imagine what was different.

'Did you bring the bucket, Nina?'

'Yes. It's in the back.'

'Are you feeling okay right now, or would you like it
with you?'

'I'm okay.' Was he trying to switch my attention to
something else?

'Why did you have the carpet removed?'

'What carpet?'

I sighed. 'The fluffy bit that goes under my feet.
Remember?'

'Perhaps I shook it out and forgot to put it back.'

'While you were changing the screws, polishing the
brackets, replacing my broken mirror, and fixing the
windscreen wiper, as well as the wobbly handle and

the tear in the upholstery, and dripping oil all over the place.'

'Exactly.'

I got up and walked round to the back. The number-plate was the same, the colour schemes hadn't changed, we even had the same stickers on the windows.

'New vehicles for old. Where's the magic lamp?'

'Same year, same model, same mileage. Believe it or not, this is our vehicle.'

I sat staring straight ahead, tight-lipped and furious. Then I snapped my fingers under his nose. 'Come on, Wolf, what are we into? Gun-running? Diamond-smuggling? Drugs?'

I glanced at my watch. It was precisely seven a.m. and the day, which had begun so promisingly, was already ruined. We had swum in the hotel pool, breakfasted, checked out, and we were about to leave for South Africa, via the Victoria Falls. This would take a few days. Days of tension, by the look of things. Wolf didn't seem in the least tired although he had been up for most of the night.

'Once and for all, tell me the truth, Wolf.'

'Relax. Just hang on to the bucket.'

I hurled the bucket out of the vehicle and clenched my fists feeling horribly aware that this wasn't my kind of behaviour. Was that what pregnancy did?

Wolf braked slowly and pulled in to the kerb. With a dead-pan face, he walked back along the track to retrieve the bucket.

'Just get rid of it, Wolf. Don't dare to bring it in here.'

'I assume you're pregnant,' Wolf said quietly. 'Pregnancy is a trying time for both parties, I've been told.' He placed the bucket on the back seat. 'Try not to make it too dreadful. You seem to have undergone a personality change. That's why I couldn't sleep last night. I spent the night renovating and servicing this vehicle. As for the so-called 'Russian', he's one of the hotel's porters and he helped me with the service. I can understand how irritated you must be, Nina. This heat, the awful nausea, but I've heard it doesn't last all that long. We could pop in to see a doctor here in Chobe, if you like.'

His story was absolutely unbelievable. 'You do remember the point of this conversation, I assume?'

'Nina, don't be too angry with me. I'm sorry that I have to be so secretive. Part of my contract work is to buy and sell for Armscor, which, in case you don't know, are South Africa's only armaments manufacturers. It's top-secret work. I even buy spare parts and fuel for weapons. And I'm not allowed to tell you even that, so keep it quiet. At least I can tell you that I love you.'

'Right.' I'd never felt so inadequate to cope. 'I just feel . . . Well, I feel I've turned into someone else.'

'Perhaps. You've never looked so lovely.'

'I don't want to be lovely. I just want to be me.'

Wolf humoured me on the long drive to Johannesburg, via the Victoria Falls and Messina. He bought an old, hand-painted chamber-pot from a junk shop in Bulawayo, and presented it to me, filled with flowers. 'Now it really is goodbye to the bucket,' he said, smiling anxiously. Lately he had been going to extraordinary lengths to make me happy.

'Half your holiday was spoiled,' he said, when we had booked into a hotel near the Falls and were sitting in the beautiful gardens eating lunch by the pool. 'I'll make it up to you, darling. I promise. As soon as we get home we must get married.'

'That's not what we agreed, Wolf. We said we'd live together first.'

'But, Nina, you're pregnant. If we don't marry I won't even be a relative of my own child. I would have no rights of guardianship. If anything happened to you, God forbid, I wouldn't even be able to take him home.'

'Don't put a guilt trip on me. I don't want to feel trapped.'

'How about a guilt trip for your child? Doesn't it have the right to a father?'

What did I have against commitment? Was it because of my parents' unhappiness? I sipped my soda and fresh lime juice and gazed out towards a group of Africans in tribal dress, who were setting up their drums for a concert.

'Right now, I don't want to hear another word about it.'

Wolf looked hurt, but I felt scared and trapped. But why? There was no stigma in being a single mother and I wasn't short of money. I had to face the truth. I was scared of myself, this new self. Once again I was changing, becoming dependent, motherly, craving Wolf's love and protection, longing for a conventional home. I was looking forward to getting back to create a nursery, rather than hunting out new investment possibilities.

'Clearly you were reared in a happy home or you wouldn't be so keen,' I argued. 'Why don't you tell me about it?'

Despite my obvious ploy to change the subject, Wolf played along. 'I was the son of a beautiful, strong woman, who ran her matriarchal family with an iron rod yet retained our love and loyalty because she was just and gentle. I was an only child, and although I was spoiled I was never lonely, I had so many friends. Most of all,

I loved to be with my father. He taught me to fish, to skate, to ski, to hunt, everything a father is supposed to teach his son, but he was more like a friend, and he adored my mother. Everyone did. Father never understood why he'd been so lucky as to marry her.'

He went on at great length about his mother. From his many descriptions over the past weeks, she didn't seem real to me, more like the good fairy in a child's story. Or an orphan's dream of a mother. I wondered why I had thought that.

After two days at the Falls we drove home. As we neared South Africa the nausea lessened and then stopped altogether. I was reborn. The nerd disappeared and Nina Ogilvie took her rightful place inside my head.

I had put my problem out of my mind when Wolf reminded me, with a statement that was totally unexpected and unwelcome.

'Nina, I think it's time I met your parents.'

I tried not to show my reluctance. I didn't want my sad childhood to contaminate my present happiness. 'My parents and I aren't close, Wolf. I've run my own life for too long.'

I might as well have saved my breath. Wolf was determined to meet them. The 'honeymoon' was over.

Chapter 21

We flew to Edinburgh where I called Mother from the hotel. Her husband, John, answered the telephone.

'Oh, Nina. What a shock to hear your voice. I'm so sorry, my dear. How did you find out?'

'Find out what?' Panic surged.

'About Rebecca's illness.'

'What's happened?'

'Oh, Lord! I hate to break the news to you like this. Your mother had a stroke ten days ago. Unbelievable, isn't it? She's recovering, but she has a long way to go. She can't manage the phone just yet. Talking is a problem for her.'

I stood in stunned disbelief, as John explained that the stroke had paralysed her right side so he had hired day and night nurses.

'You should have called me.'

'You know your mother. She was emphatic that you shouldn't be told. We can only pray, Nina.'

'I'll be right over. Can I bring someone with me?'

'Better not.'

'Will she recognise me?'

'Yes, but her eyesight is badly affected.'

'Oh, God!'

'Why are you here, Nina? Holiday?'

'Sort of. A pre-marriage honeymoon.'

'Good for you. Why didn't you let us know?'

'That's why I'm here. Should I tell Mother?'

There was a pause. 'No. I think not. Better wait. It might be too much of a shock. Come on over. She'll be so glad to see you.'

I was moved to tears by my mother's appearance. All pretence at youth had fled. She looked haggard, and deformed by her partial paralysis. I tried not to show my shock or my tears as I smiled and said the right words, complimented her on her recovery, and tried to hide my grief.

'I look old, don't I? I can read it in your eyes.'

I shook my head. 'Just ill.' I'd been asked that question so many times. Mother had always dreaded my school holidays, for her second husband had been fourteen years younger than her.

Perhaps to obviate my mother's fears I never grew beyond the gangly schoolgirl stage until long after I left school, never wore cosmetics or high-heeled shoes.

Now her humiliation hurt me like a gangrenous sore in some hidden part of my psyche. I could not get to grips with my feelings, but I had to acknowledge a deep emotional tie with my mother of which I had been unaware.

She gazed at me sorrowfully and I stroked her frozen cheek, murmuring white lies as I wept inwardly. She wanted more, much more, from me, I could read it in her eyes, but what else was there to say?

The weather and I were conspiring to present a cold, loveless canvas. Bitter, vengeful clouds raced across the sky, reminding me of lost summers, missed chances and love denied.

As I sat holding her hand and nursing her ego, little incidents, major wounds and harboured grudges rose to the surface of my mind, like rubbish from a sunken wreck newly ripped apart.

I helped with a jigsaw puzzle, which she was pretending she could manage, but I noticed she was only shuffling the pieces quietly from side to side. All the while I was trying to come to terms with the fact that although I wanted to be there helping her, I also wanted to go and never return – and both with equal and astonishing passion. Was it guilt shading my soul with sorrow? Or love? I longed to know.

That night I wanted to be loved and made love to again and again. I had to feel youth and life surging through my veins . . . and I needed to convince myself that she, not I, was dying. I remained unconvinced.

The next morning we flew to Inverness, where an icy scene greeted us both outside and within Ogilvie Lodge. I was reminded that there is no compensation for loneliness, only a slow shrivelling of the soul. My father's face was set in a grimace of welcome as I introduced him to Wolf. I could see that he had taken trouble with his clothes. When he wished, he could play the role of country squire to perfection, but his eyes mirrored his bleak existence.

'Come in. Make yourself welcome, Wolf. Lunch will be ready soon, trout and spinach. Hope you don't mind plain food. At least it's home-grown.'

Having said that, Father took a long, hard look at Wolf and folded his lips into an unspoken verdict of disapproval.

Wolf, ultra-sensitive to other people's moods, tried to woo him.

'Lawrence Ogilvie,' he murmured, staring at a painting

in the hallway. 'That's you, I assume. So you paint?
How beautifully you've caught the winter light and the
bleakness of the mountains. It's just as I saw the scene
when we drove here.'

'Hmm! Come this way. What would you like to drink?
We have some very good Scotch. A gift from a friend on
the Isle of Skye.'

'Nina tells me that you breed cattle. I'd thought of
having a shot at it in Botswana. Of course, the problems
we face there are quite different from your but either
way it's a tough business.'

Wolf was determined to demonstrate his know-how of
problems facing Scottish farmers. Perhaps he'd looked
them up, but Father remained unimpressed.

'Did you know about Mother's stroke?' I asked, inter-
rupting Wolf.

'John wrote to tell me. I don't know why. There is no
link between us.'

I gripped my father's arm. 'Dad, Mother's so ill. You
should go and see her.'

'Whatever for? It would be an impertinence.'

'To forgive?'

Sensing that we needed to be alone, Wolf announced
that he would walk down to the loch. His eyes met mine.
He understood. He always did, and I blessed him.

Scanning my father's expression I picked up his genuine
concern. 'Don't worry. I'm very happy, Father. Wolf is
the most wonderful person. When you get to know him
you'll like him. He's kind and sincere, a real champion
of the underdog, a most sensitive man, and so clued up
on ecology and wildlife.'

'Well, he certainly goes out of his way to appear
concerned and understanding, Nina. I wonder why.'

'Father, for God's sake. Try to meet him half-way.'

'Be careful, Nina.' He put one hand over mine. I was astonished. 'I can see how taken you are, my dear, but Wolf is a man with hidden agendas. Keep your money in England. You might need it. Remember that, will you?' His words put a dampener on my joy.

I halted the angry words that threatened to spill out, realising that after this I would not see my father for a long time.

'You don't trust anyone and you never truly loved me.' I tried to make light of that statement.

He smiled, a funny, tight-lipped, bitter smile and it haunted me for the rest of the day, while the three of us inspected the cattle, the sheep, and tramped around the loch, returning for tea and cake by the fire.

After supper we said goodbye and drove back to our hotel.

'Only Father can cut emotional ties so effectively and permanently,' I began angrily, when Ogilvie Lodge was still in sight. 'Everyone else learns to cope with a new set of rules, adding exes and their spouses to their wider family circle. Finally they settle somewhere between siblings and cousins. You tolerate them for the sake of the kids, and because they offer a sense of continuity in a scary world. But not in Father's case, of course. He never forgives.'

'I found him heavy-going, but he's your father so I tried.'

Our gloom lasted until we reached our hotel room and switched on the TV where we saw a replay of Nelson Mandela stepping out of prison after a twenty-seven-year incarceration.

'I have a longing to go home. Let's get out of this place,' Wolf said, throwing his arms about me.

129

'Oh, yes. First thing in the morning.'

'Tonight!'

'Let's go!'

'First things first,' Wolf said, as he pounced on me. We made love with frenetic energy, threw our clothes into our cases and called the astonished night porter.

As we sipped our drinks in the first-class cabin, I curled up close to Wolf and tried to relax, but my father's warning kept coming into my mind. He was so bitter and empty, perhaps because he had been betrayed, and his nature was unforgiving. There and then I decided to put my love first. From now on, I vowed, I would guard my home with my life, make any sacrifice necessary. I hugged Wolf's arm.

'I love you,' I murmured sleepily. 'Nothing matters except you and me.'

Chapter 22

Morgendauw, Wolf's run-down old manor, was now my home, so my first few days in the Cape were spent recruiting staff and a housekeeper, the very Irish Mrs Mallory, as capable as she was pleasant. I embarked on a massive renovation, and after three weeks' hard work, the house was beginning to regain some of its former glory.

Right in the middle of a busy morning, Joy arrived. 'Darling, this is an official invitation to a garden party next Saturday afternoon. Wolf has accepted on your behalf, but I thought I'd better check with you.'

'Sorry, Joy. Next time. Just look at this mess.'

'But I need you, Nina. This is my first proper English garden party, as in Buckingham Palace. You know the ropes. Must I beg you?' She wouldn't give in.

'Well, if it's so important . . .' Groaning inwardly, I capitulated.

'Everyone will be titled.'

'Not everyone, Joy. There's you and me, for God's sake.'

'Almost everyone.'

'What if it rains?'

'We'll do like you English, darling. We'll simply ignore the weather. You must, repeat must, wear a large hat, gloves and an absolutely super outfit. I'm counting on you.'

By Saturday I was exhausted. I had coped with plumbers, electricians, building inspectors, interior decorators, landscape gardeners, carpenters, and usually all at the same time. On top of that I'd had to go out and buy a new dress, a stupid extravagance of beaded lace in pale lilac with a large hat to match. Wolf had sensibly absented himself on a business trip to Namibia. When he called me late on Friday night I was thrilled to hear his voice.

'Come home. I've missed you, darling. Besides, I need you here.'

'I'll be landing in Cape Town around lunch-time, Saturday. That's the best I can do. I'll drive straight to the Fortunes' and meet you there. Don't be late.'

'I've never been to a garden party, let alone the Queen's.'

At precisely two p.m. on Saturday, Caesar arrived in Bernie's new Rolls-Royce.

'Joy's being daft, I'm walking there. It's only five minutes away and it's a lovely day for a walk, Caesar.'

'You'll get me into trouble,' he said bluntly.

Sighing, I climbed into the Rolls.

'Jesus!' I burst out laughing as we drove up the driveway and caught sight of Joy, absurdly dressed like a youthful bridesmaid. I should have helped her choose something more suitable. Oh, God! This was going to be ludicrous.

How dumb could anyone get? I only cottoned on when a handful of premature confetti blew into my face, and the good wishes poured in.

Joy had everything ready: the bouquet, the veil, something borrowed and something blue – her garter, as it happened. Wolf couldn't control his triumph, he looked tremendous in his top hat and tails, but I was panicking.

Bernie took my arm and led me through the rose garden to the balcony, the organist struck up, the priest stepped forward and said the right words, and for a wild, silly moment, I considered saying, 'No,' but whispered, 'I will,' instead. Wolf slipped the ring on my finger and I found myself married before I'd had time to panic.

When I signed the register, I discovered that I was now the Baroness Wolfgang von Schenk Möller. I don't believe in titles, except for those that are earned, but I guessed I could keep mine hidden, as Wolf had.

That day we did everything in style. I flung my bouquet towards the clamouring bridesmaids, took off my garter and flung that, too, and we cut the cake after the first waltz.

'I'm sorry there's no photographer,' Joy told me, when we had a moment to ourselves. 'Wolf didn't want photographs. He was most insistent.'

'Oh, who cares, Joy? Everything's perfect. You've been wonderful. Thank you.' I flung my arms around her, surprising both of us. 'Dear Joy. My dearest friend.'

To my dismay, Joy burst into tears.

Marriage to Wolf was a fairy story. I was pampered and loved, and nothing was ever too much trouble if it made me happy. Even pregnancy agreed with me, after my initial bout of morning sickness. As the months passed I became lazier, more content and filled with joyous anticipation. I was so happy I felt guilty. What had I done to deserve this wondrous bounty? Wasn't it all too perfect to be real?

Chapter 23

~~~~~~~~~~~~

'Hey, Nina, where are you?' Wolf called from the kitchen.

'Out here.'

I was sprawled in the sun by the pool, immersed in a local gardening book. Bugs were getting my roses. They were great ugly triangular things that looked and smelt disgusting. They sucked the moisture out of the stalks until the rosebuds withered and died. A whole new crop of roses had come to grief.

'I've identified the bastards. They're called stink bugs, otherwise known as *Coreidae*. And the remedy is – goodness – a swift swipe. In this day and age! You'd think science could come up with something better than that, wouldn't you?'

'Nina, you amaze me. All those years you were a whiz-kid, and here you are wallowing in domesticity as happy as a pig in pee.'

'Shit,' I said. 'You should lay off English idioms.'

Wolf crouched beside me and tickled my nose with a blade of grass.

'Hey! I have to concentrate. I'm into a full-scale war of attrition. I tell you, Wolf, you wouldn't believe the variety of African bugs just dying to munch my succulent English roses.'

'Roses are not English, darling, they come from Asia. These tea-roses are native to China.' He gazed at me quizzically. 'Aren't you bored?' he asked.

'No. Should I be?' There was never enough time, because I still worked part-time for Bertram's. For the rest, my days were filled with pleasure. All my earlier unpleasant pregnancy symptoms had vanished leaving me with a deep sense of contentment. I was longing for the birth of my child, and I had only one worry and that was Wolf, who was chronically overworked. Despite his glowing tan, there were deep shadows under his eyes and lines criss-crossed around them, but his expression was still as caring. He sat at his computer half the night, endlessly scribbling into notebooks and filing his data on to floppies that he kept locked in his safe.

I'd come to the conclusion he was a genius. He had so many irons in the fire, so many get-rich-quick schemes on the go involving a quick in and out. Most of them worked out well for him, so why was he always so keyed up? It was as if he performed his juggling acts on a high-tension wire. One slip would mean disaster. If only I could shoulder some of his load.

'I'd be happier if I could help you with your workload.' I saw his face change and hurried on. 'That was what we planned, remember? You'd be amazed how helpful I could be. Accounts are my business.'

'God forbid that I should allow my pregnant wife to overtire herself. Besides, Nina, most of my work is classified. I told you that.'

Sometimes I wondered if he used this to keep me out of his affairs.

'Come here, you MCP. Would you like to feel your baby kick? Put your hand here. Maybe he'll do it again.'

I sprawled back on the grass, propped myself on my

elbow, and felt the tiny foot kicking out from inside. 'He's restless. He takes after you.'

Wolf pressed his hand over my swollen belly. 'I can feel him. He kicked me. Can you believe it? Do you think he can hear us?' Wolf's expression was a mixture of pride and awe.

'I like to think he can.'

'Listen here, Nicholas, you mustn't kick your mother. Be gentle or you'll have me to deal with one of these days. Just you wait, my boy.'

'Nicholas? What sort of a name is that? Russian?'

'My grandfather's name. I would love to call him Nicholas.'

'Nicholas it is. But, Wolf, what if he's a girl?'

'Then we'll call her Nicola, but I'm sure he's a boy.' Wolf pressed his lips against my stomach. 'I love you both,' he murmured. 'Of course you're right about us working together, but only later. I'm thinking of ditching Armscor.

'Darling Nina,' he went on, 'I wanted to buy something to tell you how much I sympathise with your swollen state. You never complain, but it must be difficult. I couldn't find anything precious enough, so I had this made instead. It's been in my pocket all day. It's nothing.' He dropped a small packet on the grass beside me and stood up. 'See you at lunch. Bernie and I have to work.'

I watched him stride away, tall, vigorous and immensely handsome. I envied him his figure. At six months I was so ungainly.

I opened the wrapping and found a beautiful emerald and sapphire bracelet, exquisitely worked in 24-carat gold leaf chain. The note read: 'Thank you for my son.'

I was acquiring quite a collection of jewellery. Strange, I had never thought that I, of all people, would learn to value such things, but it had been given with love so I loved it.

The days passed in a heady glow of sunshine and success. We became richer as profits poured in from his many and varied business ventures, but I sometimes worried about what I had become. I saw myself as some vast, swollen fertility symbol, all belly and little else.

But then my baby was born and, like everything else in my married life, it happened with little pain and a great deal of joy. Wolf was with me throughout the birth, hovering over me, lending me strength with his own energy, showering me with love. When my son was washed and dressed and wrapped in a shawl, I held him in my arms and gloated over his beautiful dark red hair, which was long for a newborn baby, and his tiny but perfect fingers and his funny little screwed-up face. It was love at first sight.

After the birth of my son, Nicholas, I discovered that Wolf had other talents I'd never suspected. He was the perfect father. Despite the presence of Mavis, a young, local full-time nanny, one or the other of us was always with our child. We still went out into the bush for days and travelled a great deal, but Nicky went with us. Sometimes we had to walk for hours, and he would sit in his backpacker strapped on Wolf's strong shoulders.

In those wonderful, explorative days of Nicky's infancy, Wolf and I became as close as two people ever could be. Our sex brought us unbelievable heights of joy as we coaxed every ounce of pleasure from each other's bodies.

Nicky was a sweet child with a happy nature. He said his first word at ten months. Much to our chagrin it was 'Nanny'. A few months later that graduated to 'Nanny do'. He would point imperiously at whatever he wanted done or lifted or taken away, and Mavis, who adored him, did his bidding with a smile. She was never impatient with him, but later I learned that this was an African trait. They spoil their children.

It was about then that we acquired a Great Dane puppy, whom I named Brigit the Second. Nicky adored her, and although he often came off worse in their romps around the garden, he never complained.

One morning, when Nicky was almost twenty-two months old, he asked to play in the pool.

'Later, Nicky. Mummy has to finish this cake first.'

His big brown eyes gazed seriously at me. 'Later?'

'Of course.' He took his truck off to the fenced-off area of garden outside the kitchen door. Shortly afterwards I heard Brigit barking furiously. She sounded distressed. I looked around for Nicky, but there was no sign of him. Then I saw that he had somehow managed to drag a garden chair to the swimming-pool fence and throw himself over.

'Oh, God! Oh, no! Oh, God!' I raced to the pool, leaped on to the chair and toppled over the fence. Brigit, dripping with water, was guarding my soaked, frightened child. Nicky gazed at me tremulously, his bottom lip quivering, his hair wet and falling over his face, his eyes pleading for mercy.

I hugged him tightly and threw one arm around the dog's neck. Later she was rewarded with the remainder of yesterday's cold roast lamb, but it took me hours to stop shaking.

'He's strong and resourceful,' Wolf said, when I told him about the accident. 'It's amazing that Brigit managed to jump over the fence to rescue him. From now on I'll spend an hour a day teaching Nicky to swim, and meantime that fence is going up another metre. I'll call the company right now.'

Since Nicky's birth, without really meaning to, we had adopted the lifestyle of our neighbours and friends. We went shares with Bernie on the running costs of his helicopter and patronised all the best restaurants within a three-hundred-kilometre radius of Constantia, we took two long holidays a year, Europe in spring and some tropical paradise in winter. Because we would not leave him behind, Nicky had become one of the most travelled children in our set. Wolf's work for the government meant endless invitations to semi-official dinners and cocktail parties all over the Republic. We had a box at the races, we flew to Durban for the July Handicap, to Johannesburg for the Grand Prix.

In the early days I used to wonder when the honeymoon would be over. Eventually I came to believe that it would never be over.

I was wrong. Even now I can pinpoint the exact date and time when we fell out of paradise. It was 2 October, 1992, one day before Nicky's second birthday.

Chapter 24

'Nina, I've come to you because . . . well, because we're friends.'

Friendly was not a word I would use to describe Joy at that moment. Her blue eyes flashed ice.

'Joy. What a lovely surprise. Come in. I'm working in the kitchen. D'you mind sitting there?' As I took her to the kitchen, I couldn't help wondering if her lover was playing up again. 'Let's have a drink. Take a look at that!'

I had just finished making the birthday cake, with two candles and a multi-coloured toy train made of sweets and icing-sugar on the top. I was proud of it.

'Wolf's not here, is he?' Joy said, looking around nervously and ignoring my cake. 'Bernie said he's away.'

'Namibia, but he'll be back early tomorrow. It's Nicky's birthday tomorrow. You hadn't forgotten, had you? Don't you like it?'

'Good! I mean . . . Oh, yes, the cake.' Momentarily Joy looked sad. 'I have to speak to you privately. Theo wants to call in the fraud squad. Bernie won't let him because we're up to our necks in this thing.'

'Joy, please, calm down. I don't know what you're talking about.'

'I'm talking about Wolf's container business.'

'I didn't know Wolf had a container business.'

'I told Bernie he'd never tell you. Sometimes you're so uptight about things like that.'

I heard a yell from the nursery. 'Hang on, Joy. Let's see to Nicky.'

Joy followed me to the nursery.

'I've never seen a two-year-old so utterly spoiled,' Joy murmured, as I lifted Nicky out of his cot and hugged him close. Moments later he was all smiles.

Joy reached for him and I relinquished my baby grudgingly. I could hardly bear to let anyone else hold him.

'He needs changing.' I wrinkled my nose.

Joy handed him back fast. 'Isn't he potty-trained?'

'By day, yes, but not when he sleeps.'

'Sometimes I wish—' She broke off and bit her lip. 'You and Nicky make me broody. Well, it's too late now.' She looked so wistful and deprived. She had been going through another bad patch lately.

I carried Nicky back to the kitchen, put him in his pushchair while I put the finishing touches to the cake.

Joy's story poured out. 'Don't get upset, Nina. Help me! I'm scared. This scheme involves our total savings.'

'What scheme? Joy, you're not making sense. Start at the beginning.'

'Wolf has imported some advanced computer technology for missile tracking, that sort of thing. Sanctions prevent South Africa from importing this type of product, but Wolf knows some right-wing US manufacturers sympathetic to the government. Bernie got involved when Wolf needed bridging finance in a hurry. He coughed up because of the profits involved.'

'I presume you wouldn't tell me this if you weren't absolutely sure of your facts, Joy. So what's the problem?'

'Money, of course. I'm getting there.'

She began to pace up and down distractedly. 'About three years ago, Wolf bought the controlling share of a Dutch company called International Containerisation.' She turned in a swift, compulsive movement and pulled out a chair. 'He told Bernie he would use it to smuggle his money out of the country. Fairly simple with the containers being shipped all over the world,' she explained, tight-lipped and pale. 'The point is, eventually you sell the containers overseas and only repatriate part of the cash. It's a long-term project.

'Every one of our friends is transferring their capital overseas via Wolf's business. Between us, the investment amounts to several million rands. Right now he holds the lot. The containers were scheduled to be sold months ago. Wolf keeps promising the money, but we never see it. None of us has received a cent.'

'I'm sure there's a reasonable explanation.' It was an effort to sound calm. 'I'll ask him as soon as he gets back.'

'Then there's the short-term finance Bernie advanced for the tracking system. Repayment is a month overdue. Bernie has a suspicion that Wolf is going broke. That would ruin us. Oh, God, Nina. I'm sorry to burden you with this, but Bernie can't get a damn thing out of Wolf. You know how charming and convincing he can be. He promises the moon, but does nothing.'

She leaned over the table and buried her face in her hands. When she looked up I noticed how red her eyes were.

'The problem with breaking the law is that we have no recourse to lawyers or the police. Not even to foreign lawyers unless Bernie flies over. I suppose he'll have to. Even the bloody phones are tapped here, and you know how often mail is opened.'

'True.'

'Try to find out for us, Nina.'

'I'll speak to Wolf. He must have it out with you. I'm sure it's all right. Just a delay. After all, you said it was a long-term project.'

'There's a rumour going round that Wolf has created a diamond-dredging scam up at Torrabaai in Namibia. A Greek ship-owner who invested in the project is suing him for millions. Did he tell you?'

I shook my head, suddenly feeling sick.

'I always warned you about him. We never really knew his background. Take care – but please, find out what's happened to our cash.'

'How could you distrust Wolf? We're friends, aren't we? Wolf has proved himself trustworthy so many times. For God's sake, Joy, be realistic.'

She shot me a guilty smile and drove off looking haggard and old.

I felt bad about using the master key to Wolf's garden study, particularly since he had no idea that I had one. Not that I'd ever wanted to spy on him, but the insurance broker had insisted on a duplicate being available in case of fire or burglary.

Switching on Wolf's PC was virtually admitting my distrust, wasn't it? I was making a definite statement. I squirmed with shame.

'Please, God, let there be a good reason for what he's doing.'

As I had expected, Wolf had installed a password, which prevented access. I sighed and got to work, dredging up skills from my Machiavellian days when hacking was my hobby. It took me half an hour to remove Wolf's hard disk and change the pin-setting. Something I'd always thought of as a computer lobotomy, turning the hard-disk drive into a slave-drive, obedient to my own lap-top's commands. I switched on my lap-top and made myself comfortable.

Letter by letter, I began the painstaking search for Wolf's six-digit password, starting with the first letter and running through the alphabet. Half an hour later I had the word. Bosbok. I almost cried at the memory of Namaqualand and that intrepid plane that transported us up and down the coast for the next nine months before being sold for scrap. Oh, God! To think that we had come to this. I blamed myself for listening to Joy. How could I spy on my husband? Yet I could not bring myself to stop. Joy's words had triggered hundreds of queries I had put aside over the past few months.

At last I was able to key into Wolf's business files. Perhaps I'd get an insight into how he operated. There were almost a hundred ledgers, with a handful of documents in each one, so I hardly knew where to start. His business interests were varied and intricate and, far from going bust, he seemed to be making a fortune, at least with the ones I examined.

The Torrabaai Diamond Dredging operation came under the umbrella of the Trans-African Development Foundation. That was curious. A number of diamond deals in Angola were also listed under this umbrella trust company.

It was almost three a.m. when I found the container company, listed under Lübeck, for reasons I did not understand, until I learned that the main bank account was there, too, not in Amsterdam. The records showed agents in every major port, bills of lading for each cargo shifted over the past three years, plus the number, the owners, and the position and destination of every container moving between Europe, Africa and the East. Everything was carefully listed, giving a fair description of South Africa's international trade, much as one would expect: minerals, fruit and wine on the out trips, manufactured items coming in.

Yet I sensed that something was horribly suspect. For three years there had been no setbacks. The entire operation was far too simplified: no hold-ups for bad weather, no delays through strikes or penalties, no losses through damage and breakage. It was a perfectly executed business, meticulously carried out according to plan.

Does anything ever go so smoothly? I asked myself. Wasn't business – and life, come to that – mainly a scissors-and-paste job? Plans go wrong, accidents occur, one spends one's time trying to put things together again. It wasn't real. How could it be?

For a long time I sat in a state of shock. When I noticed that dawn was breaking, I reset the pin-setting on Wolf's hard disk and put it back. As I slung my lap-top over my shoulder and returned to the house, I was so stiff with tension and tiredness I could hardly move my legs.

Chapter 25

Wolf arrived home at six a.m. with a present for Nicky, which we decided to keep for the party. Nicky was still sleeping.

'You look a sight. What is it? Are you ill?' he asked, cradling me in his arms. 'Why so pale?'

'I haven't slept.' I told him about Joy's visit and Theo's threat to call in the fraud squad.

Wolf sat down and gazed at me with narrowed eyes. 'That's what happens when you try to help people,' he muttered. 'I didn't want them in at all. They insisted.'

He set about calming me and putting my fears to rest.

Finally I said, 'You've gone white. Why?'

'It's a bit of a let-down discovering that your friends don't trust you,' he said.

'I couldn't agree more. So where is Bernie's money? And the rest of it?'

'In Deutschmarks.' He looked bemused. 'I came out of yen and went into Deutschmarks. I speculate with currencies, you see. Quite honestly, Bernie's doing very well out of it. His cash has appreciated by thirty per cent over what he was due. I know he wants his cash, but every day he makes a little more profit. To hell with it!' He stood up, looking worried. 'I'm going to liquidate and pay them out. All of them. I don't need this in my life.'

'Oh. Thank God!' I almost burst into tears of relief.

'Don't you trust me, Nina?' he asked.

'Of course, but Bernie thought you were out of your depth with money problems. It's Bernie you must explain to, and the rest of them, not me.'

'Bernie's on edge. Did you hear the news?'

'What news?'

'Johan skipped the country?'

'Johan?'

'Johan du Toit, Bernie's friend. You must remember him, he tried to feed you raw impala meat at the game park.'

'I'll never forget him, but surely . . .'

'No one knew he was running into trouble. He floated his floundering group on the London stock exchange, and absconded with over a hundred million pounds. It's rumoured that his loot went into a numbered account in Switzerland. He's skipped to Venezuela with his wife and kid.'

'Good God! When did this happen?'

'The news broke late last night.'

'No wonder Joy's so nervous about you.'

'Nina, would you stick by me and come with me if I did something like that?'

'I'd stick by you whatever you did, Wolf. But I'd never agree to live in luxury on other people's hard-earned cash. No, I'd definitely give that a miss. You can never get happiness out of other people's misfortune.' I beamed at him. 'Fortunately such a situation wouldn't arise. You'd never do something like that.'

'Wouldn't I?

'No. You'd face up to your losses and start prospecting all over again. With me, of course.'

'So you'd live in poverty with me and start all over again? Remember that house in Namaqualand?'

'Of course. As long as I can live with myself, I can live with you. Oh, Wolf.' I hugged him fiercely. 'I hate anything illegal. Apart from the moral issue, I don't have the guts for it. Whether you want to acknowledge it or not, you're aiding and abetting them in breaking exchange-control laws.'

'If you think so. Darling, I'm starving. When does Mrs Mallory start work?'

'Not for another hour. I'll rustle up something.'

I sang with relief as I made toasted egg and bacon sandwiches and coffee. Belatedly, I remembered Wolf's immaculate container-business files and the three years of perfect operations. Well, Wolf was pretty smart. It wasn't impossible, was it? I decided to put it out of my mind.

'Smells good. Jesus! I'm tired. I drove all night. I was so anxious to get back. I worry about you and Nicky being alone. I've made up my mind to employ a security guard for the nights when I'm away.'

I watched him eat. 'It's not necessary, Wolf. Brigit's all I need.'

'Come to bed with me, darling,' he begged. 'I'm longing to screw you. Then I need to snatch a couple of hours' sleep before work.'

'I'll call Mavis to look after Nicky. Be right up.'

I was singing, I remember, as I hurried upstairs. Wolf was lying naked on the bed, his penis swollen and hard, and his eyes glowing with that mixture of recklessness and tenderness that turned me on so.

I took off my clothes slowly, piece by piece, our eyes locked, engulfed by an ecstasy in which joy and relief were equally intermingled. When I climbed over him I put my hands on either side of his face and gazed hungrily at him before bending over and brushing my lips on his. He was so precious to me, as precious as my son, as important as my own life. Maybe more so. When I pushed him into me I began to groan and then I burst into tears.

'Why don't you trust me?' I sobbed. 'Why didn't you tell me about the Greek ship-owner and Torrabaai? They say it's a "dirty heap" scam. I know you better than that but, Wolf, that sort of talk could ruin us.'

'Shut up and fuck,' he said tenderly. 'It really isn't important. The Greek's an arsehole. My lawyer's handling it.'

'Promise me! Promise you won't take chances just because of our lifestyle. I'd be happy in a cottage or a shack. Anything! Just as long as I have you and Nicky. Oh, my darling.'

We made love frenziedly, and when Wolf groaned and came I was so moved. We were like two people who had been long parted. How foolish I had been to worry.

I had hardly fallen asleep when Mavis woke me. I put on my dressing gown and opened the door.

'Madam, what shall I give Nicky for breakfast?'

'Oh, Mavis,' I grumbled sleepily. 'Porridge as usual. Do it now and I'll come and feed him. Be right with you.'

Wolf sat up in bed and watched me dress. 'You're lovely, Nina. Don't grow old.' He looked at me so oddly.

'I'm sure it won't happen overnight,' I teased him. 'I expect I have a couple of years left before I'm over the hill. There's no need to look quite so regretful.'

Chapter 26

'He eats well. Is this his usual breakfast?' Wolf asked.

'Absolutely his favourite,' I said, tickling my little boy's chin. Nicky gripped the arm-rests of his chair and bounced up and down, opening his mouth for more porridge.

'And lunch?'

'Oh, whatever we have,' I said, absent-mindedly.

'No, really. I'm interested. Tell me.'

I looked up in surprise. 'You think he's under-weight?'

'No, indeed. A picture of health.'

I stepped back and smiled at Wolf, making a decision to take his sudden interest seriously. He didn't spend much time in the kitchen. 'Mince and mash with veg, or fried fish and chips, or stew with boiled mutton, all sorts of veg. One thing about him, he loves his veg, especially pumpkin. Don't worry, he gets all he needs and more.'

Gazing at my boy, I felt a glow of pure happiness. Nicky was strong and tall for his age and seldom sick. I knew I was blessed. I was convinced that he was the cleverest two-year-old ever.

At that moment I said a silent prayer of thanks. A surge of guilt hit home when I remembered last night's distrust. No harm done.

'What about vitamins?'

I laughed. 'A teaspoon of vitamin syrup every morning.'

'And then?'

I stood up. 'Come!' I opened the fridge door and gave a little mock bow. 'The menu is as follows, sir. The Prince of Wales gets a mashed banana or paw-paw or any fruit before he eats his soft-boiled egg and toast. If he's still hungry he'll polish off a couple of biscuits with his warm milk.'

'You're a genius.'

'No, just a mother. By the way, I love you and I love your sudden interest in our son's diet.'

When, at last, Nicky finished his breakfast, Mavis wiped his face with a damp flannel and stood him on the floor. Brigit gave him a large wet lick that knocked him over. He rolled over on to his hands and knees and climbed to his feet enduring the dog's attention stoically, and murmuring, 'Bad Brigit.' She fawned and wiggled, and tried to make amends.

It was late November, early summer, and Morgendauw was ablaze with sunlight. The silverleaf trees were glistening as the sunrays hit the morning dew. Cape robins were making their nests in the hedge and the garden was noisy with birdsong. I opened the french windows. 'Out,' I told the dog.

Brigit rushed outside and pranced around the lawn like a clumsy colt, with Nicky running behind her. It would be months before she gained poise and dignity, but Nicky adored her.

Wolf nuzzled his mouth around my neck until I gasped. 'I have to take some papers to the air freight. I'll take Nicky for the ride. He loves to watch the planes landing.'

I remembered last weekend when we had gone to see a friend off. Nicky had created a rare scene when we left. 'I could come, but I'm preparing for the party.'

'Don't worry. Won't be long. I'll take Mavis in case I have to wait. Give her his coat. Sometimes it gets windy there.'

'What? In the middle of a heatwave?' I laughed at him.

'You know how suddenly the wind can come up.'

'You're a real old fuss-pot.'

'See you.'

He smiled. It was a smile of such compassion and tenderness. All the love in the world was mirrored in his eyes.

I followed them out, doing my mother-hen act, checking that Nicky was properly secured in the back of the Land Rover beside Mavis.

'Please come, Mummy.'

'I have to get ready for your party, my boy. See you soon.'

I gave Mavis her hundredth lesson in buckling up carefully and off they went, with Brigit cantering along behind. She gave up at the end of the lane and trotted back, looking downcast.

I finished the jellies and still had time on my hands, so I sprayed the roses. I adored gardening, and for a while I didn't notice the time passing. I surfaced later and glanced at my watch. Heavens! Almost twelve. I warmed some mince and mashed potatoes, covered the plate with a lid and placed it in the warmer. I kept myself busy tidying the house and toys until one, but then I began to get irritated. Wolf had been delayed but he should have called me. After all, we had a birthday party starting soon, even if it was only Joy and a few neighbours and their children.

By two p.m. I was fighting off a strange feeling of disaster. Wolf knew I was waiting. He had never done this before. Why hadn't he called? He knew how much I worried about Nicky and, anyway, he had promised to be back by twelve. Had they had an accident? On impulse I called the police, but no accidents on the road to the airport had been reported.

At two thirty Mavis rang me from the office of the airport manager. 'Madam,' she sobbed, 'I sat in the truck for three and a half hours. The master's taken Nicky and gone.'

Chapter 27

I parked haphazardly, then forced myself to walk and not run to the airport manager's office where I introduced myself. 'Please! Help me find my husband and my child. Perhaps he's been taken ill. Put out a call on the loudspeaker.'

'I've already done that, Mrs Möller. I sent your maid to First Aid. She was hysterical. She'll be here soon.'

He was a caring person, but I could see that he thought I was overreacting. Perhaps I was. I made an effort to be calm, but tension gripped me. I could feel the blood hurtling through my veins and my heart hammering against my chest.

But, of course, nothing was wrong. Perhaps he was waiting for documents to arrive. He could have taken Nicky to lunch. But how could he worry me so? I made an effort to pull myself together and convince myself that soon it would all be over. By nightfall Nicky would be tucked up in his cot.

Mavis returned with a nurse. She was still wailing.

'Pull yourself together, Mavis. Think carefully. What did Mr Möller say to you when he left you in the Jeep?'

'He said . . .' She swallowed hard and looked afraid of me, which puzzled me. 'He said, 'Wait there.' But, Madam, he carried Nicky's backpack, and it was very heavy. He had it in the boot. And that leather bag you gave him for Christmas. And Nicky's blanket. I didn't think. I said, "Let me carry Nicky."' She burst into tears again.

'And he said?'

'"Guard the Land Rover, Mavis. There's been a lot of thefts here." But later I saw he'd left the keys.'

As the implication of her words sank in I swayed and almost lost my balance. I felt light-headed. As if I weren't there at all. Wolf would never leave the keys. The Land Rover was his pride and joy. Why had he taken a coat for Nicky? Why his sudden interest in Nicky's diet? What if he didn't have the cash to pay Bernie and his friends? Was he bankrupt? Had he run away? Oh, God. Oh, God. No! Even to think about it was insane. We were so happy. He wasn't a cruel man. He would never deprive me of my baby. And what about Nicky? My little one needed his mother. My heart began to thump and I broke out in a cold sweat.

'Sit down, please, Mrs Möller.' The airport manager pushed me into a chair and spoke to the nurse. 'Bring a glass of cold water at once.' He glanced at Mavis. 'Bring two.'

The young airport clerk knocked at the door, wide-eyed and scared.

'Now, Mrs Möller,' the manager said, 'I've put out another broadcast. This is Sergeant Blumer who will escort you around the airport. Are you well enough to go?'

'I must.'

'Check the bookshops and the refreshment bars. Did your husband drink?'

'No.'

I was almost blinded by tears and my legs were so

stiff it was an effort to walk as I followed the sergeant listlessly. We would not find Wolf. I knew that now.

It seemed like hours later when we returned to the airport manager's office where officials were coming and going, the telephone kept ringing and the loudspeaker monotonously repeated the call for Wolf every five minutes. A nurse brought me a headache pill and a cup of sweet black tea.

'Do you have a photograph of your husband or your child, Mrs Möller?'

'Not with me.'

He looked up. 'Come in, Miss Swanepoel. Mrs Möller, this is my booking clerk on the charter-flight desk.'

A young woman in uniform nodded gravely at me.

'She has a description of a man and a toddler who left this morning at eleven forty-five on a charter flight to Walvis Bay, Namibia. Please listen to her and see if you recognise anything at all.'

The woman flushed self-consciously and read her notes woodenly. 'The man was tall, brown hair, blond streaks, blue eyes, sun-tanned, wearing a safari suit, mid or late thirties. He was carrying a little boy, a backpack and a briefcase. The child was beautiful, I remember him clearly. Red hair, big brown eyes, and he was wearing blue dungarees and a green shirt—'

'No . . . No . . .' I lurched to my feet. The last thing I heard was her singsong voice as the room began to turn. Sergeant Blumer caught me and helped me back into the chair. 'Nicky. Oh, God, that's my Nicky. Why has he taken him? Why? Why?'

The police arrived. They seemed so young and inexperienced and they asked absurd questions. Had we fought? Were we happy together? Had we ever considered a divorce? Was my husband in financial difficulties?

Was there another woman involved? The questions went on and on. Mad questions. Absurd! Insane! Wolf loved me.

I couldn't think. The right words wouldn't come as I tried to answer. My mouth dried and my lips were so frozen they could not frame the syllables.

'Shock,' I heard one of them say.

They wanted to take me to hospital.

'No.' I managed to get that word out, at least. 'My husband, Wolf, will call me. I must stay at home. He's bound to contact me. He'll explain. Please take me home.'

The police left and I told Mrs Mallory a story about an accident, and she sent the birthday-party guests home. The kids went off whining, trailing balloons and cradling their cake. Only Joy hung around, but I left her to the housekeeper and stayed in my room until she, too, left. Then I gave the staff the afternoon off and wandered around the empty house, so vast and lonely, and gathered some of Nicky's toys together, but I did not move far from the telephone. Wolf would call. He had lost our friends' money and run away. He would tell me where to come and join him. We would sort it out together. I still had some money and I could sell the house.

Meantime, my poor baby was deprived of his mother and his home. How would he sleep without his teddy? Oh, God! Where are you, Nicky? Oh, Wolf, come home. I don't care what you've done. How could you be so cruel?

I missed them both so much. I threw myself on the bed and lay dry-eyed, hardly able to bear my grief and my headache. The pillow felt like a block of cement. I hurled it across the floor and grabbed another. At that moment I saw the photograph.

I screamed and kept on screaming. Eventually I sat up, shuddering, and picked it up, but my hands were shaking so much, I had to place it on the table because I couldn't see properly.

'Be calm. Your baby needs you. Keep your wits about you.' Saying the words aloud seemed to calm me, but still I could not stop shuddering. Had Wolf done this? I returned to the bedroom and gazed at the terrible evidence. The photograph of Nicky in his high chair had been taken by Wolf two weeks ago. I had asked for an enlargement but I had not seen it since. Here it was. Nicky was looking so happy and smiling so confidently at his father. But his father had taken a red crayon and mutilated the photograph with a deep red slash around my baby's neck.

He had written in red ink over Nicky's white T-shirt: 'Keep your mouth shut.' A red arrow pointed to the slash on Nicky's neck.

Chapter 28

I was muttering to myself almost incoherently, but another part of me was watching me as if from a distance. In my detached, bemused state I was listening to my own voice.

'There's no one here. No one! Little Nicky, my sweet son, and my love . . . Gone! I must do something. What is it that I must do? I must burn the papers. There must be no documents left concerning his business. Leave nothing! Not even a fingerprint. Wolf must have no excuse to harm my baby.'

First I rubbed every polished surface, Wolf's shoes, light switches, door handles, bathroom cabinet, TV set, CDs, everything I found that he might have touched. This took me several hours. At midnight I took matches, paraffin and a galvanised bucket and hurried through the garden to his office. I threw all that I found into the bucket and set light to it: files, computer diskettes, correspondence. I opened the safe and ran out with bundles of files and papers. My anger was like the flames, all-consuming. The papers were soon reduced to ashes as my love was. I wanted it to die as I stirred the ashes with slow, deliberate movements.

Switching on Wolf's computer, I keyed in his password, Bosbok. As I had thought, he had trashed everything, but there are ways and means of recovering trashed information, so I removed his hard disk and smashed it to fragments with a hammer.

I knew I should destroy the mutilated photograph of Nicky, too. No one must discover that he was held hostage, but when I tried, I found I couldn't bear to throw his image on the fire. Smoothing it out lovingly, I placed the tear-splashed picture on the desk.

'I'll find you, Nicky. I promise you. Mummy's coming after you.' But where would I find him? My determination gave way to utter dejection and more tears.

Brigit began to growl, but I hardly noticed. Looking down I saw her hackles rising. She looked terrified. I just sat there. A man appeared in the doorway and I came to my senses too late. I stood up and stumbled across to him, but he pushed me back violently. He stepped in and slammed the door behind him. Then he locked it and put the key in his pocket. He walked to the computer and switched it on.

'Get out! Out! I'll call the police.'

'I am a policeman, Mrs Möller. I'm looking for your husband. Where is he?'

'You're foreign. You're lying. Who are you?' My voice had become too high-pitched. I tried to keep calm.

'I told you. Ah. So I'm too late. You have destroyed everything. Why?'

He shot me a grim look and began searching the office. I watched him nervously, wondering how I could get out. There was a panic button behind Wolf's desk, but he blocked the way. There was only one door and he had the key. He was short and powerful-looking, with a wide head set on a thick neck. Blond stubble hardly covered his scalp, and the expression in his blue eyes was of the utmost menace. He seemed to think he had all the time in the world. I shuddered.

'Where is your husband, Mrs Möller?' His voice was low as he moved towards me. I screamed as his hand shot out and punched me on the side of my face. Reeling back, stunned and hurt, I felt my mouth fill with blood.

It was then that Brigit sprang at him. Taken by surprise, he fell backwards. I leaped across the floor and reached the panic button by the desk. As the room reverberated to the sound of the siren, I heard a shot and saw Brigit float backwards, her skull disintegrating, blood gushing. She jerked a few times and lay still in a pool of blood.

'Bastard!' I screamed, losing control. Grabbing the nearest chair, I flung it at him, intending to kill him, but he could have been a rock. The chair splintered and my anger turned to fear as his hands closed around my throat.

'Where is Wolf Möller?'

I choked and gagged, and his hands loosened while the sirens wailed on. 'I don't know. He's gone.'

A quick push sent me sprawling on the ground. His hand caught hold of my right wrist, strong as a handcuff. A flick-knife flashed and the agony exploded in my brain as he pushed the point under my thumbnail and twisted it, while I writhed and screamed.

'Where is your husband?'

His voice seemed to come from a long way away from the cave of pain I inhabited. Then the intruder caught sight of Nicky's photograph lying on the desk. He dropped my hand and gazed at it.

'So you tell me the truth, eh? You do not know where he is. If you did you would go after your child. You would not be here. He holds your child as hostage.'

He took the picture and left as unexpectedly as he had arrived. I collapsed groaning on the floor, nursing my dead Brigit, my swelling thumb and my stifling grief.

Someone was shaking me. I became aware of pain. My head ached intolerably and my hand and cheek were swollen. Opening my eyes, I saw the blood and Brigit's corpse, and the night's events came flooding back. I frowned at a policeman, who looked concerned. Who was he? I tried to get away from him.

'Police, Mrs Möller.' He pushed his badge at me. 'You're quite safe. Your siren went off and the security company called us. What happened?'

'Someone broke in,' I muttered.

'And your dog?'

'Oh, my poor Brigit. She went for him . . . He shot her. She saved me.'

'Your neck is badly bruised. What happened to your hand, lady? I'd better call an ambulance.'

'No! Don't! I must stay here. My husband's disappeared . . . taken my son. But he'll call me . . . he must. I have to be here.' By now I was almost incoherent.

'Did your husband do this terrible thing?' He took my hand and gazed sadly at my black thumb, where the nail hung by a thread.

'For God's sake, I told you. Someone broke in.'

He helped me back to the house where two more plain-clothes detectives were searching around. One of them made coffee and brought it to me. Another took out a folder and a pen and we spent a long and painful half-hour composing a statement. I had to repeat everything several times. He was sure that I was lying and he was right. I didn't want him to know that the intruder had been looking for Wolf. When I was satisfied that my statement said next to nothing, I signed the page.

'You have to try to rest, Mrs Möller. Call your doctor, please. That hand must have attention. Is there a neighbour I can fetch to look after you?'

I shook my head.

'We've searched the premises thoroughly. There's no one here. Nothing appears to be missing. Let me help you to your room. I'll leave a policeman on guard.'

'I can manage, thanks.'

As the first glimmer of dawn touched the windows I slept briefly, only to wake to pain and nausea, but far worse was the nightmare that would not go away.

Chapter 29

Mavis came in with a cup of coffee. 'The police are back. They've been here for a while. They've searched the house.'

Again! What good could they do? I knew now that they would not find Nicky. Wolf had kidnapped him and Wolf was the cleverest man I knew.

'Tell them I'm going to take a shower. I'll be down in twenty minutes.'

These were sterner, cleverer policemen and all signs of sympathy were gone. They introduced themselves as Lieutenant Joubert and Major Barnard from the fraud squad. Joubert, the younger man, was pale and thin with sculpted features and deep-set pale green eyes. Major Barnard was very tall, with a domed forehead. Each of his features vied to be the biggest and most prominent, yet his mild brown eyes brought a kind of sanity to his face.

'Mrs Möller, you're in big trouble,' he began, in a surprisingly low-key voice. 'We've traced your husband to Walvis Bay harbour. After that there are no further sightings. He could have left by boat or driven overland to Angola. Did he have contacts there?'

I remained staring at my hands.

'Why did he take your child?'

'I shrugged.'

'Did he leave you here to cover for him?'

'No.'

'Do you know where he is?'

'No.'

'We have details of your behaviour at the airport. You were in shock, Mrs Möller. You had no idea that he was leaving. You were desperately worried about your son.'

My thumb was black and throbbing. The more I stared at it, the worse it seemed to get.

'You were tortured last night.'

'We had a fight when I tried to reach the panic button.'

'I don't think so. From your bruised neck and your maimed thumb, I think this man tried to force you to tell him where your husband is. If he finds your husband before we do, your child will be killed. Tell us what you told him, Mrs Möller.'

'That I don't know where Wolf is.'

'Is he going to send for you?'

I stared at him. 'Do you think that's likely?'

He must have picked up a trace of hope in my voice. 'No, I do not. Wherever he is, it's imperative that you find your son quickly. Co-operate with us, Mrs Möller. That is by far your best bet. We have deduced that you destroyed all your husband's files and his hard disk drive.'

I shrugged. Then I decided to lie. I said, 'No, the intruder did that.'

'That's a silly answer, I'm afraid. If he were a friend of Möller's he would not have tortured you. He is Möller's enemy. Help us to identify him before he harms your child. Be realistic.' He shook my shoulder. 'The child would be taken to force your husband to hand over the

millions he has made. Think what he did to you. Do
you want that to happen to your son? It would be far
worse, I assure you.'

I shuddered. 'I can't help you. Why don't you leave
me alone?'

'Help us to identify the intruder. If you don't you will
be obstructing justice. We know that you saw him.'

'I can do that. He was short, thick-set, bull neck,
blond stubble over his flat-topped scalp, blue eyes. His
eyes were a killer's eyes. No warmth, just menace.'

'Will you attempt to identify him from pictures?'

'Yes.'

'I'll take you down to Headquarters.'

'No, please, I must stay here.'

'Your husband won't contact you, Mrs Möller. We
are your best bet.'

My lips were pressed together, but my eyes beamed
fury.

'Why are there no photographs of your husband in
the house? Did you destroy them?'

I shook my head. 'There were none.'

'But you were married to him for three years.'

'He never allowed himself to be photographed.'

'Didn't that seem odd to you?'

'Not at the time.'

'You are a part of everything, aren't you, Mrs Möller?
All his thieving and conning.'

'No.'

'But you must have known there was incriminating
evidence on the file. Why else would you destroy
it?'

'I knew nothing about it.'

'You're covering up for him.'

'No.'

'Give me another reason why you destroyed your husband's files.'

There was a long silence.

'We know that he created a project to help local businessmen shift their capital out of the country. Unfortunately for them, that was not his true motive. Are you involved in this fraud?'

'Do I look like a cheat? And if I were, wouldn't I be long since gone?'

'We called in a locksmith to open your husband's safe, but it was empty, naturally, since you emptied it. Your silence incriminates you. I must remind you that it's ten years for fraud, Mrs Möller. I've heard there may be other, more serious charges. You had better co-operate with us or you will be considered an accessory to your husband's many fraudulent projects. He conned many millions out of his victims, so you can expect a long sentence. Do you have any suspicion as to where he might have gone?'

Their questions went on and on. I suppose they were hoping to wear me down. I fended them off, or closed my mouth. Hours later, they stood up scowling.

Barnard's voice was very expressive. It spelled out my danger succinctly as he said: 'Don't leave Cape Town, Mrs Möller.'

I buried my face in my hands. I didn't have to pretend that I was in shock. I was.

Chapter 30

Joy and Bernie arrived at lunch-time. They parked the car immediately below the steps and stood on the porch looking hostile and scared.

'We're ruined. We've had to put our house on the market,' Joy said, in an undertone. For the first time I noticed a sense of comradeship between them. Bernie was clinging to Joy's arm.

'You warned him. You helped him get away. I trusted you.'

'Joy, I only asked him where the money was, just as you told me to.'

'Don't bother to give me his reply. Just tell us where he's gone.'

'I wish I knew.'

Joy noticed my swollen cheek and bandaged hand for the first time. 'Did he beat you up? What's wrong with your cheek? And your hand?'

'Someone broke in last night.'

'There'll be plenty more. Hordes of them,' Bernie said nastily. 'They'll all want to know where Wolf is. Did you tell him?'

I shook my head. 'No! How could I? I tell you, I don't know.'

'Tell us where he is,' Bernie pleaded. 'If I could get

my hands on him, I might force some of my cash out of him.'

'You have to believe me. He's kidnapped Nicky. According to the police, he chartered a flight to Walvis Bay and then disappeared. Joy . . . Bernie . . . How am I going to find my baby?' The last shreds of my self-control were at snapping point.

'The fraud squad came.' Bernie's voice grated unpleasantly. 'They told me you covered up for him. You burned his files while he skipped with the cash. I'm telling you, Nina, you won't get away with it. There's more to this than you know. Wolf's waiting for you somewhere. You two were as thick as thieves. Well, you are thieves and I told the fraud squad as much. He made a fool of the government, and they'll put you away instead of him. You could get years.'

'Oh, please! You can't believe that, Bernie.'

Joy shot Bernie a warning look. He shut his mouth, as if realising he'd said too much, and the silence was chilling.

'Come in,' I said. 'Why are we standing here?'

'We'll never set foot in your house again,' Joy retorted. 'Don't ever try to contact us.' She shot me a glance of contempt.

As they left, the full impact of my duplicity hit me. I could have told them that their cash had been transferred to Lübeck, but if Bernie contacted the Lübeck police, Wolf would hurt my Nicky. Nothing would tempt me to risk my baby's life. Wolf had silenced me, just as he had planned.

My mood lightened slightly as I saw that there might be a lead here. I had been so shocked I hadn't thought properly. I decided to fly to Lübeck at once. I might be

n time. It seemed an eternity since Wolf had left, but
t was just twenty-four hours. I sat at the dining-room
table and jotted down what I could remember of his
background. Beeskow was his home town, and he had
studied geology at Dresden.

What if Bernie was right and the fraud squad pre-
vented me from leaving? I decided to wait until the
following evening and drive through the night to the
Namibian frontier. No one would expect me there.
Besides, it would be Sunday, and the dreaded Major
Barnard would be enjoying his day off.

I spent the rest of the day trying to plan. I organised a
freight company to pack my personal possessions, which
would be shipped home. I cashed money from my private
account and paid off the staff. A call from the building
society revealed that the bond repayment on our house was
overdue. How could that be? When I checked the statement with them on the phone I discovered that Wolf had
taken an 80 per cent bond on the house a few days earlier.

Sitting with my head in my hands, I went through
the facts I knew so far. A call to Wolf's bank manager
revealed that my husband had banked five hundred
thousand rands ten days ago, and later that day he had
issued a cheque to the Gold Coin Exchange for the same
amount. So Wolf had carried 490 one-ounce gold coins
with him. Was that possible? Of course, for it was only
just over thirty pounds in weight. That's why he'd had
Nicky's backpack. The coins were stashed in it.

The blown-up photograph, the purchase of the gold
coins, even the application for an 80 per cent bond on our
house revealed that Wolf had been planning to leave for
some time. If I could get to Lübeck fast enough I might
find him – or, at least, a trace of his next cash transfer.

*   *   *

That night I paced up and down for hours attemptin
to out-guess Wolf, trying to make sense of all that ha
happened. What did I really know about this man I ha
married? Very little, I concluded. This monster, wh
had defiled my son's picture, robbed our friends an
taken the cash I had invested in our home, was ne
the man I'd thought I loved. That person was just
false personality of Wolf's creation.

And who was the thug who had broken in last night
Why did he want Wolf? Bouts of shuddering and pani
were incapacitating me. I swallowed a tranquilliser, pulle
on a jersey and vowed to pull myself together. Nick
needed me, and I would need my wits about me t
find him.

At dawn, when my strength deserted me, I cried fo
the man I'd loved so much. I longed to feel his arm
around me, his lips on mine, his hands caressing me, hi
firm hard body on my own. Why did I still love him so
If he had returned at that moment I would have accepte
any excuse. If he called me, I would go anywhere to b
with him and Nicky. I tried to make excuses for hin
but I was forced to remember the terrible photograp
of Nicky, with the ring of red around his little throa
The image turned all my excuses into nonsense. Th
pain of Wolf's betrayal was almost more than I coul
bear. Only the need to rescue Nicky kept me going. Fo
three years I had loved an evil, unscrupulous man, an
now he had my son.

Chapter 31

Gale-force gusts buffeted the car and whipped up minor sandstorms as I drove through the night. For summer, it was bitterly cold, but I cheered up when I saw a glimmer of grey in the east. I longed for a cup of coffee, a warm bath and breakfast, in that order. After a few minutes of indecision I decided to stop at a road-house. I had time to kill since the frontier post did not open until eight.

By the time I returned to the road it was light. To the left was a desolate coastline, where gigantic rollers were breaking over jagged black rocks. To my right was a flat gravel plain stretching far into the interior. As I climbed into the car and turned on the ignition, I felt so old and tired. I couldn't remember ever feeling like this before.

Alexander Bay came into sight, a collection of gaunt square houses on a flat gravel plain where nothing green seemed to flourish. I passed through quickly, crossed the Orange river and joined a queue of ten cars. There was still an hour to endure. I wondered if I had done the right thing. Probably. In this region of diamond smugglers and terrorists, I was unlikely to excite any interest. Unless they had filed me as 'wanted' on the computer, I would soon be on a plane to Windhoek and from there to Lübeck.

It was the longest hour of my life. At last a uniformed official waved me forward. I held my pre-marriage Ogilvie passport, plus details of my permanent residence and forwarding address. The man tapped into his computer, frowned, glanced at me in surprise, and returned to his computer. The keys clicked away, his frown became more menacing, the minutes passed.

A sense of desolation settled upon me.

'Oh dear. I've left my suitcase at the hotel. I'll have to go back and fetch it.'

'Please wait there,' he said sternly. Another official slipped into the room and hovered behind me. The entire operation was so smooth and efficient. No one seemed to notice. To my confusion and fear, shame was added. My cheeks burned, my eyes watered. I had to keep reminding myself that I was the victim in this tragedy.

'Would you kindly step in here, Mrs Möller?' It was the official behind me who had spoken. His grip on my arm was very firm.

'You have no right to detain me. I am a British citizen and free to move about as I wish.' My voice had gone wrong. Or was it my sanity?

'We have every right to detain you, Mrs Möller. A warrant has been issued for your arrest. Major Barnard is flying up to collect you. You will be flown back to Cape Town where you will be formally charged.'

Locked in a stuffy, overheated cell with six local criminals, I endured a frightening and humiliating day. I had seven hours to wait, plenty of time in which to examine my many mistakes and to grieve for my son. At last Major Barnard arrived to accompany me to Cape Town.

'A very unwise move, Mrs Möller,' Barnard lectured me as he led me to the car. 'You were warned not to leave Cape Town. I'm afraid you're unlikely to get bail after this.'

'Why? I had no idea I was going to be arrested.'

'I think you did. Furthermore, your exit choice was suspect. Were you expecting to be met in Walvis Bay like your husband?' His mouth twisted into a leer.

'No! What are you talking about? Who met my husband?' Nothing made sense. I felt like Alice in Wonderland.

'Your actions could be misconstrued.'

'Tell me what's going on. Please! They said I was under arrest, but I haven't been arrested. Why? What are the charges? I have a right to know. What about Wolf kidnapping my baby? Have you done anything about that? Where is my child? Do you know? What about my rights? I've done nothing wrong.'

He turned a stony face to my pleas and I couldn't get another word out of him.

I puzzled over the innuendoes. What else had Wolf done, besides conning most of our friends and myself, and kidnapping my baby? I went through all that I had learned so far. Something far more serious than fraud was on the cards, I suspected.

We sat in the airport lounge, looking like any other couple, I assume, because no one gave us a second glance. A couple on the verge of divorce, perhaps, since we did not exchange one word. Only later, when the plane had taken off for Cape Town, and Barnard had tossed back a couple of neat whiskies, did he relent.

'I believe in you, Mrs Möller,' he said, in a voice that had become slow and deliberate. 'This may surprise you. I think you're being blackmailed by your husband. He probably took your child as a hostage.'

He didn't have to be a genius to work that out.

'I don't understand why Möller left you alive. You could be his greatest danger. My theory is that when the time came for Möller to leave, he found he could not kill you, as I feel sure he had intended to. You are a very lovely woman, Mrs Möller. Perhaps he fell in love with you.

'Furthermore,' Barnard went on, pressing home his obvious advantage, 'I believe that he married you because you were exactly right to create the social background he needed for his work.'

Barnard had been doing his homework.

'Your safest and best bet would be to put your trust in us. Turn state evidence. Most of the Western world's police are looking for Möller. Eventually they'll get him, and your son.'

'You're not very convincing, Major Barnard. You're trying to frighten me, but this man whom I married, but whom I never really knew, frightens me much more. Don't you think he reads the newspapers? He'll know . . . He'll—' I almost choked on the words. I had said too much. I stared at my hands to escape Barnard's scrutiny and to hide my fear.

'Mrs Möller, believe me, you have no choice. They'll be waiting for us in Cape Town where you will be formally charged. You will be taken into custody.' He waited, sighed and went on. 'There's a great deal that you don't know about your husband, Mrs Möller. Our intelligence sources discovered belatedly that he was working as a Soviet spy all the time he lived in South Africa. In fact, he was using Armscor as his front to send American research to the Russians. We traced your husband as far as Walvis Bay harbour. After that there are no further sightings. He could have left by boat, but here were no passenger boats in dock. The only boat to leave Walvis Bay was a Russian Fisheries research vessel, known to be involved in intelligence gathering. They picked up Möller. We have no doubt about that at all. They probably dropped him off in Angola from where he could fly directly to Russia.'

I sat there, mouth open, disbelieving. The sweat was rolling down my back and leaving great damp spots on my dress. My hands were shaking and I couldn't think. Could Wolf be a spy? Was Nicky in Russia? If so, how would I ever find him?

Chapter 32

I pulled myself together, trying to make sense out of what Barnard had said. I remembered the time I'd heard Wolf speaking a foreign language at Chobe. It had sounded like Russian. But what did spying have to do with conning people? How could he be both a spy and a con? I couldn't find any similarity between the man I thought I'd married and this other person who seemed to have co-existed in the body I had learned to love so much.

Had the Russians sent a boat to fetch Wolf? Was he *that* important?

'Mrs Möller,' Barnard repeated, 'I have to warn you that unless you co-operate with the authorities, you will be treated as your husband's accomplice and given the same sentence as he will receive *in absentia*. Only you will be here to serve yours.'

My mind was racing round with millions of thoughts, but they came to the same thing: I was trapped. I struggled to push away my anguish and listen, for I sensed that Barnard was biased in my favour.

'If only I knew what was going on, I might be able to make up my mind.'

He thought about this for a while. Then he said, 'Interpol and the CIA have been looking for Möller for some time. No one guessed that he was in South

Africa. It's rumoured that he had plastic surgery to alter his appearance. I doubt you were ever legally married. Möller was not his real name, let alone the title, but no one knows who he really is.'

'If I'm not married to him, then he has no rights at all over my son.'

'Exactly.'

'Major Barnard, if I get a long sentence will you push through the kidnapping charges and document the fact that I have custody of Nicky?'

'I can do that much for you, Mrs Möller. I'll tell you what I know, unofficially that is, because it might help you. I do realise that your baby is being held hostage to keep you quiet, however much you have denied this.'

He waited, but I said nothing.

'Möller duped local officials by pretending to help South Africa obtain items denied to us by international boycotts. He was uncovered after CIA agents arrived at Armscor to find out about computer shipments that were supposed to come here, although their real destination was the Soviet Union. It became clear that South Africa had been used as a key link in smuggling US military secrets to Russia.

'Your husband is a brilliant systems engineer and well versed in modern military technology. With a continuous supply of money from the Soviets, and Armscor's help, he was successful in obtaining whatever he wanted through bribery, blackmail and pay-offs. You see, most people would baulk at taking bribes to supply the Soviets, but they might not worry so much if the goods were destined for South Africa. It was a brilliant ploy. Through it, Möller was able to send the Russians the computer tracking system for the intercontinental ballistic missile. This put back the West's nuclear lead on the Russians by at least four years. The CIA have vowed to kill him if they find him.

'Now do you understand your position, Mrs Möller? You became Möller's accessory when you destroyed his documents.'

'But the Soviet system collapsed almost exactly a year ago.'

'Exactly, just after Möller had completed his project. No doubt he found himself out of pocket so he conned a whole lot more money to replace what he had lost, taking advantage of the local rich who were desperate to shift their cash overseas.'

Was that why Wolf had become so tense and anxious, I wondered.

'Mrs Möller, I expect you have some crazy idea of searching for your son, but listen to reason. Intelligence services from the US, Britain, West Germany, South Africa and Israel, plus Interpol, are looking for him. So far they have been unsuccessful. He was operating right under our noses for years and we never even knew his name or his identity, so how can you hope to succeed?'

'And you expect me to put my faith in you to find my son?'

He had the grace to flush. 'Naturally, we're in serious trouble with the US. Justice must be seen to be done. They've lost your husband, but they have you.'

'Stop it! Stop it!' I couldn't handle my fear.

'Möller made a fool of us,' he said, mournfully.

I remembered Bernie and the desperation in his eyes as he had said almost those exact words.

'I wish I could help you,' he added, more gently. 'I believe in you. You must trust us.'

'Oh, Jesus!' I murmured. 'Surely you realise that a man

as clever as my husband would never tell me anything. I
lived in a fool's paradise, imagining myself to be happily
married and loved.' I couldn't keep the bitterness out of
my voice. 'Even now, I'm not at all sure that I believe a
word you've said. I know he stole but, believe me, my
husband hated all Russians.'

'Your husband *is* Russian, Mrs Möller.'

After that Barnard leaned back, closed his eyes and
didn't say another word. Why should he bother? I
was entirely annihilated and suffering all the physical
symptoms of blind panic.

When I was sure that he was dozing, I scribbled a
note to my father explaining briefly that I was innocent,
that Wolf had kidnapped Nicky and telling him the facts
that I had learned from Barnard. Father must employ a
missing persons' agency to search for Nicky. Dresden,
Beeskow and Lübeck might provide some clues to Wolf's
real identity. I explained why, but my hands were shaking
so much that the note would be difficult to read.

I planned to visit the airport toilet and bribe or beg
a passenger to airmail the letter.

Then I considered my plight. They might put me on
trial for fraud and spying, and lock me away for years.
What could I do? I tried to think of a plan but my mind
fluttered around, like a wild bird in a snare, trying to
find a way out. I calmed down when I realised that there
was no way out. There was nothing to do, no point in
planning. The choice was quite simple: my freedom or
my son's life. Barnard was right. Turning state evidence
was my only escape route. Which was what Wolf had
feared and why he had taken my baby hostage.

What sort of woman would buy her freedom with
her baby's life? I had a sudden vivid image of Nicky's
crumpled face when he needed to be comforted. Was

he crying for me now? Was he with Wolf? Or had Wolf placed him in an institution?

Oh, my baby! Where are you? I won't let you down, my darling. Not if they put me away for years. And one day I'll find you.

Part Two

16 May 1994 –
11 November 1994

Chapter 33

Pollsmoor Prison, 16 May 1994

When the cell doors slammed on me I succumbed to despair. Then help came from within in the guise of a dream. I became aware of a part of me that was so cruel and strong I could hardly believe it was real, a part that could kill. I knew I must trust and nurture this deadly side of my psyche. I called it my *tokoloshe*.

I have been in prison for eighteen months, but my *tokoloshe* grows daily more deadly. I keep it chained in the deepest, darkest recesses of my mind. It has been burned by the furnace of my anger, drenched by my fears, tortured by the long, agonising wait, deformed by my own hands into a vicious tool. My *tokoloshe* is cunning. It will lead me to Wolf and my son. It will give me courage to do what I have to do. It is my strength and my strategy. It is the dark side of my soul.

Chapter 34

Our cell, which was the size of a large bedroom, housed twenty-four women sleeping on bunk beds. We came from the eroded hills of the Transkei, the sugar fields of Natal, the arid plains of the West Coast, and the Cape's squatter camps. We had stolen, whored, mugged and two of us had murdered, but we were women, and we shared the same agony at being parted from our families and particularly our children.

A late summer heatwave had turned the overcrowded prison into an intolerable hell on earth. The walls were blistering with heat and we lay on our bunks in our prison uniforms almost afraid to breathe. God knows what germs were spawning in the tepid brew that passed for air. We had been told that today we would not be working in the laundry or cleaning the prison. We did not know why, but for me inactivity was harder to bear.

I lay on my sweat-soaked pallet feeling dazed, straining to hear the voices of the warders' children playing outside, for they seemed to provide a link with sanity. I was startled out of my apathy by the wardress calling my name.

'You're to come.' She stammered a little. 'Come now. Hurry!'

Fear brought bile into my mouth as I was tossed back

in time to those terrible pre-trial months. I could see the chair, the cruel clasps, the electric wires leading up to the wall, and smell the heavy disinfectant that could never obliterate the stench of vomit, urine, sweat and blood from those who had been there before me. Oh, God! The warder was smoothing the thick jelly-like substance around my ears and the back of my knees. I could hear my own screams as I fought to keep out of the chair.

'Hurry. The Captain's waiting.'

A feeling of damp around my inner thighs shamed me into mustering my courage. I could take whatever they had in store for me. How many times had I proved that to them and to myself as the interrogators strove to make me talk about Wolf and his spying? Giving a last, despairing glance at the others, I followed the wardress out of the cell.

I was led along corridors and through gates, which had to be unlocked and locked again, to the office block where I ended my stumbling walk in the governor's office.

Captain Hendrik Vermeulen was going to seed. His shirt was soiled, his fingernails were dirty, his hair was flecked with dandruff. Life had not been kind to the Captain. I had often wondered what led a man or a woman to become a warder or a prison governor. It was hardly the sort of occupation kids dream about. Engine driver, yes. Prison governor, no.

The Captain spent a while flicking through my file, while I stood before him feeling foolish. Even after eighteen months as a prisoner I still resented standing in the presence of men who were seated.

At last he cleared his throat. His blue eyes flashed towards me and as quickly shied away, but not before I saw his bitterness.

He said, 'President Mandela, in his wisdom, has issued

several pardons to celebrate the launch of the new South Africa. You are one of the lucky recipients.'

What did he mean? A shorter sentence? I held my breath.

He paused and took a deep breath. He was trying to control his anger, but he failed and a part of it came gushing out.

'Hardly surprising, is it? Your husband being a Commie spy. I suppose you'll be in Moscow in next to no time tossing back the vodka.'

He broke off, frowning, and I pondered on what the new South Africa meant to landless, working-class whites. A slow regression into statelessness while their jobs were taken by blacks? Was this what he feared?

Unbelievably, he said, 'You're free to go at once.'

I began to shake. My knees felt wobbly and, for a moment, I thought I would fall, but I hung on to my self-control.

'I have to ask you if you require the services of a social worker, but as far as I'm concerned, you can—' He broke off warily. 'The likes of you and your husband have destroyed this country. If I had my way the traitors would be necklaced. All those in power—'

Once again he closed his mouth, looking uneasy. I knew about the pain of betrayal and I felt a glimmer of understanding.

'May I say goodbye to my cellmates?' I stammered.

He flushed with anger, while his eyes blazed with contempt. 'That won't be possible.'

Moments later I walked down a corridor thronged with newly freed prisoners, who were laughing and embracing. In one way or another they had all fought for freedom. I had not. I tried to blank my mind until I was alone in the shower. Then I gave way to joy, and the release of pain, beating my hands against the tiles until they hurt, screaming, 'Free, free, I'm free,' until the scalding water washed away my tears.

Half an hour later, dressed in clothes that were much too large for me (had I ever been this wide?), and still feeling light-headed and unreal, I staggered out of the prison gates into the arms of Joy.

'Heavens! Joy! Why ... ?' I hugged her tightly and bit back angry memories of her earlier betrayal.

'Thank God,' Joy said. 'Oh, Nina! Thank God! That's all I can say.' She hung on until she was gasping. Then she stepped back and gave me a critical once-over. 'God, but you're thin. How you must have suffered. Oh, my poor Nina. You don't have lice, do you?' She flushed and grabbed my arm as I shook my head. 'Sorry! Rightie-ho! Let's get out of here. I had no idea whether or not you'd be freed. We tried to find out, but we couldn't get a firm answer. It was always "maybe", or "there's a possibility". I came along in the vague hope ... Every morning for a week, to tell the truth. Nina! I'm so sorry about ... you know. I've missed you. Well, here you are. Let's go.'

'Where to?'

'Our home, of course. Not as grand as the last one, but we're happier. I've booked you on the evening flight to London, plus your connection to Inverness. Your father insisted that you leave the country at once.'

'Father?' I asked wonderingly. 'I thought he'd written me off.'

'Oh, Nina,' Joy said. 'You will never know how hard your father has lobbied to get you this pardon. To read his letters to the government you'd think you were Britain's leading Commie out here to fight for freedom.'

'Good God. That doesn't sound like Father.'

'You're his daughter, aren't you?'

A lump came into my throat so big it was hard to swallow.

Chapter 35

Inverness, 18 May 1994

I peered through the taxi window and tried to prepare for the moment I had dreaded: coming face to face with my father. I felt such a failure, not so much because of my prison sentence and the publicity but because I had lost my son. I should have listened to my intuition and Father's fears that Wolf was crooked. If only I had guarded Nicky better. Father must despise me for my foolishness. I should never have come home, but I had no choice. I needed his help.

It was unusually cold for May. The branches of the trees had not yet unfurled their leafy buds, leaving a stark, pristine winter beauty that I had always loved. The loch shone like a sheet of burnished steel, and above, the snow-capped Liathach mountain peak looked sombre and forbidding against the grey sky.

The trip had passed with bewildering speed. I still felt shocked. It was hardly twenty-four hours since I had been released so unexpectedly. I needed more time to pull myself together. I could not stop shivering and not only because of the cold. 'Almost there,' I whispered to the taxi driver.

No one was waiting. Saddened by a sense of anticlimax, I paid the driver, picked up my case and opened the front door.

Nothing had changed. There was the grandfather clock I used to hide in, the old Afghan rug that our first Brigit once chewed and Maria had sent to be invisibly mended, the picture of Grandmother on the wall, the homely smell of polish. Everything was shockingly familiar, except for the darkness. I had grown used to brilliant light, space and sun, and had quite forgotten about the gloom.

A woman hurried towards me. Plump and matronly, with iron grey hair and rosy cheeks, she looked the part of the housekeeper. She had fine grey eyes, and a kindly aura lay about her, but she could not disguise her unease. Perhaps she was afraid that I might change her routine or take her place.

'Good morning,' she said. 'No doubt you're Miss Nina Ogilvie. I'm Rosemary Peters, the housekeeper.' She was a local woman, I could hear. 'Your father will be pleased to see you. He's been fretting.'

Ogilvie? Not Möller? Is that what Father preferred?

'Commander Ogilvie is in his study,' Mrs Peters said. 'There's a nice fire there. Would you like coffee before lunch?'

'Yes, please. That would be very welcome.'

I pushed the door open and saw my father sitting in an easy chair, pushed close to the window for light. He was studying a book of sketches. When he looked up, I was shocked to see how he had aged. His hair had turned white, his face was paler and thinner than I remembered, yet his eyes burned with vigour and his glance was as keen and decisive as it had ever been. I forced myself to walk towards him, even to smile. So many hurts came to mind, but then I remembered what Joy had told me.

'Thank you for lobbying to get me out of prison, Father.'

He shrugged and rose unsteadily, using the strength of his arms to push himself up on two sticks.

'And thank you for putting money in my account. I only found out at Heathrow.'

'For goodness' sake, Nina. You'll be thanking me for procreating you next.'

'Maybe not.'

'Was it that bad?'

'Not prison. But losing my Nicky . . . No, even worse is my baby's loss of me. I can't bear to think of his pain.'

I took a deep breath. I didn't want to get into any situation I couldn't handle.

'It's so cold, yet it's May. I'm not used to the cold. My blood has thinned.'

Father gave an awkward laugh. 'The man's a scoundrel. I tried to warn you.' He balanced on one stick, leaned the other against a table and shook my hand. No mean feat.

'Come over here and sit down, Nina. You're standing like a soldier on parade.'

It was painful to watch Father negotiate the four yards and struggle to control his slow descent into a chair, but he would not let me help him. I sat opposite him, moving as close as I could to the fire roaring in the hearth.

'Ah, that's better. You look thinner, Nina. There's a nasty scar on your arm, I see. Otherwise there's no change. The worst scars are inside, of course, but you endured. That's the main thing.' He was making an effort to sound happy, but I could see that he was hurting.

'I'm sorry, Father.'

201

'I'm sorry, too. You were set up by Wolf and imprisoned by the government to try to draw Wolf out. It didn't work and you suffered deeply, I'm sure. I wish I could have helped you in time. Thank God you're home. I was afraid some right-wing zealots might take a pot shot at you at the airport.'

'Oh, come, Father. That's going a little over the top.'

'I don't think so. Wolf made a fool of the former government. That's why they gave you such a stiff sentence. The President's pardon could be taken by some to mean that you, too, were working for the Russians. The irony is that Wolf was a freelancer selling to the highest bidder. Clive Wattling, my former colleague at the department, backs up my opinion. D'you remember Clive, Nina?'

'Vaguely.'

'His research paints Möller as a specialist in minerals and military hardware, subjects he knew well. He sold to the highest bidder, oil to the South Africans, missile-tracking systems to the Russians, whatever he could lay his hands on. His scheme to use Armscor and sanction-busting to get the help of right-wing US manufacturers was nothing short of genius.'

It was a long speech for Father, but it explained his anxiety. He cared. The knowledge gave me a warm glow. I took his hand, although I couldn't remember ever doing that before, but he gently pulled it away.

I voiced the question I had been longing to ask. 'You were the only person to recognise that something was wrong with Wolf. How did you know? At the time I felt so hurt. Everyone else was taken in, as I was. If you remember, you said Wolf had hidden agendas.'

He continued to stare at me, in his curiously intent, yet

remote manner. He, who was so expert at reading every expression, had shuttered his soul. No one penetrated that cool, amused expression. Did anyone really know my father, I wondered. Certainly not my mother, who had given up trying and run for cover. Mother had died while I was in prison and I knew that this was another topic I must avoid, if I was to remain calm and composed.

'Nothing specific, Nina,' he said eventually. 'In my line of work one develops a sixth sense. Most people try to disguise their weaknesses by covering up. A clever man might take pains to look idiotic and vice versa. You should have asked yourself why he worked so hard to impress everyone with his loving nature. Of course, we were all prospective marks in one way or another.'

Despite my hatred of Wolf, I still squirmed to hear him so despised.

'That's enough of that bounder,' Father said, as if he sensed my feelings. 'Ah, coffee. Thank you, Mrs Peters.' He waited while the housekeeper poured it.

'You need to forget Wolf, Nina. Never use your married name. It's only an alias. I doubt it was ever real. God knows what his name is.' He laughed curtly, and again I was wounded. 'Around these parts no one has connected the jet-set spy Baroness Möller with Nina Ogilvie. Let's keep it like that, shall we?'

Suddenly I recalled my wedding. How beautifully Wolf and Joy had planned their surprise. How stunned I had been when I signed the register. And later Wolf had held me in his arms and teased, 'Can a baroness be fucked? Or do I beg for an audience from now on?' How he must have laughed at me. Cruel! Deep down, the flames of my anger were scorching my heart. I frowned at nothing in particular.

'Take my advice. Put it all behind you, Nina.'

I stared at him in shocked silence. Then I leaned forward and gripped his arm. 'Never!' I had spoken more vehemently than I had intended. 'Forget my son? What sort of a woman could do that? Wolf is cruel and evil, and Nicky must be found and brought home, just as quickly as I can. If only I knew where to start.'

Father came down hard and fast on my inadequacy. 'Is that what you plan, Nina? D'you want to leave right now? I'll give you all the money you need. I'm not exactly a pauper. Will you start searching the world, probing every haystack?'

An icy blanket of despair settled on me and I shuddered. I had only a vague idea of how to begin.

'Well, I haven't been entirely idle,' he went on. 'I'll brief you after lunch. Can it wait until then?'

'Of course. Yes, really.' Despite my tension, I forced a smile to prove it.

Chapter 36

We lunched as strangers, groping for trivial topics: the state of the crops, the poor rains, the size of the trout, anything except feelings. Out of habit Father ate frugally, but I had no appetite for steamed trout and spinach, my father's favourite food. My unease filled the dark dining room.

We arranged to meet at three in Father's office. I knew that to be late for a meeting at Ogilvie Lodge would be tantamount to treason. I spent an hour going through the cupboards where Mrs Peters had packed away my old clothes. In view of my prison sentence I guess the mothballs were understandable, but I doubted I'd ever lose the stench of them.

The fifteen cartons of clothes, household effects and the suitcases the freight company had shipped were in the attic. As I gazed at my inventory, vases, photo albums, clothes, cutlery, kitchen equipment, Nicky's clothes, I almost gagged. Oh, God! One day I might have the strength to unpack them, but not for a long time.

Father was standing with his back to the fire, balancing on his walking sticks.

'Well, here you are. Shut the door, Nina, and listen carefully,' he began, without any preamble. 'While you've been away, three of the world's top missing persons' agencies have been searching for Nicholas over three continents.'

Hope must have dawned in my eyes for he added quickly, 'Don't get excited. I have absolutely no good news at all, but their work is well documented here.' He pointed to a pile of bulky folders on his desk.

'From the moment Wolf left the aircraft at Walvis Bay, there is no further news of him or Nicky. Nor any records of a man and a young child leaving Namibia. I'm sure that he was picked up by the Fisheries boat, as Barnard believes.

'You will remember that I sent you a cryptic reply to the note you scribbled on the plane with Major Barnard. The Lübeck account had been closed before our man got there, probably before you even wrote the letter. There is no trace of a Wolf Möller at Dresden University, nor anywhere else. That is why I feel sure that was not his name.'

I felt shamed by the memory of so many shared intimacies, and fought to smash the rising image, but failed. We were lying in bed, my head on his shoulder, having made love with sensuous abandon. We were at peace with each other and utterly content. 'My dear wife,' he had murmured, 'one of these days we'll save enough to restore our home in Germany and the estates. You will be famous for your beauty – the regal Baroness von Möller. Only I shall know that you're the best fuck in Europe.'

My face contorted with pain. 'He was real enough. Real flesh and blood. What does it matter what he calls himself?' I felt myself flushing. Why did I have to fight back? Why was I rekindling an old, rebellious pattern of behaviour?

Father opened one of the files. 'You'll see here that a man using the alias of Gunther Mannheim operated in

America during the early eighties and conned several people out of a great deal of money. He also claimed to be East German. There are similarities in his and Wolf's *modus operandi*, I feel. We have a few vague descriptions of him. Nothing conclusive.'

He leafed through a bulky file. 'In the early eighties one hundred and sixteen mineral frauds were documented with Interpol that were similar to Wolf's type of operation. I have examined them all and it seems to me that some of them bear his fingerprints. It's possible that our young fledgling con was learning to fly, but he always had a bolt-hole and no one knows where that is, or who he is. That's the problem, Nina.'

He turned the page and shot me a troubled look. 'I was able to draw on old contacts to obtain this one. It's a copy of the CIA's data on Möller. They want him very badly. He's a very rich man, he's very astute, and shows immense daring and cunning. Not one of the intelligence forces has got near to finding his real identity, or his whereabouts.

'My advice to you must be to give up your quest for your son. If the experts can't trace him, then how can you?'

My fury surged. 'Of course I won't give up. Whose side are you on?' It was a cry straight from my heart.

He ignored my outburst. 'Read the files, then put them away and start again, Nina. Start a new life, create a new family. Of course, you won't be able to go back to asset management or banking after a prison sentence, however unjustly given, but many other openings exist. Or you could stay at home and do nothing, or run the farms perhaps, or start your own business. You're still young. Your life is ahead of you. We are not poor by any means. Be sensible, Nina.'

Madge Swindells

'I can't believe you're saying this, Father.' I struggled to stay calm as my temper got the upper hand. 'What sort of man could abandon his grandson?'

'I have never seen my grandson.'

Briefly I saw his pain, and guilt struck home hard. Why had I never brought Nicky home? Because of Wolf, of course. He had always thought of a thousand reasons why Scotland was out of the question whenever I mentioned a visit, but I should have insisted. I didn't because I had dreaded another dismissive confrontation between my father and Wolf.

'You were so set against Wolf,' I said to him again. 'You were right, of course.'

He shrugged. 'Water under the bridge, my dear.'

'Nina,' he called, as I walked out, cradling three bulky files, 'I'd like to know what you plan to do by midnight. Would that be possible?'

'Yes.'

As if I needed time to decide! Nevertheless, I spent a depressing evening going through the files. So many experts, all with professional training and back-up, yet there was virtually nothing to show for their efforts.

Midnight. I heard Father in the kitchen making hot chocolate and burst in on him without planning exactly what I would say.

'I shall search for Nicky, I can never abandon him. You must see that. I don't expect you to agree with my decision, but you can surely understand how a mother feels about her baby. If necessary I'll spend my whole life searching for him. I'll never give up. Never.'

'Have some hot chocolate, Nina.' Father had a way of bumping one down to earth.

'Thanks.' I sat at the kitchen table and pushed the

208

files towards him. 'I've never seen so much data saying nothing.'

'Exactly my diagnosis. Do you have any plans on how to begin?'

'Some. I've had a year and a half to think about it.'

He watched me inquiringly, but I was reluctant to put my ideas into words. Dreams have a habit of dissolving when pure reason touches them. Father wasn't short of pure reason. So what could I say? The silence was becoming painful.

'Listen, Father. Wolf has two weaknesses. One is time. Whenever he embarks on a fraud he has to get out fast before his victim or the authorities latch on to him. His second problem is laundering his cash in such a way that it will not lead his pursuers back to his base. Nowadays, governments and banks are tightening up on cash transactions. Running loot round the globe is becoming hazardous and it takes time and expertise.

'I hope to conduct some of the search by Internet. I intend to examine all documented weapons and mineral frauds, and search for Wolf's *modus operandi*, places where there is a need to bust sanctions, for instance, or smuggle in forbidden supplies. Subterfuge is something Wolf needs for his operations. Eventually I'll pre-guess a scam and catch him at it.'

Father was sipping his chocolate. 'And we can trace his loot on its convoluted trips around the globe, until we find out who and what he is and discover his lair.'

We? Hope was added to my confusion. I tried to quell this foolish fancy, but it kept surging back.

It was Father who finally broke the spell with what sounded like a rehearsed speech.

'Since you are determined to go ahead,' he began, in his brisk, clever voice with no trace of emotion, 'then I offer you my full-time help, my experience and my considerable financial resources. For obvious reasons you'll have to do the legwork. Of course, I still have my contacts in Intelligence. Some of them are getting a bit long in the tooth, but never mind.' He stared gloomily at the files. 'In view of my experience I'll take charge of our search. We might still make a team. Drink your chocolate. It's getting cold. We have a tough day ahead of us.

'Here are two points to cheer you, Nina.' Father's voice was surprisingly gentle. 'Wolf has two more weaknesses. He loved you and your son. I believe that he took the boy because he could not bear to be parted from him.'

I almost choked. 'He deprived me of my son and left me to face a prison sentence? Is that love?'

'You're alive, aren't you? Yet Wolf knew that you would eventually become his biggest danger. That's why he threatened you with Nicky's life. I'm quite sure that he would never harm his son. You are probably the only person in the Western world who knows who and what Wolf is, although you don't realise this yet.'

'Why? How could I? Although sometimes . . .' I broke off as I remembered Major Barnard telling me exactly that. 'Yes. Of course . . .'

Father's hand shot out and grabbed my wrist. 'Not now, Nina. We'll do it professionally, *in camera*, with a tape-recorder. We don't want to let anything slip through our fingers. Over the next few days, or weeks, we shall find out what it is that you know. In other words I'll debrief you. Eventually we'll piece together an image of the real man behind the smiling mask. After that we'll have to create a new personality for you. And I think plastic surgery could do a lot for that scar. How did it happen, Nina?'

I tried to tell him. 'I'd been sentenced that afternoon.

210

I was in shock. All I could think of were the terrible five years I had to endure before I could search for Nicky. I was driven to Pollsmoor Prison and taken to the showers and told to strip and shower. I didn't look round until someone grabbed me. I fought . . . Jesus . . . I fought . . . This cut saved me. Blood everywhere. The wardress had to summon help. I'm sorry, Father. I never want to talk about prison again.'

That wasn't the whole truth. Here, in this cold, austere northern home, I could not imagine the existence of overheated prison showers, or the suffering, bestial women and their sick, distorted sexual desires. Or the wardress who enjoyed watching. It was just one of the impossible memories that I would never relate.

'It's one more of the many things you'll have to put behind you. We'll start tomorrow morning at six a.m. Oh, by the way, Nina, while we're working together, I would appreciate punctuality. There's an alarm clock in your room in case you should be tempted to oversleep.'

At that moment I longed to punch him and hug him with equal intensity. Both were out of the question.

That night I spent hours awake, wondering how one old cripple and an emotionally involved amateur could succeed in finding Wolf, when the world's experts had failed.

Chapter 37

While I was grateful for Father's help, the coldness of his spirit wounded me, as it always had in my childhood after my mother left, while his assumption that I would botch whatever I attempted infuriated me. Hadn't I spent my early years trying to prove him wrong? Had nothing changed?

Father was waiting in his study, drumming his fingers on his desk. The well-known aroma of aftershave, smoke from the crackling fire, dusty papers and tobacco carried me back two decades. Father's forbidding expression was equally familiar. Why? A quick glance at my watch assured me that I was a full two minutes late.

'Sorry,' I muttered. I wondered what time he rose, for he had lit the fire, made a Thermos of coffee and carried in a tin of biscuits from the kitchen. No mean feat for him.

'Switch on that spotlight,' he said. 'And the camera, and the tape. Now sit there.' He pointed to the chair facing the spotlight. 'Begin at the beginning. How and when did you meet Wolf?'

I had to force myself to recall the events that I had so painstakingly banished. At first I thought I'd never make it. My voice rose and fell with my degree of hurt, but once I began, my first stammers turned into a flood.

I remembered Joy's dinner party, and the victims strewn

across the road, the eyes of the mugger boring into me as he pinched my breast, and Wolf's timely arrival. Then there was the river, and the lion pride that had been too near for comfort. What was it Wolf had said: 'They fear *Homo stupido* as much as *Homo sapiens*.' I had loved his foreigner's humour. Agonisingly, I relived the first time we made love in the game park. And later in Namaqualand. I could smell the sea, feel the rough sand against my back, hear the waves pounding nearby. It had been good sex. I could smell Wolf, too. Feel him, hear his voice, taste him. It was so real.

'You're still in love with that bounder.'

'Once I loved him so very deeply. He seemed genuine, while everyone else seemed so foreign, so brash, so . . . well, so brittle and artificial. Remembering hurts. That's all. Knowing what he is . . . what he did . . . I can only hate him. Once he told me that I was lucky, I hadn't learned to hate. Well, now I have—' I broke off, unwilling to reveal my intense desire for revenge.

It was a long morning, and I was grateful for the coffee and toasted sandwiches Mrs Peters brought in. My back ached, my eyes stung, my throat was getting sore.

'I'm not a political prisoner, Father. And I'm not a spy. I'm your own flesh and blood. Why the spotlights? Aren't you indulging your passion for the past just a little?'

Father's remote, unresponsive gaze locked in on me just as before.

'You don't even know when you're hurt or bewildered, or when you've picked up something that puzzles you. But it shows, Nina, perhaps in a flicker of doubt, or of pain. I shall replay the tapes each night. This way I'll get a better sense of your feelings. I might pick up something we missed. Bear with me. Now, let's get on.

'Living with Wolf, getting to know him, what surprised you most about him?'

Once again I had to bludgeon myself into the past. We had been so happy. Other people weren't happy as we were. Perhaps that in itself was suspect.

'We were nearly always on cloud nine. I took happiness for granted. There weren't many hurts, hardly any fights. A bit unnatural, now you come to think of it. But occasionally when something really annoyed Wolf he switched off. I'm not explaining very well.'

'Try harder.'

'Well . . . Wolf's eyes were remarkable. They used to glow with love and tenderness, and all the things I wanted to see there. The sun came out when he was around. But he could switch off the love. There was something unreal about the way he could do this. Like touching a light switch. As fast and effective. Only coldness was left in his eyes and this was hurtful.' I had to think this one out. 'To be more concise, it was the fact that he could do this at will that hurt me, not the fact that he did it.'

'And he did this often?'

'No, not often, but he seemed to use it to wound and control.'

'And what sort of things annoyed him?'

'Funny, silly things. Not the sort of things you'd imagine. For instance, I remember once in Namibia, I slipped and dropped a truly valuable diamond into the sea. He laughed off the loss. That was Wolf for you. Yet trifles could enrage him for hours or days. I tried not to show how hurt I was when he ignored me. Sometimes he locked himself in his office and played his favourite music, shutting me out.'

'Can you think of a specific example?'

'The first time was when we were at the game park

having dinner in the *boma*. There was an unfortunate incident. David had to shoot a maimed baboon because the black staff thought it was a *tokoloshe*. When David explained that witch-doctors used to create a *tokoloshe* by inflicting the utmost deprivation and cruelty on young children in order to make them evil, Wolf was terribly put out. He seemed to take it personally, but I couldn't think why.'

'I don't remember his exact words.' I laughed shakily. 'That night I dreamed of a *tokoloshe* with Wolf's eyes. Terrifying!' And so was the bird's nest falling on me, but I wasn't going to bore Father with that experience. Strangely, he pursued the dream at great length.

'Nina, it's possible that your subconscious was trying to warn you that Wolf was maimed, that evil had been grafted on to him in his early days. But you weren't listening, were you?'

'I guess not.' Forgetting his own advice, Father chatted on. I learned that he had been studying psychology since his accident. He was full of surprises.

'We're getting off the subject.' He pulled us up smartly. 'So when was the next time he switched off?'

'This is important.' I snapped my fingers in triumph and set about reliving an incident in Botswana. 'We were driving through a barren area. There was no game to be seen and it was so hot, with not a breath of wind. We were both suffering and rather bad-tempered. Then a flock of large birds swooped around us, snapping at midges. Wolf cheered up and told me that he had watched these same kestrels as a child. They used to catch mice and small birds, he said. He pointed out their red feet. Of course, I had to argue. I pointed out that the book said they had migrated from Siberia, not Germany, and therefore he must be mistaken. Wolf sulked for hours and accused me of spying on him. Later he apologised—' I broke off as a rush of similar instances came to mind.

'So, Nina, looking back, do you now realise that you were being taught not to spy on him? Never to question what he told you. Never to put two and two together or else you would be rejected, which, as we both know, is your Achilles' heel. Right? Wolf's façade was sacrosanct. His alias must never be violated. You learned to play this game with him because of the fear of losing his love.'

'Something like that. Yes. I hid my doubts. After a while, when something puzzled me I kept it to myself. How could I have been such a fool?'

'Rats get programmed with cheese. You were programmed with love and its withdrawal.

'Perhaps at this stage we could make our first tentative assumption,' Father said. 'Which is that Wolf was orphaned, taken away from his home and cruelly treated, probably in Siberia. It is possible – no, let's say probable – that Wolf was raised in one of the many Siberian re-educational military cadet camps. Later he was trained to commit acts he believed to be evil. It's a familiar story in post-war Europe. We are approaching the real man, Nina.'

Father's smile was like moonlight on the surface of a dark lake.

'All of us, even the most evil murderers, have goodness at our inner core. Our souls are a font of goodness and integrity and we will come to hate ourselves, and others even more, if we feel that we have lost touch with all that is pure within us.'

I glanced at him in surprise. A stranger lurked behind those shutters. A friendless, uncomplaining philosopher with ideas and beliefs that I had never before heard him voice. I had the strangest feeling that I was entering

Father's world for the first time, and that I might find the real man there. Tread softly, Nina, I cautioned myself.

It was lunch-time when Father switched off the spotlights. I blinked and stretched. I couldn't see a damn thing.

'This is awful. I'm blinded by those lights, and stiff with sitting still so long. I feel exhausted and emotionally drained. Remembering! Ugh! It hurts. It's been so real. And we don't seem to be getting far.'

'If you don't mind, we won't discuss it during our break,' he said, glancing at his watch.

Father saw the mutiny in my eyes. One eyebrow shot up, while those still-young eyes appraised my mood and found me lacking. 'D'you want to give it a break until tomorrow? Perhaps we should.'

I scowled at him. 'No! *Have* we made any monumental discoveries yet?'

'Maybe. We'll see. Now, if you'll excuse me.' He made his way to his private bathroom, which had been installed next to his study. The door slammed shut.

Chapter 38

It was like an archaeological dig. We were unearthing
fragments of Wolf's past and building a vivid picture
of him. Two weeks had passed since we began our
debriefing, but it seemed more like two years. I was
physically exhausted from days and nights of questions
and deep introspection. Reliving the past had brought the
trauma of Wolf's cruelty back into sharp focus and Nicky
back into my arms, but in some way it was also healing.

Now it was time to take a break for a few days. Father
had persuaded me to find the best plastic surgeon available
to improve my scarred arm. 'You'll thank me later, Nina,
when you get over this self-hatred of yours.'

I was astonished by his words.

Early in June I entered a private clinic for two days. I
travelled back from Edinburgh with my arm in a sling.
Although it was past eight p.m., Father had not yet
emerged from his study, so I sat alone in our austere dining
room while Mrs Peters hung around grumbling about the
roast spoiling on the warmer. Father was replaying our
tapes. How could he bear it?

I was startled by the sound of a blackbird singing in
the elm tree outside the window. Looking out, I noticed
that the leaves had sprung from the branches of the trees
and the mountain slopes were brilliant with yellow wort,

buttercups, cowslips and celandines. Around the loch were patches of pink and purple from thistles, ragged robin and water mint.

'Mrs Peters,' I called into the kitchen, 'please tell Father I've gone for a walk. I'm feeling jaded.'

'I shouldn't be surprised, lass. You should be in bed . . .' Her voice faded as the back door closed.

Outside, there was a crisp tang to the air and a sense of happiness all around. Summer had come late this year, but at last it was warm and the garden vibrated with birdsong. I walked down to the water's edge and sat on a fallen log to watch the sun set over the mountain peaks. A deep sense of melancholy touched me softly. Did Wolf ever think of me? Did Nicky ever ask about his mother and was he happy? Where were they at this moment? Nostalgia fled as my fury burned.

Quietly grieving, I became aware of two deer moving through the grass around the edge of the forest. Stately and ethereal, they glided to the water's edge in single file, like a visitation from some other more peaceful dimension. Their burnished silver bodies glistened as their limpid eyes searched for danger and found none. Slowly they bent their magnificent heads down, suppliants to nature's communion, breaking the still surface of the water, which rippled out in ever-widening circles.

Watching them, I had such a strange sense of *déjà vu*, until I remembered the dog. She had been tall, stately and silver-grey and she had crept like a living skeleton into our garden to drink thirstily from the pool. I had flung a few lamb chops her way, all I could lay my hands on in a hurry. The dog had wolfed them down and fled to the shelter of the hedge.

Days of patient feeding had brought about a transformation, and when the dog sneaked into the kitchen to stay

I was overjoyed, but my triumph was spoiled by Wolf's annoyance. 'Take it to the pound,' he had commanded imperiously.

'I most certainly will not.'

'Shall not.'

I had laughed. 'I object to a foreigner teaching me English.'

He would not smile back.

'I shall find her a home when the time is ripe. That's if I don't keep her.' I was pregnant at the time and my natural affinity with dogs was bolstered by my burgeoning maternal spirit.

Wolf had calmed down eventually and resorted to pleading. 'You can't help your hormonal urges any more than I can help my instinctive distrust of all mongrels. Be they human or not, I trust only pedigrees. Give it away, my pet. It offends me.'

'Maybe. But first it must grow strong.'

Joy had a friend whose dog had been run over, so the long, lank, skinny creature found a good home the next week, but by then Brigit, a six-week-old Great Dane, had joined our household, a gift from Wolf. Her pedigree was so long it might have stretched back to the Vikings, for all I knew or cared.

Dusk was falling. As I stood up the deer vanished and I hurried back to the house. Father was at the dining-room table, waiting to eat. 'It's so lovely outside. I forgot the time. Sorry.'

'No matter, Nina. You could do with some fresh air. How do you feel?'

'It's a bit sore, not painful. And you? How do you feel?'

'Oh, me. I'm always fine.' He brushed aside my inquiry.

Lately Father had been forgetting his obsession with time and discipline. He was more relaxed and his legs seemed to be strengthening.

'I thought of something else and it might be important, Father. For some reason I felt it was deliberately brought to my mind. Does that sound silly to you?'

'No.'

'I was watching the deer. Funny, but they looked like reindeer.'

'They are reindeer. Once, they were native to Scotland. A large herd has been released near Aviemore. They're running free on the Cairngorm mountains. They come this way sometimes. So, what is it?' He picked up the water jug and filled my glass.

'I forgot to tell you about Wolf's obsession with pedigrees and titles. I can't imagine how I missed this.'

'Three years of living with a man can lead to a lot of conversations.' Father was only half listening, his mind on carving the meat. 'You're bound to miss some things.'

'Wolf cringed when I wanted to keep a stray dog. It was lovely, too, but a mongrel. Later he told me that mongrels should be put down at birth. For Wolf, animals and people were divided into two camps, those with pedigrees, if not titles, and the common herd whom he despised. When he explained this to me, I accused him of being a neo-Nazi, which horrified him. You can't imagine my astonishment when I was told by Wolf that my own acceptance stemmed from the ancient earls of Angus. Believe it or not, he had studied the Ogilvie pedigree.'

'Perhaps as a boy he had only that to hang on to,' Father mused. 'If Wolf has a genuine title that narrows our search. Barons and counts were two a penny in that part of Europe, but the point is that they were all documented.

I'll keep this avenue of exploration for myself. It's ideal for computer work.

'I haven't been idle while you were away, Nina. I've pieced together a picture of the boy and the man. From the lies and the truths that Wolf inadvertently let fall, we can make an assumption that he was born into an old, landowning family somewhere in Eastern Europe. His father was probably a patriot in the Second World War, later returned home and eventually married. His son, Wolf, was born around 1954, at the time when Soviet purges were quashing all remaining resistance in the outlying Soviet states. It seems likely that his entire family was transported to Siberia, where his father died or was killed. Perhaps the latter, which would give him the anger he needed. From then on he was reared on tales of former greatness, the land they had once owned, the fabulous home, jewels and paintings they had once possessed. Probably he was taken from his home at puberty, or maybe younger, and sent to a military camp to be trained as a soldier. He must have suffered bitterly, but later his flair for languages, his looks and his friendly manner led to ready acceptance from his superiors, while his intellect opened the gates to university, where he might have been recruited by the KGB to be trained as an agent. Later he learned to combine spying with freelance conning.

'It's only conjecture, I know, but the image fits Wolf far better than that of a German baron, which he claimed to be. It also matches all that you had learned about him.'

'Which leaves us only half the world to search,' I acknowledged wryly.

'Come on, eat something, Nina. You're far too thin. Now,' he went on, as I reluctantly pecked at my plate, 'let's suppose that our young Wolf, recently banished to

Siberia, was heir to a title. Perhaps that's why he added a baron to his alias. Most of the families dispossessed by the Soviets vanished into obscurity, but Wolf fought back and he fought dirty. No doubt he was strengthened by the conviction that the world owed him a fortune. Does this theory make sense to you, knowing him as you do?'

'It's him. The cap fits perfectly.' I laughed triumphantly, and reached across the table to hold my father's hand. Remembering how he hated emotion I pulled back, but he held on tightly.

'We're winning, Nina. Take courage. I have the utmost faith in you. Now, eat your supper.' He grasped at normality.

A warm glow spread through me. It began in the tips of my toes and moved upwards. 'And I in you,' I muttered. I looked up and our eyes locked as we silently exchanged our mutual trust and acceptance.

Chapter 39

The days became jumbled and interlinked. I seemed to have been sitting behind the spotlights for ever. My eyes were even more swollen, my throat more sore and my voice came out in a croak, but there was no letting up.

Father had his methods for dealing with rebellious daughters. 'Bear with me, Nina,' he would say. 'I'm pretty sure that your subconscious mind had understood Wolf by the time you were married, but not for anything would you allow your conscious mind to ruin your happiness. So you covered up the truth. The evidence you didn't want to acknowledge was thrust down out of sight, but the data we need is still there, of course, and we must try to recover it.'

On 15 June, I returned to Edinburgh to have the stitches taken out of my arm. I didn't have to wait long. I was shown into the surgery where the nurse took over. Within five minutes the bandages and stitches were gone. The nurse set about rubbing my skin clean with surgical spirits. 'The doctor will see you shortly. Please wait here,' she said.

'Beautiful,' the doctor said, running his index finger down my arm. 'Really lovely. In a year's time you'll hardly see the scar. Don't get into any more fights, will you?'

Father was not alone when I returned, which was unusual.

I was disappointed for I was longing to gauge his reaction.

'They said you should go straight in,' Mrs Peters told me.

The first thing I noticed was a sense of intimacy between the two men, so I guessed that our guest was from the Department. He was short and square, and his head jutted forward so that he had to twist it at an impossible angle to look round, like a parrot. The resemblance did not stop there. His nose was more of a beak, his brown eyes were deeply hooded, but they gleamed with lively curiosity as he glanced briefly at my arm. So I was right about their close relationship. Father had never been the confiding type.

The man stood up and took my hand as we were introduced. 'We met when you were so high, Nina. Of course, you don't remember.'

'Commander Clive Wattling heads my old department, Nina. Once he was my "gopher". I never told you this, my dear, but I have retained a loose connection with the Department. Only because they need my know-how or I'd have been turfed out long ago.'

'I'm very impressed with the facts you have uncovered regarding Wolf Möller,' Wattling said ponderously. 'I'm inclined to agree with the early profile you have accessed. He wasn't Russian, but his connections were good. As an industrial spy he worked for whoever paid him and from time to time the Russians paid him handsomely. He was very well versed in military hardware and he had a degree in geology. A very clever man, I'm afraid. Difficult to track. He saw sanctions against South Africa as the necessary cover to sell US research to Russia and China. I have no doubt the South Africans covered his expenses. That's all we know about him. When the Communist system broke down he found himself without buyers and at risk. That's when he got out of the country fast.

'As for the man who broke into your home, we think he might be Boris Borovoi, a long-time member of the KGB and once Wolf's controller. He appeared to have hung on to his connections with the Russian secret police after the Soviet system crumbled. Can you identify him?' Wattling took a photograph out of his file.

'Yes! That's the bastard who shot my dog.'

'Good!' He put the picture back in the file. 'We, and our American colleagues, of course, want Möller badly, and that's why we're prepared to lend a hand to your search, be it ever so subtly, my dear,' he went on, in a kindly way. 'I wish you the greatest possible success. I would bend over backwards to help you in any personal capacity. Officially speaking, the connection is very loose.'

'I haven't told her yet, Clive,' Father said. 'Nina, you have been admitted into the holy precincts of Naval Intelligence, in a roundabout sort of way. You are my official agent and informer.'

'A spy?' Heavens!'

'Welcome aboard. It's a *quid pro quo* liaison,' my father went on. 'We pass on all we learn about Wolf Möller. In return, they give us a semi-official back-up, mainly research, should we need it.'

'More to the point,' Clive Wattling said, in his deep, grating voice, 'we have provided you with a false identity, which you badly need. You can't go around as Nina Ogilvie. Someone might link you to your married name or to your father. He's still well known in intelligence circles. There's no pay, nothing like that, and we won't be bailing you out if you break the law, although we'll do whatever we can to smooth your passage. This mission could prove very dangerous for you.'

I took a deep breath. Lately I had managed to avoid thinking about any danger involved in my search. Suddenly Wattling had brought it into sharp focus, but I could not turn back. My son needed me.

'Have a look through that, my dear.' Wattling passed me a slim folder.

On top was a passport in the name of Naomi Hunter. I opened it curiously. She was thirty-one years old, two years younger than I, and she was described as an accountant, five feet six inches tall, my height, with blue-green eyes, brown hair and no distinguishing marks. I gazed long and hard at the picture. She did not resemble me at all.

'Don't worry about the picture,' Wattling said, as if he was reading my thoughts. 'Yours will go there. Get some passport pictures taken and I'll get this back to you within twenty-four hours. You should darken your hair to match the description.'

Mrs Peters brought some coffee and biscuits, which gave me time to glance through the file.

Naomi Hunter had been sentenced to five years in June 1988 for embezzling funds from the building society where she worked. She had committed suicide while serving her sentence. She had no close relatives and by now she would have been released. Her crime had been kept under wraps by the building society and almost no one knew about the fraud.

Poor Naomi, I thought, gazing at the picture. She had paid her debt to society and she could have begun her life again. But can one ever break free of one's own condemnation?

Father broke into my thoughts. 'More coffee, Nina?'

'Mm, please.' I pushed my cup towards him.

'Now, listen to this,' Wattling said, fumbling through a file. 'The CIA, the FBI, Interpol and Goldbrick, which is a conglomerate created to combat an epidemic of mineral frauds in the US, have sent us a list of scams that occurred worldwide during the past eighteen months.' He took out a thick file and placed it on the desk. 'Go through it. You may find something that rings a bell and makes you feel that Wolf Möller might have been involved.'

'I'll be burning the midnight oil,' I said, feeling the weight of the folder.

'Enough said.' Father stood up. 'Would you drive us round the fields, Nina? I'd like to show Clive our latest progeny. Unbelievable what modern science can do for the herd. How about you meeting us in front in half an hour? I just need to wangle a few more concessions out of my friend.'

Chapter 40

After Clive Wattling had left, Father and I spent half the night going through the files. I was amazed at how gullible some investors were.

'The con-artist usually catches his victims through their greed,' Father said. 'Yet our Wolf always shows a flair for the unexpected.'

'He's bright and versatile. I always considered him a genius.'

'A bent genius.'

Around two a.m. we both came to the same conclusion. The Friends of Unita fund was right up Wolf's street.

'Look at the initials. FOU!' I smiled at my father. 'Wolf always had a sense of humour.' I picked up the file and read: 'A man claiming to be Dr Andrés Anselmo, a well-known Portuguese surgeon, formerly resident in Angola, initiated a fund to assist Unita in its drive to bring democracy to Angola. A successful fund-raising drive was launched in the States to buy military and medical equipment. Subsequently, the man impersonating Dr Anselmo disappeared with four million dollars.'

British Intelligence had typed a note stating that the real Dr Anselmo had returned to Angola to set up a mission for war casualties, but he had died of a new and virulent strain of malaria in a remote local mission station.

'Wolf's a natural for this one,' I said thoughtfully. 'He was often in Angola buying illicit diamonds. He could easily have found out about the doctor's illness.'

'Exactly.'

'What does this sentence mean: "The merchant banker concerned, David Bernstein, refused to hand over the sucker list"?'

'It means a list of those people, or suckers, who were caught by the con. A sucker list is a highly valuable commodity for any crook. Invariably the con will use this list for future scams. Some of them will probably bite again.'

Father glanced doubtfully at me. 'We need this list, Nina. David Bernstein can't release it because of the confidentiality banking laws in the States. You'll have to get out there and take it. Once we have it, we'll contact every one of them, asking them to pass on any new approaches that come their way. Whoever this con-artist is, he was working against time. He must have been concerned that the news of the real Dr Anselmo's death would reach the American press. For cons, timing means survival. That's how we'll catch up with him eventually. How about booking your flight? Be ready to leave on Monday. That gives you enough time to fix your hair and get the passport pictures to Wattling. Check out Bernstein on the Internet. See what you can find. I'll think up a reason for you to be there.'

David Bernstein's CV was daunting, I learned later that evening. He had graduated brilliantly from Yale, only to enter the Israeli Army where he slogged in the ranks for a year before being hoisted off to Military Intelligence and awarded the rank of captain. After five years he had returned to enter his family bank, for he was the sole surviving heir. He was thirty-four years of age, a millionaire, and last year a woman's magazine had voted him the fourth most eligible bachelor in the States. And I was supposed to outwit him. What a hope.

By the weekend I was packed and ready to leave. I would be travelling as Naomi Hunter, an Australian-born accountant, currently employed as an insurance-claims investigator, following up claims made by the country's biggest arms manufacturers. Several contracts for armoured vehicles had been awarded to them by the bogus Dr Anselmo. It was an excellent alibi and I blessed Father. I knew the country and the business well enough to carry it off.

'We're on the way, Nina,' Father said, as I left on Monday morning. 'You look quite different with your hair so dark, but it suits you. Good luck.'

As our driver took me to the airport, I thought about Father and how he had changed. His eyes twinkled, his voice had taken on a happy lilt, he smiled often and even called me by childhood pet names I had thought were long forgotten. 'Ninja the Terrible' was one of them.

I could not help thinking that I had been entirely confused about him. He was a philosopher and a thinker. I doubt he had ever been the bluff, outdoor squire, or the derring-do intelligence agent I had imagined. I had always loved him but, unbelievably, I was getting to like him, too.

I had five hours to kill in London, and I decided to take the plunge and do something I had been wanting to do since returning to Britain. I walked into Bertram's Bank and asked to see Eli Bertram. He could always refuse, I comforted myself, but he didn't.

It was a journey into the past that brought a lump to

my throat as I walked past Mary, his secretary, to Eli's office. Nothing had changed and neither had Eli. Maybe his white hair was a little longer, his clothes slightly more flamboyant. But his burning, youthful brown eyes had not changed at all.

'Nina, my dear, what a terrible experience. I was hoping you would come and see me. I've missed you. Come and sit down. I want to hear everything.'

While he spoke, he was holding my hand and squeezing it, and I was wondering if he would ever let go of it. A surge of warmth and a flood of memories led me to hug him tightly.

'That's better,' he said.

'I have the time to spare, Eli, but have you?'

'Yes. I'll make the time.' He called through to his secretary. 'No interruptions. And send for two coffees, please. And biscuits.' He looked up. 'You're far too thin, Nina. And why have you changed your hair? I don't think it suits you. Now, begin at the beginning.'

I was amazed that I could describe four and a half years of my life in an hour. I had always been straight with Eli. I found that I could even tell him about prison. Strangely, some of the load seemed to lift as I poured out my story. Finally I took out my most precious picture of Nicky. It was crumpled and worn from prison days.

'This is Nicky,' I said, proudly. 'I intend to find him and take him home. So for a while I'm Naomi Hunter, and I'm dark-haired because she was. To be honest, I'm a little scared about the coming encounter. Can you tell me anything to help me?' I could not bear to put away the picture, but sat there smoothing it with my fingers.

'I can tell you a hell of a lot that won't help, Nina. David's one of the most astute bankers I've ever met. He excelled in Israeli Intelligence. I don't believe that it was he who was caught by this basic fraud. I think he's shouldering the responsibility for his father. Naturally so. His father's been hanging in there, but longing to retire for years. One of the old man's favourite hobby-horses has always been pushing democracy in Third World countries. He backed this particular scheme eighteen months ago. I know because he told me. David's only been there for a year.'

'So the two of you are friends.'

'Relatives, through marriage. We don't see each other often.'

'Please don't—'

Eli held up one hand. 'Wouldn't dream of letting you down, Nina. I heard that David was reluctant to leave the Mossad, but his father put moral pressure on him to start taking over the bank. David's very liberal. His father's ultra right-wing. They have clashed a great deal.'

Eli chatted on until I had to leave to catch my plane. 'Don't underestimate the danger, Nina,' he said, as we shook hands. 'You'll be up against the world's intelligence agents and organised crime. Both are ruthless and very astute. Remember that.'

Despite Eli's warning, I left feeling optimistic.

Chapter 41

'Join me for lunch. Twelve thirty at the Four Seasons? Would that be convenient?' David Bernstein had sounded delightfully uncomplicated and friendly when I had called him from my New York hotel. His unassuming manner had disarmed me.

Father had faxed him earlier on a bogus insurance company's letterhead, choosing a name that could be easily confused with an existing insurance group. The fax had explained that the company needed proof that the contracts had been awarded to the manufacturers, and that I was also investigating any clues to the whereabouts of the bogus Dr Anselmo.

Now, as I quickened my step to follow the waiter past babbling fountains and inset lily-ponds, I wondered if I could carry off my role.

A man stood up and hovered at a table. Catching sight of him, I paused mid-step, hoping against hope that this man wasn't David Bernstein, but it was. Instinctively I knew I would never be able to handle or deceive such a man, but I was not sure why. Perhaps because of his air of quiet watchfulness and self-discipline.

He seemed unaware of his excessive share of positive male attributes. Third-generation American from Eastern European stock, I guessed, noticing his almond-shaped brown eyes, his high cheekbones and his sensual, mobile lips. He was wearing khaki trousers and an open-necked shirt, with no sign of the male adornment I detested so much. Not so much as a wedding ring.

As his hand gripped mine, I puzzled over the tentative surge of excitement that flickered in me. How long had it been since I had touched the hand of such a man? Or met for lunch? Or even held a conversation? This was all a mistake, I realised in a flash. I needed more time to convalesce from my long sojourn in prison. How could anyone keep a cool head in the face of such a man? I guessed that David Bernstein spent his leisure time fending off women.

'How are you, Miss Hunter? Welcome to New York.' His voice was deep, almost gruff, but he spoke softly as if to disguise it.

'Ah, well, hello. Thanks for meeting me,' I murmured. 'Kind of you to spare the time . . .' The waiter was holding my chair back. I sat down, wishing that I did not have to cheat the man opposite me. Suddenly I minded very much indeed.

The wine waiter appeared, and Bernstein turned his attention to the list. 'Do you like wine with your lunch, Miss Hunter?'

'Hardly ever, and not today, thanks.'

'How about freshly squeezed orange juice?'

'Perfect.'

Bernstein ordered a grape juice for himself and tried visibly and unsuccessfully to cope with his impatience while questioning me about my flight and my hotel accommodation. Small-talk wasn't his forte. The waiter produced our drinks with amazing speed and Bernstein solemnly lifted his glass. 'To our success, Miss Hunter. It seems that you and I have a common purpose. I'd like to see the so-called Anselmo behind bars. I'll offer you all the co-operation that's in my power. By the way, here are the copies of the documents you need.' He pushed an envelope towards me.

'Thanks.'

Toying with my glass, I wondered whether to be straightforward. With David Bernstein, there was little point in being anything else, I decided.

'I would like to have the list of people who were caught by him.'

He frowned. 'Everyone's after that list. What did the agent call it? The sucker list?'

'Exactly.'

'So why do you want it?'

'Same reason as others want it. Those investors have proved themselves susceptible to this type of plea. No doubt the con-man will contact them again and when he does we'll be waiting for him.'

'We?'

'My colleagues and I.'

'Banking ethics prevent me from giving you that list, Miss Hunter,' he said, almost automatically. 'Everyone on it is a *bona fide* banking client. Let's put that one aside, shall we? How else can I help you? What exactly is your brief? Is it merely to investigate the authenticity of the insurance claims? Or are you actually looking for the man himself?'

'Yes, of course. If I could discover the whereabouts of this thief, my employers would take steps to recover the money and hand him over to stand trial.'

'Tell me more about yourself, Miss Hunter. Just how far will you go to trace this con? It could be dangerous for you, but I suppose you know that. How did you fall into such an unlikely role? And why is it so important to you?'

'It's my job.' I frowned, and decided not to comment further.

Bernstein, who missed nothing, caught my reticence. There was a glint of puzzlement in his eyes, but the waiter arrived and I escaped into ordering soup and salad. His bearing was military, his expression detached, but his eyes held me in close arrest as they smilingly interrogated me.

'There's very little that I can tell you about Dr Anselmo, or whoever he was, Mr Bernstein. You, on the other hand, have a close knowledge of how this man operates. I suppose you know that the real Dr Anselmo died of malaria in Angola recently. Why didn't you check that you had the right man?'

I leaned back waiting for a reaction and was gratified to see that Bernstein looked shocked.

'Are you absolutely sure of that? My God! This business gets increasingly absurd. Of course, we checked out the doctor and learned that he was a tireless campaigner against Communism. He has launched several successful projects to help landmine victims and he was trying to assist Unita.' He lapsed into dismayed silence.

I moved on fast to keep him off the questions.

'Perhaps you should tell me your side of the story. Why did you lend four million dollars to a man you'd never even met?' I paused, hoping that I had established myself as a woman who was not affected by his undeniable sex appeal.

'Two, not four. The remainder was collected by the fund drive. He was never our client.'

Bernstein was riled and it showed. Good!

'Friends of Unita was the client and, believe you me, it was a genuine, *bona fide* non-profit-making organisation set up in the States to collect funds to assist in the spread of democracy in Africa.' He shrugged and shot me an embarrassed grin. 'I fouled up.'

'But I heard that you took over a *fait accompli*, that this scheme was in fact a hobby-horse of your bank's chairman, your father.'

He looked amazed. 'Where did you get this information?'

'I don't remember.' Damn! I had made a bad mistake. God forbid he would check on me with Eli. 'So you never set eyes on him and neither did anyone else in your bank?'

'True.' Now he was on his guard.

'Mr Bernstein, we are both on the same side. We must pool our information.'

'Okay. I'll do my best. Anselmo was supposed to come out here and give a lecture tour and slide show on the devastation in Angola. Instead he sent a party of paraplegics with a Unita official. They were in a state of shock most of the time. And for what?' A waiter arrived with our lunch. 'Is that okay?'

'Just what I needed. Thanks. Why are you so angry about this scam, Mr Bernstein? I hope you don't mind me asking.'

'I suppose it's because I hate to see other people's suffering being used in this way. This special division to back democracy in Third World countries was a long-term dream of my father's. I took over half-way, as you found out, but I should have cottoned on at once. Father has lost face, as well as two million dollars, and so have I. That's putting it mildly. So,' he ran his hand over his forehead tiredly, 'I need to find the bastard.' He laughed briefly and shook his head.

I guessed that his anger was deep and raw and it would live with him until Anselmo's impersonator, or Wolf, or whoever he was, was caught and sentenced.

He smiled. 'You're very easy to talk to. I guess I'm boring you. May I call you Naomi? Everyone uses first names here. I'm David.' He smiled disarmingly. 'I have hopes of an early success. You see, Naomi, no matter how clever these crooks are, they face a common problem. They can't use their loot unless they launder it first. That is how I shall catch him.'

I could have listened to David for ever, if I had for ever but I didn't. I even forgave him for being so damn patronising as he explained about money-laundering. Eventually my patience ran out. It was time to take a stand.

'Anselmo, or whoever he really is, is by now a past-master at laundering money,' I said, with genuine distaste. 'He will probably be using cash businesses, he might ship bogus freight around the world, he probably transfers illegal diamonds and gold for cash. You mentioned one hundred billion circling the globe at any given time. You must know that it could be as high as three. How could you possibly pick up trends and movements from the banking transactions at your disposal?'

Silence followed. I listened to the water trickling in the pond beside our table and wished I could play some other kind of woman, a soft, feminine, clinging type, but that wouldn't be Naomi Hunter.

'My apologies for patronising you.' He looked ill at ease. 'I think this meeting should continue in my office. Furthermore, I'll surprise you with the amount of information I can lay my hands on through the banking fraternity. Let's go.'

He did not pay for our lunch. Obviously he was a regular patron. When we walked out into the sunlight I saw how his black hair shone with a deep blue sheen and his eyes lit up with a reckless gleam that was more than appealing.

He moved lightly and sinuously, as only a superbly trained athlete can.

In another time and place I could fall for you, David Bernstein, I decided regretfully, as I stepped into the taxi. I'd rather be on your side than against you.

Chapter 42

On that brief and breathless drive to Bernstein's, my senses blazed as the adrenaline coursed through my veins. I felt both exhilarated and terror-stricken, sensing the energy flowing out of the man at my side and feeling disconcerted by my intense interest. I knew that it was reciprocated. But who am I? Naomi Hunter? Inexplicably, I felt a surge of jealousy at David's obvious attraction to this other woman who was also me. Then came a flicker of fear. David must never get close to me. That would be fatal.

When we left the cab, David captured my arm in a proprietorial grip and marched me firmly through the bank's foyer. His touch was like an electric shock, both thrilling and scary. I could feel the warmth of his thigh beside mine and it was strangely exciting. How could I feel like this at such a time? Had I gone crazy?

When we reached his secretary's room he relaxed his grip and smiled at the well-groomed, middle-aged woman. Round-faced, sharp-nosed and plump, she was saved from plainness by the clarity of her remarkable blue eyes.

'Naomi, meet my secretary, Taube Bach,' David said, releasing my arm. 'Miss Hunter and I are taking a headlong flight into the unplumbed depths of cyberspace. Wish us luck, Taube, and sustain us with cookies and coffee at regular intervals.'

Smiling a pseudo-meek smile, she promised to do that. 'But first,' she insisted, 'you really are going to have to deal with these routine matters. It won't take long.'

'Miss Bach runs me as well as this office.' David voiced the obvious.

Miss Bach laughed at some whispered joke he made. As she glowed and twisted her grey hair with fluttering, ringed fingers, I thought that David must be fun to work with. I wasn't quite sure how much fun I had been back in the old days. Power sits uneasily on female shoulders, perhaps because it's never enough to be the best. I had to prove my ability as a daily chore. Relax for one moment and some man beneath me would be trying to show me how to do my job. Perhaps that was why I had zoned out femininity as a sign of weakness. A silly mistake.

I watched David fend off his secretary's queries, dump all the work on her shoulders and be rewarded with a beaming smile. As he opened the door to his office and beckoned to me, his glance was frankly intimate. Then he flushed beetroot and it was the flush that got to me.

I walked into a large, gracious room overlooking the park. A desk, pushed to one side, contained a computer and an empty in-tray. For the rest it could have been anyone's living room with the green and blue floral chintz-covered settees, a moss green carpet looking newish, and a green glass bowl full of irises. Two walls were stacked from floor to ceiling with books in Russian, French, Hebrew and English, in subjects that ranged from law and banking, to archaeology and philosophy.

I turned as David called sharply, 'Naomi! Hey, why do I feel like I have the wrong name?'

'Sorry. I wasn't listening.' How could I be so foolish? I changed the subject. 'David, how did it begin? I can't imagine you being caught by anyone.'

He sprawled in the easy chair and drummed his fingers on the arm. 'I suppose there's no harm in telling you. Come and sit down. Eleven months ago, I was approached by a Boston society woman, known as Martha, who was handling the fund collection for the Friends of Unita.'

'Martha who?'

'Sorry.' He looked damned pompous when he folded his lips like that.

'You checked her out, of course.'

'Naturally. Impeccable background. She could trace her roots back to the Pilgrim Fathers. That sort of thing.

'A little over a year ago, shortly before I joined the bank, Martha came to see my father and told him what she and the fund were trying to do. She brought plans and figures to back her story. He was impressed, so he bullied the board into making this charity the first project to benefit from the bank's development fund, which he had been instrumental in setting up. As I told you, this was his dream. He wanted to push democracy. He's quaint and old-fashioned, but a hell of a guy. He didn't deserve this. Anyway, the bank agreed to back the venture with bridging finance to cover purchases, just as long as the investments kept rolling in. You see, Naomi, something touched the American investors' hearts and they responded with tens, hundreds and thousands of dollars.

'The funds were transferred to FOU's London account at Dr Anselmo's request, to buy arms, vehicles and medical supplies.'

'Why London?'

'Anselmo claimed that exchange control in Angola would cause endless delays for foreign payments and that the cash should be kept in London.'

'Sounds reasonable.'

'Yes, but within twelve hours of transfer, Dr Anselmo and the money had disappeared.'

I tried to keep my face calm while my mind churned with rage.

Chapter 43

'Disappeared without a trace,' I muttered bitterly. It was getting to sound like Wolf's *modus operandi*. Was that all I had ever been, a project?

'Come and sit here.' David pulled up a second chair, switched on his computer and connected to the Internet. Within seconds we were tracing international banking exchange routes and keying in to large deposits.

'Look here! This is my tracking record to date.'

I pondered over the detailed route traced over an atlas. Three cheques had been made out to Canadian, Belgian and South African munitions and armoured-vehicle manu-facturers. The cash amounts had been transferred the moment they were cleared. From then on the three money routes were marked as the cash circled the globe and came to rest for a few days at the Hong Kong Bank in Geneva. Co-currently, $100,000 was transferred to Maun, in Botswana, and withdrawn in cash. The following day, $50,000 dollars were handed over the counter of a specialist safari dealer to purchase a converted Land Rover, which had tanks for massive water supplies and three times the normal petrol capacity. The vehicle had left Botswana at Mukwe, bordering Angola, and no trace of it was seen again.

'One month after the cash was deposited in Geneva,

an amount of two million dollars was drawn from the same account and transferred to Prague and from there to Moscow.'

Was Anselmo yet another alias for Wolf? And was Moscow where he lived? I suppressed my excitement.

'The rest of the cash remained in a Swiss bank. I can't get further right now because of the secrecy laws, but I'm not without influence and it won't take me long to get the next step out of them.'

I felt confused and scared. How had David got so far so fast? Would he track down Wolf before me? If so, he would hand the matter over to the CIA and they would apply for extradition. Wolf would have all the time in the world to go to ground, or to hide Nicky where I would never find him. What if he found out that I was free? Would he suspect me of identifying him? Would Nicky be harmed?

'I'm right at the beginning,' David muttered. 'I'll catch up with this bastard, I promise you, and I'll do it my way. I've also put out an alert on that Land Rover.'

'For heaven's sake, David. The money's destined to circle the globe for months.' I tried to sound dismissive. 'You could grow old tracking it.'

'Hey, there, have a little faith,' he objected. 'I'm a banker, remember. You can work with me, if you like.'

'Fine by me, if you give me the investors' list.'

David shook his head.

'You're very determined to do things your way and sweep this mess under the carpet, but you're playing into the con's hands,' I said, with minimum politeness. 'He's out-thought you all along the line. Don't you see that secrecy is his ally? Someone has to contact each one of his so-called investors and warn them. As for the fund-raiser, Martha, she could provide some clues about his real identity. Give me the list so I can use it. Give me Martha's name and address so I can contact her. We're wasting time here. Bring the whole scam out into the fresh air.'

He looked offended. 'Naomi, I have to consider the bank's and my father's reputation, and my investors' privacy,' he said, in the solemn tones of a future board chairman. 'As for Martha, I'm unwilling to have a poor old woman dragged into this mess.'

'So that's it, then? A book entry? A couple of digits off next year's annual profits and a blanket cover-up?'

'Look at it whichever way you wish.' When David was angry, his voice softened in inverse proportion to his mood. Right now it was merely a mutter.

He got no further for Miss Bach came in, wanting to haul him off to deal with a problem.

'I'm not here, remember?' David threw up his hands in mock defence.

'It's the message you were waiting for.'

'Oh! Okay. Sorry, Naomi. Make yourself comfortable here. Won't be long.'

As the door closed behind him, I sat gazing at his computer. Chance had given me the perfect opportunity. David was talking on the telephone in his secretary's office as I sat down at the keyboard. My hands were shaking so much I kept making mistakes, but it took only thirty seconds to transfer all the data on FOU to an e-mail document and only a split-second to despatch the information to Father.

Hurry, Nina, hurry! My fingers sped over the keyboard. I disposed of the money routes and all David's research. FOU research covered several documents. I found Martha's name and address, memorised it, quit the programme and disposed of it. Then I keyed around for back-up documents and trashed them, too. Finally I trashed the trash. Triumph surged.

Shaking visibly, I stood up and moved to the window. David was still talking on the phone. I ventured a deep breath, but I needed much more air, a tankful of oxygen. His secretary bustled into the room with a pile of mail.

David was coming. I braced myself, pretending to be admiring the view.

'David,' I turned and held out my hand, 'it's been interesting meeting you, but I can't see any point in wasting time. You will not share your information. As for your absurd plan to trace the route of the laundered money, you could spend your life trailing after Anselmo's conjuring tricks. You'd be as effective as a car with its headlights shining backwards, seeing where you've been but not where you're going. I don't have that much time. Thank you for lunch. It was great meeting you.'

I fled before David had time to recover from my rudeness.

I called a cab, threw my things into my suitcase, checked out and drove to the airport. Once safely there I relaxed enough to put through a call to Martha Newton-Thomas in Boston and made an appointment for the following morning.

Waiting in the first-class lounge for my flight, I tried to quell a feeling of regret. I don't usually waste time with thoughts of the 'if only' category, but this time I allowed myself to feel a shaft of self-pity. I would take care never to meet up with David Bernstein again.

Chapter 44

Every city has a Martha Newton-Thomas running its charity drives, minding its business and declaiming on public morals. Naturally she lived in the oldest and most exclusive part of Boston, in a tall, narrow villa tucked away in a crescent overlooking Boston harbour among bankers and brokers. I was shown into a modern office where I came face to face with a woman of majestic proportions and imperious features, incongruously dressed in pink chiffon.

Mrs Newton-Thomas touched hands briefly while she explained that she deducted 20 per cent from every fund drive as her management fee and an extra 5 per cent if she had to appear on the board. Her spectacles and rings glittered as mercilessly as her eyes, and her many chins swung pendulously with the effort of listing the number of charity boards she chaired. She reminded me of a voracious starling, mercilessly picking at every titbit for her 20 per cent cut.

'This is where I plan my fund drives.' She showed me graphs and advertisements and explained how her excellent computer system worked.

'Now tell me again, Miss Hunter, what it is that you want? I couldn't quite understand on the telephone.'

'Dr Anselmo has malaria, I'm afraid. He asked a

colleague at the mission station to check with Bernstein's Bank and find out whether or not they had received a cash transfer to send you, to initiate another fund drive. It hasn't been received at our end, but perhaps it came straight to you. Have you heard anything about it?'

'No. I haven't heard from Dr Anselmo at all. The drive was so successful, quite honestly I was expecting his thanks. Silly of me, I suppose.'

'Now we have the job of tracing it, but with Dr Anselmo being too sick to be questioned we're having difficulties. Mr Bernstein asked me to see you. He needs a few details to get moving.'

'I'm sorry to hear about his illness. I wonder why he's sending funds when we have so much cash in the bank?'

'Actually, Mrs Newton-Thomas, investors' and bank funds have been transferred to London to buy the medical supplies and armoured vehicles Unita need.

'Mrs Newton-Thomas, did you have any written contact with Dr Anselmo in the form of a letter, a fax, a telegram or cheques? Who or what paid for your original fund drive? No doubt his latest cash transfer took the same route.'

For her bulk she was remarkably agile. She rose without effort, sat at her computer and began searching through the index.

'Early on I received two cheques from him. Ah, here we are. It was eighteen months ago, to be precise. Naturally, they weren't Anselmo's cheque. They were from one of those many seemingly innocuous aid organisations the ones where you never know if they're Catholic- or Communist-backed. Here we are, the Trans-African Development Foundation, based in Sarajevo, Yugoslavia of all places. Dr Anselmo seems to like living dangerously. The transfer was to pay for the initial advertising campaign. You get nothing for nothing, my dear, you should know that.'

I could hardly control my excitement. I stood up and leaned over her shoulder to memorise the account number. I had last seen that name on Wolf's computer when I searched his office the night Brigit died. At the time the account had been based in Lübeck.

'Which bank issued the cheques?'

The keys were tapping away and I blessed her for her efficiency. 'The Bosnaskandia, a private bank, with sub-branches in Austria, Hungary and Bulgaria. I checked them out.'

Her triumph rang loud and clear. Mine, I hoped, was less obvious.

'I distinctly remember thinking that it was a strange place for a Catholic mission to keep its cash. There was a signature and a printed name on the cheque. I made a note of it somewhere. Here we are, Gunther Mannheim.'

I was feeling breathless at my good fortune. That was the confidence trickster Father had mentioned, who had operated in the States in the early eighties. Just how many millions had Wolf scammed worldwide? Was Sarajevo the final base for all his loot? Did he live there? Was Nicky in Sarajevo? I said a silent prayer of thanks as I dredged up a smile.

My joy was short-lived when I realised that David Bernstein would soon be asking Martha the very same questions I had asked. What else could she tell him?

'Could you give me a description of the doctor, Mrs Newton-Thomas?'

'No, I never saw him. I've spoken to him on the

telephone and he seemed to be a caring, concerned person. Very wide awake. I was looking forward to meeting him.'

'But I'm sure you could describe his voice?'

'Deep, but soft. Foreign base, American intonations. He probably studied in the States.'

She had described Wolf's voice exactly, but the description probably fitted millions of men. Nothing for David in that.

'So no one actually saw him?'

'No one here, but in Africa scores of people must know him. I really had nothing to do with him. I was contracted by the Friends of Unita organisation to handle their funds collection. My commitment was to them, not him. But why are you asking these questions, Miss Hunter? There's something wrong, isn't there?'

'No. There's nothing wrong, other than the doctor's serious illness. It's one of these new strains that are resistant to all known antibiotics.'

Her eyes narrowed and the look she shot me was pregnant with suspicion. 'David Bernstein would have told me,' she muttered.

It was time for me to leave.

'You're very efficient, Mrs Newton-Thomas. You've been extraordinarily helpful,' I said, meaning it. 'I mustn't take up any more of your time.' I stood up.

She glanced at her watch.

'Oh, my dear, you can't go now. Coffee's coming. You must stay and keep me company. Now where is that maid? Wait here, Miss Hunter. It's coming now.'

She went outside, shutting the door behind her. Mrs Newton-Thomas was not the type of woman to waste her time with nonentities like me. Panic surged. She had gone to call David Bernstein. And then? I had to get out of

256

there, but a grim-faced woman was hovering with coffee and cake.

'Do sit down,' Mrs Newton-Thomas's housekeeper commanded.

I stood up, fending her off. 'Please thank Mrs Newton-Thomas. Tell her that unfortunately I have a plane to catch, so goodbye.'

'What about transport, my dear? Sit there while we ring for a cab.'

'I have a car waiting,' I lied.

I heard her calling to Mrs Newton-Thomas as I fled.

Chapter 45

———⟨𝔢𝔤⟩———

It was close to midnight by the time I reached home. When I walked into the living room Father's face lit up, which gave me a warm glow.

'I'm sorry I'm late. I did some shopping and met an old friend for dinner.'

'I got your message.'

I took off my raincoat and hung it on the back of the door. 'Feel my hands. They're frozen.' I thrust them at Father and to my surprise he rubbed them hard until the circulation came back. 'It's good to be home.'

'Glad you're safe and sound.'

'I could do with a drink. A vile and terrible day. Ugh!' I shuddered.

'Get me one, too. I was waiting for you. Let's have the whole story. I know it's late, but it's important.'

I went through my two days, step by step. 'The truth is, I feel such a failure.'

'Don't. The most you can expect from each investigation is to get a lead. Don't hope for more than that, Nina. Imagine a row of dominoes. One falls and knocks the next one down. That's what Intelligence is like. You follow each domino to the end of the row. So what's next?'

'You know as well as I do, it's Sarajevo.'

'Yes.' He sighed. 'I was afraid you'd say that.'

'It's possible that Wolf comes from the former Yugoslavia. The bankers might know him. I can't ignore this lead.'

Father frowned. 'It's extremely dangerous and, anyway, I don't suppose you'll get a visa. Sarajevo is undergoing an uneasy truce, Nina. With two peace plans discarded, all sides are bent on terrorising the government-controlled areas. There have been hundreds of one-off shell attacks. A mortar shell killed sixty-eight people in the Sarajevo market in February. Now the Russians have moved in and they, with American troops, are keeping the peace. It's a very uneasy situation. The Slavs are touting for cash. In return for the two-year use of it, they give you fifteen per cent a month.'

'So much? That's incredible.'

'They have to have Western currency for armaments. Paying the kind of interest they pay is an expensive business. They use the cash to do drug deals, which in turn pay for weapons to support their civil war. The money is washed through Austrian shell companies and these companies buy the arms they need from Hungary or Bulgaria. The transactions are disguised as legal deals and protected by total banking secrecy. The last thing the bankers want is people asking questions about these accounts.'

'Nevertheless, I must go. Wattling could help us. I'll call him in the morning.'

'I suppose it's inevitable. Now, I've got news for you, Nina. You created quite a stir. Rule one of this game is: always leave things as you find them. You should not have destroyed Bernstein's research.'

'True. But you must see that I have to stay one step ahead of the remarkably astute David Bernstein or I might lose the chance to find Nicky. How would it help us if Wolf were brought to justice? Or if Wolf suspected that

I'd played a part in his arrest? David is my enemy and that's the way it has to be.'

'Perhaps you're being over-anxious. After all, Interpol, the CIA, even the South Africans have all been after Wolf and no one has come near to discovering his nationality, let alone his lair.'

'David's different,' I mumbled.

Father shot me a perceptive glance. 'Your disappearance has been noted by the media. Martha Newton-Thomas called in the police and the press found out. She gave a statement this afternoon. It was on CNN. She told them about the missing cash and disclosed that a certain Miss Hunter had made a lightning visit to her headquarters to find out how much she knew about Dr Anselmo. It sounded as if you, together with the bogus Dr Anselmo, created the entire hoax and conned American investors of four million dollars. It didn't take the media long to find out that the real Dr Anselmo had died.

'Of course, Mrs Newton-Thomas wanted to make sure no one put the blame her way. She blamed Bernstein's Bank for transferring the cash to London before they had investigated the fund properly. She made Bernstein look foolish. He had to act fast. He held a press conference and promised investors that it was only a matter of days before the entire sum was recovered. Meantime his bank is bridging the loss. Probably be in the newspapers tomorrow.'

'Oh, God. Not a very good start.'

'Depends which way you look at it, Nina. Some might think that Naomi Hunter is an acknowledged expert in conning and money-laundering. That was our original plan, wasn't it? Notoriety might be just what Naomi Hunter needs.

*   *   *

On Sunday Mrs Peters drove to the village to buy fresh croissants and half a dozen newspapers. Father settled down to devour both with his usual enjoyment. Soon his eyes were sparkling.

'Why, Nina, listen to this! Your David Bernstein held a press conference. He claimed that several of his clients were caught by a certain Naomi Hunter and an unknown accomplice, and he issued a warning to other investors. I'll read it to you: "Naomi Hunter is at the forefront of a new era in crime. Once upon a time we had to look out for the guy with a gun. Nowadays it's the woman with the latest computer technology. With her youth, beauty and undeniable charm, it's easy to see that for Naomi Hunter the world is her oyster. She is brainy, well educated, she has the latest technology at her fingertips. She uses her laser mind to zone into the weaknesses of our financial systems. She preys upon the gullibility of the public and their woeful lack of financial expertise. She takes calculated risks, but she knows the odds."'

I frowned at the offending article. Did he really think I was beautiful? I pushed the paper aside. I hated having to be Naomi Hunter to David.

'David Bernstein is a shrewd man.' Father chuckled. What's he like?'

'Pompous, smart, arrogantly intellectual.'

'You don't like him?'

I shrugged. 'He doesn't think much of me. Why should he? He thinks I'm Naomi and he doesn't trust me.'

There was a hint of mockery in Father's shrewd eyes, but there was also anxiety. I longed to comfort him. 'Wait here, Father. I have something to show you.'

I ran upstairs to the attic, knowing exactly which crate my photograph album was packed in. I felt a need to share Nicky with Father.

'Look, here's Nicky on the day Wolf brought us home from the nursing home. And here he is on his first outing in his pram. There's Nicky in his cradle. And here he is in his high chair. I took this one because his face used to screw up like a little monkey when he was sad or thwarted. In the mornings, when I took him out of his cot, he was so happy to see me that his brown eyes glowed, so I snapped him just like that. He loved to play with Brigit. That great, clumsy dog was so gentle with him.'

We paged on. Father said very little, but I could see that his eyes were glistening. We reached the end and I placed the album on the table. 'It's the first time I've had the courage to look at those pictures. At last I feel that we're moving forward.'

'It's going to be dangerous, Nina. Perhaps worse than you realise.'

'Let's not think about the danger. I'll just keep going.' I knew that my love and my hatred would give me strength. I would hang on to both with equal intensity.

Chapter 46

'Clive's a good man. Dependable. Lucky to have him on our side.' Father slid some papers across the table to me.

I examined the coveted visa, plus permission to visit Sarajevo as an Oxfam observer, which Wattling had organised.

'How did he get this letter from Oxfam?'

'You have to work for it, Nina. Research, mainly. Most of their work is done by unpaid professionals. You've joined the ranks. Wattling agreed that you will visit major orphanages in three main former Yugoslav cities and send back details of budgets, subsidies, to what extent they rely on local and overseas charity, the children's diets, their state of health, that sort of thing. They're sending you some questionnaires. They're pleased with the arrangement.'

'What if . . . ? Father, are you still contacting the orphanages as an on-going process? I know you said . . .'

'Yes, of course. We started two years back. Our missing persons' bureau handles it. They send out monthly news-sheets with Nicky's description. Perhaps we could give them another photograph. Our search is only one of many on their files. I seem to remember you've been to Sarajevo.'

'Yes. When I was in the university skiing team we toured Eastern Europe.'

'It's one of the few places I've never visited.'

'It's a strange city, part Turkish, which is fascinating, then there's the graceful old Austrian quarter, and right next to it the ugliest proletarian city you can imagine – high-rise buildings with nothing to commend them.'

'I doubt if much of that is still standing. Nina, I still think you're wasting your time. I've already explained that the Slavs needs foreign currency. It's their lifeline. Consequently they offer total banking secrecy as a matter of national policy. They won't tell you a damn thing about Wolf's accounts.'

'You're probably right, but I have a plan. There are just a few details to attend to before leaving. I'll leave the day after tomorrow if I can get a flight.'

The 'details' involved setting up an account in Switzerland entitled the Trans-African Development Foundation and transferring fifty thousand pounds from my trust account to this account, with myself and my father as the sole signatories.

It was a week before I landed at Sarajevo airport and took a taxi to the city centre. It was cold for June, and the commuters were huddled in coats and scarves. Everyone looked bleak. The city is situated dead centre of a huge, flat plain encircled with distant mountains, like an amphitheatre. On my last visit its surroundings had been one vast, snowy plain; now there were patches of wild flowers in the grassy fields, some cattle and goats. Suddenly we were driving among blitzed high-rise blocks on either side of the road, many windows were shattered and boarded up and a few buildings had been totally destroyed. The previous vivid contrasts of architecture had given way to a depressing uniformity of rubble, dirty streets and shattered façades.

Did Nicky live somewhere here? The thought frightened me.

The Holiday Inn hotel was still standing, but a little scarred. I booked in, dumped my suitcase and took a taxi to the Bosnaskandia Bank, situated in a once-beautiful art-deco building near the Sarajevo hospital. The windows were shuttered and boarded up, but the bank was intact. Presenting my Oxfam credentials at the information counter, I was shown down a flight of stairs to the vaults, built to withstand almost any blast and temporarily converted into offices.

The manager, Michel Banski, a stocky, middle-aged man with sallow skin and thinning hair, hurried in. He held out both hands and clasped mine in his. His broad smile revealed damaged teeth held together by intricate dentistry, but his eyes shone with friendship and I warmed to him.

'*Dobrodosli*! Welcome! Welcome to Sarajevo. It's not often I have visitors from London, Miss Hunter. I only wish I could offer you something civilised in the way of refreshment. Alas, those days are past. But I am thrilled that Oxfam has sent us an observer. Our people keep suffering.'

This seemed as good a time as any to bring out my gift, six half-kilo packs of coffee. I was hoping that he would not be offended but, to my relief, he was delighted.

'That is not the only reason why I'm here, Mr Banski. I need details about an account in your bank. The Trans-African Development Foundation—'

I was cut short as Banski stood up and gave a strange little bow. His friendly smile had vanished.

'I'm afraid you are wasting your time. I have never heard this name.'

'Please hear me out, Mr Banski.' I stayed glued to my seat and produced my cheque book showing the withdrawal on the cheque stub. 'Five days ago, I transferred fifty thousand pounds from London to this account, the Trans-African Development Foundation, in Sarajevo. This was to settle a debt with the account holder. Will you please check that the money has been transferred?'

Banski's face was a picture of sullen suspicion as he began to tap into his desktop computer.

'There is no trace of the transferred cash, Miss Hunter. Do you have a deposit slip or any other proof of transfer?'

I handed him my slip.

He scowled. 'But this is not the right number for this account. It's not even the right bank. Yet the name is correct. You have made a mistake. Please wait here. I shall check on this branch number. I won't be long.'

'I only need five minutes, Michel Banski,' I murmured to myself, as I took his chair and typed the number of Wolf's account, gleaned from Mrs Martha Newton-Thomas.

Seconds later, disappointment flooded through me. The account had been opened through a nominee, an offshore company registered in the Dutch Antibes. I memorised the address, but I doubted I would find any names, even if I went there. Instructions from this company to the bank came by fax. Only one withdrawal had been made since the cash was first deposited and that was to launch FOU. The cash was out on call and interest payments were credited monthly to the account. The manager had made a note, but it was written in Serbo-Croatian. I copied it faithfully into my notebook.

There was only one other credit and that was for one

million dollars from a Sardinian bank, transferred from an account called International Trading. I copied out the account number.

I heard footsteps, switched off the computer and raced back to my chair.

Mr Banski's eyes reflected his unease. 'Why are you here? Who sent you, Miss Hunter?'

He placed my paying-in slip on the desk, but kept one hand on it. 'If you won't answer me, I shall be obliged to call the police.'

'I told you why I'm here. Have you traced my money?'

'Yes, to a newly opened account in Switzerland.' His eyes veered to his computer. Suddenly I realised that he had left it switched on. Damn!

He reached for the telephone receiver and began to dial.

'Before you call the police, hear me out, Mr Banski. I can have the CIA, Interpol, and the intelligence services of at least three more countries sniffing around your bank, asking questions, trying to get entrance to your files, within hours of my contacting them. You probably aren't aware that a highly paid spy, whom the Americans have been trying to trace for years, is a client of your bank.

'Believe me, Mr Banski, if this information were to hit the headlines, and your bank came to the attention of the world's intelligence agents, your drug barons would withdraw their cash and place it somewhere safer. You probably wouldn't survive such a run on the bank. Do I make myself clear?'

Banski looked sullen and dangerous as I stood up.

'My job is to take whatever cash comes this way, pay the interest and keep my eyes shut. That is what I do. You are a foolhardy woman, Miss Hunter, but I don't want any trouble. I am retaining your transfer slip.'

'It's all yours.' I picked up my bag and left.

Chapter 47

It was two o'clock in the afternoon when I returned to my hotel, feeling fairly optimistic and a little hungry. My first priority was to send Father my report by e-mail and ask him to check on the Sardinian bank account of International Trading and to have the bank manager's notes translated soonest.

Then I went down to the dining room. It seemed to me that I was on the verge of a breakthrough. Deep in thought, I hardly noticed the other guests as I passed along the counter with my tray. I took a sandwich, a bowl of salad and a cup of coffee, and paid absent-mindedly.

Sitting by the window, I tried to chew my sandwich but I was no longer hungry. Was Nicky getting enough to eat? The thought of him abandoned in an orphanage was almost more than I could bear. Would I recognise him if I saw him, I wondered. Two years had passed since Wolf took him away.

Suddenly I was back in my Constantia kitchen watching Nicky clamber out of his high chair as I ran towards him. He was always so impatient to be done with breakfast and play in the garden. His soft brown eyes gazed at me with love and trust, believing that I would always be there to catch him as he tottered on the seat. And I always was. I swung him up and round and placed him on the floor. As he ran outside I watched his red hair flame in the morning sunlight and heard and loved his laugh as he ran across the lawn, accompanied by the big, adoring dog.

The image vanished as I became aware of someone looming over me. I blinked hard and frowned up into David Bernstein's hostile eyes. I felt riled by the spasm of comfort his sudden appearance triggered off.

'So here you are. I might have guessed you'd pitch up like the proverbial bad penny.'

'Don't be trite, David.'

He looked away, but not before I'd seen anger and hurt glinting in his eyes.

'It's a tough world, David. Dreams don't work out and no one is quite what they seem to be. Haven't you learned that yet?'

'Just talk,' David muttered, pulling out a chair and sitting next to me.

'About what?'

'About why you lied to me, why you destroyed my research and stole the list of investors. Not that it helped you. I have other lists and a photographic memory. You committed a criminal offence and I want to know why.'

'You can't prove that.'

'Are you denying it?'

I didn't answer, not wanting to tell more lies.

He sighed. 'Damn you, Naomi. Why don't you lie?'

'Would that make you feel better?'

'You're cool, I'll give you that. I was about to hand you over to the FBI, but I checked up on you with friends in the business and learned that in June nineteen eighty-eight, you were sentenced to five years for embezzling funds from a Perth building society where you worked. Despite your gracious appearance you're an ex-con, caught red-handed with your hands in the till, jailed for fraud.

Australian. My God! You really hoodwinked me. You've only been out a year. Is it so hard to go straight, or are you bent on self-destruction? Did your boyfriend, the bogus Dr Anselmo, send you to wipe out the trail? Don't you realise that cleaning up after your accomplice makes you as guilty as he? You'd have got ten years at least if I'd handed you over.'

'You still can, David.'

'The trouble is, I can't help feeling sorry for you. Perhaps you need help. This con-man seems to have some power over you. You don't seem to me like a criminal type. Listen, Naomi. I've offered a five-hundred-thousand-dollar reward for information leading to the arrest of the bogus Dr Anselmo. That cash will be yours if you identify him for me. I'm prepared to forget what you did if you tell me what you know about this man. Otherwise . . .'

'That's unworthy of you, David.'

He had the grace to flush. 'What is this man to you? Can't you see what he's doing to you?'

'You've got it wrong, David. I intend to bring him to justice, but first I have to find out who he really is and where he is. I didn't want to deceive you, but I would break any rules or laws to find him. Don't ask me more questions because I'm not going to tell you a damn thing.'

When David frowned every feature was brought into play: his eyes narrowed, his bottom lip was thrust out, his jaw tightened, and his brow wrinkled. To me he looked like a ham actor trying to look tough. I could never take his anger seriously. I smiled at him.

'You knew this man personally.'

It wasn't a question so I kept quiet.

'You were his partner?'

'Partner in crime? No, never.'

'Then he stole something from you.'

'Spot on, David. He stole something precious.' I could hear the bitterness in my voice.

'And you would do anything to get it back?'

'Yes, David. Believe me. Anything.'

'Money should never be that important.'

I gazed at my cup.

'Naomi, trust me. I want to help you.'

'If I believed that, I'd believe anything. You can't help me, except by keeping away from me.'

'Now who's being trite? D'you know where this man is?'

'If I did, I'd be there.'

'Do you love him?'

I shook my head.

'Did you take the rap for him?'

'Yes. Now get off my back, David.'

I pushed my chair away and stood up. 'Please excuse me, I have an appointment.'

His hand clutched my wrist. How strong he was. His grip was like a handcuff.

'You can't frighten me, David. Let go.'

'How could someone like you get so hard and so mistaken? Be careful, Naomi. I'm probably a fool to say this, but I'd like to help you. If you should run into something you can't handle, you know where to find me.'

He let go of my wrist and sat hunched over his chair, his face too close to mine, gazing into my eyes.

'Why, David?'

'I'd like you to stay out of prison long enough to settle down and lead a normal life.'

I shut my eyes tightly, resisting the impulse to tell him my story and enlist his help. I had no defence against his kindness, but I knew that if I wanted to find Nicky before

Wolf took cover I had to keep one step ahead of David Bernstein.

'Just forget me, David. Goodbye.'

It was time to visit the local orphanage. The hotel receptionist gave me the address. I returned to my room to fetch a coat and check the e-mail, and found that Father's reply was already waiting.

Well done, Nina. Be careful! I have discovered that the Bosnaskandia Bank is owned by a consortium containing a number of bad boys from the East and the West. I suggest you move to another hotel and leave Sarajevo as soon as possible.

The bank manager's note reads: 'All the faxed instructions received to date were anonymous, referring to credits on the way. They were sent from Vienna, Prague, Paris, Rome and Istanbul post offices. The last communication, received in October '94, informs us that the client is closing his account on 1–10–95. He will send written instructions later concerning the transfer of his capital.'

Lastly, Nina, the International Trading account is one of the many local accounts into which Vittorio Cassellari's laundered loot goes. He is one of the most dangerous men in the drug business. Love, Father.

I trashed the message and called the porter to order a taxi to take me to the orphanage.

It was an old, rambling, broken-down house in the Austrian sector. There was a plane tree in the middle of the front lawn with several tyres hanging from ropes and this cheered me.

I asked the driver to wait, and went inside to find the

matron. No one could locate her, so eventually a young nurse showed me round.

I don't know what I'd been expecting, but not these rows of cots where children sat apathetically still and quiet, with absolutely nothing to do. Bleak eyes, running noses, scabby skins and a strong smell of urine surrounded me. They had all wet their cots.

'When do they get out to play?'

The nurse spoke very little English. 'Excuse . . . ?'

'When is their playtime? They do play sometimes, don't they?'

She shrugged.

I began to feel anger mounting. It began somewhere in my solar plexus and it churned my stomach and burned my cheeks and my eyes.

Bending over a cot I picked up a little red-haired boy and held him close to me. He smelled badly of vomit and urine and he began to cry, so I put him back.

'Excuse me.'

The nurse hurried away while I crept from cot to cot, wondering who would ever take the time to talk to these little mites. Who would teach them to play, to laugh, to run? Were they ever naughty?

The nurse returned with the matron, who took my arm and accompanied me through the dormitories. She looked sad as she tried to explain. 'We have two hundred children. We don't have enough money to feed them, so two of my sisters are engaged full time in collecting funds. We are too short-staffed to look after them properly. We can only supervise one play group at a time, with one nurse in charge. The rest of my staff handle medical care, washing, cooking, feeding and, to be honest, we are all exhausted. There is no time to give any of them personal attention or to teach them to talk.'

'Just one person with a blackboard could do so much,' I whispered.

'Why don't you send us help, my dear? We need volunteer workers. We don't have the facilities to engage extra staff.'

'I'll suggest that in my report to Oxfam.'

As we passed the cots I continued my search for another small, silent, red-headed boy. When I had completed my research and assured myself that Nicky was not there, I offered a prayer of thanks to whatever saint was supposed to watch over children and left.

My driver was waiting. 'You were followed here. I don't want trouble.'

He frowned as he pointed across the street to a parked car. I caught a glimpse of David's profile.

'No trouble, just a curious friend, I promise you. Take me back to the hotel, please.'

How dare David spy on me? Maybe he suspected that I was not Naomi Hunter. I knew that I had to find out.

Chapter 48

I waylaid David in the lobby. 'Why are you following me, David? Do you still believe that I stole Unita's money? Or do you think I will lead you to Dr Anselmo?'

'I want to know who you are.'

'You do know. An ex-con, caught with my hands in the till. Those were your words. It's true, I did serve time for fraud and other crimes. There's nothing else you could possibly want to know about me.'

'So you say. Yet you spent your afternoon touring the local orphanage and I heard that you were upset. You intrigue me, Naomi. You can't leave before tomorrow afternoon. There are no flights, so neither can I. Let's put our differences aside. Have dinner with me tonight. Please.'

Why not? I had nothing else to do.

'Where?'

'Daire's, in the Turkish quarter. I'm told the food's marvellous. See you in the foyer at eight.'

The nightclub was in the basement of what had once been a granary. It was decorated Renaissance style and the floor-show of gypsy dancers was entertaining.

'David knew a great deal about Yugoslavia and the background to the civil war and I listened to him through an exotic dinner of *skamplignje*, a spicy squid dish, *begova corbar*, soup, and *bakalava*, a light pastry with jam.

Eventually he said, 'Just what did you hope to get out of Michel Banski?'

I shrugged and then stared at my hands. 'I'm not going to discuss this with you, David.'

'I want to know why you're here. I went through Martha's computer after you ran away. There was only one entry of any interest, the Trans-African Development Foundation. The cheque for the original payment to launch the fund came from this account in Sarajevo. Not really enough information to bring you here. Something tells me that the name of this account was not new to you. It linked this bogus Anselmo with the man you are looking for. Isn't that so?'

'No, David. Is this why we're having dinner? You could have asked me in the hotel foyer this morning.'

'Of course.'

'So why didn't you?'

'I wanted to invite you to dinner.'

'I think you're being underhand.'

'Look who's talking. We have to have this out, Naomi, and it might as well be now. I've been checking on you. There was no mention of any other person being involved in your building-society misadventure. I don't believe this Anselmo con-artist was ever in Australia.'

'Don't mince words, David. Theft's theft, not misadventure.'

'The trouble with you is that your past and your personality are totally at variance with each other. I don't believe you're Naomi Hunter. I don't believe you've ever seen the inside of an Australian prison. Who exactly are you looking for? Why can't you tell me?'

I remained silent. Looking around, I wondered if I should get up and leave.

'Whoever he is, you said he took something precious from you and left you to take the rap for him.'

'No. I said he stole my money.'

'Naomi, I have a very good memory.'

My cheeks were burning and I was feeling uneasy. What was David after? Why was he delving into the past?'

'I've been very busy this afternoon, Naomi. Michel Banski told me that you are here as an Oxfam observer, reporting back on the state of the country's orphaned children. How does an ex-con get into those sort of circles?'

'Leave it, David, or I'm going. One or the other.'

'Perhaps you'd rather dance than talk.'

'Why not?'

'Never forget that I'm on your side, Naomi. You don't have to worry about me. But if I were you I would worry about Michel Banski. If he thinks you have obtained any leads, he might warn those concerned.'

Clasped in David's arms I almost forgot who I was supposed to be. He was a superb dancer and, once again, my longing for him surged.

'Hey, Naomi,' he whispered in my ear around midnight, 'you're a hell of a dancer.'

When he nuzzled my ear with his lips I thrilled to him and briefly responded, remembering sadly that he was strictly out of bounds.

'David, I'm here under duress. Nothing else.'

I longed for a chance to be Nina Ogilvie. I had the feeling that David and I would go well together.

'Come on, Naomi. You can't deny your feelings for me, and you know how I feel about you. Despite our differences we make a pretty good pair. Let's be friends.'

'Our differences, as you call the gulf between us, are so vast we could be of different species. Furthermore, the carrot-and-stick deal you put to me earlier today is hardly the basis for friendship. I hate being spied on. And you coerced me into coming here tonight, yet you talk about friendship.'

He stopped in the middle of the dance floor and glared at me. 'You are absolutely right. I'm at fault and I admit it. I was silly enough to think that we might rise above the circumstances we find ourselves caught up in. Let's sit down.'

As we moved towards our table we heard a loud but distant whistling, which became a shriek. It became even louder. The band stopped playing as the terrible high-pitched scream raced towards us. Then came absolute silence.

David's expression changed to one of horror. He hurled me towards the stairs. I fell heavily against the wall, too shocked to think, as David fell over me, holding my ears.

The sound of the explosion was like nothing I had ever experienced. It hit me like blows to my head and my stomach. I was stunned by the blast.

Moments later I was struggling to breathe as thick dust replaced air. It was pitch dark. I was face down on the floor with a dead weight on my back. I couldn't move. I panicked and heaved and clawed at the floor, trying to pull myself from under the burden. Then, pushing down, I realised that it was David.

'Get off me,' I yelled, but my voice came tinny and faint as if from a distance. There was a sound like an alarm clock in my ears.

'Get off,' I sobbed. Sanity returned and so did my hearing. I pulled myself together. Putting my weight on my elbows, I slithered out from under David and felt for his head. My hands became warm and sticky. Blood. Just how badly was he hurt? Cupping his chin in my hands I yelled at him. 'David, David. Can you hear me? Are you all right'.

There was no reply.

Panic surged. 'David, speak to me.' There was a soft groan.

Then I heard him whisper, 'Get out, Naomi. Emergency door . . .'

When I tried to stand I began to choke. Plaster was falling around us, and glass was splintering in the distance. I could hear groans and cries for help, but I couldn't see a thing and each breath of dust choked me. I tried to remember where the entrance was. Somewhere behind the stage, I seemed to remember.

A red haze lit the room. Fire! It had started on the stage. We could die here. The dark shapes of people stumbling around aimlessly were silhouetted against the glow. Now smoke was added to the dust.

Emergency door? I hadn't noticed one. Then I decided that it was probably along the passage behind the toilets. The toilets were next to the bar. And the bar was . . . ? At last I got my bearings. We could move along the wall to the corner and if we kept going, we might make it.

I bent down and touched David, ran my hands over him. A lump of concrete lay beside his head and another piece was on his legs, pinning him down. Panting and heaving I shouldered it off him.

'David!' I yelled.

The room was rapidly filling with smoke and my eyes were burning so badly I could no longer see.

'We've got to get out – fast.'

Wrapping his arms around my neck, I tried to pull

him up, but it was impossible. He was too heavy. Sitting him up against the wall, I got into a crawling position and backed into him, pulling him over me, gripping his arms tightly. I tried to stand, but could not. I began to shuffle my knees along the wall, keeping close to it, trying to avoid the panic-stricken survivors.

'Get out, Naomi. Leave me.' He had surfaced again.

'Shut up and move. Try to help me. If you could hang on to my neck I could use my arms.'

'I think I could stand,' he muttered.

Together we struggled up. Gripping his arm around my shoulder, I stumbled forward and felt his weight lighten slightly as his legs strengthened. Flames were roaring, people were screaming. I needed to pant, but there was no air, only smoke. It was raining plaster around us, and the heat was intense.

We reached the corner, but ahead of me I could see a mass of bodies pressing against the locked door. They were yelling and hammering against it. The main entrance was engulfed with flames. We'd never get back that way. I sank down against the wall, and David collapsed beside me.

'David. I admire you,' I croaked. 'I always have. I don't know why I'm telling you that. I wish things could be different between us. But now—'

I heard sirens. The door burst open with a crash. Water smashed into the hall from a dozen hoses. The firemen looked like beings from outer space as they loomed through the smoke.

I was propelled down the passage to the fresh air and left on the grass. David came next, but he had blacked out again. Nurses and stretcher bearers were moving between survivors under hastily erected arc-lights. The nurse took one look at David and summoned the stretcher bearers. 'Go with him,' she said in English.

The hospital was modern and efficient and the nurses reassured me as I sat outside the X-ray unit. Finally David was wheeled out and I hurried along behind the stretcher, still coughing, until we reached casualty where they transferred him to a bed.

A young woman in white hurried in. 'Don't worry too much. It looks worse than it is. I'm his doctor, Anna Babic. There's plenty of stitching to be done, as you can see, and multiple bruising, but the X-rays show there's no real damage, apart from his concussion. He's had a bad gash on his head from falling debris, but he should regain consciousness soon. If so, he'll be able to leave in a few days.'

'He was conscious for a while in the nightclub.'

'That's good news. You don't look too good yourself. Take a shower and have a rest here and we'll do the documentation later.'

'Naomi,' David said, when I woke much later, 'you never cease to amaze me. Thank you for getting me out.'

'You saved me first. Don't you remember? You threw yourself over me so that the concrete fell on you, so thank you, too, David.' I felt embarrassed.

I sat up and smoothed my hair. 'I must look a sight.'

'True, but a lovely sight.'

I looked at him in amazement. Perhaps he still had concussion. I glanced at my watch. 'I'm glad you're better, David. I'm leaving this afternoon.'

His hand reached out and gripped mine.

'How will I find you?'

'You won't, David. It's goodbye. There's no future for us. Better to stop now before we've even started.'

I bent over and kissed him on his lips.

'I suppose you know that I love you, Naomi. One of these days I'll find out who you really are.'

'I'll pretend you never said that.'

Later, when I was safely on the plane reliving our goodbye, I realised how much I longed to see David again.

Chapter 49

'As Naomi Hunter,' Father was saying, 'the successful con, you'll be trusted. It gives you the right background to penetrate Vittorio Cassellari's world. If they want your advice, you can give it. When it comes to finance you're streets ahead of the competition.'

'True.' This was no time for being modest.

It was good to be home, however briefly. My next task was to engineer a meeting with Vittorio Cassellari. He had paid Wolf's Trans-African Development Foundation a million dollars, so presumably he must either know him or know of him. I could see how worried my father was as he briefed me for my role as Naomi Hunter, the rich, unscrupulous woman who had successfully defrauded American investors and was now setting herself up as a money-launderer for Europe's most wanted hoodlums.

'Between us, we can provide the trappings of wealth you'll need to convince the underworld that you are a highly successful con-artist.'

'But as a route to Cassellari? I wonder. I was thinking of a more direct route.'

'I don't agree. Wait for him to come to you. It's safer. The night you came home from South Africa, you told me that Wolf's biggest problem was laundering his cash in such a way that it would not lead back to his base.

Cassellari must have the same problem. Several of his financial advisers are serving long prison sentences right now for laundering his money. Lately governments and banks are tightening up on cash transactions. Running loot around the globe is becoming hazardous. It takes time and expertise. These people need to specialise in their own fields. So who can they turn to? There's none they can trust and few really know the game. You're a woman, so they'll feel they can intimidate you. They won't fear you might steal from them. You'll be filling a market gap.'

'I suppose you're right.'

'Listen carefully, Nina. I've done some research on Vittorio Cassellari. You must know what you're letting yourself in for. He was once a penniless teenage crook. From stealing from warehouses along the Panama Canal, he graduated into heavier crime, but he never saw big money until he turned to drug trafficking. He was first arrested and convicted in nineteen sixty-eight after being caught with cocaine. One of the officers who arrested him was killed shortly afterwards. The others were bribed until all the charges were dropped. This was the pattern Cassellari followed. Arrests were always followed by charges being mysteriously dropped until, in the late eighties, a particularly obstinate Italian prosecutor would not give in. He was murdered. From then on, anyone who confronted or threatened Cassellari was wiped out. He's responsible for almost a hundred deaths. Be careful. If Cassellari's gang were to discover that you were connected to British Intelligence or to me, they would kill you without a second's remorse. They'll put you through a third degree, particularly over your laundering plans. Be prepared and let me know as soon as he makes contact, but be patient. Even if you wait a month, it's worth it.

'There's just one thing that bothers me, Nina, and that is the possibility that Michel Banski warned Cassellari that you had knowledge of the cheque paid into Wolf's account.'

'I'm sure Banski will keep quiet. It was his error. Why should he publicise his mistakes? He knows I won't tell.'

'Let's hope you're right. You must try to live the role of Naomi Hunter. You're a rich, successful woman, who's taken on the world and won. You're clever, resourceful, shrewd and entirely without scruples. Remember that! Get some glitzy clothes, get into the role, and be careful. Never forget who you're supposed to be. You'll be in with some very rough guys. On the surface they're strictly legitimate. The richer they are, the more you should suspect them, unless they own a couple of oil wells or inherited their wealth. I'll be checking for you as soon as you send their descriptions over. Be sure to let it fall, here and there, that you'll do anything for a quick profit, but that you specialise in money-laundering.'

I had a sudden flash of fear. 'And how will you know where I am?'

'By nightly e-mail communication wherever you are. Make it a rule. If I don't hear from you I'll know something's wrong. Now, listen. You will need to open a bank account in the name of Naomi Hunter. I suggest Monaco as your base.'

'Makes sense.'

'You'll need to purchase or rent an apartment, buy a car, and so on. Be ostentatious.'

'Clever,' I said. 'Very clever.'

Father smiled briefly. 'Because it's publicised that you have millions of dollars tucked away, all kinds of people will try to interest you in various get-rich-quick schemes.

Most of them will be outside the law, but you'll keep your money to yourself and captain your own ship.

'Now, Nina, here are some addresses. You have already called the Aiglon Estate Agency who have three properties to show you.'

'When did you do that?'

'When you were in Sarajevo. Buy the most ostentatious and hopefully it will be the most expensive. It will be bought by your trust company, which is called Thornton Fidelity Trust, and the initials, TFT, will be printed on the trust cheque account. The account will remain in London.'

'But do we have this much money, Father?'

'We'll manage. Frequent the best hairdressing salons, gamble nightly at the casino, oh, and you have been accepted as a member by the Monaco Sports Club. Your fees are paid in advance. It's a very good place for you to make contacts. I have an informer there, by the way. And then there's the casino, which is a famous money-laundering venue.

'The Monaco Mercedes agency has a brand new white convertible awaiting delivery. You ordered it from New York. Shop around for a good local designer and make sure your clothes are noticed and that they're designer stuff. None of your tweed suits. Got that?'

'Absolutely.'

Why was Father's voice so hoarse? I asked, 'What's wrong?'

'The truth is, I'm beginning to worry about you. Be careful. Trust no one. Look here, Nina. I don't usually take charge as I have this time. You're more than capable of handling this type of thing. The way you got to see Michel Banski was very clever. Well done! But in this case I know you, and I know you'll fight shy of wasting money. That's not the way Naomi must operate. You must never lose sight of who you're supposed to be.'

'Don't worry, Father.' I crouched beside his chair and put my arm around his shoulders.

For the first time I felt the loneliness of this sad, controlled, clever man, who was playing such a crucial role in the quest for my son. His grandson, I corrected myself. I thought how he had taken on the role of adviser, leader, supporter, healer, spending hours each day at his computer, engaged in research for me, how he never complained about his disability. For the first time I recognised the tragedy of a man who could not easily show his love, but who loved nonetheless.

'I love you, Father,' I said.

'Of course you do,' he said briskly.

'I can't help remembering those terrible days and nights when I grieved for my baby. I endured by hanging on to hope against all reason. Suddenly reason is on our side and I can see the way ahead. Thank you, Father.'

'We'll get there, Nina, I promise you.'

Chapter 50

Dressed in a beaded Valentino black lace cocktail dress, I arrived at the Monte Carlo casino and, as usual, made first for the cashier and then the bar. A month had passed since I had begun to spend alternate nights there, waiting to be 'discovered'. Sooner or later I'd meet the big boys, I felt sure. I knew that large sums of dirty cash were laundered regularly through gambling.

Officially, management claimed that their strict surveillance made it impossible for the Mafia to get a hold on the casino, but the truth was that this tiny state's closeness to Italy made it particularly vulnerable. With luck I, too, would be pulled into organised crime.

Armed with a glass of tonic water, I entered the hallowed fount of Monaco's wealth and marvelled at the way in which the panelled walls, thick velvet curtains and chandeliers had achieved a hushed, almost holy atmosphere. Sounds were muted and controlled, and the guests reacted by assuming grave, awed expressions as they placed their bets. I paused at the main roulette table where a swarthy-faced, hawk-eyed man was peering intently at the revolving wheel as if it had some special secret that he ought to be able to unravel.

To me, gambling is strictly for fools. I have never felt any sort of fascination for roulette, baccarat or *chemin de fer*. If I win I feel guilty, and if I lose I feel much worse, so either way there isn't much in it for me. Nevertheless, I had to wait there, so I hung around, placing an occasional bet, admiring the winners, trying not to look too bored, and continually reminding myself that I was Naomi Hunter. Naomi might have thrilled at the opportunity to pit her wits against mindless chance but for me it was one big yawn.

I stood at the roulette table for half an hour, watching the swarthy-faced man become increasingly desperate as he doubled up on his system. Chronic gamblers often believe in the fallacy (called the Monte Carlo doctrine) that each particular play in a game of chance is not independent of the others, and that a series of outcomes will balance out in the long run by exact, alternate possibilities. Most of the gambling systems are based on this fallacy, and I knew that casino operators were happy to encourage them.

I glanced at my watch. It was half past ten. A long night lay ahead. To pass the time I decided to try my hand at the black-jack table and chose the one with the highest stakes, Naomi style. Here, at least, I could memorise the cards as each hand was exposed.

When we were three-quarters of the way through the pack and I had memorised the used cards, the croupier dealt me an ace, the last. Ah-ha! I bet ten thousand francs and waited for my second card. It was a jack. As the croupier placed his cards face up on the table, I scooped up my winnings. I managed to win three more times, before taking a break. Of course, the winnings belonged to Father, since I was gambling with his money, and for the same reason, had I lost I would have felt obliged to replace it. Clearly I was in a no-win situation. What a bore.

It was then that I stepped back, collided with a spectator and spilt my drink on the floor.

'Let me replace it,' he said, rubbing his wet sleeves. 'I was crowding you.'

What was that accent? Russian?

'My clumsiness. Sorry. Please don't bother.'

'I insist, Ms Hunter. I'll see you on the terrace. It seems quiet there tonight.'

He was tall and swarthy, with reckless, renegade brown eyes and an air of wild sensuality, which had something to do with his flared nostrils, wide full lips and high cheekbones. Cossack roots, I guessed. He was barely forty, but his air of studied contempt gave the impression of someone older. As he walked towards the bar I noticed the grace and economy of his movements. He was fit and very strong, and he reminded me of a leopard stalking its prey.

I walked out on to the terrace and shivered with the damp breeze. I peered over the balustrade at the mist-shrouded waves breaking on the rocks below. The casino lights created evanescent rainbows in the spray. I watched, fascinated, and did not hear the man's return, but suddenly he was there beside me, standing far too close, invading my space with his intimate, powerful presence.

'You were drinking tonic water, but I know that you like martinis. Perhaps you felt you had to keep your wits about you. Don't worry. With me you can relax, Naomi. I want to be your friend.'

An Arctic bear could not have growled more deeply or more menacingly. Or so sexually. I hastily banished that last thought as he handed me a dry martini with an olive. Was he one of the recent influx of high-rollers from Russia?

'You've made me curious. Who are you? How do you know my name?'

His smile was extraordinary. It began with a beam of warmth in his eyes, then his face crinkled into a patchwork of lines, and finally his lips opened in a rueful grin.

'I am Sergei Romanovitch, jewellery designer by profession, but nowadays I seldom have the time. I want to put some business your way. Naturally, one does a certain amount of – shall I call it research? – before offering a partnership. By the way, Naomi, that is a very beautiful necklace you are wearing. Where did you get it?'

'It was a gift from someone who was once very close to me.' I almost choked on the words.

'He had excellent taste. Those are flawless diamonds with perfectly matched black star sapphires, a gift that is both rare and beautiful. Will you come with me to my home? I live nearby. I have matters that I wish to discuss with you but only in private.'

'What could be more private than here? No one wants to brave the cold. I can't say I blame them. Hard to believe it's August.'

Sergei took off his blazer and put it around my shoulders. There was a pleasant, musky smell about it, intermingled with lemon verbena. He was wearing a tightly fitting short-sleeved black T-shirt and through the thin fabric I could see the strength in his arms and neck, rock-hard muscles that only years of intense physical labour could have produced.

'You'll be cold.'

'Please! I was reared in Siberia. I can't talk about this project here, Naomi. I have to show you certain objects.'

'Perhaps tomorrow evening. Yes, why not? I'd be delighted. Right now, I'm tired.' I wanted to check him out first.

'I'm sorry, Ms Hunter, but it must be tonight. Drink up. Let's go.'

I shrugged and smiled. 'Very well.' Sergei gripped my arm and led me through the casino to the car park, where he opened the door of a black Maserati sports car. Moments later we were gliding through the main street to the highway. When we reached the summit of the ridge overlooking Monte Carlo, he turned off near the Monaco Sports Club into a cul-de-sac. Wrought-iron gates slid open and we drove towards a house that took my breath away. It was built on a large rock, so that the granite slopes seemed to be part of the architecture. From below, in the car's headlights, it looked like a series of jutting ledges and angles in a deep reddish ochre, reminiscent of Corsican cliffs. The garage doors slid open and we swept in. As they shut silently behind us I experienced a sense of fatalism. I had entirely lost control of the situation.

Chapter 51

The house was extraordinary, like its owner, I decided, as I followed Sergei on a tour of the ground floor. The design was open-plan, with each large room set at a different level and angle. The décor was plain white, which set off Sergei's remarkable collection of Russian icons. The Persian rugs on the white tiles looked old and rare.

'Collecting icons is my hobby, Naomi. The one you are looking at is thirteenth century, from Constantinople. And this one is Siberian. I found it in a long-abandoned church. My biggest problem was discovering from whom I could purchase it. No one wanted to be responsible.'

'So what did you do?'

'Naturally I stole it. Our country's heritage is leaving Russia by shiploads each week. Most of it is smuggled out through the Ukraine to Odessa, or via Hungary to the West. I was determined to have my share. In Russia, the genuine article is becoming increasingly hard to find.

'Let's get back to business. I brought you here to show you something. But first, what will you drink?'

'A martini would be lovely.' Drink in hand, I followed him around, admiring his superb collection of icons, but when we reached his bedroom and he led me inside, I had a moment of misgiving. Icons instead of etchings? It was a typically male bedroom, I noticed, Spartan in its furnishings.

Sergei was striding across the room. He pushed a large mirror along sliding rails, revealing a door to a walk-in safe. I followed him into a small anteroom without windows, lined with glass-enclosed shelves. Six costly pieces of jewellery were displayed on velvet boards. I held my breath as I bent over the beautiful gems. Sergei handled each piece reverently as he told me its history.

'So you deal in antique Russian jewellery?'

'At present, yes. This one is not Russian.'

He picked up a three-stranded diamond and ruby necklace from its black velvet board. Something about the careless way he handled the piece made me suspect that it was worthless, but I was entranced at the beauty of the design and the flawless craftsmanship.

'So where's the original?'

He chuckled. It was a deep-throated, pleasant laugh. 'So you know a fake when you see one.'

'Not really. Sorry to disappoint you. I guessed from your irreverence.'

'I was right about you, Naomi. You're very smart. I want you to go to Prague and buy the original. Use your client's cash to buy the necklace. You will pay for it in cash and repay your client in a cheque drawn on a famous London auction house. We split the profits and you get your laundering fee as well.'

I turned away from Sergei, pretending to admire a necklace, but I was trying to hide my shock.

'What makes you think that I . . . ?'

'You've been hanging around the sports club and the casino for a month, touting for business. You've had a few nibbles but that's not what you're after. You're waiting for the big boys, I assume. I need their dirty cash, too, but for quite another reason – as temporary capital. I'm cleaned out and I have to start again. I want to propose a deal, Naomi. I can put you in touch with someone very big indeed.'

'There's only one problem, Sergei, I don't know what you're talking about.'

'For instance,' he said, ignoring my denials, 'I am a close friend of the once-lovely Carla Maria Lo Bello. She's the long-term mistress of Vittorio Cassellari. I have noticed you talking to her often. I know that you are trying to make her acquaintance. You never will without my help.'

'Why are you spying on me?'

'Naomi, don't be so naïve. It's public knowledge that you conned the American public out of millions and got away with it. No trace of the cash was ever found. Now here you are, touting for business. The rumour is that you launder money very effectively. I need you and I can help you. Let's make a deal.'

So Father had been right when he'd insisted that eventually the criminals would come to me. At that moment I experienced such a strong sense of fatalism that my arms came out in goose-pimples.

'So trust me, my lovely Naomi,' Sergei was saying. 'Carla does. She'll begin in a small way to test you. Maybe a million dollars, which would be enough to purchase this necklace. A dealer in Prague is anxious to sell it to me.'

'Why should I want to share my business with you?'

'Because you need to launder your dirty cash and I can provide you with the means to do this. And then there's

301

another reason. The profits will be large and I will give you a share. This particular necklace might fetch double what we'll be paying for it. I'll pay you ten per cent of my profit.'

'Since I have the cash, Sergei, why do I need you?'

He laughed. 'You have no idea what's wanted, what's available or what to offer. How about it, Naomi?'

His deal made sense. It was a good method of laundering cash because my client would receive a *bona fide* auction-house cheque.

'Sergei, I'll try to use you as often as I can, but it won't be all the time. I have to change my money routes all the time. You must understand that. And there's another problem. I could be cheated by the dealers. I wouldn't know a fake from the genuine article.'

'I'll teach you, Naomi. Trust me. We'll start now.'

Sergei wanted to tell me about all the lovely pieces currently on offer in Europe, their background, their design, and their past and present owners, but it was almost three a.m. I leaned back in a roomy settee and momentarily closed my eyes. Then I felt Sergei shaking my arm.

'Come, Naomi. I must take you home.'

I stirred as I felt his lips on mine. Then sanity returned. Pushing him away, I stood up, suddenly wide awake, glaring at him.

'I was merely sealing our bargain. From now on I promise to behave. You're dying of boredom. I'll drive you back to your car.'

I laughed. 'I was tired, not bored, Sergei. No hard feelings, I hope.'

As he drove me to my car near the casino I marvelled at my awakening libido. I had to admit that Sergei was a fascinating man.

Chapter 52

Once again I was on hallowed ground, my alternate-nightly beat, the coveted Monaco Sports Club where Europe's super-rich let down their hair: oil sheikhs, film stars, noblemen and billionaires, rubbing shoulders with crooks and scavengers. The club fees would keep working family for years, I guessed, but who cared anyway? Such thoughts were as out of place as sensible shoes or hot dogs for supper, and certainly not in keeping with Naomi Hunter's acquisitive nature.

I struggled to be her, inhaling the balmy air with a sense of satisfaction, noting the heady scent of costly perfumes, rare wines, vintage brandy and Havana cigars, the latter drifting up from a group of men in earnest conversation by the swimming pool. The bar was pandemonium, everyone trying to out-shout the neighbouring groups, so I wandered outside to the terrace.

I, too, was one of the scavengers, an ex-con touting for business, but this was my night for feeling optimistic. Sergei had spoken to his friend.

My background was perfect. I had a lovely apartment overlooking the harbour and the Princess Grace Rose Garden, a brand new Mercedes convertible and a wardrobe full of designer clothes. I knew I looked the part of successful woman in my midnight blue shot silk Dior dress with a deep *décolleté* and a long flared skirt. It suited me and set off the emerald necklace given to me by Wolf one birthday.

I lingered, watching Monaco's lights strung like jewels around the bay. In the yacht harbour, the masthead lights swayed to and fro with the gentle swell.

Returning to the crowded lounge, I found an empty settee in a corner beside the window. The black-clad waiter shot me an inquiring glance, so I ordered a martini.

A tall man, so black that his features hardly showed in the muted lights, stalked into the room and flung himself into a chair. He was a government minister from Zaïre, flamboyantly rich from dubious sources. Trailing him came two beautiful lookalike Spanish tarts, who serviced the rich clientele at a bayside hotel. He had dressed them alike in yellow designer dresses with petal skirts. The yellow brought out their swarthiness and the ultra-youthful design made them look *passé*. Business must be bad at the hotel, I thought, watching their uneasy efforts to please their bored patron.

A group of Saudi Arabian oilmen dominated the centre of the room with noisy argument. Further off, I identified an American pop star, an actor, a British banker, a French estate agent and an Italian mobster. The remainder were unknown to me. Given time I would probably get to know most of them, but time was the one requirement I did not have.

I was startled to see an imposing, once beautiful woman making her way towards me. She was wearing a black satin suit in the latest cut, which accentuated her willowy figure. In contrast, her hair was a thick mass of white waves caught up in a chignon. She looked around haughtily and, moments later, hovered over me with a slightly hostile look in her imperious brown-black eyes.

'May I join you?' She sank gracefully beside me, bringing a scent of Joy perfume and the rustling of nylon as she crossed her shapely legs. Late sixties, well groomed and preserved, a beautiful figure despite her age, probably Italian.

I smiled cautiously.

Her hand touched my arm lightly as she said, 'I hope you don't mind . . . I may seem a little impertinent, but I'm sure I've seen you before somewhere. It bothers me. Haven't we spoken here once or twice? You are always alone. You must be a stranger to Monaco. After all, a girl with your looks could not remain alone for long. Perhaps I should introduce you to some of my friends. Tell me, what is your name, my dear?'

'Naomi.'

'Naomi Hunter? Ah, I thought so. I read about you in the newspapers a little while ago. I was hoping that I was right, because . . . Well, it may sound a little odd, but I need your help.'

Thank you, Sergei. I tried to hide my excitement.

She nodded to the waiter. 'What are you drinking, Ms Hunter?'

'A martini, very dry, with an olive. And please call me Naomi.'

'And you may call me Carla. I like your Western habit of using first names. So refreshing. My name is Carla Maria Lo Bello. I live in Rome some of the time, but I move around. The truth is, I'm restless.'

When she smiled her eyes lit up and she looked much younger. She used her hands a great deal when she talked and they were well shaped, with long, tapered fingers that sported a number of rings. 'My dear, I've decided to throw myself on your mercy. The truth is, I have fallen upon hard times. You see, darling,' once again her elegant hand touched my arm, 'I have this lover. This wonderful man, and we have been, well, what do you say in English?'

She paused long enough for me to feel obliged to supply the word.

'Intimate?'

She burst out laughing. 'Well, yes. That part we take for granted, darling. But we have also been a family. Always . . . From Monday until Friday. For weekends he went to his lovely mansion in Sardinia where his two sons and three daughters live. It is the daughters I fear the most. They hate me. Three months ago this man of mine suffered a heart-attack, which has confined him to his Sardinian estate.' She turned her lovely eyes on me and did her best to assume a tragic expression. She failed. 'Naturally, being an honourable man, he wishes to see that I am secure.'

'Naturally.'

'Now that he is incapacitated and might even die, he is afraid that his children, who have taken over the business, might discover the amount that he is settling on me. After his death they might even try to recover it. For that reason he wants me to find a way to cover up this gift. How do you say . . . ?'

'Launder the money.'

'Exactly. You are a straightforward woman, Naomi. I have faith in you. Would you consider doing this for me, for a small professional fee?'

'My small professional fee is five per cent.'

I heard her sigh softly – with relief or regret?

'How much is involved, Carla?'

'A million dollars for the first payment.'

'And how will the donation be made?'

'He will pay the dollars in cash. Of course, there may be more later.'

'I'm sure I can help you, Carla. It's easy enough to turn the cash into a cheque in any currency, but it's more important to make it look as if you raised the money yourself.'

'That is what my lover says.'

'I'll put my thinking cap on. When would you like me to help you?'

'As soon as you're ready.'

'One last question. What is your lover's business?'

'Is that important?'

'It would help me to make my plans.'

'He has many interests – shipping, wholesaling, distribution, many products.' She waved her hands to take in the whole world. 'I will have the cash sent to you. Give me your address before you leave. But meantime . . . Come, my dear. I will introduce you to some of my friends.'

I gave her my card as she led me outside to the group of men beside the pool, who hardly bothered to be polite. They were talking about currency speculation, a subject on which I could hold my own. While I tossed in a few comments I was analysing their faces, trying to memorise their names, faces, accents and mannerisms, which would enable Father to find their true identities. Perhaps his paid waiter informer could supply their fingerprints, too.

Each one of them looked like a caricature of a crook. Strange, that. Why did police always look the part, too? And undertakers. Really weird. And what was it that branded my companions? Their predatory eyes? Or their prematurely lined faces? What if they weren't Mafia at all, but my bankers? In that unlikely case I would transfer my account elsewhere, I decided, smiling inwardly. I hung around until one a.m., and then I went home.

No matter how late it was, I always reported to Father by e-mail. Lately my letters had been full of fears that our plan wasn't working. Father always gave the same answer: 'Be patient, we'll soon get a nibble at the bait.' At last I had a major breakthrough to report. I was about to launder a million dollars for Vittorio Cassellari, the man who had put a million dollars into Wolf's Sarajevo account. We were getting somewhere at last.

Chapter 53

It was past midnight and I was on my usual beat, trying to look as if I enjoyed gambling. I was pocketing some chips when a waiter arrived with a martini on a tray.

'I didn't order anything.'

'It's from the gentleman over there. He sent this note.'

I looked up and saw David. He winked and looked away, and so did I, but one brief glance was enough to send my blood racing, my eyes smarting, my hands trembling. I fumbled to open the note. 'Must see you. Come to the yacht basin. There's a boat called *La Belle*, which is moored at the quay immediately below the bus stop. I'll wait there.' I scribbled, 'Yes!' in bold letters across his note. 'Give him this,' I told the waiter.

Nothing could keep me from him. I walked through the night, unhurried, loving the smell of the fresh sea mist. At midnight in Monaco only the mountains are dark. Lights twinkle under a midnight blue sky.

Why was I hurrying to meet David? Perhaps because I was sick of hungering for him and all that that entailed: nights of longing, dreams of lust, the passive state of being without love, where every joy turned tasteless. Enough was enough.

David was crouched on a pile of planks. He stood

up and caught hold of me, pulling me roughly against him.

'You'll never know how much I missed you, Naomi.'

The dear, familiar sight of him, and the urgency of his desire, took me by surprise, releasing a flood of feelings. Once again I was running out of control.

'Hurry,' he muttered, clutching my hand, and leading me up the gangway. He pulled me into a cabin and lifted my skirt in clumsy, fumbling movements.

'I nearly went crazy when you left. Oh, God. I love you, Naomi.'

'I love you. I love you,' I heard myself muttering.

As we wrenched off our clothes, I gasped at the force of my passion. We fell back on the bed, arms wrapped around each other, lips and tongues mingling, bodies intertwined.

'Naomi, darling.' David groaned.

Then it was over and I was lying on his shoulder loving the sight of him, wishing the night could last for ever. I felt sad about all the lies that were still to come and the gulf that must always keep us apart.

Oh, God! Help me! Help me! There's no place for love in my life.

I lay there for a long time, clutching David, not wanting to speak, knowing that we had reached a point of no return.

We made love several times that night, but dawn came bringing sanity. I felt damp and soiled and furious with myself. I must have gone crazy. I sat up and glared at him. 'Let's forget this ever happened.'

'No, never.'

'It's only lust. You don't know me. I don't know you. This mistake won't happen again.'

310

We frowned at each other. I had never seen David look so tense, or so concerned. He kept running his hands through the stubble of his hair while shooting despairing glances my way.

'Are you sure that's what you want, Naomi? For how long can you keep lying to yourself? Why can't you accept that you love me?'

'I'm going to shower. Where's the bathroom?'

David pointed to a quilted pink door with gold thread all over it.

'Enough to make you puke at this time in the morning,' I grumbled. For the first time I looked around.

'Ugh!' The room was huge, the bed enormous, and the décor was pink and gold and very glitzy.

'The bed was soft, wasn't it?'

I could see that *La Belle* was an ocean-going yacht that must have put someone back several millions.

'Whose boat is this?'

'Belongs to a Syrian merchant who hires it out, so it's mine for a while.'

'And how did you find me?'

'Not very difficult. I have good banking contacts. I picked up your trail through a credit check put out by the garage where you bought your convertible. Then I thought, Where else would you look for criminals laundering their cash? I was going to wait every night for a week. This was the second night.'

'Well done,' I said flatly.

In the bathroom I considered my position. I had been extremely foolish. It would not happen again. I scowled at my reflection in the mirror. Stupid bitch! What was more important? My son's life, or an affair? My eyes blurred with tears until I couldn't see my reflection.

I took a scalding hot shower, then drenched myself

with ice-cold water, needing to punish myself and drive out weak emotions. Pulling my comb through my hair, I tried to work out why everything had gone so horribly wrong. The cabin was empty, and I was about to leave when David returned with two mugs of coffee.

'Oh, thanks. Just what I need. David, listen, I think I'm getting somewhere. Things are moving at last. A woman called Carla has asked me to launder a million dollars. She's giving me the money in cash tonight. The night before last I met Sergei Romanovitch at the casino and I went to his home. He wants me to team up with him, using the money I'm laundering to buy Russian antique jewellery for auction in Britain. This way Carla will get a cheque from the auction house in return for her dollars.'

'Carla who?' David said sharply.

'Carla Maria Lo Bello. Sergei says he doesn't have the cash to buy the pieces on offer right now. Also that dealers would put up their prices if they recognised him.'

'What if he's setting you up with fakes, Naomi? The seller could be his accomplice. This woman is linked with one of the biggest drug dealers in Europe. Try to think what he would do if you lost his money. It's a phoney story and you're being conned. Don't do it.'

'I must.'

'You're a hard-headed, stupid bitch. Is there any point in begging you not to?'

'None at all, David. Sooner or later I'll meet someone who will lead me to . . . to the man who set us up.'

'But are you any better than him, Naomi? You're breaking the law daily and kidding yourself that it's permissible. You look so angelic,' David said moodily, 'but the truth is, you're the opposite. You work for the worst kind of criminal and you stand to make a great deal of money out of it.'

'In this case the end justifies the means,' I said primly.

'The end never justifies the means,' David retaliated. 'How much will you make from this deal with Sergei and Carla?'

'That's my business.'

'I'm making you my business. I'm determined you'll see the error of your ways. Do you wonder that I lose faith in you, Naomi? So many lies, so much secrecy, and so much profit as the end result.'

'God, David, you can be so self-righteous. I've told you, nothing counts except finding . . . our Anselmo con.'

'For revenge?'

'That, too.'

'To recoup your losses?'

'You could put it like that.'

'You have no possible justification for what you're doing.'

One of these monsters is bringing up my son, David. I need to get him back fast. That's enough justification for me.

'Yes, David, I believe that I do.'

'Is revenge that important?'

I hesitated. 'Yes, it is.' I was tempted to blab out everything and implore him to help me, but common sense prevailed. 'David,' I began tentatively, 'if you knew that I was breaking the law because of something bad that had happened to me, would you help me do what I have to do?'

'Not if it means helping these criminals to launder their money.'

'Isn't love unconditional? Wouldn't you break the law

to help me with something that was far more important to me than my own life?'

'No.'

'But, David, suppose you had a child and it was threatened. Wouldn't you do anything at all to safeguard your child?'

'Forget it, Naomi. I would never give in to criminal demands.'

'You have a lot of learning ahead, David.' I felt sadness weighing me down.

David saw my expression and this made him angry. 'Don't try to bamboozle me. It's greed that's driving you – greed for money, greed to get back what Anselmo owes you. You even believe the comforting lies you tell yourself. I've told you that I'll find this man for you. If it's revenge you want, I promise you he'll get a life sentence. Leave it to me. You can work with me, if you like.'

'No, David. You shouldn't have come looking for me. Just keep away.'

David insisted on walking me to my car to say goodbye. I drove away, confused by warring emotions: shame, guilt, compassion. If only I could confide in David, but our priorities differed.

David's fears of Sergei proved unfounded, although I had a few uneasy moments when I paid over Carla's one million dollars to an antique jewellery dealer in Prague to purchase the necklace and other chosen pieces. There were no hitches and I caught the next flight to Heathrow, wearing an exquisitely designed diamond and ruby necklace and the rest of the jewels, once owned by Princess Marie of Hesse.

Sitting in the first-class cabin, I gnawed my fingernails and promised myself in future never to lay out more than

I could repay, just in case I was stuck with a fake while Sergei and the dealer absconded with my client's cash. Little and often would be my guideline.

A neat Scotch did nothing to dispel my anxiety. Had I been conned? This arrangement with Sergei seemed too good to be true.

The jewellery fetched four million pounds when the items were auctioned. I took my five per cent fee, which included my cut of Sergei's profits, and netted me almost fifty thousand pounds. Not bad for two days' work. The cash went into the kitty to help reimburse my father.

The following evening, when I gave Carla her cheque drawn on a leading London auction house she looked very satisfied.

'My lover has other amounts for you to work on,' she whispered, leaning close to me so that her hair brushed my cheeks and I inhaled her marvellous perfume. 'Ten million dollars this time. Can you handle it?' Her eyes were glittering with anxiety.

'Child's play, dear Carla.'

'But, Naomi, please remember that he is a very exacting and efficient man. One might call him a perfectionist. He comes down hard on those who fail him. Don't come unless you are sure you can cope.'

She looked concerned, but did she really care, I wondered?

Sergei had been right. Her lover's name *was* Vittorio Cassellari and I was to spend the weekend at his Sardinian stronghold.

Chapter 54

A sensation of floating interrupted my light sleep when the Air France Boeing began its slow descent towards Sardinia. I watched the emerald green island materialise out of the afternoon haze, and the dark blue shimmer of deep water change to turquoise as we descended over offshore shallows. Moments later we were circling the western beaches with their rash of millionaire hotels, splendid residences and the blue oblongs of swimming-pools. We raced through the dark green mountains of the interior and saw the late-afternoon sun flash its gold on bright snakes of tumbling rivers and streams. The sun had already set on the other side of the mountain and we swooped into violet shadows to land at Elmas in Cagliari.

'Hope you enjoy your stay, ma'am,' the immigration officer said, with a smile. I only had hand baggage so I went directly to the barrier where a small crowd awaited the passengers. A placard said, 'Naomi Hunter, welcome.' It was held by a stocky uniformed driver with a lined leathery skin and an anxious expression.

'That's me. Here I am.'

'Welcome, welcome. I am Alberto.' He gripped my hand with his calloused one. I winced, handed over my bag since he insisted, and allowed him to take my arm and guide me through the crowd to the exit. The car, a black Mercedes SL600 with shaded windows, was parked in a non-parking zone and an airport official was guarding it. He saluted as we arrived.

As we moved off along the hibiscus-fringed beach road towards the north, I leaned back and made an effort to put my fears aside and enjoy the beauty of the scenery. I could not help admiring the magnificent mansions we passed. Night fell, lights twinkled, but the rush of air was still warm and scented.

Alberto remembered the old days and told me about them at great length. 'There were no houses or pools when I was a boy. You could put up a shack near the beach and live happily for next to nothing. All this has changed. Well, that's modern life for you, eh? There are advantages and disadvantages.'

Alberto was in a philosophical frame of mind and his heavily accented voice droned on and on.

Forty-five minutes later we turned on to a hairpin road up a steep slope into a thickly overgrown indigenous forest, and almost total darkness. Eventually we emerged on to a plateau overlooking the forest and the sea. Before us was a gate set into a tall, razor-topped wire fence where an armed guard with a Rottweiler scanned the car. Moments later the gate swung open, and then came the scent of tobacco flowers, honeysuckle and lemon verbena as we drove through a shrubbery towards distant twinkling lights. We passed floodlit tennis courts, where a group of youngsters were watching the players, and an Olympic-size pool shimmering turquoise.

The exterior of the Cassellari home was painted rosy pink and it looked gay and busy, with overhanging balustrades and nooks where flowers and cherubs lurked. There were sun blinds in deep red, and huge pots of scarlet and rose bougainvilleas. The french windows were flung open and I could hear someone playing Mozart proficiently. I had not envisaged a home so full of charm and gaiety, and my Calvinistic conscience rebelled.

I had hardly emerged from the car when I was welcomed with extraordinary deference by an old-fashioned, black-clad housekeeper. She led me through corridors hung with art treasures to a large room overlooking the pool.

'You'll have a magnificent view of the sea and the forests in the morning,' she said, in a thick provincial Italian accent. 'I'll leave you to change. Would you like me to run your bath?'

'No, thanks. I'll take a shower.'

'Shall I unpack?' She eyed my one suitcase with disapproval.

'I'll do it.'

'Plenty of drinks here. I mix you a gin and lime, perhaps? Or a cocktail?'

'Really, I'm fine.'

She gave up with a sigh. 'Dinner is at eight. Signor Cassellari insists that everyone be on time, yes? The dining room is down the stairs and on the left.' She gave an odd little curtsy and left.

I took a fresh lime from the fruit bowl, squeezed the juice into some tonic water and sat on the balcony, looking out across the pool. The moon had risen, a huge golden orb poised over the sea and its paler reflection.

'Naomi Hunter,' I murmured. 'I am Naomi Hunter. I am tough, resilient, grasping and very, very good at my job. I am about to enter the inner sanctum of one of the world's most powerful drug dealers, but this does not faze me. I am only concerned with how much I can charge Cassellari when he puts his deal to me.'

When I felt sufficiently competent to play my role, I hung up my dress and had my shower.

Vittorio Cassellari met me at the dining-room door. He was a small man with a glaring simian resemblance. His hair was thick and black, clipped black hairs protruded from his ears and nostrils, his eyebrows met across his lined, leathery forehead and the lower part of his face was obscured by a trim black beard. The most striking thing about him was his eyes, which sparked energy and a fierce intensity. They were dark brown, set against unusually clear whites, and they did not seem to belong to his face.

'Ah, Miss Naomi Hunter, my dear young lady. What a pleasure to meet you, and what a surprise.' His deep voice had hardly a trace of an Italian accent. He took my hand and led me into a room decorated in blue and white that was as costly as it was tasteful.

'How can anyone be so lovely and yet so wise?' he purred. 'Carla has told me of the wonderful help you gave her. Likewise you saved me considerable embarrassment. You will learn that I know how to show my gratitude. There is a great deal of business that I can put your way, my dear, but we will talk about these things later.'

The guests were on the terrace, except for one man, standing on the other side of the dining room pouring himself some sherry from a cut-glass decanter.

'Come and meet Miss Hunter, Boris,' Cassellari called, catching hold of his arm.

The man turned abruptly, and I found myself staring into the steely eyes of the intruder who had shot Brigit, a lifetime ago, in my Constantia home.

'Naomi, meet Boris Borovoi.'

Leaden-footed and with my mouth set in a rigid

grimace, I took a few steps forward and shook his hand. His eyes narrowed and his mouth flickered into the faintest smile.

Would he remember what I had looked like almost two years ago? Our encounter had lasted for only a few minutes, but I had never forgotten an agonising second of it. Of course, it had been dark and the room badly lit.

'How do you do, Mr Borovoi?' I said. Were his eyes mocking me? No, surely it was my imagination. If he had recognised me, would he give me away? Of course he would.

'We've met before, Miss Hunter. Do you remember?'

'I'm not sure,' I heard myself stammer.

Now Borovoi would tell Cassellari who I was. And then?

'And where did you two meet?' Cassellari sounded like a kindly old uncle, but I knew otherwise. I shuddered.

'At the casino a few nights back. I must congratulate you on your winning streak, Miss Hunter.'

He turned away, leaving me to wonder why he was protecting me and for just how long he would continue to do so.

Chapter 55

'This way, Naomi. Everyone is on the terrace. It's delightful there at this time of the evening.' Cassellari led me towards the doorway, before turning to speak to his housekeeper.

I hesitated. The aroma of old sherry and pure malt whisky, the lavish surroundings and Carla's beautiful dress and jewellery nauseated me. It was so absolutely wrong. Here were the dregs of the human race. I looked away to where the moon's ghostly reflection glittered and shimmered. A few lights flickered from yachts passing the island. Exotic, scented shrubs and tobacco flowers filled the balmy air with their fragrance. There's no justice in this world, I reflected bitterly.

Carla smiled, looking delighted. She beckoned me to her. I was surprised that she was there, but why? Hadn't I long since realised that her story was fiction? Tonight she looked regal and beautiful, in a black brocade dress with a high neck and puffed sleeves. As if in a dream I crossed the terrace and shook hands as she introduced me to everyone present, but my concentration was flawed. Listening to the small-talk, I felt alienated. Their world of parties, fashions, first nights and constant travel was foreign to me. Besides, Borovoi's face had brought a vivid recall of that terrible night when we last met. I could not banish the image of Brigit dead in a pool of blood.

Borovoi had been described by Major Barnard as a former agent of the KGB, but since the Soviet system had collapsed, he might well be a banker, I reasoned. Or perhaps he was part of the move to link Russian and European drug interests. Or had he remained with the Russian police? In which case, was he still after Wolf? And did that make us allies? No, I decided emphatically.

'You shivered.' Borovoi touched my arm. 'You feel cold, Miss Hunter. We are up in the mountains where it is always cooler at night. Australians are used to something hotter, yes? Come inside. With your permission, Signor Cassellari . . .' Taking me by the arm, he led me inside.

'You look frightened,' he muttered close to my ear. 'Don't be. We are in each other's hands, Mrs Möller. I am trying to sell Cassellari half of my bank. Do you understand me?' He hung on to my arm and gave me a slight shake. 'Pull yourself together.'

I glanced over my shoulder, but the others were still on the terrace. 'You know who Wolf Möller is and you know why I am looking for him, Mr Borovoi. If I help you, you must help me.'

'I agree.'

His fingers were digging into my arm. 'Remove your hand or it's no deal.'

'That's better!' His low chuckle of derision annoyed me as I moved away from him. His bank? What bank? And did that mean that he was no longer connected with the Russian police? Nothing made sense.

Everyone followed us inside where we clustered around an antique ebony table while Carla fussed over her seating plan. She was opposite me, on Cassellari's right while I was on his left. Next to me was Cassellari's son, mis-named Angelo, who looked to be around forty with his hard, toffee-brown eyes, fancy moustache and greasy, crinkly hair. He had his father's features, which was his misfortune.

Beside him was Frans Aquitton, from Panama. I studied him surreptitiously, memorising his name and face: blue eyes too close together, under a thatch of ash blond hair, and a disappointed mouth. At the end of the table was Carla's son, Paolo, who had inherited his mother's beauty, but who had a warmer, more sensuous appeal. Beside him, and almost opposite me, sat Cesare de Sica, an Italian of around Cassellari's age, whom I guessed was his financial adviser. A man to beware of. I noted his shrewd grey eyes, pinched features and mobile lips; he smiled often, spoke little, but missed nothing. Lastly, there was Borovoi.

It didn't take long to realise that I was being tested. If I passed I would be accepted into their circle. If I failed, God help me. Cassellari welcomed me ostentatiously, proposing a toast in my honour. 'I think you've all heard of Miss Naomi Hunter, sitting here beside me, who walked off with a cool four million under the eyes of the FBI and the bankers. You're probably wondering how she did it. Well, so am I. Tell us, Miss Hunter, how did you evade the charges?

It was a question I had anticipated. 'Don't explain, don't complain,' was my motto. Cassellari and company were waiting for my reply.

I smiled with more confidence than I felt. 'Really, it was a mistake. There was no such crime. Just a story the press created. The FBI soon realised this and let me go.' Pleading innocence was a good line. Hadn't everyone in Pollsmoor constantly whined that they were not guilty?

'All kinds of people made this mistake, Miss Hunter,'

Cassellari muttered. 'American philanthropists to the tune of four million dollars, for instance. That's why the FBI investigated.'

The kindly-uncle act was becoming an effort.

'You can talk freely. You are among friends here, my dear.'

I should be so lucky. There was a long silence. I had to speak. What else could I do? I stumbled through a naïve explanation of something that had never happened. 'The police could never find a link between the Friends of Unita scam and myself.'

No one seemed to find that very satisfactory so I embroidered slightly. 'The FBI's main problem was that there was nothing to link me to the cash. They could not follow the trail. They had no idea who was the final recipient, nor who set up the many bank accounts the cash travelled through.'

Borovoi cut in. 'Miss Hunter does not wish to divulge her home territory,' he said. 'No doubt she chose her bank's domicile with the utmost care. Had she chosen any one of the private-enterprise banks in Russia, the authorities could not have discovered who set up the account, or how much it contained. Ah-ha! I can see from your eyes that I'm getting warm, aren't I, Miss Hunter?'

I nodded, and tried to look annoyed. Borovoi had saved me again. Why?

Dinner was excellent, lobster bisque, pâté, roast partridges and lastly cream puffs, but I was too tense to eat. I toyed with my food, wishing I could escape from Angelo's foot nudging mine, followed by his groping hand under the tablecloth.

While Borovoi was boasting about the advance in

democratic banking in his country, Angelo took the opportunity to whisper in my ear, 'You are very beautiful, Naomi. You turn me on. Perhaps we could meet later?'

'It could never get that much later.'

His foot continued to caress mine.

The conversation increased as the wine flowed, and it was about money, naturally, and the increasingly high cost and risk of laundering it. The guests asked me every question they could think of, other than the one they wanted to ask: *Was I for real?*

'Our problem,' Cassellari began, looking at me, 'is that the rules of the game are changing. It's getting tougher daily. Some of our best agents are in prison. Men with powerful legitimate businesses. Even some brokers on the New York stock exchange. Four were sentenced recently, getting from twenty to forty years.'

'It's a powerful deterrent,' de Sica admitted. 'No one wants to take this kind of risk. The FBI have been following a paper trail all over the States and Europe, even to wire-tapping some big institutions.'

'Take the case of René Laurent, one of our associates,' Cassellari added. 'His cash went round the globe several times over a period of months, but the Feds caught up with him.' He seemed to lose track of his story as he paused to gaze at me suspiciously.

'Yet you, Miss Hunter, outwitted all of them,' Angelo muttered.

That was my cue to present my credentials again.

'You need the financial know-how. That's all. The problem is, almost everything that's documented can be traced. In a way, it's similar to a fox hunt. The fox can circle the globe several times over many years, if he has the stamina, but what's the point of this if he leaves a trail that can be followed by the hunters, *ad infinitum*, as your associate did? So what does our fox do? He breaks the trail as often as he can. He wipes out his scent by lying low in a river, or paddling upstream, or even climbing a tree. The latter is not always successful, of course.'

'If it were only so simple,' Paolo answered, looking more contemptuous than amused.

'What do you know about it?' Angelo snarled at him, and not for the first time. There was no love lost between them, I realised. Instinctively I knew I had to do better than this.

'Banking, finance and broking services leave a paper chain and that's how these men get caught. Let's imagine we're talking about a million-dollar cash payment. In South Africa, for instance, you could walk into the Gold Coin Exchange and buy a million dollars' worth of gold coins with cash, no questions asked, and carry the gold out in a suitcase.'

'You'd need some help,' Paolo muttered.

'True. But there's no computer on earth that can trace your footsteps as you emerge from the Exchange. You have broken the paper trail. You can take your coins anywhere without fear of being traced. The point is to break the trail as often as possible – change the amount, change the currency, change into other mediums. All this can confuse the enemy totally.'

I seemed to be winning at last. De Sica was nodding his approval and, after a cautious moment of watching his adviser, Cassellari followed him.

'Another safe bet is to move into one of the many private banks that have mushroomed in Russia, or an adjacent East European country. Pakistan recently legislated to protect the secrecy of foreign cash deposits. In Czechoslovakia there are a hundred and fifty new banks and no fraud squad. Poland offers a stable background, a convertible national currency and the right to transfer money abroad.'

Borovoi was looking agitated. He said, 'Gentlemen, the whole of Eastern Europe is one big launderette, so why are you trying to launder your money in America? Surely it's the most dangerous place in the world for you.'

I had to back him. I had no alternative.

'My own choice, Signor Cassellari, is Russia. More than a thousand new private-enterprise banks are ready and able to launder your cash, no questions asked. Total privacy guaranteed. How else can they get foreign currency?'

'Getting the cash to Russia is dangerous.' Cassellari shot me a disapproving glance. 'Sooner or later there will be a leak and then *whoof*! That's the end of it. Armed robbery is the norm there. Then there's the danger of the bank going bust, or defrauding you . . . Add to that the incredible power the police have to wipe out crime, and specifically money-laundering, and you have a situation fraught with danger.'

'The real winners will buy their own bank and set up a courier service from a sea port to the bank. It's easy to send your currency on your own ships to Odessa. Two hundred thousand US dollars is sufficient to register and set up a bank in Moscow. Personally I would advise a partnership with a Russian national. I could do some research for you, find the right man for the job.'

'Brave words, young lady. We'll see if you succeed with our first joint attempt.'

I caught my breath. Had I passed?

'You must understand that the risks are high, Signor Cassellari. Half of your business undertaking consists of money-laundering. It's just as important as earning the cash. I would expect a ten per cent cut. Double my normal rate.'

Angelo's foot stopped pressing mine as he anxiously scanned his father's face.

Cassellari burst out laughing. 'You really are an ambitious young woman, Naomi.' He used my first name unexpectedly. 'I'll discuss terms with you tomorrow.'

As I gazed into his implacable eyes I felt a tremor of anxiety. Outsmarting Cassellari would lead to early annihilation. I would hand everything over to Borovoi at my first opportunity, but meantime use the project to probe his connection with Wolf.

Cassellari's hand reached out and squeezed mine. After a short pause, I squeezed back. He gave me a look in which admiration and suspicion were equally matched. I felt only the latter as I beamed back at him.

By the time I arrived for breakfast, Borovoi had left. I felt relieved enough to swim and play tennis with Angelo, which kept him at a safe distance. The rest of the weekend was spent discussing strategy and terms with Cassellari and de Sica. We finally agreed that I would test my ideas by ferrying ten million dollars from Odessa to Moscow, depositing the cash in a suitable free-enterprise Moscow bank.

On behalf of Cassellari, I would begin negotiations to purchase a licence to set up a bank, or otherwise find a suitable partner for him. He and his advisers would follow when the legwork was done. If I succeeded I would receive 5 per cent of the final deposit. The air was potent with menace as they warned me against failure.

I flew back to Monaco, feeling satisfied that I was moving towards my goal at last. I had time to kill, something I liked to avoid for my thoughts went back to

Nicky and the last time I had seen him, looking so excited about the trip to the airport and his coming birthday party. 'Mummy's on the way, Nicky,' I whispered. 'God willing, I'll find you somewhere in Russia.'

Chapter 56

On my first evening in Odessa I explored the beautiful old city, much of which had been built in Venetian times. As I stood on the famous Potemkin steps, looking down on the harbour crowded with ships of all nations, I wondered if Nicky lived somewhere in the Ukraine. I was thrilled to think that I might be in the same country as my son, but also frustrated that I did not know where to start looking.

Soon I began to worry that I might miss the call while I was sightseeing, so I returned to my hotel room, determined to stay there. I sat there for days, until eventually I began to have trouble sleeping. I would calculate the odds of ever finding Nicky. Around dawn I would be exhausted enough to take a brief nap and then the whole sorry routine would start again. I had my food sent up, and I spent my days hugging the television set. My only relief from gloom was plugging the modem of my lap-top into the telephone and sending my nightly report to Father and reading his latest letter to me.

On the sixth morning, I woke with a start to hear the telephone ringing in a strange, high-pitched tone. Where was I? After a split second of panic I remembered and groped for the receiver.

'Hello.'

'Naomi Hunter?' It was a woman's voice.

'Yes.'

'The address you want is sixteen Petrovka Street. Ask for Mikhail Voy-na-Kry-na. Come at once, please.'

The name sounded more Slav than Russian. I wanted to ask her how to spell it, but an impersonal click terminated the conversation. I wrote it down phonetically, hoping I had remembered the sounds correctly.

At last! But why had it come on a Saturday? The implications made me feel uneasy for it meant that I had to guard the dollars until Monday when I could get them to the bank. But at least I could swing into action.

It was a lovely August morning, still cool, with a white mist drifting over the sea. Dressed in holiday gear, jeans, a T-shirt and sandals, I emerged from the hotel and called a taxi. It was sheer heaven to get out of my room and drive through the city. I decided that to arrive luggageless in a taxi at a dockside location and then to leave shortly afterwards carrying two heavy suitcases would be to invite the suspicions of the driver, so I paid off the driver a block away.

I hurried along the shabby Petrovka Street adjoining the dockside until I found number sixteen, a dingy basement apartment. A man hovered in the doorway. He was stocky and weathered, with cunning blue eyes, fleshy lips and straw-like hair.

'I am Mikhail. Come in, come in.' He pulled me through the doorway by one arm and gazed nervously up and down the road before shutting the door. Then he shook hands solemnly. 'And you are?'

'Naomi Hunter.'

'Welcome, Miss Hunter. We must be quick.'

A nervous, swarthy woman, whom I took to be his wife, hovered behind him, watching contemptuously as he handed me two British-made, scuffed and much-labelled suitcases. I insisted on inspecting the contents, and only closed the suitcases when I had assured myself that the hundred-dollar notes amounted to five million dollars per suitcase.

'Okay, that's fine. Well done. Would you please call me a taxi, Mikhail?'

'There is no telephone here.'

'What about your neighbours?'

He shook his head. 'My job is finished. Now it is your turn.' Unbelievably he walked out of the room, leaving me with his wife.

'Madame, where is the nearest telephone?'

She scowled. 'No English.' That was a lie. She had spoken to me on the telephone, I recognised her voice.

She opened the door and slammed it behind me, clearly glad to get rid of me.

I felt nervous as I set off towards the nearest bus stop. I had heard that armed gangs patrolled the streets demanding protection money so that taxi drivers were never without a spare carton of cigarettes, a bottle of vodka or a few dollars to pay off their 'protectors'.

There was no sign of a taxi or a bus stop. It was past eleven, the August sun was reaching its zenith and I was sweating profusely as I climbed a steep, cobbled road towards the city. I had just stopped for a rest when a police car drew up beside me.

'Madame is a tourist?' the police officer asked, in passable English. From his expression I assumed that tourists and delinquents were virtually indistinguishable.

'Yes. Where can I find a taxi?'

'To where?'

'To my hotel – the Cosmopolitan.'

'May I see your passport and visa?' He examined

my papers with intimidating interest. 'You have been in Odessa for five days and yet you have no sun-tan. What have you been doing with yourself?'

'I was ill – food poisoning.'

'Madame, please get into the car. I shall take you to your hotel via a trip to Headquarters. There is a militia post nearby.'

This was the moment I had dreaded. I climbed into the back seat while my suitcases went into the boot. I had to do something.

'Listen!' I leaned forward to mutter in his ear. 'Is your radio switched off? Can I talk? You must know that there's no law against bringing Western currency into the Soviet Union. Your country needs dollars. I have ten million dollars in those suitcases. It is my job to deliver the cash to the Moscow headquarters of the International Bukharin Bank as soon as possible. I'm sure the bank would be grateful for your protection.'

'Madame is a courier?'

'Yes, that's it exactly.'

'That is not a suitable occupation for an unarmed, defenceless woman. In Russia there are no laws against depositing large sums of cash as yet, but we prosecute money-launderers. It is for you to prove that this is not drug money. I will take you to your hotel and we shall telephone the director of the bank after I have examined the contents of the suitcases.'

Clearly he was a policeman, not a mugger, but some of the police were corrupt, I knew. What if he stole the money? My life wouldn't be worth much when Cassellari found out.

I leaned back trembling. I hadn't told Borovoi about this trip, sensing that the fewer people who knew the safer I would be. Mikhail's refusal to call a taxi had been suspicious. Perhaps he had notified the police. But since he, too, was a courier, what possible advantage would that be to him?

Ten minutes later, when Inspector Anatoli Zhoglo had introduced himself and confirmed that the suitcases contained exactly ten million dollars, I became convinced that he, Mikhail and Borovoi were in some way connected. He asked me for the name and telephone number of Bukharin Bank, called them and asked to speak to Borovoi.

The conversation was brief and I wished I could have understood what he was saying. When he put down the telephone, his manner had changed altogether. 'Miss Hunter, I have decided to help you.'

Help me? He was busy helping himself, taking bundles of dollar notes from the suitcase.

'This is my fee of five thousand dollars to which the bank president has agreed,' he told me, without a trace of shame. 'He will pay five again in Moscow. I am your bodyguard, Miss Hunter. The *mafiya* know about the consignment. You are not safe. Please pack your things, we are moving elsewhere. I'll wait downstairs.' He gave a funny, old-fashioned sort of bow, but he could not control the gleam of satisfaction in his eyes.

As soon as he had gone, I called Borovoi.

'He is an inspector in the local police force,' Borovoi told me. 'I've just checked. He was tipped off. An inspector would never undertake traffic-patrol duties. We don't have much choice since he has threatened to arrest you for money-laundering unless I pay for protection. There are always dangers in this business.'

Inspector Zhoglo took me to his home for the weekend. He lived in a cottage by the sea on the outskirts of Odessa. His wife, Theresa, provided me with marvellous meals and his two children, a boy of twelve and a girl of ten, took me swimming daily in a pretty, sheltered bay. I was not surprised when 'Uncle' Mikhail came round for a drink the following evening. It was going to be all right, after all, I decided. I couldn't wait to reach Moscow. It was almost time for Boris Borovoi to tell me all he knew about Wolf.

Chapter 57

———~~⌒⌒~~———

The head office of Bukharin Bank was located in a four-storey building just off Pyatnitskaya street.

The lift was being repaired and we climbed four flights of stairs, only to be stopped by heavily armed, grim-faced security guards, with an air of authority reminiscent of KGB days. They examined my identification papers.

The central doors swung open and a fresh-faced young man strode out and shook hands with me and then Zhoglo.

'You have the money?' he said, in almost accentless English.

I nodded. 'I am Naomi Hunter. I was expecting to meet Mr Borovoi here.'

'Come in, come in. My congratulations. Mr Borovoi won't be long.' He went to take the suitcases, but Zhoglo held on to them.

'Only to Borovoi. Those were my orders,' he growled.

We passed into a hastily thrown-together office, with new, steel-legged beige Formica desks, brand new wall-to-wall carpeting, and some hideous modern reproduction paintings propped against the walls. The chairs were still flecked with plastic packing material, the pictures were still covered in plastic sheeting and the desks were thick with foam dust. Clearly everything had been delivered a matter of hours earlier. Instant banking. Nevertheless, tracklights on the ceiling, a large piece of modern metal sculpture, a Persian rug, plush sofas, and vases on occasional tables, plus several computers and rows of telephones showed that, give or take a couple of days, this bank would look impressive. Cassellari would be satisfied if and when he came here.

Even the secretaries looked newly acquired, kitted out in smart clothes and shoes that could only have been bought in Western-currency stores in Moscow. I guessed they had received lessons in smiling, and clearly they were finding this an effort, although they kept trying.

As we stood around, Borovoi came bounding in. 'My dear Miss Hunter.' He enfolded me in a crushing embrace. 'Welcome, my dear, and congratulations.'

'This is Inspector Anatoli Zhoglo, my guardian angel. He would like to get back to his job as soon as possible.'

Zhoglo was paid, clapped on the shoulder and shown to the door, with the promise of further assignments in the near future.

'An interesting young man. We could do worse than to ask him to set up our courier service. He has the contacts, the experience and the nerve. Now, Nina, let's get down to business. If you had let me know you were coming I would have been ready.'

I laughed. 'I can see we weren't expected for a couple of days. Never mind the furniture. Have you received your banking licence yet?'

'Everything is completed, Nina.'

I exhaled with relief.

It was all over bar the negotiations. Borovoi wanted too much for the half share of his bank and my negotiating skills were weakened by his insistence that he was protecting me and my real identity. His were weakened by the fact that I knew he had put this bank together in a matter of weeks for an outlay of two hundred thousand dollars for the deposit and licence, plus the rent of the building, the renovations, the furniture and any bribes he had been forced to pay to speed up the red tape. Finally we settled for a million dollars. The other nine million would be Cassellari's first deposit.

I made out the deposit slip, which was signed and stamped, but I wanted much more than this. I knew that the most dangerous criminal activity in the new Russia was taking place inside the thousands of newly established private banks. They were under-capitalised and they offered hardly any protection to the depositor. Like this bank, many were fronts for criminals.

I listed my demands to Borovoi, talking and writing at the same time. 'First, I need to have this deposit slip signed by you, as director of this bank. Next, I want a personal letter from you acknowledging receipt of the cash. Then I need Cassellari's share certificates for half of the holding company. Have you set up the holding company yet, Mr Borovoi?'

'Nina, Nina, relax. You can't foresee every hazard. Cassellari's best security is his reputation for instant annihilation of those who try to double-cross him.'

He grinned and slapped his knee, rather overdoing it, I decided, as I pushed the handwritten list towards him.

'Now, Mr Borovoi, no doubt you will remember a certain night in Sardinia. We made a pact. I have kept my side of the bargain, so start talking.'

'You are going to be disappointed, Nina. I have no idea where or who Wolf Möller is.'

My disappointment felt like a physical blow. I was shocked and it showed.

'You know that Möller was a brilliant industrial spy. When I was in the KGB I was his controller, but I never saw him. That was how Möller operated. The initial contact to supply us with American research came from him. He always operated by telephone and later by fax and e-mail. In the early days he used many go-betweens, but we never met the real man. He spoke Russian perfectly and I assumed that he had spent at least a part of his childhood in Russia, perhaps Siberia.'

'But, Mr Borovoi, if you were in the Russian police and Wolf was working for you, why didn't you know where to find him when he disappeared?'

'When the Soviet system broke down, his network did, too. We were unable to get funds to him to meet our obligations, so he diverted the last shipment to the Chinese. He was well paid by them, I assume. I wanted to prevent this at all costs, but I was too late. My dear, I was sorry to hurt you. Until I saw the picture of your baby son I thought you were his accomplice. You must understand that we wanted that shipment badly.'

I decided to ignore his apology.

'Major Barnard told me that Wolf was picked up by a Russian fisheries search trawler.'

'Not true, Nina. He has never allowed himself to be seen by any Russian agent. He has always been a freelancer, trusting no one. We believe that he made his way overland to Cairo.'

With my baby? Had Nicky survived the journey? I began to feel sick. I had to get out of there. I stood up and forced myself to shake his hand. 'Not much information for all the work I have done for you, Mr Borovoi. You owe me.'

'I acknowledge my debt.' He bent and kissed my hand

flamboyantly. 'Please call me Boris, Nina. We are friends, aren't we?'

Never, but I would keep that to myself.

'I need the papers I listed for Cassellari. I'll remain in Moscow as long as it takes.'

'You are most welcome, Nina. Perhaps I can show you Moscow's special attractions?'

I longed to say no, but sitting in my hotel room would not help me to find Wolf.

I remained in Moscow for ten days until I had the documents I wanted. True to his word, Borovoi took me to the ballet and opera, and wined and dined me generously.

Before I left I contacted Inspector Zhoglo again. He had already planned a fast courier service to transport incoming cash to the bank's Moscow headquarters. He and Borovoi deserved each other, I decided, and left them to sort matters out.

I flew back to meet Cassellari in Sardinia, knowing that I had done a good job for him. He and his henchmen were delighted with their acquisition.

'You've done well, Naomi. There's plenty more work for you now that you've proved yourself to be reliable.' Cassellari paid me my cheque with a flourish.

I decided to take my courage in both hands and press for some of the answers I badly needed. 'Have you thought of trying Sarajevo?'

'Where the hell is that?'

Not a good start.

'Bosnia, for God's sake.'

He scowled at me.

I marvelled at his strange standards. Murder was acceptable, but blasphemy was not.

'There's a civil war there, Naomi.'

'That's why the interest is so high. Drug money is financing their civil war. They offer very high interest rates, but you have to invest for a two-year period.'

'Forget it! I like my cash to be around when I need it.' Cassellari's scowl became more intimidating as he lost patience with me.

I persisted. 'Does the name Trans-African Foundation mean anything to you?'

'No.' De Sica shot me a strange look, part suspicion, part irritation.

'How about Wolf Möller?'

'What is this? Twenty questions? Can we get down to business, Naomi? I want to discuss another approach. I don't want all my cash to go through Russia. There's another five million that needs to be processed. How do you suggest we play it this time?'

I sighed. I hated this work. It was both boring and dangerous, involving long periods of waiting around for moments of intense danger, but I had to play along with Cassellari. He had a link with Wolf.

'I want to find a new approach. I'll come back to you in a couple of days' time when I've sorted something out. Okay?'

It was sheer bliss to get back to my Monaco apartment, which lately had been beginning to feel like home. I switched on the computer and keyed into the incoming e-mail. There was a message from Father.

Dear Nina, An American private detective has been inquiring about you in the village. He obtained photographs of you from the local rag, the one taken of you when you won the women's canoe marathon. He has not had the nerve to come here yet. With Wattling's help, I traced his employer – it is David Bernstein. Co-currently, the Mossad are making inquiries about you through official channels. I've asked Wattling to release certain info revealing your connection with British Intelligence. It might be an easier role for you to play than that of a con, in view of your friendship with DB. Clearly DB suspects that you are not NH. Hopefully, he'll pick up the intelligence connection without learning of the South African fiasco. Take care. Love, Father.

I switched off and remained sitting there, thinking of David. I knew that I loved him, but my love was tinged with shame and guilt. I was afraid he would condemn me for my past. 'Afraid' was too weak a word. I lived in fear of losing him when he found that I was, or had been, Möller's wife and that I had systematically cheated him from day one. If only I could confide in him.

Chapter 58

For me, far worse than the hazards of money-laundering were the compulsory periods of fun. I had to be seen to be enjoying my supposed wealth, or else I would be suspect. I divided my leisure hours between lazing in the sun in Sardinia and the Caribbean, attending Monaco's rich parties, or gambling my wealth away at the Monaco casino.

Every wasted hour hurt me, but I never knew just when I might come face to face with Wolf. I knew there was a link between him ans Cassellari. So I kept in with Cassellari's friends, jet-setted to concerts in Tel Aviv, or wherever, moving with the fashionable set, simply because it made sense for Naomi to do this. They were hell-bent on extracting the most satisfaction out of every minute, living each day as if it were their last, a realistic assumption, I guessed. Invitations poured in for dinners, for private cinema shows, which I avoided for they were both blue and boring, and for parties at all times of the day and night. Most of Europe's rich and titled had holiday homes around the Mediterranean coast and they all gave or attended parties as a nightly ritual. I had to be seen, and I had to keep looking for Wolf, so I became a nightbird, allowing myself no more than an hour at each party and moving on until just before dawn.

A once ravishing but now ravaged dark-haired woman surged towards me triumphantly. 'My dearest Naomi,' she bellowed. Who was she? Where was I? Panic surged for I could not remember.

Glancing uneasily at my pocket diary lying open in my handbag, I saw that I was in the lavish Monaco home of Princess Nabila, a recipient of massive oil revenues. She shook hands, put her log-heavy arm around my shoulders and led me to her guests. One by one I met a team of robed negotiators and two beautiful film starlets, tagging along for a profitable ride.

Uniformed stewards were helping the guests to roast beef, turkey, caviare, oysters, crayfish and a vast selection of salads. I wasn't hungry, so I nibbled a crisp. The trick was to be seen to be there but to leave privately. Fifteen minutes later, I was driving to the next ordeal.

It was three a.m. and I was walking to the car park, feeling pleased to be leaving the last party for the night, when I bumped into Sergei Romanovitch in the dark.

'Naomi, my sweet, I'd given up trying to find you. This is fate. Come back with me, I have some urgent work for you.'

I sighed inwardly as I was shepherded to his car.

Half an hour later I sank into an easy chair in Sergei's office. 'A martini before we get to work?'

'At four a.m.? No, thanks. Anything soft will do. When do you sleep, Sergei?'

'Hardly at all. I don't need much sleep. Are you going to pass out on me again?'

'Soon, but not just yet. Let's be brief.'

He handed me a drink and smiled intimately. 'I have a very comfortable bed.'

'Thanks, but no. Let's get on with it.'

'Follow me.'

He led me to his office. Flinging open the door, he pointed to three icons hanging on the opposite wall. 'Feast your eyes, Naomi. I like to gaze at these while I work.'

There were places for four icons, but the third was empty. Vertical in shape and larger than usual, they depicted the story of the birth of Jesus. They were lovely, but cracked with age. The first showed Joseph and Mary begging for a room at the inn. Next was the newborn baby lying in a manger and the wise men offering their gifts. After the empty space, came the fourth, a gruesome image of Roman soldiers slaughtering infants. The colours had darkened with age but the deep crimson blood was vivid enough.

'As you can see, one is missing, Naomi. Can you guess which one?'

'Possibly the flight to Egypt.'

'Exactly. These icons are early fourteenth century, originally from Constantinople, created as a series of panels to separate the Eucharist from the congregation in a church that has long since disappeared. To have the entire set would be to own a priceless treasure. That is one of the reasons why I asked you here tonight. I suspect that the missing icon has been discovered in Turkey, of all places, and bought by a Moscow dealer. I want you to go to Moscow and purchase the icon on my behalf and bring it back to Monaco.'

'Why don't you go yourself?'

'I cannot return to Russia right now. I'm a wanted man. That is partly why I need you, quite apart from your amazing supply of dollars. Also I'm well known to this particular dealer. If he were to recognise me, the price would rocket. He would understand how much I long for his icon and how valuable this collection would become if I were to own the complete set.'

'But why me? There must be dozens of people you could send. I'm sorry to sound doubtful, but for starters I don't speak Russian. Secondly, this is not my field. It's hardly a money-laundering operation.'

'I disagree. I'm sure that Cassellari is keeping you busy. I don't suppose he wants to trust the Russians with all his cash. I'm sure he has asked you to be . . . well, versatile.'

'You must be psychic, Sergei.'

'One of my customers is a director of a rich American art gallery. They will pay a great deal for the complete set, and what could be more useful to you than their cheque? So, please, can we get down to business?'

'What exactly is your connection with Cassellari?'

'It's confidential. Naomi, listen to me.' Sergei put his hands on my shoulders and held me at arm's length, staring intently into my eyes. 'You're being too inquisitive. In our line of business one asks only what is strictly necessary.'

'It's strictly necessary for me to stay alive.'

'Come and sit here beside me.'

I guessed he would make a pass, but I had not anticipated his sudden attack – or my own reaction. A sharp pull propelled me into his arms. His mouth forced my lips apart while his arm pulled my right leg over his knees. I struggled, but thrilled to the soft stabs of sexual awakening that pierced my stomach. His hand tightened around my back as he pulled down the shoulder strap of my dress, revealing my breast. He was too strong to push away. Holding me back, he pressed his lips on my nipple. For a moment he tugged like a baby. The sensation let loose poignant memories as well as a hot flood of lust. I struck out at his face angrily. He let go abruptly and sat up.

'How dare you?' Salvaging my modesty, I hauled up my dress.

'No bra. I like that, and your nipples are large. You have nursed a baby, Naomi. I like that, too. I find you very exciting. I would like to paint you.'

'You've made a bad mistake, Sergei. I keep my life tidily in different compartments. I never mix business with sex.'

'So which one shall we choose?' He was laughing at me.

'I'm leaving.'

'I'm sure you'll suffer as much as I.' He took an envelope out of his pocket. 'Here is your air ticket. The art dealer's name and address, a hotel voucher and travelling expenses in dollar traveller's cheques. Take a taxi to the dealer, don't try to walk around that area, particularly when you are transporting the icon. Our usual arrangement. Is this agreeable to you?'

I nodded.

Sergei flipped open the desk drawer and drew out a full-colour drawing of the icon. 'The missing icon looks something like this. Don't let the dealer fob you off with the wrong one. D'you want to take this with you, or can you memorise it?'

'If you give me a few minutes. Did you draw it?' I took it to the light in the corner and studied it.

'Yes.'

'You're very good. Are you sure these are the correct colours? You're not guessing about the subject matter, are you?'

'Yes, to your first question, and no, to the second. Naomi, I'm sorry. I mistook your signals. Am I forgiven yet?'

I gazed at him, watching his lips curl in a sardonic smile while his eyes gleamed with amusement.

351

'As long as you remember that there's no place in my life for that sort of thing.'

'I swear I never heard anything so sad.' Now he was openly teasing me.

He drove me to my car in silence. He parked and came round to help me out. His arms encircled my waist. Unexpectedly his lips brushed mine and came down hard on my neck as he bit me.

'I shall dream of you tonight, Naomi.'

I pushed him off angrily, feeling absurdly conned and knowing I'd been caught off-balance again.

Chapter 59

I leaned back against the lift wall, thankful to be almost home but conscious of a web of pain tightening around my forehead. I stared at my haggard reflection. I'm getting old, I decided.

The lift doors opened and I hurried to my apartment fumbling for my key. I wanted nothing more than to throw myself on to my bed and shut out the world for at least eight hours, but as I swung open the door I saw that someone else had got there before me. There were clothes on the back of the chair and David's wiry black hair lay against my pillow. He sat up, instantly wide awake, and stared at me silently. How fierce and remote his brown eyes were. I leaned over him, kissed him on the mouth and smothered him with light kisses. 'Thanks for coming.'

He thrust me away and pushed himself up on one elbow. 'Where the hell have you been?'

'For God's sake, David.' I straightened up wearily and took off my jewellery, laying it on the dressing-table piece by piece. Then I took off my shoes. 'How did you find out where I live?'

'You let me walk you back to your car, didn't you? Anyone can get your address from your car registration number.'

'Sometimes I don't think.'

'You don't have a talent for subterfuge, that's all.'

David climbed out of bed and caught hold of my arm, twisting me round fast. He was naked. Caught off-guard I swayed and felt myself caught up and pulled tightly against him. Despite my annoyance, lust took over. David tugged at my clothes, looking anguished, wrenching the straps of my dress over my shoulders.

'I knew you were being pawed. I sensed it. Who the hell is he, and what did he do to you?'

'Hey, ease off, David. What's with this jealous husband act?'

'Why are you flushing?'

'Leave it alone, David. Sergei made a pass. That's all.'

'Liar!' He pushed up my chin with his thumb. 'Look at your neck. And look at your breast. He bit you here. Damn you, Naomi.'

'Sergei was over-confident. Perhaps because he's a very sexy man. When he realised I was seriously unwilling, he gave up.'

'Why is it that I can't believe you?'

David tried to pull my dress down and it tore. I heard the pattering of tiny beads hitting the dressing-table as the fabric ripped.

'Oh, God! What are we doing to each other?'

I caught his head in my hands and pulled him to me, needing his lips on mine, feeling a surge of love that threatened to drown me, pushing my fingers through his hair. He picked me up and carried me to the bed. Thrusting my arms around his neck and my lips on to his, my libido burst through the bars I'd erected, blotting out reason. I craved all of him, his sex, his body, his mind and his love. I think I told him all of this, perhaps

I even said, 'I love you,' in the next turgid hour. Or was it two?

Did David know who I was, I worried later, as I lay on his shoulder. I was sure that he suspected the truth. What would he do if he knew for sure? Perhaps there would be some compensation in being able to be myself again. It had been an incredible strain living a lie, acting the role of the hard-boiled, selfish, grasping Naomi, for whom men were mere stepping stones to her ambitions.

'Darling?' His voice disturbed my thoughts.

'I thought you were asleep, David.'

'I thought you were, too, until I heard you sigh. I can't sleep much lately. I never stop worrying about you, night or day. It's a permanent ache in my guts. I can't carry on like this.'

'That's tough.'

'Stop trying to pretend you're so hard-boiled. You aren't like that, and you aren't fooling me.'

I scanned his face in the cold dawn light, noticing now he had changed. Sadness and caring showed in his eyes and in the tight lines around his mouth. I couldn't help him. He had fallen for a person who didn't exist.

'You don't have to do this. Listen to me. I'm almost there. I'm catching up with your enemy. Another month, perhaps. That's why I've taken leave. I have my old contacts in the Mossad and my computer. I'm only hanging around in Monaco in case you need me. Once and for all, understand that I'm on your side. Work with me. Tell me who you really are. Trust me.'

'You're coming down hard on the wrong girl, David.'

David looked exasperated. I watched him run his hand over his stubbly hair, frowning until his eyebrows met in a thick black line.

355

I felt sad for him, but I knew I could not trust him to put Nicky's welfare first, even before his desire to bring Wolf Möller to justice.

'I don't trust anyone,' I told him, and watched his eyes narrow with anger. He got up and dressed.

He picked up his car keys, then paused in the doorway.

'I suppose it's only natural that you've become paranoid after what you've been through, but I think you ought to know who your friends are. Don't be such a damn fool, Nina.'

I felt glad when he had gone. I was wrong to have loved him. I had to keep my mind free from emotional clutter in order to find my child. Nothing else mattered. It took a few minutes before I realised that he had called me Nina.

Chapter 60

❦

Just before dusk I landed at Moscow's Sheremetevo international airport. The air was cool but not cold, and a shimmering silver twilight lay around the birches and pines of the surrounding woods. It was so calm and peaceful, not even a whisper of a breeze stirring the branches. That great Russian space was all about me, perhaps because the terrain was so flat. No plane took off or landed while I waited in the bare reception hall. The silence gave an impression that I was far from civilisation.

I had long since discovered that Russians never smile or laugh unless something extraordinarily funny occurs, and certainly never for politeness, but I am always depressed by their dour indifference. They stamped my declaration form without glancing at it, and passed my bags without opening them, which cheered me. This was going to be an easy job, I felt sure.

Moscow, like Johannesburg, I discovered, has magic in its peculiar evening light, which transforms the distant Moscow skyline into a golden city, but the light fled as my taxi drew closer and I felt a pang of disappointment as we passed mile after mile of squat, ugly apartment blocks.

I had been booked into the National Hotel, which looked vaguely Victorian with the old-fashioned lamp-post right in front of it, although the travel agent had assured me that it had been built at the beginning of this century.

The driver led me past the reception desk to a special room for foreign tourists. I sat at a desk opposite a shabbily dressed but extraordinarily lovely woman, with auburn hair, the palest skin and gleaming amber eyes under a smooth wide brow. She handed me my keys gravely and explained about the hotel's rules and routine. At my request, she booked me for the ballet that night, which took her some time for she had to shop around for a ticket. Then she directed me to a dilapidated lift, while the porter followed with my bags.

My room was vast, and reminded me of Sergei's house, for the ceiling seemed much higher than any hotel room I had ever been in. Heavy dark velvet drapes hung over lace curtains. Crocheted doilies lay everywhere, even on the overstuffed chair backs, again reminding me of Victorian England. Who cared? I had enough space, a comfortable bed and a small but adequate bathroom. Shortly afterwards I discovered that the food was superb, so I was content to while away the hours until my appointment.

At eleven a.m. the following morning, I took a taxi to the address Sergei had given me. I was driven past the Museum of the Revolution, the Pushkin Museum, the Operetta, and the Tchaikovsky Concert Hall to reach the Maximov Gurov Gallery, which was situated near the Hotel Metropole.

My troubles began when Gurov produced icon after icon, none of which resembled Sergei's drawing.

After sitting there for an hour I was feeling distraught.

'It's not at all what I'm looking for. I have clearly explained to you that the icon must match my décor.'

Maximov Gurov, the art dealer, sighed. There was a

ook of the bloodhound about him, with his hanging,
bloodshot brown eyes, his soulful expression, his long
ace and leathery, sagging skin.

'But, Madame, it is both authentic and beautiful. It
nce belonged to the Tsar's family . . .'

The dealer's enthusiasm matched that of a tired tour
guide as he recited the icon's history. This was the twenty-
ourth icon we had viewed. Each item had been brought
rom the back, one at a time, unwrapped as lovingly as a
newborn child, and reverently placed on a stand.

'Hm! I'm sure it's rare, but as I told you, I'm no
connoisseur of icons.' I stared disdainfully at a striking
image of the Madonna, with a smile like the Mona Lisa's.
would have loved to be able to buy it.

'I'm looking for something costly to match my décor,
bottle green and purple. Those are the colours of my
oom.'

Rancour flooded his eyes, but he kept his voice even.
'Perhaps you need something to lighten such a colour
cheme,' he suggested tactfully.

'On the contrary, I want something to match it.'

'Well, I'm afraid I have no such item.'

I could see how much it was costing him to let me walk
ut with my traveller's cheques intact in my purse. By
now his eyes looked even more haggard and his fleshy
mouth sagged.

'It has to be expensive and exactly what I want, Mr
Gurov.' I was unwilling to fail on my first project. 'If you
ind something I'll be at the National Hotel until noon.'
glanced at my watch. 'My goodness, it's late. I must
o back and collect my things. I'm leaving today. Nice
meeting you, Mr Gurov.'

'Wait a minute, Miss Hunter. Let me think. Perhaps I
an still find a way to match your remarkable décor.'

I stared hard at him, but his face seemed devoid
of irony.

'Valya,' he called to his assistant, 'bring coffee for
Madame. This will take a while.' Presumably he'd found
the right colour scheme at last. I blessed Sergei for his
faithful reproduction.

Half an hour later Gurov returned, looking even more
nervous and dishevelled.

'Ah, Miss Hunter, come to the back, please.'

I held my breath and tried to look calm. There was the
selfsame icon that Sergei had drawn for me, in muted
bottle green, on a dark, shadowy, purplish background
with delicate touches of gold here and there. Although
Sergei had drawn a faithful reproduction of the colours
I was unprepared for the impact of something so beautiful
and so meaningful. The Virgin Mary, clutching the infant
Jesus, sat huddled over the donkey. Joseph's body language
expressed his fear and haste as they fled. I checked the
points Sergei had mentioned: a gold bell hanging from the
donkey's neck, and gold thread on the Madonna's veil, the
evening star and the new moon shining equally brilliantly
in a midnight blue sky.

It was exotic and desirable and I fell in love with it
there and then. With a start I pulled myself together. I
had probably upped the price considerably with my rapt
adoration.

The deal was quickly concluded in US dollars, a thousand below my ceiling. I felt pleased with myself as the
precious icon was wrapped and placed in the centre of
my suitcase, well cushioned with sweaters and a pillow
brought for the purpose.

I drove back to my hotel and deposited the suitcase at
reception. I had time for a little shopping, which always

addened me, for there was only my father and me to
shop for. Gazing into a toy-shop window I saw a robust,
grinning grizzly bear. Nicky would be four in exactly three
weeks' time. Did he still play with teddies? Did he still
play? 'Oh, God, let me find my child.'

I stood gazing at the toys, tears streaming down my face,
overcome with sadness for him and for myself. Would I
ever find him? I began to feel so cold. It was the strangest
feeling, as if a cold front had wrapped itself around me like
a snake and was tightening its grip. I shuddered. Hardly
knowing what I was doing, I walked into the shop.

It was the most remarkable bear, large and sturdy, with
bright intelligent eyes and thick coarse hair. Real bear's
hair, I was told. All the more reason not to buy it, but I
heard myself say, 'Please wrap it. It's a birthday present
for my son. I will give it to you one day, Nicky, I promise.
Even if you're much older, one day you will hold this bear
in your arms.'

I was still crying as I paid.

This was not madness, I told myself, as I hugged Mr
Bear and waited for a taxi. This was positive thinking.

Eight p.m. I had arrived at Sheremetevo airport well in
time to get my ticket and find something to eat. A pie
and some beer would do me nicely. Better still, two pies. I
felt cold and tense as I queued to get my seating card
and hand in the suitcase.

The booking clerk pushed a form towards me. 'Read
this, please.' She turned her attention to the computer.

It was a form listing items that were not allowed out
of Russia. I pushed it into my pocket, knowing that I
was breaking the law. But how else could I gatecrash
the *mafiya*? No doubt this was why Sergei sent me. If
Customs took as much care with passengers leaving as

they had on my arrival everything would be all right, reasoned.

On impulse I decided to take the bear as hand-luggage I watched my suitcase trundle off along the conveyor be with a sense of relief. Now I had nothing to do excep wait. I went to buy a paperback and find a restaurant.

It was almost nine when I passed through Passport Control. I felt drowsy from the beer and the warmth and happy to be going home. The passport official wa taking a long time. I frowned at him.

'Why the delay?'

He shrugged and looked away.

A Customs official arrived and took my arm. 'Pleas step into this office, Miss Hunter.'

I could hardly come to grips with reality when h marched me firmly towards an office behind Passpor Control. It said, 'Inquiries' in five languages.

'Please wait here.'

Since they had taken my passport I had no choice. Bu they had not taken my hand-luggage, which held m lap-top computer. I quickly plugged into the telephon and e-mailed Father telling him of my detention an my fears.

Half an hour later another official appeared.

'What's going on? I demand to see someone who speak English. I have a plane to catch. Do you speak English?'

'Please come this way, Madame.'

He led me to a room where three men stood waiting Perhaps they were Customs. A spot check? My suitcas lay open on the table, the icon was unwrapped and lyin on my clothes. Even at this hazardous time I could onl blink lovingly at it.

'It's so lovely, isn't it?'

'Yes. It is very lovely.'

I looked round at the man who had spoken. He had
ntered the room silently behind us. He was short, with
square head that had a flat top, from which a mop of
black hair sprouted. Light amber eyes peered from under
wide, domed forehead. For some reason his eyes made
me feel afraid.

'I am Colonel Andrei Trenzin. Good evening, Miss
Hunter.'

'Thank God you speak English. Is there a problem?
Could you explain it to me? You see, I don't want to
miss my plane.'

'This icon is the problem. It is not only lovely but it is
stolen and also unique. So unique, in fact, it is not allowed
to be taken out of Mother Russia, so you have broken the
law on two counts, as a receiver of stolen property and by
attempting to smuggle it out of Russia.'

'I bought it today. I simply walked into a shop and liked
. I had no idea of its background. I have the receipt and
description here.'

'But you did not declare it.'

'I didn't realise that I had to.'

'The form you were given at the ticket desk specifically
told you to list any works of art bought by you.'

'Look,' I said determinedly, 'I'm sorry I didn't read
the pamphlet. I'm a tourist, for God's sake. The icon
was for sale and I bought it. The dealer should have
warned me.'

'Where did you buy it, Miss Hunter?'

I hesitated. 'It was a shop fairly close to my hotel. The
receipt is in my bag. No doubt it will tell you the name of
the gallery. I saw one that matched my décor so I walked
in and bought it. I demand that you return my passport.
have to catch my flight. Keep the damned icon, but it
cost a great deal. I shall sue for the return of my cash.'

'That is out of the question. You will be taken int custody, searched, fingerprinted, formally charged an later questioned. These are very serious charges.'

'I would like to see the British Consul.'

'But you are Australian.'

'Nevertheless . . . I have contacts there. Meantime, won't answer any questions. I believe I have been se up.'

'At this stage I don't know if we shall involve foreig embassies. Come this way, Miss Hunter. I don't thin we need to handcuff you. After all, you have no plac to hide.'

My head was spinning and my heart hammering again my chest but I struggled to pull myself together and kee calm as I was escorted to the police car waiting outside

Chapter 61

My cell was bare but clean, and the small barred window, set high in the wall, enabled me to see daylight dawning, but after a night of anxiety my fingers were gnawed and I was exhausted with tension. I had no idea when they would charge me, or what they were planning to do with me. I hung on to the knowledge that Father and Wattling would swing into action to find out where I was and push for my release. The thought that David, too, would try to find me comforted me.

No one came or passed by. The building was silent. Where were the nightly cries and mad laughter that had vibrated through Pollsmoor? I reminded myself of how people used to disappear for decades in Russia. They could send me to Siberia and deny ever having heard of me. So far I had only seen the wardress who had brought my supper and accompanied me to the lukewarm showers. There was no point in trying to talk to her because she could not speak English.

At two p.m. the cell door swung open and the wardress beckoned to me. I combed my hair, grabbed my bag and followed her along the passage to a door where a guard stood on duty. He pointed to a bench along the wall and we sat down.

Another hour passed. My wardress was used to waiting. She slumped against the wall and fell into a trance-like state, her head lolling back, her arms folded on her lap. I fidgeted, crossed and uncrossed my legs, smoothed my hair with my fingers, shivered and pulled my coat tighter around me, while I examined every possible question that came to mind and reached no sensible conclusion. At last the door swung open.

The guard beckoned to me and I entered, squaring my shoulders. It was a large room with a huge Persian carpet and little else. A long polished table filled one end and two men were sitting there: Colonel Trenzin, who had arrested me at the airport, and another uniformed man who had been with him. He stood up and pulled out a chair for me, but I remained standing.

'How dare you hold me, Colonel Trenzin, without charging me, or allowing me access to a lawyer and the embassy—'

I broke off in astonishment as Boris Borovoi walked into the room, wearing the uniform of a police colonel. He nodded to me and sat at the end of the table.

'You are acquainted with Colonel Boris Borovoi, Mrs Möller,' Trenzin said.

'Please sit down, Nina,' Borovoi said. 'You're making me feel awkward. You don't need the embassy's help, you're about to be released. I'm sorry it took me so long to get here. You've had a bad fright. My apologies, but I was in Europe. I was called back to identify you after your arrest.' He nodded to Trenzin. 'Yes, she is definitely Nina Möller *née* Ogilvie.'

I slumped into the chair, feeling confused.

'So now you know my secret, Nina. I'm a colonel in the Russian state police. My job is to try to infiltrate local organised crime, mainly through their money-laundering operations, which is my speciality. My colleagues and I have set up this bank and, with your help, wooed Cassellari to join us. Unbeknown to him, his money-laundering operations will be under surveillance from now on. He is linking Europe's criminal gangs with those of Russia. Through him, we hope to infiltrate our own criminals. I know that this information is safe with you. After all, your position is as precarious as mine.'

I tried to look calm despite my intense relief. 'So why was I arrested?'

'Because of your own stupidity, Nina. Rule one of this game is never to confide a thing. Colonel Trenzin received a tip-off from an Israeli source that Nina Möller was in Moscow to purchase a certain rare icon for Sergei Romanovitch, but that your real motive was to launder a million dollars on behalf of a Sicilian gangster, namely Vittorio Cassellari. Would you like coffee, Nina?'

I was unable to speak. My blood was pounding in my head and it was hard to breathe as I tried to deal with the hurt and bewilderment Borovoi's words had let loose. I struggled to be calm enough to think. Three people had known why I was coming to Russia: Father, David and Sergei. Would Sergei ... ? No, he needed the icon badly. Besides, he had no idea who I really was. That left David.

'Tell them to hurry up with the coffee,' Borovoi said. Trenzin spoke rapidly to his assistant who left the room.

'I understand your motivation, Nina. You will stop at nothing to find your child, and in your position I'd do the same. But, rightly or wrongly, you've joined the world of international gangsters, laundering their cash and breaking the law.'

David's words. I leaned back and closed my eyes.

'Colonel Trenzin had the art dealer watched.' He sighed.

'I have informed my colleagues that you are infiltrating these organised gangs in the hope that you will discover the identity of Wolf Möller, who has kidnapped your son, and that you are liaising with British Intelligence and working with me.'

Borovoi broke off as a woman entered, carrying a tray full of steaming mugs.

'Here's your coffee, Nina. You look as if you need it.'

We sat in silence for a few minutes. Borovoi was watching me quietly. I guessed that he knew that he'd just tipped my world upside down. Could David do this to me? Had he? No, I didn't believe it. *Believe it, Nina. Wolf betrayed you, so why not David?*

'I hope you understand the risks you've been taking, Nina, particularly with Bernstein and Cassellari. Bernstein was in the Mossad. I doubt he's fully broken his links or his allegiance. After all, your father hasn't. Bernstein would never condone breaking the rules and you have put yourself in danger by liaising with him. Conversely, if Cassellari were to find out that you are the daughter of a British Intelligence chief you would be killed immediately. For safety, don't tell Sergei Romanovitch who you really are. Trust no one, except me.'

I was astonished that he knew so much, but on second thoughts felt I shouldn't be.

'I want you to keep me informed, Nina. Work with me, not Bernstein. He has different priorities from yours. I'll be in touch constantly. As for your money-laundering, I suggest you stay with a safe route that has been proved to work for you. Place the money in the Bukharin Bank. We will do the rest. I'm there to protect you.'

I exhaled softly. *But you own the bank, Borovoi, so you, too, are suspect since you are lining your own pocket at the expense of the state.*

There were so many loose ends. So many facts that
didn't tie up.

'There's something you must know. Möller has stolen
a great deal of money from Romanovitch and ruined his
reputation. When he finds Möller he will kill him. That
would not serve our purpose, which is to bring him to
trial. You must make sure that we find Möller first. Your
son will be returned to you the moment we find him. You
have my word on this. You will be in Monaco by late this
afternoon. Right now, the guard will give you your suitcase
and your toy bear. Is it for your son?'

I nodded, unable to speak for a moment.

'So we guessed. I don't mind telling you that it brought
tears to our eyes. Even policemen have hearts, Nina.'

I didn't believe him. I tried to push away my hurt and
concentrate on my triumph. Sergei had worked with Wolf.
He knew him. At last I was on the right track.

Chapter 62

On my arrival at Nice Airport I faxed David: 'Safely back. Meet me at my apartment at 9 p.m.' Then I collected my car and drove to Monaco, where I parked above the yacht basin.

Glancing at my watch I saw that it was almost nine. David would have left by now and I had at least half an hour to search his files. A party on a nearby yacht was in full swing, the guests' cars had caused a minor traffic jam and angry security men were trying to unravel the mess. As the guests sauntered up the gangway, their laughter seemed to intensify my lonely state. Had David betrayed me? I shrugged off the hurt. I was here to find out.

There was no sign of a guard on David's boat. Perhaps he had slipped off to the party. I mounted the gangway unchallenged and crept into the cabin David had converted to an office. Switching on the computer, I searched his documents.

Three new developments point to Latvia as Möller's domicile. First: the Land Rover purchased in Maun on the day Möller went missing with the Friends of Unita (FOU) millions, has turned up in Tel Aviv. A party of students returning from a Baltic tour contacted a local dealer to sell their vehicle, which has since been positively identified as the one bought by Anselmo in Maun. The students said they had purchased it in Riga shortly after their truck broke down. The Riga dealer claims to have bought the vehicle for cash some months ago from an unknown German tourist.

Second: a cargo plane, grounded in Sweden for repairs, was found to contain a parcel of diamonds, Tanzanite gems and emeralds believed to be of Central African origin. No one has claimed the gems, but they were air-freighted from Riga and addressed to an Amsterdam gem wholesaler who claims to have no advance knowledge of the parcel. They are being retained by Customs.

Third: a number of Krugerrands (one-ounce gold coins made in South Africa, and negotiable currency in many countries) are in circulation in Latvia, although no one seems to know their source.

Latvia! It made sense. It would explain a great deal about Wolf's background and his attitude to life. Excitement surged as the importance of David's research hit me.

I was not surprised when I saw my name heading a file. It contained a report from David's private detective, giving a CV of my life until the time of my trial, ending with the paragraphs:

A son, Nicholas, was born on 3–10–90 at the Kingsley Nursing home. Subsequently, Nina Möller reported that her child had been kidnapped by her husband. Father and child were traced as far as Walvis Bay, Namibia, but they have not been heard of since. Later it was learned that her husband, the so-called Baron Wolfgang von Möller, had been involved in fraud scams and industrial spying for the USSR.

Unable to discover the true identity of her husband, the SA authorities arrested Nina as his colleague, but *she served only eighteen months of her six-year sentence. While she was in prison, her father, Commander Ogilvie of Naval Intelligence, now a paraplegic, successfully applied to have her marriage annulled on the grounds of a false name and identity given by Möller. The Court of the Hague legalised Ogilvie's rights to the sole custody of her natural son, Nicholas Ogilvie.*

Father and daughter have been searching for the child ever since. Nina is believed to be using an alias, provided by British or Naval Intelligence, who confirmed that she has some viable link with them, but I can get no further information.

NB Under the circumstances one must assume that the criminal who impersonated Dr Anselmo is Wolf Möller, Nina's husband.

Keying to the next page I read:

Steps taken to extradite Nina Ogilvie.

October 9. Colleagues in the Mossad have formally applied for the extradition of Naomi Hunter to stand charges of . . .'

The boat gave a lurch and shuddered. Someone was walking up the gangway. I switched off and raced out of the cabin. I hid in the store and heard someone walk into the office and close the door.

Chapter 63

I tried to keep emotion at bay on the drive to Sergei's home. From now on I was on my own, trusting no one, although I would pretend to play along with the Russian police and with Sergei.

Arriving at Sergei's home, I rang the bell and waited.

Moments later he bounded out and caught hold of me, whirling me round, carrying me inside and behaving like an idiot. Was all this enthusiasm for the missing icon or for me, his missing courier, I wondered. The icon, I decided finally, as I watched him lovingly unwrap it.

Shortly afterwards I was confronted by two images and I could not fathom which intrigued me more. The icons hanging in sequence at last, which in itself was a miracle for each had made a hazardous, lonely journey through five centuries of wars and upheaval. Or the man himself, gazing as if entranced at the icons' poignant imagery. His head was thrown back, his throat moving with the force of his emotion, his fierce eyes blazing with joy.

'Mere money can never repay you, Naomi,' Sergei said, passing me a cheque. It was for the full purchase price, plus 10 per cent.

'But surely they will be auctioned?'

'Not this time, Naomi. For me, the icons are a reminder of man's eternal quest to find the sacred fount within himself, expressed as a need to create and covet beauty. Tell me, have you ever wanted anything as much as I desired this icon?'

'No,' I lied. 'Or maybe only money.'

There was a quiet chuckle close to my ear. 'I think you are lying.' His hands caressed my breasts. 'You have beautiful breasts. I told you that you had suckled a child. I like that. Stay with me tonight, Naomi. We shall make love and then we'll make our plans. Say you will stay.'

I craved love, but not his. I shuddered. I knew I needed comfort, an outlet for my impassioned love, and a shoulder for my sadness. Of the three men in my life, Sergei was the only one who had not lied to me. I did not have to guard my back when he was around. 'I suppose it always was inevitable, Sergei.'

I could feel his body trembling with desire, and smell the musky scent of his hot longing, yet subtly I sensed that this man would never want the same woman twice.

Sergei was a skilled and passionate lover, as I had known he would be. I cried out when my body reached the fierce and final climax and the essence of me spilled out over him in drops of exquisite sensations. Only then did I feel a fleeting sensation of shame, knowing that I was only groping for compensation for the loss of something infinitely precious to me.

Oh, David, it should be you.

It was midnight when Sergei woke me. He was lying sprawled half over me, one leg flung over my hips. For a moment I thought it was David and I almost cried with disappointment. Moments later, when I felt his tender thrust into my innermost place, I shuddered and gave myself up to him.

Later, as we lay entwined, drenched with his sex, Sergei told me about my jewellery: every piece, every gem, and every occasion for which it had been made.

'That is how I found you, Nininchka. You wore your jewellery, at the sports club and at the casino and I knew that you were Wolf Möller's wife.'

I climbed out of bed, unwilling to reveal my dawning horror. I felt numb as I stared out of the window, watching the lights twinkling from passing boats and occasional patches of phosphorescence lighting the darkness. I felt strangely drained. Everything Colonel Borovoi had told me was a lie. He knew Sergei and vice versa, so he knew that Sergei knew my true identity. I tried to understand what was going on. Who had betrayed me, and why?

'Why did you stay so long in Moscow, Nina?'

'I have never been there before. I fell in love with the city. I did some shopping.'

'What a secretive woman you are, my little Nininchka. You remind me of the sea.' Sergei stood up and came close behind me until his body fitted against mine. He wound his arms around my shoulders. 'You are deep and dark and very mysterious. Sometimes your eyes light up momentarily, but not often. In your own way you are as relentless as the sea, and as mindless. You are compelled to act out your role of motherhood, propelled by your instincts to regain your son – your pristine instincts.'

'So you know?'

'I knew that Wolf Möller had a son. I made the emerald and sapphire bracelet he gave you for the occasion. It was Borovoi who told me you are searching for your child. We shall find him, Nininchka, by working together,' he whispered. 'I promise you. We make the perfect combination. I know how Wolf Möller operates and you can recognise him. You have brought me the icon and now I will find your son for you.'

'I find it hard to believe that you never saw Wolf.'

'Once I knew him well. We were in the same prison camp for juveniles in Siberia, but we were children. He was always known as Wolf because he was fast and silent and very smart, and also because he would not tell anyone what his real name was. Once he confided in me that his parents were shot because they were titled. I suppose he was afraid he would be killed if he told anyone.

'Years later he contacted me because he had Angolan diamonds for sale. He used the name Wolf again, Wolf Möller this time, but we never met. It was always the telephone, or the fax, or a go-between.'

'But you made the jewellery for him, so you must have known where he lived.'

'No. I assumed that he lived in Angola, or close by.'

Sergei's eyes beamed reassurance and kindliness, yet he did not mention his own reason for wanting to find Wolf.

'You are not being straightforward with me, Sergei. Why do you want Wolf so badly? Colonel Borovoi said Wolf stole millions of dollars from you.'

'Not dollars, Nina, diamonds, half a billion dollars' worth and not from me, but from the Russian state, but I was ruined because of the theft. It's a very complicated story.'

'If we are going to work together, you must tell me everything.'

He sighed. 'Let's get up. I'll tell you over breakfast.'

I took a leisurely shower, dressed, and found Sergei in his kitchen laying out fruit and cheese and home-made brown bread, which he said he had baked. He was full of surprises.

'Eat and listen well, Nininchka. All my life I have loved jewellery and beautiful gems, with too much passion perhaps. So I became an expert gemmologist.

'Here?'

'Don't interrupt. No, in Russia, but later I studied in Germany and Holland. Eventually I saved enough to start my own workshop, designing beautiful things. Möller used to supply me with smuggled diamonds and other precious stones from Africa. I wasn't able to take all that he offered. My workshop and my jewellery shop did not have that large a clientele. It was an arrangement that suited us both, but I never met him. He was always cautious.'

'So what went wrong?'

'Tch! I shall lose track if you keep on prodding me. You don't understand how it is in my country. Everything is run by committees. It's very tedious, but as a Russian I can never forget my roots, so when Kromdragmet, the committee that exports Russia's gems, asked me to join them, I agreed. Later they voted me vice-president.

'Now, listen, Nininchka, here comes the crunch. We Russians are at the mercy of De Beers' world marketing cartel, who control diamond marketing worldwide. Russia is permitted to sell only five per cent of its diamonds on the open market. This is far too little for us because we badly need foreign currency, but if we sell more diamonds and defy De Beers' control we are penalised.'

'That seems so unfair.'

'We hit on a brilliant plan. Early this year we shipped over five hundred million dollars' worth of diamonds in five lots to be cut and polished prior to selling them. I set up a diamond-cutting workshop in San Francisco and signed security for the polishing and cutting equipment. We planned to have the diamonds stolen, and returned to us so we could sell them on the open market, which would double our diamond sales.'

'Sounds foolproof.'

'I thought it was. It was I who suggested bringing in Wolf Möller to fake the theft. Colonel Borovoi of the state police was brought in as well, because he had worked with Möller in the old days. He was Möller's liaison when Wolf worked as a freelance agent for the KGB.'

'Was that the first time you met Borovoi?'

'Yes. Borovoi contacted Wolf and arranged the theft. Wolf was supposed to deliver the stones to me at my hotel in San Francisco, but he never came. He disappeared with half a billion dollars' worth of uncut stones.

'I was sacked from Kromdragmet and the committee refused to release the cash to reimburse me for the diamond-cutting equipment. Naturally, after such a loss, the diamond-cutting firm went bankrupt and so did I. Fortunately I hadn't signed personal security for the purchases so I still have my home. I'm starting again, buying and selling old jewellery to build up capital. Naturally I wish to find Wolf Möller. He must reimburse me.'

'Listen, Sergei. Colonel Borovoi wants to find Wolf badly. If he knew how to find him a few months ago, then why can't he find him now?'

'Wolf has fled. Can you blame him? Now, Nininchka. Wolf always sold his diamonds through the Brussels Diamond Circle. I have found you a job there. You start on Monday. When he comes you will recognise him and you will call me. I shall be nearby.'

When Sergei went into his office to take a call, I scribbled a note thanking him for the payment, adding, 'Going home for a few days. See you sometime next week.'

Chapter 64

Sergei's love-making had only succeeded in anaesthetising me for one night. I flew back to London, where I had some shopping and banking to do, and caught a later flight to Inverness. I arrived at ten to find Father sitting beside a blazing log fire in the morning room. He scanned me anxiously.

'It's good to see you, Nina. You had me pretty worried for a while.'

'I'm okay. It wasn't so bad.'

I hung my raincoat on the back of the door and warmed my hands in front of the fire. Nothing had changed except Father, I thought, in a moment of nostalgia. I bent over him and kissed his cheek. There was the same Persian rug, the thick black sheepskin by the hearth, the brass canister full of tongs and shovels, the roomy old couches and books piled all over the place. If I looked long and hard enough I might find my old copies of *Ivanhoe* and *Kidnapped*. I remembered how Brigit and I used to huddle by the fire until she crawled into the embers to keep warm, but that was centuries ago.

'Let's have a snack by the fire. Are you hungry? Mrs Peters made a steak and kidney pie. It's in the fridge. You can warm it in the microwave. Or perhaps you ate on the plane.'

'I'm not hungry, thanks. I could do with a drink. How about you?'

'Likewise. You look as if you could use one.' Father struggled to rise.

'Stay there. I'll get it.'

I poured two neat whiskies and pulled up a chair to join him by the fire.

'Glad you're back.' His hand reached out and squeezed mine. 'I was never much good at expressing my feelings. I was so afraid for you. I wish to God I'd never let you embark on this search.'

I glanced at him in surprise. He was gazing towards the fire, and the flames reflecting on his cheeks made him look ruddy and sun-tanned. He looked happier.

'So what can you tell me, Father?'

'Well, I must say, your David Bernstein impressed me no end.'

'You spoke to him?'

'He came here.'

'When?'

'While you were in Russia, David brought me his research as well as details of your arrest. We can go through it in the morning. He'd persuaded his Mossad colleagues to apply for your extradition as Naomi Hunter, wanted for questioning for the Unita scam. That's when we learned that the Russian police had not arrested you. David's Mossad friends discovered that Borovoi was holding you in an old disused prison, which is used as a warehouse nowadays. David had plans to come and get you out of there, but Borovoi released you.'

How had I managed to get everything so wrong? I had badly misjudged David. Strangely I felt no guilt, only sadness.

'Why? Just why?'

'You can work it out, Nina. What did they ask you to do?'

'Co-operate with them in identifying Wolf. Evidently the police – no, rather, Borovoi has no idea what Wolf looks like.'

'And you said you would?'

'Yes. In return for Nicky's safe and immediate delivery to us.'

'Would you have trusted a bunch of criminals enough to co-operate?'

'No. But isn't Borovoi still a colonel in the police?'

'One foot in each camp, according to Wattling's latest report. So many of them have, since the fall of the Soviet system. Well, that's your answer, Nina. They wanted you to believe that you were working with the police. So they promised you Nicky.'

'Yes, of course.'

'I wouldn't set much store by their promises.'

'No. I have a problem. I feel that I'm not getting anywhere, Father. Somewhere I went wrong. I'm in a cul-de-sac. It's bugging me, but I can't quite work it out.'

'I think we should go along with David's plans. I must say, I like David, Nina.'

'Yes, I suppose you would.'

'We have a lot in common. He's someone I'd be proud to call my son-in-law.'

'What are you saying?' My calm deserted me. 'Not another word on the subject. I have promised myself to trust no one until I have Nicky safely home. Emotions have no place in my life right now—'

I broke off and gazed at the flames, trying to work out why I had been so eager to believe Borovoi. 'It's more than that, really. I could never forgive David for falling

Madge Swindells

in love with a woman like Naomi Hunter. He has no idea what I'm really like.'

'You flatter yourself, Nina. You're not that good an actress. He guessed who you were weeks ago. He told me he was waiting for you to trust him enough to tell him of your own volition. Somewhere along the line you've got things horribly wrong.'

'I really don't want to talk about David. Do you mind?'

'Now, don't get emotional on me, my dear. I could never handle women's tears. Your mother was always crying when we first married. I could never understand why. Of course, now I do. I've had plenty of time to sit and think about it.'

'Mother longed for fun. It was too bleak here. She was city born and bred.'

'I didn't keep her cooped up. She was free to go to London whenever she wanted. I suppose that was one thing I did right.'

'I wonder.'

'I never understood her. I suppose that was our problem. I never had contact with women, other than the occasional romp in the hay. My mother died when I was barely into my teens, I had no sisters and I attended a boys' public school. Nothing prepared me for the trauma of suddenly finding myself cooped up with one, and soon there were two, after you came on the scene. I'm not trying to make excuses. Just explaining.'

'There's nothing to explain. It was long ago. It doesn't matter any more.'

'I think it does. You were a lonely child, Nina, always seeking affection. I left you to your mother and that was my mistake. There is nothing in my life I regret as much as my neglect of you, Nina. I long for a second chance, but it's too late now.'

To hide my expression, I stood up and poured myself some coffee from the pot on the warmer. The aroma of my father's favourite blend brought back more memories. Taking my mug I went to the fire and stood toasting my back. I sensed that Father wanted to talk, but didn't know how to begin.

After a while I said, 'I wish I had been with Mother when she died. I always blamed her for my broken childhood. I could never forgive her for leaving you, or for taking me away from my home. By the time I left school, I was sure I'd broken all emotional ties with her. I was wrong. There's some invisible link between mother and daughter. It's like a hotline to your soul, conveying all the guilt and love and anger. I wasn't the daughter she wanted.'

'The blame's not hers at all. It's mine, Nina. Your mother came from an Orthodox Jewish family. I swept her off her feet and she ran away from home to marry me. I had no experience with Judaism, or with women. I didn't understand what she was giving up. She never went home after we married because they never forgave her.

'When I met her she was studying political philosophy. I gave a lecture on British foreign policy at her university. I remember how she heckled me. That's what attracted me to her.'

'Good God! Mother?'

'Yes. I've always felt that I received rough justice when I was partially destroyed, because I had destroyed her.'

'No . . . please!' The words were torn out of me. 'Don't think like that. No one deserves such a punishment. You call that justice?'

'Once she asked me to convert. An Ogilvie! I remember

how I laughed at her. I took her to the library and showed her our family ancestry. The ancient heritage of kings and warriors, bound in neat navy leather. It's meaningless. I know that now. There's no point in history unless you can use it to improve the lot of the living.

'She wanted to bring you up Jewish. Did you know that? She said you were Jewish. Regrettably I refused. I only gave in over your name. So she began to pine. To look at her you'd think that parties and fashion, and later on lovers, were the extent of her interests. Triviality was her defence against her world.

'You might consider examining your Jewish roots once in a while, Nina. I would be pleased, particularly now that David Bernstein has entered our lives. I have no doubt you and he will sort things out eventually.'

For some reason, I found Father's words comforting.

He had switched off in his abrupt way. I sensed this was all the emotion he could take for one night. I felt much the same.

Later, I lay in bed, remembering. On winter weekends, before his accident, Father would join the local hunt and return late, his eyes blazing with vigour and joy, his horse snorting and lathered. The hunters would return with their wives for drinks and dinner and there would be laughter and jokes, while the smell of roasting game wafted up the stairs.

Longing to join in, I used to take a rug and hide in the cupboard above the stairs from where I could sprawl across the landing and peer through the banisters, retreating to my eyrie at the sound of footsteps. Father looked magnificent in a kilt, and Mother would wear the latest fashion, her dresses and her beauty goading the other wives into a seething, uneasy comradeship as they exchanged views on her spendthrift ways and her frequent excursions to London.

During quiet moments, their whispered comments would drift up to me in snatches for the hall and surrounding balcony had the accoustic properties of a whispering gallery. To my annoyance laughter drowned most of their words. When Father sang, in his rich bass voice, my happiness was absolute. I loved him so dearly, but always from a distance. Had he any idea how much his lonely daughter used to worship him? How I still worshipped him? Or the anguish I suffered when he was brought back from hospital, maimed for life?

That was when the light in his eyes began to fade. I used to watch his heroic fight to survive as a vital, living person and I would will him to be strong, and try in vain to interest him with stories of my own daily events. Then came the day when my mother told him we were leaving and his eyes became bleak and remote.

I never forgave my mother for her cruelty, just as I had never stopped longing for my father's love. Now, for the first time, I understood my mother. I wished I had penetrated her defences.

After a while I forced myself to examine my progress in my search for Nicky, which, I had to admit, was almost nil. I went back over my search step by step.

Meeting David Bernstein had been a breakthrough because his money-laundering research had linked the Unita scam with Wolf. This had led to Martha Newton-Thomas and the discovery that Wolf's Trans-African Foundation account had been transferred to Sarajevo. Examining the Sarajevo account had led me to Cassellari, but I had not progressed since then. I was indeed in a cul-de-sac. Why had I imagined that working with Cassellari would ultimately lead to Wolf? It had not, at least not yet, and I was in a hurry. I would have to go back to Cassellari and find the reason why he had paid a million dollars into Wolf's account. There had to be a way to make him reveal the link between them.

Chapter 65

A cold front from the sea had crept over the island, but higher up in the Sardinian hills the sun was still shining. The sunlit clouds stretched out to the north, east and south, glistening golden, cerise and white under an azure sky. Sitting on the balcony of Vittorio Cassellari's home, one had the impression of being in heaven. No wonder Cassellari had delusions of godlike powers. I might get the same if I lived here long enough.

I shivered and tightened my coat around me, aware that I was incubating a bad dose of flu. My throat was sore, my neck stiff and even my ears ached. Where was Cassellari? He was over an hour late for our appointment.

Enforced waiting is the pits if you're trying to keep anxiety at bay. Perhaps because of my flu, my defences were low. Anxiety about my child and doubts of ever finding him zoomed into my mind. I shivered and sneezed and cursed Signor Cassellari for being late.

Pull yourself together, Nina! I went inside, took out my notebook and began to list the possible reasons for Cassellari's payment of a million dollars to Wolf's company. The most likely explanation was a payment for drugs, but the thought of Wolf being involved with drugs was abhorrent. It could have been for arms or for diamonds, but neither alternative seemed likely. Eventually I leaned back and visualised my favourite daydream.

Wolf is sitting unaware as I approach him obliquely. I pull out my handgun, point it at him and he turns, stunned and flinching. I say, 'Wolf, I loved you, but you betrayed me. You took away my reason for living. You took my child hostage and threatened to harm him. You left me to face a prison sentence. I was tortured and kept in solitary confinement. Did you know that? Did you ever care? You cheated me. Even our marriage wasn't real. Yet I loved you so.' Then I squeeze the trigger, slowly, keeping my hand steady, aiming between his eyes.

At one o'clock Cassellari's housekeeper came to tell me that lunch was served. Cassellari was not too pleased to see me. I could see that he was used to doing the summoning and not the other way around. Nevertheless, he was a courteous host and I kept the conversation to small-talk as we ate smoked salmon and caviare with a magnificent salad.

'Now, Naomi, just what is your problem? You do look pale. Is something wrong?' Cassellari's voice hardened as he shot me a suspicious glance.

I shuddered inwardly. 'I have flu. I don't feel well. In fact, I got out of bed to come here, but I felt it was important.'

Would he buy my story? I was counting on his incredible conceit to help me.

'Signor Cassellari, I'm worried about de Sica. You know how conscientious I am about my work.' I forced myself to gaze anxiously into his eyes.

He frowned.

'I know he handles your money-laundering, but you

should have asked me. He's made a terrible mistake. You could lose out and that would be bad for you.'

'Hey, hey, slow down! What you are talking about, Naomi?'

'Your cheque for a million dollars, which you paid to the Trans-African Development Foundation. I know you get top interest rates in Sarajevo but, believe me, you've fallen into a trap. The fund is run by a crook who defrauds his clients of their cash. One of his pseudonyms is Gunther Mannheim. He conned millions from gullible businessmen in South Africa. Most of their cash is in that same bank account. I don't want you to lose out. I've come here to warn you. Perhaps I can help you.'

'How touching, Naomi. But how would you know all this?'

'It's my business to know these things. That's why you pay me.'

His small brown eyes showed his distrust, but there was something else, too. Amusement, perhaps.

'You should have let me launder this cash for you, Signor Cassellari. You know you can trust me.'

'Don't worry.' He patted my hand. 'De Sica and I go back a long way. I'll call him.'

That was the last thing I wanted. I gazed at my plate and tried not to look anxious.

De Sica arrived shortly afterwards, looking angry. He sat down, poured himself a glass of wine and scrutinised me contemptuously.

'It wasn't that sort of a deal, Nina,' he said, when I had finished explaining. 'As a matter of fact, Angelo set the whole thing up. An old Russian peasant, who had managed to get some of his land restored to him, wanted to sell us his farm. We bought it. End of story.'

'Old? How old?'

'Gnarled, toothless, almost senile, but cunning.'

'I don't understand why you would want to buy his land. In fact, I don't believe you.'

I stared Cassellari straight in the eyes without a flinch. 'I came here to help you,' I said, standing up and trying to look insulted.

'Sit down, Nina.' Cassellari's smile gave me the shivers. His was not a face for smiling. 'This Russian had planted out the estate in poppies. Of course, it was the opium we wanted and that's what we paid for, but it was disguised as a land deal. It was all above board, so we paid him a cheque.'

'And you made it out to the Trans-African . . . ?'

'No, Naomi. It was an uncrossed cheque made out to Piotra Gregov.'

'That was the landowner's name?'

'Obviously.'

'Why uncrossed?'

'He didn't have a bank account,' de Sica said. 'I told you, he was a peasant type. He wanted to pass on the cheque. He said he was buying land somewhere outside Russia.'

'Do you know where?'

'No.'

I sighed. 'Where was this old man's land?'

'Place called Biryuchek, on the Caspian Sea. Perfect for transport. Why all these questions? Don't you trust me?'

'Oh, yes. Yes, I do. I'm so relieved. I'd hate to see you lose out on a deal.'

'Hey, there! Perhaps you need some more work. Are you short of money, Naomi? You know how much I value your services. I'll contact you in a couple of days' time.'

'Well, thanks. I can always do with more work.'

I could see that de Sica was puzzled. He was about to ask me how I knew about the cheque when I led the conversation back to money-laundering and the way the world's governments were tightening up on their restrictions. Even the Russians were giving the police draconian powers to deal with money-launderers. It was only a matter of time before they brought in restrictive laws. Perhaps we should find an alternative route to Borovoi's bank. As soon as I could I left them pondering.

I sat on the plane, sipping a neat Scotch, thinking about my next move, but feeling light-headed as my temperature soared. I decided that I should not be seen asking questions about the sale of the sixty thousand hectares planted with opium in Biryuchek. Wolf might live there, or have contacts in that area. It would be better to employ a detective agency and let them trace Piotra Gregov's present whereabouts.

I took a cab from Nice airport and plotted my next moves on the drive to Monaco. Father would know of a good agency for me. Despite my sore throat and headache, I could hardly contain my surging optimism. Was it possible that Wolf had at last committed a supreme error *by leaving a trail between his aliases and his real personality*? Could he be that careless? Dare I hope?

It was a relief to get home. I took a warm bath and climbed into bed, falling asleep instantly. At one a.m. the telephone woke me.

'Who is it?'

'Who's speaking? What number is that?'

'Oh, Sergei, it's me. I've got a sore throat. I've almost lost my voice.'

'Where the hell have you been?'

'Home. What's it got to do with you, Sergei?'

'You're supposed to start work at the Diamond Circle tomorrow morning.'

'I'm sick. I've got flu. Tell them I'm taking the day off. I'll start the next day. Honestly, Sergei, I'm dying.'

'Well, I hope we don't miss out on sighting Wolf.'

I said goodbye and replaced the receiver. The chance of Wolf returning to his old haunts was hardly likely. Surely he knew that Sergei was looking for him, but I might as well play along.

Chapter 66

The days dragged by as I marked time at the Brussels Diamond Circle and tried to throw off the flu. I was sitting at the switchboard when a call came for me. It was the German detective agency my father had recommended.

'Haape, here, Miss Ogilvie. I'm sorry, but we have been unable to trace the whereabouts of Piotra Gregov. It's true that he sold his estate to Vittorio Cassellari's company, International Trading, based in Sardinia, but he took his money and left. He told no one where he was going. No one has heard from him. We sent a Russian-speaking agent to question his friends and neighbours, but there was no luck at all. It seems he was determined to kick the dust of Mother Russia off his feet for ever.'

I thanked him and replaced the receiver. 'Shit!' I sneezed into my tissue and cursed again. My search had been looking so favourable. The disappointment was hard to bear.

Then I had another idea. What if David was right in his presumption that Wolf came from Latvia? What if Father was right about Wolf inheriting a title? It was worth a try. I called back the agency.

'Listen. I have an idea. I want you to send an agent to Latvia to check the deeds office for all land, mine or building sales over the past six months. Search for anyone who sold anything to Piotra Gregov for a million dollars.'

'That's a bit of a tall order, Miss Ogilvie. Have you any idea what's involved?'

'Okay, start with titled families. Would that make it easier?'

'Well, I don't think—'

'Just do it! Call me back as soon as you have news.' I replaced the receiver.

It was almost four when the outside doors swung open and a uniformed messenger walked in. He approached hesitantly carrying a letter. 'I'm looking for Miss Naomi Hunter.'

'That's me.'

The sudden draught seemed to blow right through me. I shivered and tried to swallow, but the pain was intense. I signed the messenger's receipt book and opened the envelope.

David's handwriting. My heart lurched. 'Meet me outside the De Witt Diamond Centre between midnight and one a.m. tonight. Urgent.' Below was an address and a hand-drawn map showing the way.

I memorised the directions, put the note into the shredder and got on with my work.

Why would David want to meet me here, I wondered. I glanced at my watch. Midnight. I was dead on time. Visibility was poor in the misty drizzle, but I could see a gaunt six-storey building at the end of the road and as I drove closer I saw the name, *De Witt Diamond Centre*, on a brass plaque beside the main entrance. Further off, a car was parked under a leafless plane tree. There were no other signs of life.

I parked by the kerb and saw the car's door open. A figure stepped out, bent to retrieve a sack from the back seat and locked the car. I wasn't quite sure how I knew it was David, but I did. As he hurried towards me, with his familiar, loping stride, I realised how much I had missed him and I regretted my suspicions.

Oh, David, if only I could tell you how I feel about you. I got out of the car and flinched as the cold drizzle hit my face.

'Let's go,' he said, by way of greeting. Taking my arm, he led me briskly round the corner, and the next, until we were one block away from the De Witt building and at the entrance to a large yard. He bent over the padlock and fiddled with a key. The gate creaked open and we walked through.

The drizzle was penetrating my clothes and David was acting like a stranger, which depressed me more than the rain. I sneezed. Shit!

We crept between the cars until we reached the fence, which lay under a line of fir trees and separated the car park from the building.

'Get down,' he muttered.

'What for?'

He swore under his breath, so I crouched by the fence and watched him cut a hole big enough for us to crawl through. He might have warned me. It was goodbye to my new Italian shoes. I could feel the heels grating deep into the gravel with every step. As I crawled through the hole, I felt my stockings rip.

'Okay, hold this,' he murmured, as I straightened up. He handed me his raincoat, and I saw that he was wearing black jeans and a sweater. He took a webbing ladder out of the sack with two hooks attached to one end.

'Oh, no. Please. You'll hurt yourself.'

'Ssh, Nina. Wait here and keep quiet.'

The hooks were hardly the size of my hand, but David was trusting them to hold his weight. He flung them at the first floor burglar bars and they hung in there. Moments later he was climbing up the webbing. Clinging precariously to the bars he tossed the ladder up to the next level.

Amazing! I could see that he was an expert in breaking and entering. In a matter of minutes he had disappeared over the last ledge on to the flat roof. The drizzle turned into a downpour as I waited, shaking with icy-cold shivers.

Five minutes later the back door opened, and David beckoned to me. 'Sorry, we can't put the lights on.' He flicked his torch on and off. 'Try to get your bearings when the light shines. This way. These old buildings are just waiting to be burgled. It wasn't too difficult to dismantle the alarm, since it's on the roof. I got the building plans from the deeds office.'

'You took a chance.'

'No. I came here yesterday, pretending to be a client, and checked out the wiring.'

'Why are we here?'

'It's rumoured that part of the Russians' stolen diamonds are here at de Witt's, being cut and polished for an unknown client. Friends told me. Come on, Nina.'

So we weren't pretending any more. Suddenly I felt as light as air, as if a millstone had fallen from my shoulders.

'David, I want you to know that I only deceived you because . . .'

'Sh! The past is over. Forget it. Keep up. You're wasting time.'

'I can't see a bloody thing. I'm blind in the dark. Always have been.' I blinked hard and my watery vista cleared a little.

The torch flickered ahead giving a pool of light. I stepped into it, unwilling to move further, but the light went off again.

'This way.' I blundered into the darkness. 'Fuck!' My shins had collided with a chair.

'Ssh! Quiet.'

'Sorry.'

I followed the will-o'-the-wisp light as it danced across the room and blundered into David. It was his turn to curse.

'Hold the torch, Nina. Shine it down on these files. I'll go through them.'

There were ten filing cabinets with four drawers each and we examined every file. Two hours later my back was aching, my flu was making me light-headed and the torch felt as heavy as lead, but we were on the last cabinet.

A whistle brought me wearily back to life.

'Okay, here we are. B B Investments. What d'you think that stands for?'

'I have no idea.'

'Your friend Boris Borovoi, what else? He and his wife are the sole directors of this company, according to the letterhead, but I knew that anyway. The company owns some real estate outside Russia, half the Bukharin Bank in partnership with Cassellari, and other assets in Russia. I've been doing my homework while you've been sitting around wasting time at the Diamond Circle.'

'Yes, it is a waste of time, but Sergei still thinks Wolf will pitch up there.'

'Your Romanovitch isn't very bright. He still thinks Wolf stole the diamonds, but he didn't. Borovoi did. It was easy for him to blame Möller for the theft. Möller's the ideal scapegoat.'

'Are you sure?'

'I am now. Before it was just a theory. According to this receipt, B B Investments owns the batch being cut and polished here, which is valued at a hundred million dollars. That's only part of what was stolen. Here's a copy of De Witt's receipt for the gemstones, and here's a quote for the job in hand. And here's an agreement that De Witt will accept payment in diamonds.

'I want you to take these receipts and letters to Romanovitch. You'll have to explain what it all means. You may find him sexy but, as I said, there's not much between his ears. Artistic type, that's all. Typical woman's man.'

So he knew I had spent time with Sergei. Silence would be my best defence, I decided.

'Nina, I'm convinced that Borovoi impersonated Möller when arranging to steal the Russian diamonds for Romanovitch. It would be easy for him to do this, since Wolf always communicates by telephone and e-mail. Borovoi has worked with Möller in the past so he knows the man's style and so does Romanovitch.'

'But why are you so concerned that Sergei should know the truth?'

'I'm anxious to set one against the other. You can't fight both of them at the same time, Nina. Let them fight each other.'

'Oh, yes. Of course you're right. You know this business well, don't you? Can we go now, please, David? I feel sick. And can we have some light this time? I'm badly bruised and I feel so odd.'

As I followed the flickering light, I was aware of his disappointment. He had expected me to be far more enthusiastic, but I felt so damned ill.

Sitting in my car, David revealed his amazing plan. He looked so smug and happy about it. He had every right to be pleased with himself, so why wasn't I? What is it with you, Nina? Are you so arrogant you wanted to find your son yourself? No! It was something else, but I couldn't put my finger on it.

'Listen, Nina. I've persuaded some philanthropic banks back home, including our bank, to set up a fund to help maintain democracy in former Russian satellite states. We plan to offer substantial cash injections and we'll begin with the Balkans. We've even persuaded the IMF to send observers, so we're able to state that this is a joint IMF–private enterprise endeavour.

'We'll put on lectures by various bankers, experts and economists, and, of course, we can't avoid the politicians. All those Balkan landowners, whose estates have been restored to them, will be encouraged to apply for substantial cash loans to turn their farms and mines into viable economic propositions. Well, what do you think?'

'It's a brilliant idea, David. But is it for real? Will they get the cash?'

'Of course. It's exactly what we had in mind when we were stung by that Friends of Unita scam.'

'I'm impressed, David. You're very tenacious. I can't tell you—'

'Don't bother. I'm enjoying nailing that bastard. I can't wait to hand him over. The police of six nations will be waiting to catch him. The plan is that you will be there, too, perhaps hidden behind one-way glass, because only you can identify the bastard. Once he fills in the application forms, we'll have established his true identity and his address. Very neat, don't you think?'

'Mm, maybe. Wolf doesn't lack the capital to develop his estates himself. He's spent half his life stealing it.'

'True. That's a possible flaw, but can you see him turning down the offer of loaned cash at very low interest rates?'

'No. Not really. Why should he? You're right. I think this is going to work. Thank you, David.'

'I'm overwhelmed by your enthusiasm.'

'I'm sorry. I've had flu for days. I can't shake it off. I feel terrible.'

'You should stay in bed. You're wasting your time at the Exchange. I've just come back from Riga, where I held a couple of get-togethers. The landowners are eating out of our hands. Any one of the men I've spoken to could have been Wolf Möller.'

'What can I say? It's a very clever idea. Thank you, David.'

'I'm going to launch the conference with a cocktail party, to be held at a prominent hotel in Riga. Once Wolf has been arrested, we'll fetch Nicky from his home and fly him to Scotland. Make sure to bring the documents you need proving you have sole custody. You have them, I assume.'

'Yes.'

'End of story. Sound good to you?'

'Yes. And Wolf? What will happen to him?'

'I guess Interpol, the CIA, the Mossad and the South Africans will fight over him. Eventually he'll stand trial in the States. If he lives that long. He'll be torn apart, I should imagine. Listen to me, Nina. Don't go back to the Diamond Circle. Just disappear. I'll find you a

safe house until the conference. I'll look after you. You
need a new name, and a new country. How about Mrs
Bernstein?'

I laughed, then wished I hadn't. I pulled my scarf
around my throat and croaked, 'What a reason to marry.
You make it sound very matter-of-fact. Maybe I'll hold
out for the candlelit dinner and a ring.'

'You're prevaricating.'

'David, listen to me. If you still want to marry me after
I've found Nicky and taken him home, then my answer
will be yes. I love you and I long for us to be married,
but I'm not sure if you'll still feel the same way about
me. I would like you to propose to me one day, but not
yet.' I reached out and squeezed his hand.

As we said goodbye, I tried to think of something
significant to say – a summing-up. We had come so
far together, but I knew I had to go the rest of the way
alone. I would decide what was best for my child. That
was my God-given right.

Chapter 67

The call from Heinrich Haape, owner of the German detective agency came three days later, sooner than I had anticipated.

'We have the information you want,' the detective told me in a dry, expressionless voice. 'It will cost a little more than originally anticipated and it will be delivered as arranged. Payment on delivery in cash, in dollars, is preferred. Can you meet our representative at the Café Vienna, which is quite near the Brussels Diamond Circle, at eleven a.m. this morning? Would that be convenient?'

I tried to curb my excitement. 'Quite convenient, thank you. I'll be there.'

Just before eleven, I wandered into the Café Vienna and searched around for a table. The place was full, but shortly afterwards a table became vacant. I asked the manageress to send my guest to my table and ordered coffee while I waited.

Shortly afterwards, a tall, seedy-looking man, with balding gingerish hair, large brown sun marks on his skin and pale grey eyes blinking myopically through thick lenses, made his way towards me. He bowed, clicked his heels and held out his hand to shake mine. Clearly he was playing safe.

'Ah, hello, Miss Ogilvie. Nice to meet you at last.'

His voice was familiar and I realised that I had been speaking to this same person on the telephone. Obviously a one-man show.

'You are Heinrich Haape?'

'Yes, indeed. I hope I'm on time.' He turned to the waitress, who was hovering with the cake trolley.

'Ah, cake. Black Forest, yes, that one, thanks.'

I ordered the same with coffee and tried to be polite while he discussed the weather, the late trains and our warming planet for a full five minutes.

'You have some information for me,' I cut in as soon as I could. I could hardly take my eyes off his briefcase. I longed to grab it and dive into it.

'There was a matter of dollars we mentioned, if you remember. You said you would pay me on delivery.'

'Of course.'

'You have the cash with you?'

'Yes.'

'Well, then . . .' His analytical blue eyes glittered with impatience.

'You haven't yet given me the information. But never mind. You were highly recommended. Here's half.' I passed over an envelope and almost died of tension as he slowly counted the notes.

'I'm sorry that the assignment cost a little more than our original estimate.'

'It doesn't matter.'

'You see, I was afraid you might need photographs for identification purposes. I obtained two, as well as some family details.'

He'd read my anxiety. Damn! 'Can we please get on with it?'

'I'm so afraid that it might be the wrong person.'

I felt shocked. 'How do you know?'

'I have worked with your father on and off for years.'

He passed over the papers, giving full details of the sale of sixty thousand hectares of farming land, excluding all mineral rights, to Piotra Gregov. And the seller was: Baron Marius Wolfgang Tyler. And there was his address, written in Latvian, German and English. I recognised the word 'Morgendauw' in all three versions.

At last! Thank you, God! At last! My breast was heaving with the force of my hammering heart.

The detective handed me two photographs. One was of Wolf and Nicky trailing over a field towards a dam, carrying fishing rods and a bucket. The next was of Nicky sitting on Wolf's shoulders, his arms wound around his father's neck as they left the lake. Wolf was holding both rods and the bucket, which looked heavy now.

'Madame, are you all right?'

'I'm fine,' I gasped. 'Just lovely.' My son had not been abandoned in an orphanage, or hurt, or simply lost. He was happy and looked after. At that moment nothing else counted.

'And the rest of the money?'

I would have paid him anything.

'Have it all.' I thrust a packet of dollars into his hands. It was double what he had wanted, for I had anticipated further demands.

'Madame, I asked around and learned that Baron Marius is a highly regarded citizen of Riga. He's on the city council, chairs many charities, that sort of thing. He's known as a devoted father to his little boy, Nicholas. The story is that he lost his wife in Europe when the boy was only two.'

Suddenly his hand stretched out and covered mine. He said, 'I, too, have been looking for Nicky for two years. I run the missing person's agency your father contacted to try to find his grandson. I am so sorry that I failed you before. It wasn't for the want of trying, I assure you.'

I hung on to my cool. 'Thank you,' I managed to stammer. 'Good day to you.' Clutching my bag, I stumbled to the ladies' room.

I had not yet shed any tears, I had been so strong. Not when Nicky was kidnapped, nor when I was arrested. Even the shock treatment had provoked screams, never tears, but now I could feel them coming. The dam wall had broken and a river of tears was flooding my soul. I sat on a chair and buried my face in my hands. Some time later I realised that a woman was bending over me. I don't know who she was. She went away and the waitress came in with a cup of coffee and two aspirins, which I refused. She left, too.

Remembering belatedly that Ogilvies never cry, I washed my face.

'These aren't tears,' I muttered aloud. 'Not real tears. How could they be when I'm so happy? It's salt water to flush out my wounds.'

And now what? I called a taxi to take me to my hotel where I e-mailed Father. Then I returned to the Diamond Circle. I continued with my work. I did not want Serge to notice that I was changed in any way.

Chapter 68

On the night before I left for Riga I invited Sergei to dinner. I chose a restaurant specialising in gypsy cuisine and music, for I wanted to talk to him in the least likely place Borovoi would come to.

'Nininchka, you have revealed a hidden side to your character. So you're a romantic under your stern exterior. A candlelit dinner and gypsy music! What a surprise! I would never have guessed you cared from the way you have been treating me.'

He reached for my hand, and as his strong, but shapely fingers crept over my palm, swords of pleasure pierced my stomach. I knew now that I loved David, truly, irrevocably and for ever, which had nothing at all to do with the fact that Sergei was the sexiest man I'd ever met. I would never again make love to him, and perhaps that made him all the more desirable. Or had we just become good friends over the past months?

Sergei's knowledge of antique jewellery was immense. He kept me enthralled with stories of the intrigue that had dogged the history of each famous piece.

I kept my story until we were sipping liqueur brandy by the fire.

'I'll never forget the time we made love, Sergei.'

'The first and last time, cruel Nininchka.'

411

'And I remember how you told me that Wolf and you had been in a camp together as children. I couldn't help remembering that Wolf would hardly ruin a boyhood friend.'

'Was he loyal to you, Nininchka?'

'In a way. I'm still alive.'

Sergei threw back his head and roared with laughter. 'D'you expect so little from your men that to stay alive proves their loyalty?'

Damn! Not a very good beginning. I couldn't help laughing with him.

'The point is, stealing the diamonds from you would be totally out of character for Wolf,' I persisted.

Now I had his interest. His expression of benign affection slipped off his face in a split second.

'What's going on, Nina? Come to the point. Have you been seeing Wolf?'

'No. It's just that I knew him well once. Wolf would steal from the government, but would he steal from you?'

'He stole from you, didn't he?'

I sighed. 'Yes.'

I flinched as I gazed into those implacable eyes. The light, the laughter and the friendliness had been entirely extinguished.

'Don't look at me like that, please. Trust me, Sergei. One hundred million dollars' worth of uncut diamonds have been delivered to the De Witt's Diamond Centre. Here's the receipt for them, the valuation certificates, the quotations for the work to be done, and so on. You'll note that the owner had to barter part of the consignment to cover the cost of cutting and polishing the rest.'

'And the owner is?' he whispered, reaching for the rest of the papers.

'BB Investments. It's a company registered in Prague. There are only two directors, Colonel Boris Borovoi, hence the initials, and his wife, Zelda. There you are. I photocopied the documents in their offices. Keep it all. It's easy to get into the building. Find out for yourself. I'm merely trying to warn you of the danger you're in, just as you did me.'

'What danger?'

'Borovoi set you up, lost your fortune, stole from you, ruined your reputation, drove you into liquidation. Why shouldn't he kill you, too, if he suspects that you may find out about him?'

'Why are you telling me this, Nina?'

'I care for you. Surely you know that.'

He frowned and stood up, as if he could no longer bear to keep still.

'As they say in the West, you could have fooled me. No, that is not why you are telling me, Nininchka. You have some other reason. I do not know what it is, but I believe that this evidence is real. I'll check out everything and then I'll come back to you. Maybe to love you. We'll see.'

He left abruptly. I finished my liqueur, paid the bill and drove home.

Once safely back in my apartment I sent Father the latest news then e-mailed Colonel Boris Borovoi.

Good news, Boris. David Bernstein, together with leading American bankers and delegates from the IMF will be holding a conference in Riga, Latvia, starting 1 November 1994, to facilitate loans and strengthen ties between the Baltic states and the West. The idea is to push home democracy with low-interest loans. Delegates will give details of their estates, and I will

413

be there hidden away to identify Wolf Möller. With luck we'll see him and learn his true identity. It is vital that you keep in touch with me so that Möller is sent to Russia to stand trial. I am afraid that he may be too leniently treated in the West and that my child might slip through my fingers if Möller is given enough time to send Nicky away. Let me know where you will be staying in Riga, so I can make arrangements for you to gain access to the conference.

I sent the message and switched off, but remained gazing at the black screen, plotting, just as I used to plot my chess games, trying to keep several moves ahead, anticipating all possible variables of my opponents' reactions. I had to have any number of retaliatory moves and I badly needed someone to second-guess me. If only I could tell Father, but that was impossible. This was something I had to do alone.

Chapter 69

As the opening day of the bankers' conference, dawned, I arrived in Riga to find that David had booked a suite for us, including an extra bedroom for Nicky. He was being very positive about his plan.

The venue for the conference was the Hôtel de Rome, Kalku Street, in Riga. David had been here for two weeks, coping with applications and finalising details. He had already called in the builders to erect a cubicle with one-way glass behind the reception desk from where I could watch the delegates filling in their questionnaires and filing their requests for financial backing.

There were twelve men and women in David's team and at nine precisely we opened our doors to receive a steady stream of visitors. From then on, everyone was kept busy answering questions, providing translations and helping applicants to fill in their forms.

At noon the rain began, a steady downpour that made the foyer dark. It was freezing in my cubicle. So far, twenty-seven families had put in their claims. According to David, most would benefit from loans to push their ideas.

I was doodling on my pad, thinking about Nicky and the pictures the detective had given me, when I suddenly had the strangest feeling that Wolf was near. I looked up curiously. No one was in the foyer, but moments later he strode in, crossing the marble floor on rubber-soled shoes that squished with water.

The thought that flashed through my mind was that I loved him. The love seemed to rise up from the depths of my being, as unexpected and dangerous as a tidal wave threatening my life. I pulled myself together fast. I did not love him. It was merely the memories that the sight of him had resurrected. That, plus the knowledge that he had guarded Nicky so well.

As I watched him, the questions that had been walled up for years almost erupted into words: Why, Wolf? How could you leave me?

I was sweating yet freezing cold. I ran my tongue over my dry lips and hung on to the desk-top for support as I gritted my teeth. Not a sob, not a cry, not a glimmer of reaction must show for David was right beside me.

I tried out a yawn, fiddled with my pencil and doodled figures on my pad, while part of me watched Wolf carefully, willing him not to go to the book and write down his real name.

The porter beckoned to him and handed him a pen, and Wolf shrugged and turned away. He took a form, studied it and asked for several more. Then he went to the information counter in the next room.

I bent down towards the floor, away from the camera, and fumbled in my bag, producing a tissue and a pseudo-sneeze. It was the supreme effort of my life to sit up straight, assume a bored, watchful expression and continue to gaze blankly at the door.

Three more visitors signed and filled in forms. Wolf was spending a long time talking to a bank official. Eventually he walked out, telling the receptionist in English that he would bring back the forms the following day.

So he was here, virtually hooked, and no doubt he would attend the cocktail party. What was I going to do? My indecision was agonising.

David invited me to a local nightclub. He desperately wanted a romantic evening, but I simply could not get into a romantic mood. I was too worried. I tried to explain and I think he understood. Most of the time, I was imagining quite another scene: *Nicky alone, waiting for his father who never, ever returns. Instead two strangers come to take him away. Okay, so one of them is his mother, but a stranger nonetheless.*

It hardly seemed good enough for Nicky.

'Wolf will be lucky to get off with anything less than life,' David said.

What if Wolf brings Nicky to the cocktail party? Would he try to escape? Would Nicky see his father captured?

And what will I tell Nicky about his father when he's older? How will I explain that he is serving a life sentence? Nicky loves Wolf. I could see that in the photographs. He wasn't abandoned or neglected. Wolf has loved him dearly. Doesn't that count for anything?

'When will you marry me, Nina?'

'If you still want me when I have Nicky back in my arms, I'm yours. Get a special licence if you like.'

'Now it's my turn to grumble. You're not being very romantic.'

I reached out and squeezed his hand. 'Our time will come, David. I'm sure it will.'

The man I had most hoped to avoid flew into Riga early on the following morning. He checked into the hotel we were using, naturally, and came straight into my cubicle to threaten me.

'Pretty neat,' Colonel Borovoi said, looking at the one-way glass cubicle that surrounded me. 'You can see the entire foyer and they can't see you. Have you seen Möller yet?'

'Yes. He didn't reveal his identity, but he will. He's coming back.'

'Your Bernstein has taken most of the ground floor. Must have cost a packet. When does the conference officially open?'

'The day after tomorrow with a cocktail party. That is where we'll nab Wolf.'

'But, Nina, just how much does your Bernstein know about me?'

'Only that you're in charge of the investigation to find Wolf and bring him to trial. In other words, the truth.'

'Hm! I suppose he wants to make sure the US gets Möller first.'

'I guess so, but he hasn't said as much to me.'

'I'd like to remind you of your promise and our agreement, Nina.'

'I haven't forgotten.' I tried out a friendly grin, and noticed that his eyes remained cold while his lips returned my smile.

'I no longer trust you, Nina.'

'Why not? This is as good a plan as any to find Wolf's real identity.'

'What makes Bernstein so sure Möller is Latvian?'

'He traced the stolen money to Riga. Now, if you don't mind, I'm busy.'

'What did you tell Sergei?'

'About what – this conference?' I frowned.

'About the diamonds at De Witt's.'

'I don't know what you're talking about.' He had caught

me by surprise, and my bowels cramped with fear. I hoped it didn't show.

'I think you do.' His hand shot out and gripped my arm. I struggled to shake him off, but his fingers dug into my flesh. Should I scream? If I did, half the hotel would come running. David would probably start a fight.

'Someone broke into De Witt's. The files were photocopied and the wires cut. Strangely, it happened on the same night you went home with flu. Sergei was with me that night, but yesterday he had these documents in his possession.'

'Did he give them to you?' Cold dread seized me as I realised that I had made an error.

'I think you broke into De Witt's with David Bernstein.'

'That's not true. I went home with flu. Now, let go of my arm or I'll scream. Where is Sergei?'

'Where you'll be if you try to double-cross me.'

Fear for Sergei swamped all other emotions. 'What happened to him?' I noted the hysteria in my voice and I tried to calm myself.

'I arrested him and sent him to Moscow to await trial, but he was shot while resisting arrest.'

I could no longer pretend. I pressed my fingers on my forehead and closed my eyes. Bastard! Bastard! I screamed silently.

For a few moments grief stopped me from thinking clearly, but unexpectedly and blessedly, cold hard logic took over, and with it came the idea for which I had been searching.

'I liked Sergei. I'm so sorry, but I'm sure it wasn't your fault. This is my plan, Boris. You must attend the cocktail party as one of the guests and I will identify Wolf to you alone. Then you must do what must be done. Do you understand? You must force him to tell you where my child is hidden and get him back to Russia to stand trial. Only then will I be able to go home and live in peace with myself, knowing that justice has been done.'

Colonel Borovoi looked relieved. 'We understand each other, Nina. I've always admired you. You're a tough woman. You can count on my support.'

'You must come as a delegate, not as a policeman, or they'll thwart you. I don't think David knows what you look like. Don't come down here again until I have an alias for you. I'll make a badge and find a suitable address. I'll send the details to your room. Be sure to be at the opening tomorrow night at eight. It's to be held in the cocktail lounge on the third floor. Don't be late. We won't have much time.'

'Don't try to double-cross me, Nina,' he muttered. He wasn't sure, I could see that. I hadn't convinced him of my sincerity, but he would come. I felt sure of that. I needed him, and he needed to be there.

Colonel Borovoi shot me one last frown, turned abruptly and left.

'There will be time to mourn you later, Sergei,' I whispered. 'Right now, my first priority is revenge.'

Chapter 70

I had this dread that when I confronted my child, my beloved Nicky, he would not remember me. What if our meeting was no more meaningful than passing a child in the park? Would we be strangers? Common sense told me that it would be like this, but emotionally I hoped that my love would win through.

Nicky had been two when Wolf kidnapped him, now he was over four. No child could remember that far back. Thus I reasoned with myself as I paused at a T-junction and took the road to Baldone.

My palms were slippery on the steering wheel and I was panting slightly while my heart hammered as fast as the car's pistons, or so it seemed. Fields and woods and small stone houses flew by. Eventually I came to Lecava and turned left towards Vecumnieki. Soon there were no more houses. It was dark, but the full moon seemed extraordinarily bright. If the map and the directions I had been given were correct I should be getting close. I slowed and searched the right-hand side for signs of a gate, but there was nothing I could see. Pulling to the side, I drove forward at a snail's pace.

I saw lights twinkling through the trees, long before I saw the gate. The house was large and rambling in art-deco style with a light blazing in the porch. Was it a private home? I parked the car and examined the entrance: two tall stone pillars flanked an ornate, wrought-iron gate that stood open.

When I read 'Morgendauw' I knew I had arrived. How could he? That name was ours, not his. But so was Nicky.

After blowing my nose vigorously and combing my hair, I felt better. I started the engine and drove along a well-kept gravel road between lawns and shrubs. Wolf had always had good taste, I remembered.

I parked and glanced at my watch. Eight p.m., a perfectly reasonable time to arrive, although this was hardly a normal social visit, so why worry?

What would I find? A mistress and more children? A new wife who adored her step-son? I was afraid to ring the bell, but at last I plucked up courage and heard loud chimes echoing around. A child called out, and a voice answered. I heard footsteps running to the door, which opened after some puffing and heaving at the lock.

There stood Nicky. Dear, sweet Nicky, dressed in striped pyjamas and slippers with a bright red train tucked under his arm. My son had hardly changed in the past two years. He was tall for his age and he looked happy. His brown eyes still twinkled with fun, he had Wolf's full, mobile lips, my hair, that same sweet angel's smile . . . Oh, God! I love him so, but I must stay calm.

'That's a fine train, Nicky.'

'You're English,' he said shyly.

'Yes, I am. You understand English well.'

'Yes.'

'Did your daddy teach you?'

'Yes. We speak English all the time. Only my nanny speaks German.'

'Can I come in?'

He ignored that question, but reached up and took my hand.

I crouched down and wrapped my arms around him. He didn't seem to mind. 'Oh, Nicky, I'm so happy to find you, darling. I've been looking for you for a long time. Do you know who I am?'

'You look a lot like my mummy,' he admitted, escaping from my arms. 'I have a photograph of her next to my bed.'

'That's because I am your mummy. Oh, Nicky, sweetie, give Mummy a hug.'

'I remember you,' he said politely, but I could see that he didn't. He gave me a hug all the same. Something about the close connection seemed to get through to him. He hugged me more tightly and his hands reached up and grabbed my hair, as they used to do.

Nothing is ever lost to the mind, I know. Every memory is carefully recorded in our subconscious, to be triggered off by all kinds of stimuli, perfume, perhaps, or the feeling of someone's body. Nicky dropped his train and wound his arms tightly around my neck, his legs crept around my waist, and his head nuzzled my cheek.

'Don't cry, Mummy,' he said. 'I remember you, really I do. Only your hair is different. I knew you'd come because I asked God to send you. And here you are.'

'Yes, here you are,' a well-remembered and once-loved voice said behind me. 'My one big mistake personified.'

'Nicky remembers me.'

'Do you think so? He loves women, perhaps because he's missed a woman's touch. Well, come in and sit by the fire. Nicky will get cold in the draughty hall. He's just had his bath.'

He showed me into a graceful room with huge windows

where green silk curtains hung half open. A crystal bowl of hyacinths stood on a broad window-sill.

I sat on a chintz sofa and Nicky climbed on to my lap and stared into my eyes, and stared and stared. He turned to his father and spoke in German.

'He says you are beautiful. Nicky, it's bed-time,' Wolf said, decisively. He picked him up, carried him to the hall and called out in German. A woman's voice replied.

I didn't want Nicky to go, but I wasn't going to beg. He would soon be mine.

Wolf returned and sat opposite me. 'And now? What next?'

'I've kept myself going for years visualising this moment, Wolf. You sitting there unarmed and caught unawares, just as you are now. And me, drawing out my gun like this, pointing it at you, like this. And then I say to you, "Wolf, I loved you, but you betrayed me. How could you do that? You took away all meaning to my life. You left me to face a prison sentence. I was tortured, did you know that? Electric shocks and solitary confinement. You never cared." This scene kept me going. I promised myself that I would play it out.' I put the gun in my pocket. 'Of course it's not loaded.'

'I knew that. Guns terrify you.'

'That was the old Nina. I've changed. I could have killed you, but I don't want my son to be an orphan.'

It was so much more than that, but I didn't have time to explain to Wolf about my own personal discoveries: that love is all there is to live for and revenge is only for losers.

I said, 'Furthermore, I don't particularly relish the thought of explaining to Nicky why his father is serving a life sentence. That's why I've come here with a deal, Wolf. Give me my child willingly. Help him to make the change. Tell him it's what you want. Tell him you'll come and see him often, and mean it. If you will do all that, I'll help you to get out of the mess you're in.'

'What makes you so sure I need help? I don't see that I'm in a mess at all.'

'I'm here, aren't I? Your position is hopeless. Everyone is closing in on you. All they needed was your real identity and now we've found you.'

'We?'

'My father, David Bernstein and I. Truly a joint effort.'

'Who knows my identity besides the three of you, Nina?'

'Father recorded the evidence. Don't worry, it's safe unless something happens to one of us.'

'Do you really believe that I would kill you? You still don't know me, do you? I've never killed anyone in my life. I never will.'

'I don't have to know you. The past is finished. Our marriage was never legal and you have no right whatsoever to Nicky. His real name is Nicholas Ogilvie and I have custody and guardianship.'

He flinched. This time I'd scored a hit.

'Nicky is heir to a great title, a great heritage and a fortune to go with it.'

'A *stolen* fortune.'

'It was stolen from my family. It was my duty to restore our line, nourish our fields, build up our herds, as my family had done for generations. It fell upon me to repair the damage done to us by the Nazis and the Soviets. You must see that.'

There was that light in his eyes again. I remembered it so well, but now I understood his mission. I made a mental note to tell Father how right he'd been.

'Who is this David Bernstein? Are you married to him?' Wolf looked angry and deprived, and this amazed me.

'Not yet, but I think we'll marry soon. You cheated him with your Unita scam.'

'*That* Bernstein.'

'Yes. Not a man to cross, I promise you.'

'And he loves you?'

'Yes.'

'And Nicky?'

'He wants to help me bring him up. Listen to me, Wolf. There's a long trail of vengeful people after you. I won't list them since you know who they are. I have only to give them your true identity and that's the end for you. I doubt you'd live long enough to stand trial. If you go into hiding you would lose everything you've gone to so much pain to steal back. You'd always be afraid for Nicky.'

'It was you who found us, Nina. How did you trace me?'

'You made an error. You linked your real self with your crooked aliases.'

'Sarajevo,' he whispered softly. 'I should never have underestimated a woman's resources when she's fighting for her child.'

'Yes, Wolf. And I saw you when you attended the conference today. I was sitting behind one-way glass waiting to identify you.'

'So I'm through?'

'No. I can't destroy someone whom my son loves so dearly, someone who cared for him so well. Wolf, listen to me. I have a plan.'

'I could always rely on your plans,' he said wistfully. He broke off and sat gazing at the fire. 'Remember Namaqualand? You saved me that time.'

'I always suspected you'd set me up.'

'No, never! I was caught. I loved you, Nina. I still do. I intended to bring you back here, but your staunch morality crashed my plans. Typical!' His face expressed bitterness and longing. 'Where were all of you moral people in the West when we were robbed, my father shot, my mother starved to death?'

'Spare me the sob story, Wolf. Let's get down to some hard bargaining.'

He sighed. 'I'm listening.'

'We must be quick. David will be searching for me. I don't have much time.'

Chapter 71

It was crisp and clear and not too cold, a lovely winter evening. I leaned over the balcony of the hotel's second-floor cocktail lounge, watching the steeples and turrets of the lovely old city of Riga glow in the moonlight. In the background, a string band was playing old-fashioned tunes.

Would Wolf come? Would he keep his side of the bargain? Borovoi, too, had a role to play in this evening's charade. Would he try to rewrite the script? Lastly there was David, a stickler for morality.

Did he love me enough to bend the rules for me and for Nicky?

A steady stream of cars was moving around the hotel as the drivers searched for parking. Anyone who was anyone was intent on coming, with or without an invitation. Perhaps I should warn David. I went to look for him and found him in the small room behind the bar, which he had converted to his temporary office. At the sight of his worried frown and his hunched shoulders, which revealed his tension, I felt a great wave of love for him. With it came anxiety. What would he do?

I said, 'The delegates have brought masses of extra people, friends and family, by the look of things. We'll be swamped.'

'How will you find Möller if we get too crowded?'

'Don't worry. If Wolf's here, I'll find him. Where will your men be, David? I mean, if I need help, how will I find them?'

'They'll find you,' he prevaricated. 'All you have to do is identify Möller. Leave the rest to me.'

'To you? That's not in the script. What if he pulls a gun on you?'

'I'll shoot him.'

'David, you're not thinking about my feelings at all. How can we live with that? You'll be Nicky's stepfather. Have you really thought out the future implications of killing his father?'

David swore under his breath. He stared at his desk for a full thirty seconds. 'I guess you've got a point,' he said, accepting defeat gracefully, which was one of the many qualities I loved in him.

When he picked up his radio and spoke into it in Hebrew, I noticed the ear-plug for the first time.

'How many of you are there?'

'Enough.'

Feeling exasperated, I went back to the cocktail party. Wolf should be waiting for me near the bar, if he were coming. That thought brought out the butterflies in my stomach again. Then I caught sight of him leaning over the balcony, gazing towards the old city.

I sauntered past and paused next to him.

'The old city looks beautiful in this mellow moonlight.'

'It's not the moonlight, it's the city. It's just beautiful.'

'You always knew best and I always gave in to you. That's because I believed in you. You sure as hell fell off your bloody pedestal,' I snarled.

'A domestic quarrel will do us a lot of good, I should think.'

I brought myself smartly back into line. 'Where's Nicky?'

'In the car with his nurse. Just below. Look, over there, the car beside the fountain. I left his clothes and his toys with the porter as arranged. So you won, Nina.'

'No, Wolf. This way both of us are winning.'

'You won't forget your many promises.'

'I won't do a Wolf on you, if that's what you mean.'

I shot him a scathing glance and moved on, trying to guess which guests were police, but I couldn't see anyone who looked right for the role, except for a very macho woman with a crew-cut, but she was knocking back the champagne. I circled the room, glass in hand, trying to look as if I was enjoying myself. Eventually I returned to the bar.

There was no sign of David. Wolf was talking to a group of businessmen he obviously knew well. His friends looked affluent, and a little tipsy. The music seemed to swell and surge around me, the laughter grew louder, I began to feel claustrophobic. The truth is, I was scared. There are always two sides to a bargain. My part of the deal was nowhere around. Then David came up behind me. His hand squeezed mine. Stay with me, David, I pleaded silently.

I think we both saw him at the same time: a small boy with tousled red hair and frightened eyes. He was trying very hard not to scream or cry, but I could see that Borovoi was hurting his hand, and from the way he was being held, I guessed there was a gun held against his back.

How had he known where to find Nicky? And where

was the nurse? What the hell had gone wrong? This wasn't part of my script at all.

No one had noticed, which seemed unbelievable to me. Nicky caught sight of me and his mouth moved. He was framing the word 'help', but no sound came. What a brave little boy he was. I stood dumbstruck. Borovoi should never have done this. A spark of outrage was kindled in me as I stepped towards them.

'Where is Wolf?' Borovoi muttered. 'Bring him here, or I'll kill the boy.'

My mouth was open, but no sound came. I gestured towards the bar. Borovoi was intrigued: he had never set eyes on Wolf. In that split second I threw myself forward, propelling my body between Nicky and the gun, knocking it upwards so that the bullet smashed into the ceiling. I landed over Nicky, shielding him, squashing him, feeling the fluttering beat of his heart against my hand, which was trapped between the floor and his chest.

I twisted my head round, expecting to see Borovoi's gun levelled at my back. It was.

The guests were screaming and pushing away, jostling each other like sheep as they tried to get out. I heard the shot and saw Borovoi's face explode, just as Brigit's had.

David was hurtling towards him, hands pointing straight out as he fired three more shots, which spun Borovoi around and propelled him backwards against the wall. He twisted towards me, spraying blood, and fell down, jerking. I gathered Nicky in my arms and scrambled away from the twitching body. David was leaning over us, his face twisted with outrage.

'He was using his own son as a shield to get away.'

I was sitting on the floor, rocking Nicky, my back turned to the corpse, sheltering my baby from the sight of the blood, repeating over and over again, 'I never meant him to be killed. That wasn't the plan. I never meant that at all. I swear it.'

I would probably be saying that for the rest of my life, I realised.

'It's all right, Nicky darling. It's all right. There, there, don't be scared.' I held him close and rocked him gently as we sat on the floor. 'You're safe. Mummy's got you.'

Nicky hid his face in my dress and hung on hard. He was so silent. Too silent. Too shocked to cry.

A man with a gun was leaning over Borovoi's body. He felt his pulse and called to a waiter to fetch a tablecloth to cover him.

'Are you Nina Ogilvie, the mother of this child?' He had a strong American accent.

'Yes,' I whispered.

'And is this man the father of your child?'

'Yes.'

'The man you knew as Wolf Möller?'

'Yes!'

'Can you formally identify him for us?'

'I know him only as Wolf Möller. Of course that's not his real name. It's him. He kidnapped my son,' I muttered. 'Thank God Nicky's all right.'

The CIA agent helped to cover the corpse and lead the guests away.

'I guess you'll do,' I heard an old familiar voice say. 'You'll do just fine for Nicky.'

Nicky looked up. 'Daddy,' he yelled.

'Go!' I shrieked to Wolf. 'For God's sake, go.'

Where was David? I glanced round cautiously and saw him standing right behind me. His eyes and cheeks had turned bright red, which was as close as he ever came to crying, I guessed.

'Is that your official statement, Nina? Are you telling us that this dead man on the floor is Wolf Möller, the father of your child?'

'Yes.'

He knelt beside the corpse and flicked the cloth down and then up again.

'You'd best get Nicky out of here,' he ground out, through lips taut with fury. 'He's as shocked as hell and no wonder. Take him to our room. I'll call a doctor. You go ahead. I'll be right there.'

I hung around, gripping Nicky to me. I had to know what he would say.

David called one of his colleagues over. 'Get everyone out of here and down to the ballroom, Hank. Every last one. They can carry on there. Lock the door. Round up the local police. They're somewhere around. They should have heard the shots. Tell them we nailed the bastard. He fell into our trap.'

He sighed and bent over the corpse again. 'His name tab says Baron Peter Podnieks – one of the delegates?' He looked up and saw me standing there, still rocking Nicky. 'What do you think, Nina?'

David was staring at me so coldly. He looked so hurt. I felt for him, but this was no time for weakness.

'Are you asking me? You set this up.'

'Did I? It seems to me I'm just an amateur round here.'

'You set a trap for Wolf Möller and you caught him. Justice has been seen to be done and I have my son. Well done! Now, let it go, for God's sake, David,' I murmured. Then I scrambled to my feet, hugging Nicky in my arms, and carried him up to our room.

Mr Bear was sitting on the pillows.

'This is your bear, Nicky. I bought him in Moscow

'or your last birthday. I was still looking for you then.
I love you, Nicky. I hope you're not too big for bears.'

Nicky was shivering violently.

'Where's Daddy? I want my daddy.' His voice came
out in a whimper.

'Hush, Nicky. Daddy's coming soon. We're all going
o Scotland for a holiday, and Daddy will visit us there.
Didn't he promise you?'

'Yes.'

'And he'll come to see you often. He promised you
hat, didn't he? It's our secret.'

I scrambled into bed and held him in my arms. He
held me tightly, just as he used to do when he had
nightmares. His shuddering gradually subsided. By the
ime the doctor came Nicky seemed much better, so he
gave him a light tranquilliser and left a few more, in
case we needed them.

He wanted to chat. 'I've heard the story going the
rounds. You're a brave woman, Miss Ogilvie. No one
seems to know much about this Baron Peter Podnieks.
Evidently he spent most of his time in Switzerland.
He was a sick man, I've heard. So what are your
plans now?'

'We're flying to Scotland first thing in the morning to
spend a few weeks with my father. After that I'll play it
by ear.'

David arrived and stood pointedly holding the door
open. The doctor got the message and left.

'You let Möller off the hook,' he said coldly. 'You
planned this, didn't you? You got hold of one of the
delegates' badges for Borovoi. You'll be found out when
hey check the real owner of the name.'

'No, David. The real Podnieks died in a car accident in Switzerland a couple of decades back. There

435

are no living relatives. I think I might just get away with it.'

'Why, Nina? We've been working for months to put Wolf behind bars.'

'You, perhaps. I wanted only my son.'

'You have to tell me the truth. Do you still love Wolf Möller?'

'No, but I no longer hate him, David. Do you know why? I'm grateful for the way he's brought up Nicky. At least he was able to love one person in his life. Look how peacefully Nicky's sleeping. It's strange, David, but for years I thought I wanted to take revenge. I used to dream about it, and write about it, but then I met you and I fell in love and the hatred in me disappeared. Suddenly I could love again. Are we still together, David?'

'Do you care?'

'More than you'll ever know. God, I'm so tired all of a sudden. I seem to be falling asleep as I sit here.'

'I love you, but it's not going to be as simple as you think. There's something you don't know. After you fled to Namibia and were arrested there, the CIA broke into your home and found some fingerprints, mainly from Wolf's office. They won't match up. This could be a problem for us.'

Us! With that simple word David had answered all my questions.

I looked at my thumb, which was scarred for ever, and I remembered the way Brigit died, and Borovoi's butcher's hands around my neck, squeezing, hurting. He had searched the office, touching everything, leaving his prints.

'He was destined for the role, David.'

I began to smile. The smile became a giggle and then I was laughing. I couldn't stop.

'Shock,' I heard David mutter.

He didn't get the joke, but I did.

SNAKES AND LADDERS

Madge Swindells

Marjorie Hardy has three assets – brains, courage and beauty – but this isn't nearly enough, she discovers, when she falls in love with Robert MacLaren, heir to a Scottish whisky empire. Her family is poor and her accent and upbringing are totally wrong for Robert's calculating stepmother. Finding herself alone and pregnant after a final summer fling with Robert in Corsica, Marjorie decides to keep her baby and fight for her daughter's rightful inheritance of the famous Glentirran estates. From her humble position in a local typing pool, she wonders how she will ever succeed.

Marjorie's dream sets her off on the long, tough road of business, from selling advertising space to co-ownership of a highly successful publishing company. She finds happiness with Hamish Cameron, the chairman of a rival distillery, but in life's game of Snakes and Ladders, Marjorie is soon thrown undeservedly back into the mire. Eventually she throws a six and gets her foot on the ladder to success. Fired by the need for revenge she reaches the top, but the price she must pay is a high one . . .

In *Snakes and Ladders*, Madge Swindells tells a fascinating story of a woman's intense love for her daughter and her first lover, and of her search for her true self.

HARVESTING THE PAST

Madge Swindells

When twenty-seven-year-old Arion St John is transferred from the Pretoria police force to the small town of Silver Bay, one of the prettiest on the Cape Province, to investigate a local kidnapping, he thinks it a strange coincidence to be returning finally to the place where he was adopted aged three. Perhaps, he thinks, as well as finding the beautiful sixteen-year-old Mandy September, who has disappeared without a trace, he will also have an opportunity to discover his roots.

But Ari finds the townsfolk determinedly set against him before he has even begun his investigation, and determinedly loyal to the fabulously wealthy Angelo Palma, a fishing magnate who lives above the village and who at one time or another seems to have been a benefactor to nearly all its inhabitants. Ari soon discovers that he is a doppelgänger of Angelo's grandson Rob – who seems to be constantly protected by the Palma's sinister housekeeper Ramona – and that he is disturbingly attracted to Rob's exquisite but fragile wife Kate.

Stubborn to get to the bottom of Silver Bay's secrets, and with the help of the few local people who come to trust him, Ari gradually unearths a twenty-eight-year-old skull, a long buried crime, and an extraordinary tale of blackmail and double-cross. And, as Ari comes to realise, only when he and Silver Bay have harvested their past can the crimes of the day finally be solved.

Set against the background of the fledgling democratic South Africa, with all its new difficulties and uncertainties, HARVESTING THE PAST is a powerful and compelling novel which brings its characters and its country vividly to life.

THE SENTINEL

Madge Swindells

Liza Frank had always assumed she was white. Accustomed to the privileges of South Africa's apartheid system, the shock news that she is to be reclassified as 'coloured' comes as a crushing blow, forcing her to flee onto the harsh streets of Johannesburg and cutting her off from her childhood sweetheart Pieter – for mixed-race relations are strictly forbidden.

Joining the army in an attempt to forget, Pieter finds his Afrikaner background soon makes him a pawn in a racist system he has never really questioned. And when he is asked to eliminate an ANC member, formerly a childhood friend, his resolve is tested as never before. Sentinel to values that are rooted in prejudice, only through the rediscovery of love can Pieter begin to atone for his actions . . .

Reaching its gripping climax as the chains of apartheid are being stripped away, *The Sentinel* is a tremendously powerful story of loyalty and love, with characters as much in turmoil as the country they all feel is their own.

Other bestselling Warner titles available by mail:

☐	Snakes and Ladders	Madge Swindells	£5.99
☐	Harvesting the Past	Madge Swindells	£5.99
☐	The Sentinel	Madge Swindells	£4.99
☐	Summer Harvest	Madge Swindells	£5.99
☐	Song of the Wind	Madge Swindells	£5.99
☐	Shadows on the Snow	Madge Swindells	£5.99
☐	The Corsican Woman	Madge Swindells	£5.99
☐	Edelweiss	Madge Swindells	£4.99

The prices shown above are correct at time of going to press, however the publishers reserve the right to increase prices on covers from those previously advertised, without further notice.

WARNER BOOKS

WARNER BOOKS
Cash Sales Department, P.O. Box 11, Falmouth, Cornwall, TR10 9EN
Tel: +44 (0) 1326 372400, Fax: +44 (0) 1326 374888
Email: books@barni.avel.co.uk.

POST AND PACKING
Payments can be made as follows: cheque, postal order (payable to Warner Books) or by credit cards. Do not send cash or currency.

All U.K. Orders   **FREE OF CHARGE**
E.E.C. 7 Overseas   25% of order value

Name (Block Letters) _____

Address _____

_____

Post/zip code: _____

☐ Please keep me in touch with future Warner publications
☐ I enclose my remittance £_____
☐ I wish to pay by Visa/Access/Mastercard/Eurocard   Expiry date

☐☐☐☐☐☐☐☐☐☐☐☐☐☐☐☐☐☐   ☐☐☐☐